Spacewreck Diary...

I went outside again.

God, so beautiful, so lonely, so vast. Haunting, that's the word I want. The beauty out there is haunting. Sometimes I think I'm a fool to go back. I'm giving up all of eternity for a pizza and a bed and a kind word.

NO! What the hell am I writing! No. I'm going back, of course I am. I need Earth, I miss Earth, I want Earth. This time it *will* be different.

Karen! Earth! I have to have courage, I have to risk pain, I have to taste life.

I am *not* a rock. Or an island. Or a star....

More mind-expanding messages inside from today's greatest science fiction writers

Also edited by Isaac Asimov, Martin H. Greenberg, and Joseph Olander
THE FUTURE IN QUESTION

SPACE MAIL

----

edited by

Isaac Asimov,
Martin H. Greenberg,
and Joseph Olander

Introduction by Isaac Asimov

FAWCETT CREST • NEW YORK

SPACE MAIL

Published by Fawcett Crest Books, a unit of CBS Publications, the Consumer Publishing Division of CBS Inc.

ISBN: 0-449-24312-5

Printed in the United States of America

First Fawcett Crest Printing: July 1980

10 9 8 7 6 5 4 3 2 1

ACKNOWLEDGMENTS

CONTENTS

MEMOS

New York City
Late 1979

General Reader
Anywhere

Dear G. R.,

In calling you "Reader," I am not being entirely accurate, and I hope you will forgive me.

After all, when I call myself "Writer," which I surely am from a professional standpoint, I tend to obscure the fact that I am a reader, too. The only reason this doesn't lead to serious misunderstandings is that all of us assume that almost everyone, regardless of what else he or she does, is a reader.

And in calling you a "Reader," I tend to obscure the fact that you are a writer, too. Everyone who is a reader is apt to be a writer, at least on occasion.

You yourself, General Reader, if I may continue to use the term without prejudice, write on occasion. You may not be a professional writer in the sense that you make a major portion of your livelihood out of your writing—but you write.

You write innumerable letters to friends and families; chatty letters to old college roommates; morose complaints to your sister; hurried scrawls to your mother; careful lies to some mistrusted acquaintance.

You also write business letters to associates; dunning letters to those who owe you money, diplomatic letters to those to whom you owe money, peremptory letters to those who have in one way or another wronged you, soothing letters to those whom you have wronged, imperative letters ordering equipment, convoluted letters portraying carelessness as innocence and misjudgments as virtue.

In fact, in these letters you write—doing so without ever once thinking of yourself as a writer—you may well run the whole gamut of emotion, tension, persuasion, prevarication, and exclamation.

Nor is it only letters that you and I (casual writer and professional alike) are involved in as manufacturers of the written word. It may be that you keep a diary—or write yourself

9

notes—or send memos up and down the communications line of an organization—or write more or less formal reports on whatever line of business you are engaged in—or fill out blanks under various forms of bureaucratic compulsion—

All this is universal. What I do in writing a formal "story" is very particular, and even artificial.

Why not, then, tell a story as it so frequently tells itself in the writings of nonprofessionals—in the form of letters, diary entries, memos, reports, and so on?

In actual fact, it is occasionally done. It may seem to some an odd device, but from my remarks I hope you see it is not. It is the very stuff of human nature, and in this book, Martin and I have selected a clutch of the best examples of such stories that we could find.

Read and enjoy—and then watch your own day-to-day writings and see if there is not a story in them, too. In other words, General Reader, it may be that you are a General Writer as well.

Sincerely,

Isaac Asimov

LETTERS

*Unfortunately, the late Cyril Kornbluth (1923–58) is often
thought of primarily as a collaborator of Frederik Pohl. But
he was much more than that, and his individual efforts were
frequently of the highest quality. Particularly outstanding are
his short-story collections and the novel* The Syndic *(1953).
Although he never won a major award in the field during his
lifetime, he shared a Hugo in 1973 for a story finished by Fred
Pohl from a fragment they had worked on many years before.
Kornbluth's voice was an important if a cynical one in science
fiction, and he is sorely missed.*

"I Never Ast No Favors" (The Magazine of Fantasy and
Science Fiction, *April 1954) has a little of the flavor of* The
Syndic, *and tells the story of a criminal with a most unusual
problem.*

I NEVER AST NO FAVORS

By C. M. Kornbluth

Dear Mr. Marino:

I hesitate to take pen in hand and write you because I
guess you do not remember me except maybe as a punk kid
you did a good turn, and I know you must be a busy man
running your undertaking parlor as well as the Third Ward
and your barber shop. I never ast no favors of nobody but this
is a special case which I hope you will agree when I explain.

To refresh your memory as the mouthpiece says in court,
my name is Anthony Cornaro only maybe you remember me

better as Tough Tony, which is what they call me back home in the Ward. I am not the Tough Tony from Water Street who is about 55 and doing a sixer up the river, I am the Tough Tony who is going on seventeen from Brecker Street and who you got probation for last week after I slash that nosy cop that comes flatfooting into the grocery store where some friends and I are just looking around not knowing it is after hours and that the grocery man has went home. That is the Tough Tony that I am. I guess you remember me now so I can go ahead.

With the probation, not that I am complaining, the trouble starts. The mouthpiece says he has known this lad for years and he comes from a very fine churchgoing family and he has been led astray by bad companions. So all right, the judge says three years probation, but he goes on to say *if*. If this, if that, environment, bad influences, congestered city streets, our vital dairy industry denuded—such a word from a judge!—of labor...

Before I know what has happened, I am signing a paper, my Mama is putting her mark on it and I am on my way to Chiunga County to milk cows.

I figure the judge does not know I am a personal friend of yours and I do not want to embarrass you by mentioning your name in open court, I figure I will get a chance later to straighten things out. Also, to tell you the truth, I am too struck with horror to talk.

On the ride upstate I am handcuffed to the juvenile court officer so I cannot make a break for it, but at last I get time to think and I realize that it is not as bad as it looks. I am supposed to work for a dame named Mrs. Parry and get chow, clothes and Prevailering Wages. I figure it takes maybe a month for her to break me in on the cow racket or even longer if I play dumb. During the month I get a few bucks, a set of threads and take it easy and by then I figure you will have everything straightened out and I can get back to my regular occupation, only more careful this time. Experience is the best teacher, Mr. Marino, as I am sure you know.

Well, we arrive at this town Chiunga Forks and I swear to God I never saw such a creepy place. You wouldn't believe it. The main drag is all of four blocks long and the stores and houses are from wood. I expect to see Gary Cooper stalking down the street with a scowl on his puss and his hands on his guns looking for the bad guys. Four hours from the Third Ward in a beat-up '48 police department Buick—you wouldn't believe it.

We park in front of a hash house, characters in rubber boots gawk at us, the court officer takes off the cuffs and gabs with the driver but does not lose sight of me. While we are waiting for this Mrs. Parry to keep the date I study the bank building across the street and develop some ideas which will interest you, Mr. Marino, but which I will not go into right now.

All of a sudden there is a hassle on the sidewalk.

A big woman with gray hair and a built like Tony Galento is kicking a little guy who looks like T.B. Louis the Book, who I guess you know, but not so muscular and wearing overalls. She is kicking him right in the keister, five-six times. Each time I shudder, and so maybe does the bank building across the street.

"Shoot my dawg, will you!" she yells at the character. "I said I'd kick your butt from here to Scranton when I caught up with you, Dud Wingle!"

"Leave me be!" he squawks, trying to pry her hands off his shoulders. "He was chasin' deer! He was chasin' deer!"

Thud—thud—thud. "I don't keer if he was chasin' deer, panthers or butterflies." *Thud.* "He was my dawg and you shot him!" *Thud.* She was drawing quite a crowd. The characters in rubber boots are forgetting all about us to stare at her and him.

Up comes a flatfoot who I later learn is the entire manpower of Chiunga Forks' lousiest; he says to the big woman "Now Ella" a few times and she finally stops booting the little character and lets him go. "What do you want, Henry?" she growls at the flatfoot and he asks weakly: "Silver Bell dropped her calf yet?"

The little character is limping away rubbing himself. The big broad watches him regretfully and says to the flatfoot: "Yesterday, Henry. Now if you'll excuse me I have to look for my new hired boy from the city. I guess that's him over there."

She strolls over to us and yanks open the Buick's door, almost taking it off the hinges. "I'm Mrs. Ella Parry," she says to me, sticking out her hand. "You must be the Cornaro boy the Probation Association people wired me about."

I shake hands and say, "Yes, ma'am."

The officer turns me over grinning like a skunk eating beans.

I figure Mrs. Parry lives in one of the wood houses in Chiunga Forks, but no. We climb into a this-year Willys truck and take off for the hills. I do not have much to say to this lady wrestler but wish I had somebody smuggle me a rod to kind of even things a little between her and me. With that built she could break me in half by accident. I try to get in good with her by offering to customize her truck. "I could strip off the bumper guards and put on a couple of fog lights, maybe new fender skirts with a little trim to them," I say, "and it wouldn't cost you a dime. Even out here there has got to be some parts place where a person can heist what he needs."

"Quiet, Bub," she says all of a sudden, and shields her eyes peering down a side road where a car is standing in front of a shack. "I swear," she says, "that looks like Dud Wingle's Ford in front of Miz' Sigafoos' place." She keeps her neck twisting around to study it until it is out of sight. And she looks worried.

I figure it is not a good time to talk and anyway maybe she has notions about customizing and does not approve of it.

"What," she says, "would Dud Wingle want with Miz' Sigafoos?"

"I don't know, ma'am," I say. "Wasn't he the gentleman you was kicking from here to Scranton?"

"Shucks, Bub, that was just a figger of speech. If I'd of wanted to kick him from here to Scranton I'd of *done* it. Dud and Jim and Ab and Sime think they got a right to shoot your dog if he chases the deer. I'm a peaceable woman or I'd have the law on them for shootin' Grip. But maybe I did kind of lose my temper." She looked worrieder yet.

"Is something wrong, ma'am?" I ask. You never can tell, but a lot of old dames talk to me like I was their uncle; to tell you the truth this is my biggest problem in a cat house. It must be because I am a kind of thoughtful guy and it shows.

Mrs. Parry is no exception. She says to me: "You don't know the folks up here yet, Bub, so you don't know about Miz' Sigafoos. I'm old English stock so I don't hold with their foolishness, but—" And here she looked *real* worried. "Miz'

Sigafoos is what they call a hex doctor."

"What's that, ma'am?"

"Just a lot of foolishness. Don't you pay any attention," she says, and then she has to concentrate on the driving. We are turning off the two-lane state highway and going up, up, up, into the hills, off a blacktop road, off a gravel road, off a dirt road. No people. No houses. Fences and cows or maybe horses, I can't tell for sure. Finally we are at her place, which is from wood and in two buildings. I start automatically for the building that is clean, new-painted, big and expensive.

"Hold on, Bub," she says. "No need to head for the barn first thing. Let's get you settled in the house first and then there'll be a plenty of work for you."

I do a double take and see that the big, clean, expensive building is the barn. The little, cheap, run-down place is the house. I say to myself: "Tough Tony, you're gonna pray tonight that Mr. Marino don't forget to tell the judge you're a personal friend of his and get you out of this."

But that night I do not pray. I am too tired. After throwing sacks of scratch feed and laying mash around, I run the baling machine and I turn the oats in the loft and I pump water until my back is aching jello and then I go hiking out to the woodlot and chop down trees and cut them up with a chain saw. It is surprising how fast I learn and how willing I am when I remember what Mrs. Parry did to Dud Wingle.

I barely get to sleep it seems like when Mrs. Parry is yanking the covers off me laughing and I see through the window that the sky is getting a little light. "Time to rise, Bub," she bawls. "Breakfast on the table." She strides to the window and flexes her muscles, breathing deep. "It's going to be a fine day. I can tell when an animal's sick to death and I can tell when it's going to be fine all day. Rise and shine, Bub. We have a lot of work ahead. I was kind of easy on you yesterday seeing you was new here, so we got a bit behindhand."

I eye the bulging muscles and say "Yes, ma'am."

She serves a good breakfast, I have to admit. Usually I just have some coffee around eleven when I wake up and maybe a meat-ball sandwich around four, but the country air gives you an appetite like I always heard. Maybe I didn't tell you there was just the two of us. Her husband kicked off a couple of years ago. She gave one of her boys half the farm because she says she don't believe in letting them hang around without a chance to make some money and get married until you die. The other boy, nineteen, got drafted two months ago and since then she is running the place on her own hook because for some reason or other it is hard to get people to work on a farm. She says she does not understand this and I do not enlighten her.

First thing after breakfast she tells me to make four crates from lumber in the toolshed, go to the duckpond and put the four Muscovy ducks in the crates so she can take them to town and sell them. She has been meaning to sell the Muscovy ducks for some time since the word has been getting around that she was pro-communist for having such a breed of ducks when there were plenty of good American ducks she could of raised. "Though," she says, "in my opinion the Walterses ought to sell off their Peking ducks too because the Chinese are just as bad as the Roossians."

I make the crates which is easy and I go to the duckpond. There are four ducks there but they are not swimming; they have sunk. I go and tell Mrs. Parry and she looks at me like I was crazy.

"Yeah," I tell her. "Sunk. Down at the bottom of the pond, drownded. I guess maybe during the night they forgot to keep treading water or something."

She didn't say a word. She just strides down the path to the duckpond and looks into it and sees the four ducks. They are big, horrible things with kind of red Jimmy Valentine masks over their eyes, and they are lying at the bottom of the pond. She wades in, still without a word, and fishes them out. She gets a big shiv out of her apron pocket, slits the ducks open, yanks out their lungs and slits them open. Water dribbles out.

"Drownded," she mutters. "If there was snapping turtles to drag them under...but there ain't."

I do not understand what the fuss is about and ast her if she can't sell them anyway. She says no, it wouldn't be honest, and I should get a shovel and bury them. Then there is an awful bellering from the cow barn. "Agnes of Lincolnshire!" Mrs. Parry squawks and dashes for the barn. "She's dropping her calf ahead of time!"

I run along beside her. "Should I call the cops?" I pant. "They always get to the place before the ambulance and you don't have to pay them nothing. My married sister had three kids delivered by the cops—"

But it seems it's different with cows and anyway they have a different kind of flatfoot out here that didn't go to Police Academy. Mrs. Parry finally looks up from the calf and says "I think I saved it. I *know* I saved it. I can tell when an animal's dying. Bub, go to the phone and call Miz' Croley and ask her if she can possibly spare Brenda to come over and do the milkin' tonight and tomorrow morning. I dassn't leave Agnes and the calf; they need nursing."

I stagger out of the cowbarn, throw up two-three times and go to the phone in the house. I seen them phones with flywheels in the movies so I know how to work it. Mrs. Croley cusses and moans and then says all right she'll send Brenda over in the Ford and please to tell Mrs. Parry not to keep her no longer than she has to because she has a herd of her own that needs milking.

I tell Mrs. Parry in the barn and Mrs. Parry snaps that Mrs. Croley has a living husband and a draft-proof farmhand and she swore she din't know what things were coming to when a neighbor wouldn't help another neighbor out.

I ast casually: "Who is this Brenda, ma'am?"

"Miz' Croley's daughter. Good for nothing."

I don't ast no more questions but I sure begin to wait with interest for a Ford to round the bend of the road.

It does while I am bucking up logs with the chainsaw. Brenda is a blondie about my age, a little too big for her dress—an effect which I always go for, whether in the Third Ward or Chiunga County. I don't have a chance to talk to her until lunch, and then all she does is giggle. But who wants conversation? I make a mental note that she will have the room next to mine and then a truck comes snorting up the driveway. Something inside the truck is snorting louder than the truck.

Mrs. Parry throws up her hands. "Land, I forgot! Belshazzar the Magnificent for Princess Leilani!" She gulps coffee and dashes out.

"Brenda," I say, "what was that all about?"

She giggles and this time blushes. I throw down my napkin and go to the window. The truck is being backed to a field with a big board fence around it. Mrs. Parry is going into the barn and is leading a cow into the field. The cow is mighty nervous and I begin to understand why. The truckdriver opens the tailgate and out comes a snorting bull.

I think: well, I been to a few stag shows but *this* I never seen before. Maybe a person can learn something in the country after all.

Belshazzar the Magnificent sees Princess Leilani. He snorts like Charles Boyer. Princess Leilani cowers away from him like Bette Davis. Belshazzar the Magnificent paws the ground. Princess Leilani trembles. And then Belshazzar the Magnificent yawns and starts eating grass.

Princess Leilani looks up, startled, and says: "Huh?" No, on second thought it is not Princess Leilani who says "Huh?" It is Brenda, at the other kitchen window. She sees me watching her, giggles, blushes and goes to the sink and starts doing dishes.

I guess this is a good sign, but I don't press my luck. I go outside, where Mrs. Parry is cussing out the truckdriver.

"Some bull!" she yells at him. "What am I supposed to do now? How long is Leilani going to stay in season? What if I can't line up another stud for her? Do you realize what it's going to cost me in veal and milk checks—" Yatata, yatata, yatata, while the truckdriver keeps trying to butt in with excuses and Belshazzar the Magnificent eats grass and sometimes gives Princess Leilani a brotherly lick on the nose, for by that time Princess Leilani has dropped the nervous act and edged over mooing plaintively.

Mrs. Parry yells: "See that? I don't hold with artificial insemination but you dang stockbreeders are driving us dairy farmers to it! Get your—your *steer* off my property before I throw him off! I got work to do even if he hasn't! Belshazzar the Magnificent—*hah!*"

She turns on me. "Don't just stand around gawking, Bub. When you get the stovewood split you can stack it in the woodshed." I scurry off and resume Operation Woodlot, but I take it a little easy which I can do because Mrs. Parry is in the cowbarn nursing Agnes of Lincolnshire and the pree-mie calf.

At supper Mrs. Parry says she thinks she better put a cot in the barn for herself and spend the night there with the invalids in case there is a sudden emergency. "And that don't mean," she adds, "that you children can be up half the night playing the radio just because the old lady ain't around. I want to see the house lights out by 8:30. Understand?"

"Yes ma'am," Brenda says.

"We won't play the radio, ma'am," I say. "And we'll put the lights out."

Brenda giggled.

What happens that night is a little embarrassing to write about. I hope, Mr. Marino, you won't go telling it around. I figure that being a licensed mortician like you are as well as boss of the Third Ward you are practically like a doctor and doctors don't go around shooting their mouths off about what their patients tell them. I figure what I have to tell you about what happened comes under the sacred relationship between a doctor and patient or a hood and his mouthpiece.

Anyway, this is what happens: nothing happens.

Like with Belshazzar the Magnificent.

I go into her room, I say yes, she says no, I say yes *please,* she says well okay. And then nothing happens. I never been so humiliated and I hope you will keep this confidential because it isn't the kind of thing you like to have get around. I am telling you about it only because I never ast no favors but this is a very special case and I want you to understand why.

The next morning at breakfast I am in a bad temper, Brenda has got the giggles and Mrs. Parry is stiff and tired from sleeping in the barn. We are a gruesome threesome, and then a car drives up and a kid of maybe thirty comes busting into the kitchen. He has been crying. His eyes are red and there are clean places on his face where the tears ran down. "Ma!" he whimpers at Mrs. Parry. "I got to talk to you! You got to talk to Bonita, she says I don't love her no more and she's going to leave me!"

"Hush up, George," she snaps at him. "Come into the parlor." They go into the parlor and Brenda whistles: "Whoo-ee! Wait'll I tell Maw about *this!*"

"Who is he?" I ask.

"Miz' Parry's boy George. She gave him the south half of the farm and built him a house on it. Bonita's his wife. She's a stuck-up girl from Ware County and she wears falsies and dyes her hair and—" Brenda looks around, lowers her voice and whispers "—and *she sends her worshing to the laundry in town.*"

"God in Heaven," I say. "Have the cops heard about this?"

"Oh, it's *legal*, but you just shouldn't *do* it."

"I see. I misunderstood, I guess. Back in the Third Ward it's a worse rap than mopery with intent to gawk. The judges are ruthless with it."

Her eyes go round. "Is that a fact?"

"Sure. Tell your mother about it."

Mrs. Parry came back in with her son and said to us: "Clear out, you kids. I want to make a phone call."

"I'll start the milkin'," Brenda said.

"And I'll framble the portistan while it's still cool and barkney," I say.

"Sure," Mrs. Parry says, cranking the phone. "Go and do that, Bub." She is preoccupied.

I go through the kitchen door, take one sidestep, flatten against the house and listen. Reception is pretty good.

"Bonita?" Mrs. Parry says into the phone. "Is that you, Bonita? Listen, Bonita, George is here and he asked me to call you and tell you he's sorry. I ain't exactly going to say that. I'm going to say that you're acting like a blame fool.... No, no, no. Don't talk about it. This is a party line. Just listen; I know what happened. George told me; after all, I'm his mother. Just listen to an older woman with more experience. So it happened. That don't mean he doesn't love you, child! It's happened to me. I guess it's happened to every woman. You mustn't take it *personally*. You're just sufferin' from a case of newlywed nerves. After you've been married two years or so you'll see things like this in better focus. Maybe George was tired. Maybe he got one of these flu germs that's goin' around.... No, I didn't say he was sick. No, he seems all right—maybe looks a *little* feverish.... Well, now, I don't know whether you really want to talk to him or not, you being so upset and all. If he *is* sick it'd just upset him— oh, all right." She chuckles away from the phone and says: "She wants to talk to you, George. Don't be too eager, boy."

I slink away from the kitchen door thinking: "Ah-*hah!*" I am thinking so hard that Mrs. Parry bungles into me when she walks out of the kitchen sooner than I expect.

She grabs me with one of those pipe-vise hands and snaps: "You young devil, were you listening to me on the phone?"

Usually it is the smart thing to deny everything and ast for your mouthpiece, but up here they got no mouthpieces. For once I tell the truth and cop a plea. "Yes, Mrs. Parry. I'm so *ashamed* of myself you can't imagine. I always been

ike that. It's a psy-cho-logical twist I got for listening. I can't
eem to control it. Maybe I read too many bad comic books.
But honest I won't breathe a word about how George
ouldn't—" Here I have the sense to shut up, but too late.

She drills me with a look and the pipe vise tightens on
ny arm. "Couldn't *what, Bub?*"

"Like Belshazzar the Magnificent," I say weakly.

"Yep," she says. "I thought that's what you were going to
say. Now tell me, Bub—how'd you know? And don't tell me
you guessed from what I said. I been using party lines for
hirty years. The way I was talkin' to Bonita, it could've been
anything from George hitting her with a brick to comin' home
drunk. You picked a mighty long shot, you picked it right
and I want to know how you did it."

She would of made a great D.A. I mumble: "The same
hing happened to me last night. Would you mind lettin' go
of my arm, Mrs. Parry? Before it drops off?"

She lets go with a start. "I'm sorry, Bub." She walked
slowly to the barn and I walk slowly beside her because I
hink she expects it.

"Maybe," I say, "it's something in the water."

She shakes her head. "You don't know bulls, Bub. And
what about the ducks that sank and Agnes dropping her calf
before her time?" She begins to breathe hard through her
nostrils. "It's hexin', that's what it is!"

"What's hexin', ma'am?"

"Heathen doings by that old Miz' Sigafoos. She's been
warned and warned plenty to stick to her doctoring. I hold
nothing against her for curing the croup or maybe selling a
young man love potion if he's goin' down to Scranton to sell
his crop and play around a little. But she's not satisfied with
that, I guess. Dud Wingle must of gone to her with a twenty-
dollar bill to witch my farm!"

I do not know what to make of this. My mama of course
has told me about *la vecchia religione*, but I never know they
believe in stuff like that over here. "Can you go to the cops,
ma'am?" I ast.

She snorts like Belshazzar the Magnificent. "Cops! A fat
ot old Henry Bricker would know about witchin'. No, Bub,
I guess I'll handle this myself. I ain't the five-times-great-
granddaughter of Pru Posthlewaite for nothin'!"

"Who was Pru—what you said?"

"Hanged in Salem, Massachusetts, in 1680 for witchcraft.

Her coven name was Little Gadfly, but I guess she wasn't so
little. The first two ropes broke—but we got no time to stand
around talkin'. I got to find my Ma's trunk in the attic. You
go get the black rooster from the chicken run. I wonder where
there's some chalk?" And she walks off to the house, mumbling. I walk to the chicken run thinking she has flipped.

The black rooster is a tricky character, very fast on his
feet and also I am new at the chicken racket. It takes me half
an hour to stalk him down, during which time incidentally
the Ford leaves with Brenda in it and George drives away
in his car. See you later, Brenda, I think to myself and maybe
you will be surprised.

I go to the kitchen door with the rooster screaming in my
arms and Mrs. Parry says: "Come on in with him and set him
anywhere." I do, Mrs. Parry scatters some cornflakes on the
floor and the rooster calms down right away and stalks
around picking it up. Mrs. Parry is sweaty and dust-covered
and there are some dirty old papers rolled up on the kitchen
table.

She starts fooling around on the floor with one of the
papers and a hunk of carpenter's chalk and just to be doing
something I look at the rest of them. Honest to God, you
never saw such lousy spelling and handwriting. *Tayke the
Duste off ane Olde Ymmage Quhich Ye Myngel*—like that.

I shake my head and think: it's the cow racket. No normal
human can take this life. She has flipped and I don't blame
her, but it will be a horrible thing if she becomes homicidal.
I look around for a poker or something and start to edge
away. I am thinking of a dash from the door to the Willys
and then scorching into town to come back with the men in
the little white coats.

She looks up at me and says: "Don't go away, Bub. This
is woman's work, but I need somebody to hold the sword and
palm and you're the onliest one around." She grins. "I guess
you never saw anything like *this* in the city, hey?"

"No, ma'am," I say, and notice that my voice is very faint.

"Well, don't let it skeer you. There's some people it'd skeer
but the Probation Association people say they call you Tough
Tony, so I guess you won't take fright."

"No, ma'am."

"Now what do we do for a sword? I guess this bread
knife'll—no; the ham slicer. It looks *more* like a sword. Hold
it in your left hand and get a couple of them gilded bulrushes

from the vase in the parlor. Mind you wipe your feet before you tread on the carpet! And then come back. Make it fast."

She starts to copy some stuff that looks like Yiddish writing onto the floor and I go into the parlor. I am about to tiptoe to the front door when she yells: "Bub! That you?"

Maybe I could beat her in a race for the car, maybe not. I shrug. At least I have a knife—and know how to use it. I bring her the gilded things from the vase. Ugh! While I am out she has cut the head off the rooster and is sprinkling its blood over a big chalk star and the writing on the floor. But the knife makes me feel more confident even though I begin to worry about how it will look if I have to do anything with it. I am figuring that maybe I can hamstring her if she takes off after me, and meanwhile I should humor her because maybe she will snap out of it.

"Bub," she says, "hold the sword and palms in front of you pointing up and don't step inside the chalk lines. Now, will you promise me not to tell anybody about the words I speak? The rest of this stuff don't matter; it's down in all the books and people have their minds made up that it don't work. But about the words, do you promise?"

"Yes, ma'am. Anything you say, ma'am."

So she starts talking and the promise was not necessary because it's in some foreign language and I don't talk foreign languages except sometimes a little Italian to my mama. I am beginning to yawn when I notice that we have company.

He is eight feet tall, he is green, he has teeth like Red Riding Hood's grandma.

I dive through the window, screaming.

When Mrs. Parry comes out she finds me in a pile of broken glass, on my knees, praying. She clamps two fingers on my ear and hoists me to my feet. "Stop that praying," she says. "He's complaining about it. Says it makes him itch. And you said you wouldn't be skeered! Now come inside where I can keep an eye on you and behave yourself. The idea! The very idea!"

To tell you the truth, I don't remember what happens after this so good. There is some talk between the green character and Mrs. Parry about her five-times-great-grandmother who it seems is doing nicely in a warm climate. There is an argument in which the green character gets shifty and says he doesn't know who is working for Miz' Sigafoos these days. Miz' Parry threatens to let me pray again and the green character gets sulky and says all right he'll send for him and rassle with him but he is sure he can lick him.

The next thing I recall is a grunt-and-groan exhibition between the green character and a smaller purple character who must of arrived when I was blacked out or something. This at least I know something about because I am a television fan. It is a very slow match, because when one of the characters for instance bends the other character's arm it just bends and does not break. But a good big character can lick a good little character every time and finally greenface has got his opponent tied into a bowknot.

"Be gone," Mrs. Parry says to the purple character, "and never more molest me or mine. Be gone, be gone, be gone."

He is gone, and I never do find out if he gets unknotted.

"Now fetch me Miz' Sigafoos."

Blip! An ugly little old woman is sharing the ring with the winner and new champeen. She spits at Mrs. Parry: "So you it was dot mine Teufel haff ge-schtolen!" Her English is terrible. A greenhorn.

"This ain't a social call, Miz' Sigafoos," Mrs. Parry says coldly. "I just want you to unwitch my farm and kinfolks. And if you're an honest woman you'll return his money to that sneakin', dog-murderin' shiftless squirt Dud Wingle."

"Yah," the old woman mumbles. She reaches up and feels the biceps of the green character. "Yah, I guess maybe dot I besser do. Who der Yunger iss?" She is looking at me. "For why the teeth on his mouth go clop-clop-clop? Und so white the face on his head iss! You besser should feed him, Ella."

"*Missus* Parry to you, Miz' Sigafoos, *if* you don't mind. Now the both of you be gone, be gone, be gone."

At last we are alone.

"Now," Mrs. Parry grunts, "maybe we can get back to farmin'. Such foolishness and me a busy woman." She looks at me closely and says: "I do believe the old fool was right. You're as white as a sheet." She feels my forehead. "Oh, shoot! You do have a temperature. You better get to bed. If you ain't better in the morning I'll call Doc Hines."

So I am in the bedroom writing this letter, Mr. Marino, and I hope you will help me out. Like I said I never ast no favors but this is special.

Mr. Marino, will you please, please go to the judge and tell him I have a change of heart and don't want no probation?

Tell him I want to pay my debt to society. Tell him I want to go to jail for three years, and for them to come and get me right away.

Sincerely,
ANTHONY (TOUGH TONY) CORNARO

P.S. On my way to get a stamp for this I notice that I have some gray hairs which is very unusual for a person going on seventeen. Please tell the judge I wouldn't mind if they give me solitary confinement and that maybe it would help me pay my debt to society.

In haste,
T.T.

Chan Davis wrote a small number of excellent science-fiction stories, most of which appeared in the magazines in the mid-to-late 1940s. A mathematician by training and trade, he has lived in Canada for many years. In addition to the present selection, his most notable works are "The Nightmare" (1946), one of the first post-Hiroshima warning stories and still one of the best, and "Adrift On the Policy Level" (1959), a scathing attack on the bureaucratic mind.

"Letter to Ellen" (Astounding Science Fiction, June 1947) has lived in the shadow of Lester del Rey's famous "Helen O'Loy." But it belongs in the sunlight, because it is one of the most compassionate and beautiful stories you will ever read.

LETTER TO ELLEN

By Chan Davis

Dear Ellen,

By the time you get this you'll be wondering why I didn't call. It'll be the first time I've missed in—how long?—two months? A long two months it's been, and, for me, a very important two months.

I'm not going to call, and I'm not going to see you. Maybe I'm a coward writing this letter, but you can judge that when you've finished it. Judge that, and other things.

Let's see. I'd better begin at the beginning and tell the whole story right through. Do you remember my friend Roy Wisner? He came to work in the lab the same time I did, in the spring of '16, and he was still around when I first met you. Even if you never met him, you may have seen him; he

28

was the tall blond guy with the stooped shoulders, working in the same branch with me.

Roy and I grew up together. He was my best friend as a kid, back almost as far as I can remember, back at the State Orphanage outside of Stockton. We went to different high schools, but when I got to Iowa U. there was Roy. Just to make the coincidence complete, he'd decided to be a biochemist too, and we took mostly the same courses all the way through. Both worked with Dietz while we were getting our doctorates, and Dietz got us identical jobs with Hartwell at the Pierne Labs here in Denver.

I've told you about that first day at the lab. We'd both heard from Dietz that the Pierne Labs were devoted now almost entirely to life-synthesis, and we'd both hoped to get in on that part of the work. What we hadn't realized was quite how far the work had got. I can tell you, the little talk old Hartwell gave us when he took us around to show us the lay of the land was just as inspiring as he meant it to be.

He showed us the wing where they're experimenting with the synthesis of new types of Coelenterates. We'd heard of that too, but seeing it was another thing. I remember particularly a rather ghastly green thing that floated in a small tank and occasionally sucked pieces of sea moss into what was half mouth, half sucker. Hartwell said, offhand, "Doesn't look much like the original, does it? That one was a mistake; something went wrong with the gene synthesis. But it turned out to be viable, so the fellows kept it around. Wouldn't be surprised if it could outsurvive some of its natural cousins if we were to give it a mate and turn it loose." He looked at the thing benignly. "I sort of like it."

Then we went down to Hartwell's branch, Branch 26, where we were to work. Hartwell slid back the narrow metal door and led the way into one of the labs. We started to follow him, but we hadn't gone more than three steps inside when we just stood still and gawked. I'd seen complicated apparatus before, but that place had anything at the Iowa labs beat by a factor of one thousand. All the gear on one whole side of the lab—and it was a good-sized place—was black-coated against the light and other stray radiation in the room. I recognized most of the flasks and fractionating columns as airtight jobs. A good deal of the hookup was hidden from us, being under Gardner hoods, airtight, temperature-controlled, radiation-controlled, and everything-else-controlled. What heaters we could see were never burners, always infrared banks.

This was precision work. It had to be, because, as you know, Branch 26 synthesizes chordate genes.

Roy and I went over to take a closer look at some of the gear. We stopped about a meter away; meddling was distinctly not in order. The item we were looking at was what would be called, in a large-scale process, a reaction vat. It was a small, opaque-coated flask, and it was being revolved slowly by a mechanical agitator, to swirl the liquids inside. As we stood there we could barely feel the gentle and precise flow of heat from the infrared heaters banked around it. We watched it, fascinated.

Hartwell snapped us out of it. "The work here," he said dryly, "is carried out with a good deal of care. You've had some experience with full microanalysis, Dietz tells me."

"A little," I nodded, with very appropriate modesty.

"Well, this is microsynthesis, and microsynthesis with a vengeance. Remember, our problem here is on an entirely different level even from ordinary protein synthesis." (It staggered me a little to hear him refer to protein synthesis as ordinary!) "There you're essentially building up a periodic crystal, one in which the atoms are arranged in regularly recurrent patterns. This recursion, this periodicity, makes the structure of the molecule relatively simple; correspondingly, it simplifies the synthesis. In a gene, a virus, or any other of the complex proteinlike molecules there isn't any such frequent recursion. Instead, the radicals in your molecule chain are a little different each time; the pattern almost repeats, but not quite. You've got what you call an a-periodic crystal.

"When we synthesize such a crystal we've got to get all the little variations from the pattern just right, because it's those variations that give the structure enough complexity to be living."

He had some chromosome charts under his arm, and now he pulled one out to show to us. I don't know if you've ever seen the things; one of them alone fills a little booklet, in very condensed notation. Roy and I thumbed through one, recognizing a good many of the shorthand symbols but not understanding the scheme of the thing at all. When we got through we were pretty thoroughly awed.

Hartwell smiled. "You'll catch on, don't worry. The first few months, while you're studying up, you'll be my lab assistants. You won't be on your own until you've got the process down pretty near pat." And were we glad to hear that!

Roy and I got an apartment on the outside of town; I didn't have my copter then, so we had to be pretty close. It was a good place, though only one wall and the roof could be made transparent. We missed the morning sun that way, but I liked it all right. Downstairs lived Graham, our landlord, an old bachelor who spent most of his time on home photography, both movie wires and old-fashioned chemical prints. He got some candid angle shots of us that were so weird Roy was thinking of breaking his cameras.

At the lab we caught on fast enough. Roy was always a pretty bright boy, and I manage to keep up. After a reasonable period Hartwell began to ease himself out of our routine, until before we knew it we were running the show ourselves. Naturally, being just out of school, we began, as soon as we got the drift of things, to suggest changes in the process. The day Hartwell finally approved one of our bright ideas, we knew we were standing on our own feet. That's when the fun really began.

Some people laugh when I say "that kind of drudgery" is fun, but you're a biochemist yourself and I'm pretty sure you feel the same way. The mere thought that we were putting inert colloids in at one end and getting something out at the other end that was in some strange way *living*—that was enough to take the boredom out of the job, if there'd been any.

Because we always felt that it was in our lab and the others like it that nonlife ended and life began. Sure, before us there was the immense job of protein synthesis and colloid preparation. Sure, after we were through there was the last step, the ultramicrosurgery of putting the nuclear wall together around the chromatin and embedding the result in a cell. (I always half envied your branch that job.) But in between there was our stage of the thing, which we thought to be the crucial one.

Certainly it was a tough enough stage. The long, careful reactions, with temperatures regulated down to a hundredth of a degree and reaction time to a tenth of a second; and then the final reactions, with everything enclosed in Gardner hoods, where you build up, bit by bit, the living nucleoplasm around the almost-living chromosomes. Hartwell hadn't lied when he said the work was carried out with care! That was quite a plant for two young squirts like us to be playing around with.

Just to put an edge on it, of course, there was always the possibility that you'd do everything right and still misfire. Anywhere along the line, Heisenberg's Uncertainty Principle could shove a radical out of place in those protein chains, no matter how careful you were. Then you'd get a weird thing: a gene mutating before it was even completed.

Or Heisenberg's Principle might pull you through even if your process had gone wrong!

We got curious after a while, Roy especially. Hartwell had told us a lot; one thing he hadn't told us was exactly *what we were making:* fish, flesh, or fowl, and we weren't geneticists enough to know ourselves. It would have been better, while we were working, to have had a mental picture of the frog or lizard or chicken that was to be our end product; instead, our mental picture was a composite of the three, and a rather disconcerting composite it made. I preferred to imagine a rabbit, or better yet, an Irish terrier puppy.

Hartwell not only hadn't offered to tell us, he didn't tell us when we asked him. "One of the lower chordates," he said; "the species name doesn't matter." That phrase "lower chordates" didn't ring quite true. There were enough chromosomes in our whatever-they-were's that they had to be something fairly far up the scale.

Roy immediately decided he was going to get the answer if he had to go through twenty books on genetics to do it. Looking back, I'm surprised I didn't have the same ambition. Maybe I was too interested in chess; I was on one of my periodic chess binges at the time. Anyhow, Roy got the genetics books and Roy did the digging.

It didn't take him any time at all. I remember that night well. He had brought home a stack of books from the library and was studying them at the desk in the corner. I was in the armchair with my portable chessboard, analyzing a game I'd lost in the last tournament. As the hours went by, I noticed Roy getting more and more restless; I expected him to come up with the answer any time, but apparently he was rechecking to make sure. About the time I'd found how I should have played to beat Fedruk, Roy got up, a little unsteadily.

"Dirk," he began, then stopped.

"You got it?"

"Dirk, I wonder if you realize just how few chordate species there are which have forty-eight chromosomes."

"Well, humans have, and I guess we're not so unique."

He didn't say anything.

"Hey, do you mean what I think you mean?" I jumped to my feet.

If he did, it was terrific news for me; I think I'd had the idea in the back of my mind all the time and never dared check it for fear I'd be proved wrong. Roy wasn't so happy about it. He said, "Yes, that's exactly what I mean. The species name Hartwell wouldn't tell us was *Homo sapiens*. We're making—robots."

That took a little time to digest. When I'd got it assimilated I came back, "What do you mean, robots? If we made a puppy that wagged its tail O.K., you'd be just as pleased as I would." (I was still stuck on that Irish terrier idea of mine.) That wouldn't give you the shudders. Why do you get so worried just because it's men we're making?"

"It's not right," he said.

"What?" Roy never having been religious or anything, that sounded strange.

"Well, I take that back, I guess, but—" His voice trailed away; then, more normally, "I don't know, Dirk. I just can't see it. Making humans—what would you call them if not robots?"

"I'd call them men, doggone it, if they turn out right. Of course if they don't turn out right—maybe I could see your point. If they don't turn out right. Killing a freak chicken and killing an experimental baby that didn't quite—succeed—would be two different things. Yeah."

"I hadn't thought of that."

"Then what the heck *were* you thinking of?"

"Aw, I don't know." He went back to the desk, slammed his books shut.

"What's bothering you, Roy?"

He didn't answer, just went into his bedroom and shut the door. He didn't come out again that night.

The next morning he was grim-faced, but you could see he was excited underneath. I knew he was planning something. Finally I wormed it out of him: he was going to take a look around Branch 39 to try and find some human embryos, as confirmation. Branch 39, as you know, is one of the ones that shuts up at night; they don't have to have technicians around twenty-four hours a day as 26 does. Roy's plan was to go up there just before closing time, hide, and get himself locked in overnight.

I asked him why the secrecy, why didn't he just ask to be shown around. "Hartwell doesn't want us to know," he said, "or he would have told us. I'll have to do it on the QT."

That made some sense, but—"Heck, Hartwell couldn't have expected to keep us permanently in the dark about what we were making, when all the dope you needed to figure it out was right there in the library. He must have wanted simply to let us do the figuring ourselves."

"Uh-uh. He knew we could puzzle it through if we wanted, but he wasn't going to help us. You think the lab wants to publicize what it's doing? No, Hartwell must be trying to keep as many people as possible from knowing; he hoped we'd stay uncurious. I'm not going to tell him we've guessed, and don't you."

I agreed reluctantly, but Roy's play-acting seemed to me like just that. Roy was deadly serious about it.

Later I got the story of that night. He'd gone up to 39 as planned, and hid in the big hall on the second floor; that was the place with the most embryos, and he thought he'd have the best chance there. Everything went O.K.; the assistant turned out the lights and locked up, and Roy stayed curled in his cabinet under a lab table. When the sounds had died down in the corridors outside, he came out and looked around.

He didn't know quite how to start. There were all sizes and shapes of gestators around. When he had taken out his flash and got a good look at one, he remained in as much of a quandary as before. It didn't seem to be anything but a bottle-shaped black container, about twenty centimeters on a side, in the middle of a mass of tubing, gauges, and levers. He could guess the bottle contained the embryo; he could guess the tubing kept up the flow of "body fluids" to and from the bottle; he could recognize some of the gauge markings and some of the auxiliary apparatus; and that was all. Not only was the embryo not exposed to view but he didn't see any way of exposing it. There was a label in a code he couldn't read. Nothing was any help.

The gestators were simple enough compared to the stuff he worked with, but he had a healthy respect for that sort of thing and didn't want to experiment to try to figure them out. If you meddled with a gestator in the wrong way, there was the chance that you'd be ruining a hundred people's work; and there would be many more wrong ways than right.

He made the circuit of the lab, stooping over one gestator after another, considering. After a while the moon rose and gave him a little more light. That was not what he needed.

A key turned in the lock.

Roy, hoping he hadn't been seen, ran back to his hiding place. He left the cabinet open far enough so he could see. A figure came in the door, turned to close it, and strode toward the center of the hall. As it passed through a patch of moonlight from one of the windows, Roy recognized the face: Hartwell.

He must have been working late in his office and come down for a look at his branch's products before leaving. Be that as it may, his presence cinched the thing: whatever embryos he looked at would be from our branch. Roy watched breathlessly while the other went from bench to bench, peering at the code labels. Finally he stopped before one, worked a lever, and peeked in through a viewer in the side, which Roy hadn't noticed. He looked quite a while, then turned and left.

I don't need to tell you that Roy didn't lose any time after Hartwell left in taking a look through that same viewer. And I don't need to tell you what he saw.

Reading back over this letter, I can see I'm stretching the story out, telling you things you already know and things that aren't really necessary. I know why I'm doing it, too—I'm reluctant to get to the end. But what I've got to tell you, I've got to tell you; I'll make the rest as short as I can.

Roy was pretty broken up about the whole thing, and he didn't get over it. I think it was the experience in the gestation lab that did it. If he'd just asked Hartwell for the truth, straight out, the thing would have stopped being fantastic and again become merely his business; but that melodrama up in Branch 39 kept him from looking at things with a clear eye. He went around in a half daze a good deal of the time, pondering, I suppose, some such philosophical problem as, When is a man not a man? It was all terrible; robots were going to take over the world, or something like that. And he insisted I still not tell Hartwell what he'd learned.

Then came the payoff. It was several weeks later, the day after Roy's twenty-sixth birthday. (The date was significant, as I learned later.) He told me before we left the lab that Hartwell had asked him to come up after work to talk with Koslicki.

I raised my eyebrows. "Koslicki, huh? The top man."

"Yes, Koslicki and Hartwell both."

He looked a little worried, so I ventured a crack. "Guess they've got a really rugged punishment for you, for trespassing that night. Death by drowning in ammonium sulphide, perhaps."

"I don't know why you can't take things seriously."

"Oh? What do you think they want to talk to you about?"

"No, I mean this whole business of—"

"Of making 'robots,' yeah. Roy, I do take it seriously, darn seriously. I think it's the biggest scientific project in the world right now. You take the kind of work we're doing, together with the production of new life forms like those experimental Coelenterates we saw, and you've got the groundwork for a new kind of eugenics that'll put our present systems in the shade. Now, we select from naturally occurring haploid germ cells to produce our new forms. In the future we'll *make* the new forms.

"We can make new strains of wheat, new species of sheep and cattle—new races of men! We won't have to wait for evolution any more. We won't have to content ourselves with giving evolution an occasional shove, either; we'll be striking out on our own. There's no limit to the possibilities. New, man-made men, stronger than we are, with minds twice as fast and accurate as ours—I take that plenty seriously."

"But they wouldn't be men."

This was beginning to get irritating. "They wouldn't be Homo sapiens, no," I answered. "Let's face it, Roy. If I were to get married, say, and have a kid that was a sharp mutation, a really radical mutation, and if he were to turn out to be a superman—that kid wouldn't be Homo sapiens, either. He wouldn't have the same germ plasm his parents had. Would he be human or wouldn't he?"

"He'd be human."

"Well? Where's the difference?"

"He wouldn't have come out of somebody's reagent bottles, that's the difference. He'd be—natural."

I could take only so much of that. Leaving Roy to go to his conference with Koslicki and Hartwell, I came home.

There I finished up the figuring on some notes I'd taken that day in the lab, then I turned the ceiling transparent and sat down with my visor. I'd just added a couple of new wires to my movie collection, so I ran them over—a couple of ballets, they were. No, none of the wires I've shown you. I've thrown out all the movies I saw *that* night.

I was sitting there having a good time with the "Pillar of Fire" when Roy came back. He made a little noise fumbling with the door. Then he slid it back and stood on the threshold without entering.

Switching off the visor, I glanced around. "What's the take, Jake?" I corned cheerfully. "Did Koslicki give you a good dressing-down? Or did he make you the new director?"

"...I'll play you a game of chess, Dirk."

This time I took a good look at him. His shoulders were stooped more than usual, and he looked around the room as if he didn't recognize it. Not good. "For crying out loud! What's the story?"

"Let's play chess."

"O.K.," I said. He came in and got out the men and the big board, but his hand shook so I had to set up his men for him. Then, "Go ahead," I told him.

"Oh, yeah, I've got white."

Pawn to king four, knight to king bishop three, pawn to king five—one of our standard openings. I pulled my knight back in the corner and brought out the other one; he pushed his pawns up in the center; I began getting ready to castle.

Then he put his queen on queen four. "You don't mean that," I said. "My knight takes you there."

"Oh, yeah, so he does," Roy said, pulling his queen back—to the wrong square. He was staring over my shoulder as if there was a ghost standing behind me. I looked; there wasn't. I replaced his queen.

Finally, still keeping up the stare, he began, "Dirk, you know Hartwell told me—"

"Yeah?" I said casually. I knew it had been something important. Roy hadn't been *this* bad the last few weeks. Whatever it was, he might as well get it off his chest.

Roy, however, seemed to have forgotten he'd spoken. His eyes returned intently to the board. His bishop went to king three—where I could not take it—and the game went on.

"You're going to lose that bishop's pawn, old man," I remarked after a while.

I think that was what triggered it. He said suddenly but evenly, "I'm one."

"I'm two," I said, apropos of nothing. My mind was still on the game.

"Dirk, *I'm one*," he insisted. He stood up, upsetting the board, and began to walk up and down. "Koslicki just told me. I'm one of the . . . Dirk, I wasn't born, I'm one of the robots, they put me together out of those goddamned chemicals in those goddamned white-labeled reagent bottles in that goddamned laboratory—"

"What?"

He stopped his pacing and began to laugh. "I'm just a Frankenstein. You can pull out your gun and sizzle me dead; it won't be murder, I'm just a robot." He was laughing all through this and he kept on laughing when he'd stopped.

I figured if he was going to blow up he might as well blow up good and proper. He'd make some noise, but old Graham would be the only one disturbed. "So," I said, "how did you feel going through the reaction vats over in 26? Did the microsurgery hurt when they put you together?" Roy laughed. He laughed harder. Then he screamed.

Deciding that enough was enough, I yelled at him. He screamed again.

"Shut up, Roy!" I shouted as sharply as I could. "You're as human as I am. You've lived with yourself twenty-six years; you ought to know whether you're human or not."

After the first couple of words he listened to me O.K., so I figured the hysterics were over. I tried to sound firm as I said, "Are you through with the foolishness now?"

Roy didn't pass out, he simply lay down on the floor. I sat down beside him and began to talk in a low voice. "You're just as good as anybody else; you've already proved that. It doesn't matter where you started, just what you are here and now. Here and now, you've got human genes, you've got human cells; you can marry a human girl and make human babies with her. So what if you did start out in a lab? The rest of us started out in the ooze on the bottom of some ocean. Which is better? It doesn't make any difference. You're just as good as anybody else." I said it over and over again, as calmly as I could. Don't know whether or not it was the right thing to do, but I had to do something.

Once he raised his head to say, "Roy Wisner, huh? Is that me? Heck no, why didn't they call me Roy $W_{23}H$? ... I wonder where they got the name Wisner anyway." He sank back and I took up my spiel again, doing my best to keep my voice level.

After several minutes of this he got up off the floor. "Thanks," he said in a fairly normal tone. "Thanks, Dirk. You're a real friend." He went toward the door, adding as he left, "You're human."

I just sat there. It wasn't till he'd been gone a couple of minutes that I put two and two together. Then I raced out of that room and to the stairs in nothing flat.

Too late. Graham's door was open downstairs, and the light from inside shone into the hall, across the twitching body of Roy Wisner.

Graham looked at me, terrified. "I thought it was all right," he stammered. "He asked me for some hydrocyanic. I knew he was a chemist; I thought it was all right."

Hydrocyanic acid kills fast. One look at the size of the container Roy had drained, and I saw there wasn't much we could do. We did it, all right, but it wasn't enough. He died while we were still forcing emetic down his throat.

That's about all, Ellen. You know now why I never spoke much to you about Roy Wisner. And you've probably guessed why I'm writing this.

Roy was one of the experiments that failed. He was no more unstable mentally than a great many normally born men; still, a failure, though nobody knew it until he was twenty-six years old. The human organism is a very complex thing, and hard to duplicate. When you try to duplicate it you're very likely to fail, sometimes in obvious ways and sometimes in ways that don't become apparent till long afterward.

I may turn out to be a failure, too.

You see, I'm twenty-six now, and Koslicki and Hartwell have told me. *I* wasn't born, either. I was made. I am, if you like, a robot.

I had to tell you that, didn't I, Ellen? Before I asked you to marry me.

                                                          — Dirk

Born in England and now a Canadian citizen, Patricia Nurse is a recent addition to the ranks of professional science-fiction writers. In fact, this story, from the July–August 1978 issue of Isaac Asimov's Science Fiction Magazine, *is her first professional sale.*

This is an "inside sf" story, a form that is difficult to do well, and even more difficult to sell, because the writer cannot assume too much information on the part of the reader. However, in this case ...

ONE REJECTION TOO MANY

By Patricia Nurse

Dear Dr. Asimov:

Imagine my delight when I spotted your new science-fiction magazine on the newsstands. I have been a fan of yours for many, many years and I naturally wasted no time in buying a copy. I wish you every success in this new venture.

In your second issue I read with interest your plea for stories from new authors. While no writer myself, I have had a time traveler living with me for the past two weeks (he materialized in the bathtub without clothes or money, so I felt obliged to offer him shelter), and he has written a story of life on earth as it will be in the year 5000.

Before he leaves this time frame, it would give him great pleasure to see his story in print—I hope you will feel able to make this wish come true.

Yours sincerely,
NANCY MORRISON (Miss)

Dear Miss Morrison:

Thank you for your kind letter and good wishes.

It is always refreshing to hear from a new author. You have included some most imaginative material in your story; however, it is a little short on plot and human interest—perhaps you could rewrite it with this thought in mind.

Yours sincerely,
ISAAC ASIMOV

Dear Dr. Asimov:

I was sorry that you were unable to print the story I sent you. Vahl (the time traveler who wrote it) was quite hurt as he tells me he is an author of some note in his own time. He has, however, rewritten the story and this time has included plenty of plot and some rather interesting mating rituals which he has borrowed from the year 3000. In his own time (the year 5015) sex is no longer practiced, so you can see that it is perfectly respectable having him in my house. I do wish, though, that he could adapt himself to our custom of wearing clothes—my neighbors are starting to talk!

Anything that you can do to expedite the publishing of Vahl's story would be most appreciated, so that he will feel free to return to his own time.

Yours sincerely,
NANCY MORRISON (Miss)

Dear Miss Morrison:

Thank you for your rewritten short story.

I don't want to discourage you but I'm afraid you followed my suggestions with a little too much enthusiasm—however, I can understand that having an imaginary nude visitor from another time is a rather heady experience. I'm afraid that your story now rather resembles a far-future episode of *Mary Hartman, Mary Hartman* or *Soap*.

Could you tone it down a bit and omit the more bizarre sex rituals of the year 3000—we must remember that *Isaac Asimov's Science Fiction Magazine* is intended to be a family publication.

Perhaps a little humor would improve the tale too.

Yours sincerely,
ISAAC ASIMOV

Dear Dr. Asimov:

Vahl was extremely offended by your second rejection—he said he has never received a rejection slip before, and your referring to him as "imaginary" didn't help matters at all. I'm afraid he rather lost his temper and stormed out into the garden—it was at this unfortunate moment that the vicar happened to pass by.

Anyway, I managed to get Vahl calmed down and he has rewritten the story and added plenty of humor. I'm afraid my subsequent meeting with the vicar was not blessed with such success! I'm quite sure Vahl would not understand another rejection.

Yours truly,
NANCY MORRISON (Miss)

Dear Miss Morrison:

I really admire your persistence in rewriting your story yet another time. Please don't give up hope—you can became a fairly competent writer in time, I feel sure.

I'm afraid the humor you added was not the kind of thing I had in mind at all—you're not collaborating with Henny Youngman by any chance are you? I really had a more sophisticated type of humor in mind.

Yours truly,
ISAAC ASIMOV

P.S. Have you considered reading your story, as it is, on *The Gong Show*?

Dear Dr. Asimov:

It really was very distressing to receive the return of my manuscript once again—Vahl was quite speechless with anger.

It was only with the greatest difficulty that I prevailed upon him to refine the humor you found so distasteful, and I am submitting his latest rewrite herewith.

In his disappointment, Vahl has decided to return to his own time right away. I shall be sorry to see him leave as I was getting very fond of him—a pity he wasn't from the year 3000 though. Still, he wouldn't have made a very satisfactory husband; I'd have never known where (or when) he was. It rather looks as though my plans to marry the vicar have suffered a severe setback too. Are you married, Dr. Asimov?

I must close this letter now as I have to say goodbye to Vahl. He says he has just finished making some long overdue improvements to our time frame as a parting gift—isn't that kind of him?

Yours sincerely,
NANCY MORRISON (Miss)

Dear Miss Morrison:

I am very confused by your letter. Who is Isaac Asimov? I have checked with several publishers and none of them has heard of *Isaac Asimov's Science Fiction Magazine*, although the address on the envelope was correct for *this* magazine.

However, I was very impressed with your story and will be pleased to accept it for our next issue. Seldom do we receive a story combining such virtues as a well-conceived plot, plenty of human interest, and a delightfully subtle brand of humor.

Yours truly,
GEORGE H. SCITHERS,
Editor,
Arthur C. Clarke's Science Fiction Magazine

Ray Russell (1924–   ) is an important and relatively unknown figure in the history of science fiction. Long associated with Playboy, *he was responsible (along with one or two others) for opening that important market to science-fiction writers, and the magazine has now published many notable stories in the field. He was also the uncredited editor of the excellent* Playboy Book of Fantasy and Science Fiction *(1966) and its many successor volumes. As a writer, he has published in many genres and markets, although many of his best fantasies and sf stories can be found in* Sardonicus and Other Stories *(1961).*

*"Space Opera" (*Playboy, *December 1961) is a terrific story. We only wish that* The Planetary Evening Post *had seen fit to publish it.*

SPACE OPERA

By Ray Russell

The Editor
The Planetary Evening Post
Level 78
Building K-6 (Old Section)
New York, New York (Zip Code: AAB/00142534786c)

Dear Sir:
    Your letter was most appreciated, but I am very sorry you did not like "Vixen of Venus." Too melodramatic, you say, and today's readers will have nothing to do with melodrama.

But, my dear sir, life itself is flagrantly melodramatic! The lady I described in "Vixen of Venus" is an almost literal transcription of an actual lady I encountered there in my travels. However, that is water under the bridge, as you "Earthworms" say (ha-ha, no offense).

My purpose in writing to you again is to sketch briefly an article I would like to do for you. It is completely factual, though I fear it may strike you as extravagant. A deep-dyed villain figures prominently in the piece, also a fair maiden in distress, not to mention a righteous, retribution-dealing father right out of the admirable Victor Hugo of your own culture. And, yes, I'm afraid there will even be a tricky twist ending.

If you have read this far, perhaps you will read further. The proposed article, which we might call "The Star of Orim," concerns a series of fascinating events that occurred in my own galaxy, 75/890 (I trust you have no editorial taboo against foreign settings). The chronicle begins on the planet Orim, and our antagonist, the Sargian warlord Zoonbarolario Feng, accompanied by a beautiful young lady who hates him (it would be well to establish this immediately), is discovered in a magnificent Orimese palace. To point up their relationship, we might have them leaving a bedroom together. They make an oddly contrasted pair as they walk through the high-ceilinged, luxurious rooms of the palace. Feng is an enormous man—massive and powerful—with thick black hair and beard; his eyes are like an eagle's, and his nose is a formidable promontory that looks impressive on the coins that bear his likeness. In his black tunic, red robe and hip-high boots of shining xhulq, he is indeed an imposing figure. The girl is his complete opposite. She is small and slight, with fair skin and with hair red-gold as a dying sun—I'm sorry, but there *is* hair like that, you know, especially among the Orimese. Her young body is covered only by the most gauzelike pale rosy silk, cut in a pattern that leaves much of her smooth skin exposed. Her small, bare feet whisper on the marble floor.

Feng is in a good mood. As they walk, he chatters amiably in his rumbling basso. "Conquering your planet has been rich in rewards. Not only do I capture the most gifted scientist in the galaxy, but I find that he has an extremely beautiful daughter. A double prize!" This speech is reconstructed, and if the exposition is too crude for you, I can smooth it over in the finish.

As they approach the laboratory, they are saluted by two slender officers in the skintight black uniform of Feng's personal guard. One of them opens the door. Feng and the girl enter a huge room of glass and metal where a small forge glows and platoons of test tubes and retorts bubble and hiss. At the end of a long aisle, a gray-haired man sits on a high stool and looks at a gleaming metal star in his hand.

Feng walks up to him, and the girl follows. The black-bearded conqueror greets the scientist with condescending joviality. "Good evening, Torak," he booms. "What have you there?"

The old man ignores Feng, looks past him at the girl. "Vola," he whispers gently. "Vola, my child."

The girl's voice is faint and husky. "You look tired, Father. You work too hard."

"You, my dear—how are you?"

She lowers her eyes. "I'm all right. Don't worry about me."

Feng laughs. "That's right. Don't worry about her. She's in good hands!"

Does Torak lose your sympathy, dear sir, because he allows his daughter's virgin virtue to be rent asunder by this brute, impaled on the insatiable saber of his lechery? You must, then, be made aware that prior to her ravishment, Torak had watched, with taped-open eyes, an unedited ten-hour educational film, in living color, three dimensions and deafening multiphonic sound, of the legendary Six Hundred Sacred Tortures of Sarg, the featured roles played not by professional actresses but, at the tops of their voices, by the late-lamented lovely, young, naked, pink virgin daughters of other scientists of other planets. Do you continue to wonder why he permits Feng to plunder his daughter's beautiful body and his own brilliant mind?

Feng gets straight to business. "Now, then, Torak," he bellows, "I demand an answer! How soon will the project be finished?"

"It *is* finished, my lord," Torak answers in a lifeless tone and holds up the flat piece of metal cut in the form of a four-pointed star.

"This—" asks Feng, "this is it? The new metal?"

"The new metal. The invincible metal. Yes, this is it."

Feng chuckles. "I see you've made it into the shape of the

Star of Orim, the symbol of your people. A very clever comment, Torak—but your rebel's propaganda is wasted on me, I fear. Here, let me have that." He snatches the metal star from Torak's hand. "I shall notify my entire staff to assemble here immediately. The tests will begin at once."

"Tests?"

"Of course," Feng smiles. "You didn't think I would take your word for it, did you? Why, for all I know, this shiny new stuff of yours might collapse like tinfoil in a baby's fist. Nothing would please you more, would it?" He laughs again. "No, my friend, I am not such a fool. I have not conquered almost the entire galaxy to be finally outwitted by a rebel scientist. This metal shall be thoroughly tested, I assure you. And my own scientists shall conduct the tests." Feng's eyes grow suddenly sharper. "If it is all you claim it to be, then the last stronghold in the galaxy shall yield before me—the planet Klor!"

Now, somewhere in through here, we will have to sandwich the information that, for years, Feng had been looking forward to the day when the whole galaxy would be his. Slowly, planet by planet, he saw his dream coming true, but always the planet Klor resisted his mighty navies. Perhaps in a footnote we can remind your readers that Klor is a world almost completely underwater; most of its people are fishlike depth creatures. And Feng's engineers had despaired of building amphibious ships versatile enough to fling themselves from the base planet, Sarg, across the black emptiness of outer space and down into the watery depths of Klor. Such ships would have had to be made of metal as light as spaceship alloy and yet as pressure-resistant as a bathysphere. Moreover, it would have had to be resistant to heat and cold and radiation. But back to our scene in the laboratory:

The scarlet-robed emperor grasps the metal star and repeats, "Yes, the tests will begin at once." He turns and strides out of the room.

When the door clangs shut, Vola buries her face in her father's chest and breaks into uncontrollable weeping. "Oh, Father! It's been so horrible! That man is a beast—a filthy beast!"

Torak's hands clench as a father's indignation rises in him. "Vola, be brave. We must both be brave."

As you pointed out in regard to "Vixen of Venus," dialogue is not my strong point. I realize this and am perfectly willing to do the piece in straight reportorial form, should you so desire. However, since I have begun my outline in this style, I shall continue so:

Sparks fly in the darkened laboratory, as a group of dark-goggled men recoil from terrific heat. A powerful ray is bombarding the small piece of star-shaped metal. "See, my lord!" says one of the men. "The upper side of the metal is white-hot, while the underside—"

"Yes?" hisses Feng.

"The underside is cool to the touch! Incredible! Your captive scientist has achieved perfect insulation." He turns off the ray, and they all remove their goggles. "That concludes the series of tests, my lord. This piece of metal was subjected to powerful explosives, searing acids, atomic radiation, great pressure, and now—withering heat. Nothing affects it! It is completely impervious."

Feng smiles. He turns to Torak. "My congratulations. You have not failed me. You shall have an honored place in the scientific hierarchy of my empire." Abruptly, he turns to his chief engineer. "Great quantities of this metal must be produced and made into the spaceships you have designed. You will work with Torak. I shall expect you to begin tomorrow. And remember, gentlemen, the conquest of Klor means the conquest of the galaxy!" He walks away as the scientists and generals bow. At the door, he turns to a figure in the shadows. "Come, Vola," he says. (We can play down this sex element if you wish.)

During the days that follow, Torak forces himself to be oblivious to his daughter's tears. While she languishes in the arms of Feng, submitting silently to the legendary Seven Hundred Sacred Perversions of Sarg, the old scientist supervises at foundries where ton after ton of the molten new metal is poured from monstrous blast furnaces. Captive slave-workers from the far reaches of the galaxy labor day and night without sleep until they drop from exhaustion and are flogged into consciousness again. When they die, they are replaced by others. And often at Torak's side is the exultant Feng, who slaps him on the back and praises him.

As soon as the sheets of metal roll from the foundries, they are rushed to the shipyards, where already the armada of amphibious destroyers is growing. Feng himself supervises the construction of the largest of these, his flagship. His escutcheon, the flaming sword of Sarg, is deeply etched on its gleaming prow; rich draperies and costly furniture—the loot of a thousand plundered worlds—are carried aboard to embellish his cabin. It is only a matter of months (incidentally, I am using Earth time throughout) before the fleet is finished. Poised and sparkling in the sun, the ships stand ready for embarkation.

Feng and his highest officers stand on a great platform repeating a ritual that has taken place before the conquest of each new planet. Martial music blares from a phalanx of glittering horns. The people of Orim cheer—with Sargian guns at their backs—as Feng, resplendent in his battle armor made completely of Torak's new metal, declaims his customary ritual speech. (I have a copy of this for verification.) His big, rough voice thunders over the loudspeakers in phrases heavy with emotionalism and light on logic. Often "the glories of Sarg" and the greatness of "our sacred galactic empire" are spoken of, but no attempt is made to define or examine these terms. Feng emphasizes the importance of conquering Klor, the last remaining planet in the galaxy which still struggles in "a barbaric darkness unilluminated by Sargian glory." He tells why he has ordered not only his generals but also his eldest statesmen and savants to accompany him in his flagship on this mission: "It is fitting that the chiefs of the Sargian Empire be present at the momentous conquest of the last planet." The speech ends with the mighty exclamation, "On to Klor!" and the trumpets drown the unenthusiastic applause.

On the gangplank of his flagship, Feng pauses and turns to Torak. "Upon my return, you shall be decorated for your services to Sarg. And you, Vola"—he smiles at the unresponsive girl—"be prepared for a night of revelry on my return. Missions of conquest never fail to excite my blood, and although the water-dwelling females of Klor may turn out to be lovely"—he winks knowingly at his generals—"I fear that, as proper entertainers to an emperor, mermaids may have certain...disadvantages, eh?" He laughs at his joke (too coarse for your readership?) and enters the flagship, followed by his generals and key statesmen.

Soon there is a terrific roar and a searing blast of rocket fire as the fleet shoots upward and dwindles to a swarm of tiny specks in the clear blue sky of Orim.

During the months of the voyage, the black wine of Sarg flows freely in the imperial flagship. Feng toasts his empire, his generals and himself. He toasts each planet, each star, each comet they pass. He toasts Torak, he toasts Vola, and he toasts the nearly forgotten women of his youth. He sings ribald Sargian ballads, and he swears fantastic oaths. All this can easily be expanded into several pages.

At length, the armada approaches Klor. As his flagship hovers above the flooded planet, Feng draws his jeweled ceremonial sword and points dramatically to the objective. His voice roars through the intercoms of every ship:

"Attack!"

Down they plunge, the flagship leading. Cleanly, Feng's ship cuts the surface of the water and his fleet follows, creating a series of immense splashes and vast, ever-widening ripples.

Through the transparent dome of his ship, Feng marvels at the exotic weeds and pouting giant fishes of Klor. Triumph sings in his veins.

Then, suddenly, the cries of startled men reach his ears. He turns, and his eagle's eyes bulge with shock....

If we do this as a serial, what better place for a break? But that is up to you, of course. And now let me quickly limn the final scene, which takes place back on Orim:

Torak drops a four-pointed metal star into a glass. It floats slowly to the bottom. He turns to his daughter, who is gazing pensively out of the laboratory window. Tenderly, he asks, "Is anything troubling you, my dear?"

There are tears in her eyes. "I was thinking of the people of Klor, that's all."

Torak smiles slightly—for the first time in many, many months. "I wouldn't spend my tears on them, if I were you. In fact, I see no reason for weeping at all."

"You don't? Father, how can you say that?"

"Feng," says Torak grimly, "will never molest you again."

"What do you mean?"

"And never again will he subjugate an entire galaxy. By this time, the armada should have reached Klor." Torak verifies this by a glance of his calendar. "Feng is dead."

Vola fears for her father's sanity. She is silent as he continues, "Dead. Floating in the waters of Klor, with all his officers, his ministers and his navy."

He looks up and sees the fear in her face. "No, my dear, I'm not mad. You see, I created a very wonderful metal. A metal both light and strong, resistant to heat and cold and pressure and radiation. A miraculous metal. And Feng was smart. He tested it thoroughly. Yes, he put my metal through every possible test—except one. One so simple, so basic that it never occurred to him. And so he built his fleet and plunged it into the seas of Klor without knowing...."

Torak turns to regard the glass from which the metal star of Orim has vanished. "Without knowing," he says, "that this rather remarkable metal *dissolves*—in water."

Now, *there,* sir, even you must admit, is a natural! And true—every word. But that is not all—in fact, the greatest revelation is yet to come.

For suppose we say—or at least hint—that shrewd Feng, the galaxy killer, the scourge of 75/890, the man who never trusted anybody in his life, took the characteristic, routine precaution of wearing, under his ceremonial armor of Torak metal, a conventional depth suit (not because he suspected anything specific, but because suspicion was his natural state of mind), that Feng, in other words, *survived the disaster!*

Perhaps we may even use a title like "Feng Is Still Alive!" or "Feng Is Still Alive?"—a time-tested attention getter. We can imply that the indestructible Zoonbarolarrio Feng, after the demolition of his navy, made his relentless and lonely way to one of Klor's few shreds of dry land—say, the south polar region of Fozkep—where even now he plots new conquests, like your own Napoleon of yore at Elba. You will say, perhaps, that nobody will believe such an assertion, and I would be inclined to agree with you, but what does that matter so long as they buy your magazine? And speaking of buying brings me to the touchy but unavoidable question of payment. I am in most desperate need of large sums and would expect your highest rates, on acceptance, should this article be commissioned for your pages. So *please* let me hear from you by return warpmail, since I urgently require every bit of ready cash I can muster.

Yours sincerely,
Z. GNEF
P.O. Box 9,000,053
75/890

*Born in 1930, William Sambrot is a long-time professional
writer who sold consistently to the "slicks" (The Saturday
Evening Post, Collier's, etc.). Although his science-fiction and
fantasy output has been relatively small, there are enough
stories for an excellent collection,* Island of Fear and Other
Science Fiction Stories *(1963). Perhaps his finest story in the
field is "Night of the Leopard" (1967).*

*"The Invasion of the Terrible Titans" is from the October
1959 issue of* Cosmopolitan.

THE INVASION OF THE TERRIBLE TITANS

By William Sambrot

*Mr. George Papadoukalis
Ocean College Alumni Association
Ocean City, California*

DEAR MR. PAPADOUKALIS:

Herewith, written in some haste, is my report on Pacific
Underwater College's "Terrible Titans," the incredible group
of athletes which has flattened every rival (including yourself) in the coast league.

I regret you found it necessary to insist upon this report
before taking up the matter of the additional funds I requested by wire last night. The results of my efforts in your
and the alumni's behalf will speak for themselves next season. You have but to read the following to realize that much
more than mere money is at stake. I know you will be more
than generous.

In the event you still have some doubts after reading this,

may I ask you to review the score of the last game O.C. played
with Pacific: 112 to 0, was it not? Bear with me.

As a starter, I attempted to get some fingerprints of Sam
Bama, Pacific's star, and the first of the Terrible Titans to
enroll there. You will be as surprised as I to discover the
man has no fingerprints. I mean to say, his fingers are blank,
smooth expanses of skin. Furthermore, when I casually
handed him my solid silver (plated) cigarette case (the one
our grateful alumni gave me several seasons ago when I
uncovered the flagrant case of proselytism going on at B.U.),
he fumbled with it and acted generally like someone who's
never even seen a cigarette, let alone a solid silver (plated)
case. But, as I say, no fingerprints. Keep this in mind.

Bama, I might add in passing, speaks rather cultured English with a strong Oxford accent. His eyes are somewhat
pinkish and his hair quite white. Albino characteristics.

However, I've never before met an albino somewhat over
seven feet tall, lightning fast and weighing three hundred
pounds. He has no neck to speak of, massive sloping shoulders, and arms surely no thicker than my thighs. Also, he
has a pronounced body odor—something like a musk ox.
(They have one at the zoo, and for purposes of comparison I
went around there. Oddly enough, after some hours of sniff-
ing, I discovered the closest similar odor came not from the
musk ox, but from a yak. The significance of this failed to
dawn upon me until just last night.)

Pacific's phenomenal athletic record this season can be
laid at the door of one man—Professor Harold Crimshaw.
You may well ask what a professor of physics has to do with
your being unmercifully trounced in the bowl last New
Year's, but the facts, as uncovered by me, are these:

Professor Crimshaw, a bachelor in his late forties, is a
specialist on cosmic-ray research. He often spends his spare
time and what funds he can drum up trudging about the
higher mountains of the globe, capturing cosmic rays and
measuring their intensity. As you might guess, very few people are interested enough in captured cosmic rays to finance
expeditions, so up until the winter before last Professor Crimshaw operated on a strictly low budget.

I say up until the winter before last, because after that,
things suddenly changed. He arrived back on the campus
shortly after the holidays, accompanied by a small dark man

with a beard and a huge box, punched with air holes, which must have weighed well over three hundred pounds.

Also, the box (as I was able to ascertain myself) gave off a powerful odor. In fact investigation disclosed that Professor Moriarty of biology inquired if perhaps Professor Crimshaw hadn't brought back a live musk ox. The question remained unanswered. The small bearded man was equally inscrutable.

Shortly after that, Moriarty, Dr. Evans (president of P.U.) and Dr. Smythe-Smythe, head of the language department, on loan from Oxford University, were all seen going into Professor Crimshaw's bachelor quarters. I have since managed to gain entry by a ruse and can testify that even to this day a strong odor, as of a penned-up musk ox or yak, still permeates the atmosphere.

By careful (and guarded, of course) inquiry I have learned that shortly thereafter one Oscar Grossgudt, a wholesale butcher and one of the few alumni of P.U. worth a line in Dun & Bradstreet, was seen lingering about Crimshaw's quarters. Subsequently, one of his delivery trucks made daily deliveries to Crimshaw's home; but whatever was delivered was concealed beneath a canvas wrapper. Suffice it to say, however, that discreet queries disclosed the fact that quantities of bones were carted away daily—say, about that left over from half a haunch of well-gnawed beef.

George Sneedely, P.U.'s football and wrestling coach, along with his assistant, Daniel McGurk (known to you as "Goon" McGurk), were seen entering and leaving Crimshaw's quarters frequently. On one occasion McGurk was seen noticeably limping and holding his shoulder, although Sneedely seemed in the best of spirits. In fact he was smiling, something he hasn't done since '45, the year Pacific won one and tied one (although losing twelve).

It was less than a month afterward that Sam Bama was enrolled officially at P.U. as Crimshaw's protégé. He was (and is) amiable, quick-witted, with an I.Q. of 128. (Rorschach not available.) Well-liked by all, including the girls, most of whom preferred not to date him.

In his first football game, as the alumni of State well know, he scored every time he was given the ball, which, mercifully, was only seventeen times. Sneedely is a kind-hearted chap, retiring Bama to the bench only after he was informed during the half that two of the opponent defenders suffered severe skull fractures, incurred as Bama stepped on their heads. Fortunately he was not wearing shoes.

After the game Bama gladly granted press interviews, winning the scribes' hearts with his easy banter. He skillfully parried all queries as to his prep school, although hints were dropped by Sneedely that Bama was a transferee from "overseas."

It was directly after this first game that Crimshaw's great expedition to measure cosmic rays was announced. He was given special leave of absence. Where he was going was left unmentioned, however. Clippings enclosed.

I can tell you that after considerable checking I was able to learn that money for this expedition (a large sum in fact—please note) had been advanced by a small clique of P.U. alumni, consisting in the main of Oscar Grossgudt and one Pete DeLassio, a gentleman connected with a gambling syndicate, the same syndicate which took all bets in advance on the entire schedule of P.U. and which really cleaned up, as doubtless you know.

The expedition was organized with great secrecy, but I have since learned that the entire staff of the manual arts department worked overtime building ten stout packing cases, complete with air holes.

The expedition returned last summer, slipping quietly into town late one evening. However, there were frequent complaints that evening by the citizenry that howls and roars were coming from the direction of the freight yards. A sound, as one local put it, exactly like feeding time at the zoo.

And last autumn, of course, P.U. fielded their incredible "Terrible Titans" which remained unscored upon—but why am I telling you this? You know what they did to the rest of the league.

To a man, the Terrible Titans all look amazingly alike—each a little over seven feet tall, each weighing well over three hundred pounds. They are all albinos, I can say positively, even though (as I can prove) they wear colored contact lenses. Also, in order to further conceal their identical appearance, each has his hair dyed a different shade, and some even have their skin darkened. They use prodigious quantities of deodorants and are quite popular with the girls.

Earlier I mentioned that Professor Crimshaw, winter before last, had returned with a small dark man with a beard and a huge box. This little man vanished about the time of the great expedition and just as mysteriously reappeared when the expedition returned.

By great good luck I ran across the little dark man only last night. He was in a pub, unnoticed, morose, drinking whiskey sours and obviously disliking them. I fell into deep conversation with him, and what he had to say was startling indeed; no amount of whiskey sours could account for it. It has to be true. It all fits.

He is a Sherpa: one of those breed of slight, tough men who make a business of climbing the high mountains of the Himalayas. Between whiskey sours he sobbed out his desire to go back; he says he is one of the few men alive who knows the haunts of the Yeti—the abominable snow men, so called; those giant, strangely manlike creatures of myth (or mystery?) who roam the inaccessible peaks. He speaks their language, he says. They are shy, nimble creatures but extremely intelligent withal. Loyal to a fault, they would follow him anywhere, he assures me.

Many were the times, he says, they spent bounding about the great peaks, chasing yaks for food and fun. But, alas, all too humanlike, once they tasted the dubious joys of civilization, they forgot the old ways. They became decadent; they looked upon him, their old friend, as old-fashioned—in a word, a cornball (an epithet much favored at P.U. this season).

He longed to go back, he sobbed. Back to his yaks and untutored Yeti.

And so we're going back, Mr. Papadoukalis. Fortunately, I have my credit card. I'm writing this from San Francisco International Airport. We expect to reach Katmandu, India, on or about the twelfth of the month.

Please wire sufficient funds to outfit a good-sized expedition to reach an altitude of approximately twenty-six thousand feet. Also, make sure you include enough to cover the cost of at least eleven good-sized packing cases, strong enough to hold over three hundred pounds each.

Mum's the word, and come next season we'll have a surprise for Pacific, if you follow me, and I'm sure you do.

Yours in haste,
J. PONDER
Prop., Ponder Detective Agency

Judith Merril (1923–   ) was (she has not produced much fiction in recent years) a major figure in science fiction, both as a writer and as one of the leading anthologists in the field. Her anthology England Swings SF *(1968) was a major event in the history of the "New Wave" in science fiction, and she produced twelve highly regarded volumes of "Best of the Year" stories from 1956 to 1967.*

"That Only a Mother" (Astounding Science Fiction, *June 1948) is a deservedly famous story in science fiction, and one of the truly great first stories of all time.*

THAT ONLY A MOTHER

By Judith Merril

Margaret reached over to the other side of the bed where Hank should have been. Her hand patted the empty pillow, and then she came altogether awake, wondering that the old habit should remain after so many months. She tried to curl up, cat-style, to hoard her own warmth, found she couldn't do it any more, and climbed out of bed with a pleased awareness of her increasingly clumsy bulkiness.

Morning motions were automatic. On the way through the kitchenette, she pressed the button that would start breakfast cooking—the doctor had said to eat as much breakfast as she could—and tore the paper out of the facsimile machine. She folded the long sheet carefully to the "National News" section and propped it on the bathroom shelf to scan while she brushed her teeth.

57

No accidents. No direct hits. At least none that had been officially released for publication. *Now, Maggie, don't get started on that. No accidents. No hits. Take the nice newspaper's word for it.*

The three clear chimes from the kitchen announced that breakfast was ready. She set a bright napkin and cheerful colored dishes on the table in a futile attempt to appeal to a faulty morning appetite. Then, when there was nothing more to prepare, she went for the mail, allowing herself the full pleasure of prolonged anticipation, because today there would *surely* be a letter.

There was. There were. Two bills and a worried note from her mother: "Darling. Why didn't you write and tell me sooner? I'm thrilled, of course, but, well, one hates to mention these things, but are you *certain* the doctor was right? Hank's been around all that uranium or thorium or whatever it is all these years, and I know you say he's a designer, not a technician, and he doesn't get near anything that might be dangerous, but you know he used to, back at Oak Ridge. Don't you think...well, of course, I'm just being a foolish old woman, and I don't want you to get upset. You know much more about it than I do, and I'm sure your doctor was right. He *should* know..."

Margaret made a face over the excellent coffee, and caught herself refolding the paper to the medical news.

Stop it, Maggie, stop it! The radiologist said Hank's job couldn't have exposed him. And the bombed area we drove past...No, no. Stop it, now! Read the social notes or the recipes, Maggie girl.

A well-known geneticist, in the medical news, said that it was possible to tell with absolute certainty, at five months, whether the child would be normal, or at least whether the mutation was likely to produce anything freakish. The worst cases, at any rate, could be prevented. Minor mutations, of course, displacements in facial features or changes in brain structure, could not be detected. And there had been some cases recently, of normal embryos with atrophied limbs that did not develop beyond the seventh or eighth month. But, the doctor concluded cheerfully, the *worst* cases could now be predicted and prevented.

"Predicted and prevented." We predicted it, didn't we? Hank and the others, they predicted it. But we didn't prevent it. We could have stopped it in '46 and '47. Now...

Margaret decided against the breakfast. Coffee had been enough for her in the morning for ten years; it would have to do for today. She buttoned herself into interminable folds of material that, the salesgirl had assured her, was the *only* comfortable thing to wear during the last few months. With a surge of pure pleasure, the letter and newspaper forgotten, she realized she was on the next to the last button. It wouldn't be long now.

The city in the early morning had always been a special kind of excitement for her. Last night it had rained, and the sidewalks were still damp-gray instead of dusty. The air smelled the fresher, to a city-bred woman, for the occasional pungency of acrid factory smoke. She walked the six blocks to work, watching the lights go out in the all-night hamburger joints, where the plate-glass walls were already catching the sun, and the lights go on in the dim interiors of cigar stores and drycleaning establishments.

The office was in a new Government building. In the rolovator, on the way up, she felt, as always, like a frankfurter roll in the ascending half of an old-style rotary toasting machine. She abandoned the air-foam cushioning gratefully at the fourteenth floor, and settled down behind her desk, at the rear of a long row of identical desks.

Each morning the pile of papers that greeted her was a little higher. These were, as everyone knew, the decisive months. The war might be won or lost on these calculations as well as any others. The manpower office had switched her here when her old expediter's job got to be too strenuous. The computer was easy to operate, and the work was absorbing, if not as exciting as the old job. But you didn't just stop working these days. Everyone who could do anything at all was needed.

And—she remembered the interview with the psychologist—*I'm probably the unstable type. Wonder what sort of neurosis I'd get sitting home reading that sensational paper* ... She plunged into the work without pursuing the thought.

February 18.

Hank darling,

Just a note—from the hospital, no less. I had a dizzy spell at work, and the doctor took it to heart. Blessed if I know what I'll do with myself lying in bed for weeks, just waiting—

but Dr. Boyer seems to think it may not be so long.

There are too many newspapers around here. More infanticides all the time, and they can't seem to get a jury to convict any of them. It's the fathers who do it. Lucky thing you're not around, in case—

Oh, darling, that wasn't a very *funny* joke, was it? Write as often as you can, will you? I have too much time to think. But there really isn't anything wrong, and nothing to worry about.

Write often, and remember I love you.

Maggie.

SPECIAL SERVICE TELEGRAM

FEBRUARY 21, 1953
22:04 LK37G

FROM: TECH. LIEUT. H. MARVELL

     X47–016 GCNY
      TO: MRS. H. MARVELL
       WOMEN'S HOSPITAL
       NEW YORK CITY

HAD DOCTOR'S GRAM STOP WILL ARRIVE FOUR OH TEN STOP SHORT LEAVE STOP YOU DID IT MAGGIE STOP LOVE HANK

February 25.

Hank dear,

So you didn't see the baby either? You'd think a place this size would at least have visiplates on the incubators, so the fathers could get a look, even if the poor benighted mommas can't. They tell me I won't see her for another week, or maybe more—but of course, mother always warned me if I didn't slow my pace, I'd probably even have my babies too fast. Why must she *always* be right?

Did you meet that battle-ax of a nurse they put on here? I imagine they save her for people who've already had theirs, and don't let her get too near the prospectives—but a woman like that simply shouldn't be allowed in a maternity ward. She's obsessed with mutations, can't seem to talk about anything else. Oh, well, *ours* is all right, even if it was in an unholy hurry.

I'm tired. They warned me not to sit up so soon, but I *had* to write you. All my love, darling,

Maggie.

February 29.

Darling,

I finally got to see her! It's all true, what they say about new babies and the face that only a mother could love—but it's all there, darling, eyes, ears, and noses—no, only one!—all in the right places. We're so *lucky,* Hank.

I'm afraid I've been a rambunctious patient. I kept telling that hatchet-faced female with the mutation mania that I wanted to *see* the baby. Finally the doctor came in to "explain" everything to me, and talking a lot of nonsense, most of which I'm sure no one could have understood, any more than I did. The only thing I got out of it was that she didn't actually *have* to stay in the incubator; they just thought it was "wiser."

I think I got a little hysterical at that point. Guess I was more worried than I was willing to admit, but I threw a small fit about it. The whole business wound up with one of those hushed medical conferences outside the door, and finally the Woman in White said: "Well, we might as well. Maybe it'll work out better that way."

I'd heard about the way doctors and nurses in these places develop a God complex, and believe me it is as true figuratively as it is literally that a mother hasn't got a leg to stand on around here.

I *am* awfully weak, still. I'll write again soon. Love,

Maggie.

March 8.

Dearest Hank,

Well, the nurse was wrong if she told you that. She's an idiot anyhow. It's a girl. It's easier to tell with babies than with cats, and *I know.* How about Henrietta?

I'm home again, and busier than a betatron. They got *everything* mixed up at the hospital, and I had to teach myself how to bathe her and do just about everything else. She's getting prettier, too. When can you get a leave, a *real* leave?

Love,
Maggie.

May 26.

Hank dear,

You should see her now—and you shall. I'm sending along a reel of color movie. My mother sent her those nighties with drawstrings all over. I put one on, and right now she looks like a snow-white potato sack with that beautiful, beautiful flower-face blooming on top. Is that *me* talking? Am I a doting mother? But wait till you *see* her!

July 10.

...Believe it or not, as you like, but your daughter can talk, and I don't mean baby talk. Alice discovered it—she's a dental assistant in the WACs, you know—and when she heard the baby giving out what I thought was a string of gibberish, she said the kid knew words and sentences, but couldn't say them clearly because she has no teeth yet. I'm taking her to a speech specialist.

September 13.

...We have a prodigy for real! Now that all her front teeth are in, her speech is perfectly clear and—a new talent now—she can sing! I mean really carry a tune! At seven months! Darling, my world would be perfect if you could only get home.

November 19.

...at last. The little goon was so busy being clever, it took her all this time to learn to crawl. The doctor says development in these cases is always erratic...

SPECIAL SERVICE TELEGRAM

DECEMBER 1, 1953
08:47 LK59F

FROM: TECH. LIEUT. H. MARVELL
        X47–016 GCNY
    TO: MRS. H. MARVELL
        APT. K-17
        504 E. 19 ST
        N.Y. N.Y.

WEEK'S LEAVE STARTS TOMORROW STOP WILL ARRIVE AIRPORT TEN OH FIVE STOP DON'T MEET ME STOP LOVE LOVE LOVE HANK

*   *   *

Margaret let the water run out of the bathinette until only a few inches were left, and then loosed her hold on the wriggling baby.

"I think it was better when you were retarded, young woman," she informed her daughter happily. "You *can't* crawl in a bathinette, you know."

"Then why can't I go in the bathtub?" Margaret was used to her child's volubility by now, but every now and then it caught her unawares. She swooped the resistant mass of pink flesh into a towel, and began to rub.

"Because you're too little, and your head is very soft, and bathtubs are very hard."

"Oh. Then when can I go in the bathtub?"

"When the outside of your head is as hard as the inside, brainchild." She reached toward a pile of fresh clothing. "I cannot understand," she added, pinning a square of cloth through the nightgown, "why a child of your intelligence can't learn to keep a diaper on the way other babies do. They've been used for centuries, you know, with perfectly satisfactory results."

The child disdained to reply; she had heard it too often. She waited patiently until she had been tucked, clean and sweet-smelling, into a white-painted crib. Then she favored her mother with a smile that inevitably made Margaret think of the first golden edge of the sun bursting into a rosy predawn. She remembered Hank's reaction to the color pictures of his beautiful daughter, and with the thought, realized how late it was.

"Go to sleep, puss. When you wake up, you know, your *daddy* will be here."

"Why?" asked the four-year-old mind, waging a losing battle to keep the ten-month-old body awake.

Margaret went into the kitchenette and set the timer for the roast. She examined the table, and got her clothes from the closet, new dress, new shoes, new slip, new everything, bought weeks before and saved for the day Hank's telegram came. She stopped to pull a paper from the facsimile, and, with clothes and news, went into the bathroom and lowered herself gingerly into the steaming luxury of a scented bath.

She glanced through the paper with indifferent interest.

Today at least there was no need to read the national news. There was an article by a geneticist. The same geneticist. Mutations, he said, were increasing disproportionately. It was too soon for recessives; even the first mutants, born near Hiroshima and Nagasaki in 1946 and 1947, were not old enough yet to breed. *But my baby's all right.* Apparently, there was some degree of free radiation from atomic explosions causing the trouble. *My baby's fine. Precocious, but normal.* If more attention had been paid to the first Japanese mutations, he said...

There was that little notice in the paper in the spring of '47. That was when Hank quit at Oak Ridge. "Only 2 or 3 percent of those guilty of infanticide are being caught and punished in Japan today..." *But* MY BABY'S *all right.*

She was dressed, combed, and ready to the last light brush-on of lip paste, when the door chime sounded. She dashed for the door, and heard for the first time in eighteen months the almost-forgotten sound of a key turning in the lock before the chime had quite died away.

"Hank!"

"Maggie!"

And then there was nothing to say. So many days, so many months of small news piling up, so many things to tell him, and now she just stood there, staring at a khaki uniform and a stranger's pale face. She traced the features with the finger of memory. The same high-bridged nose, wide-set eyes, fine feathery brows; the same long jaw, the hair a little farther back now on the high forehead, the same tilted curve to his mouth. Pale...Of course, he'd been underground all this time. And strange, stranger because of lost familiarity than any newcomer's face could be.

She had time to think all that before his hand reached out to touch her, and spanned the gap of eighteen months. Now, again, there was nothing to say, because there was no need. They were together, and for the moment that was enough.

"Where's the baby?"

"Sleeping. She'll be up any minute."

No urgency. Their voices were as casual as though it were a daily exchange, as though war and separation did not exist. Margaret picked up the coat he'd thrown on the chair near the door, and hung it carefully in the hall closet. She went to check the roast, leaving him to wander through the rooms by himself, remembering and coming back. She found him, finally, standing over the baby's crib.

She couldn't see his face, but she had no need to.

"I think we can wake her just this once." Margaret pulled the covers down and lifted the white bundle from the bed. Sleepy lids pulled back heavily from smoky brown eyes.

"Hello." Hank's voice was tentative.

"Hello." The baby's assurance was more pronounced.

He had heard about it, of course, but that wasn't the same as hearing it. He turned eagerly to Margaret. "She really can—?"

"Of course she can, darling. But what's more important, she can even do nice normal things like other babies do, even stupid ones. Watch her crawl!" Margaret set the baby on the big bed.

For a moment young Henrietta lay and eyed her parents dubiously.

"Crawl?" she asked.

"That's the idea. Your daddy is new around here, you know. He wants to see you show off."

"Then put me on my tummy."

"Oh, of course." Margaret obligingly rolled the baby over.

"What's the matter?" Hank's voice was still casual, but an undercurrent in it began to charge the air of the room. "I thought they turned over first."

"This baby"—Margaret would not notice the tension—"*This* baby does things when she wants to."

This baby's father watched with softening eyes while the head advanced and the body hunched up propelling itself across the bed.

"Why, the little rascal." He burst into relieved laughter. "She looks like one of those potato-sack racers they used to have on picnics. Got her arms pulled out of the sleeves already." He reached over and grabbed the knot at the bottom of the long nightie.

"I'll do it, darling." Margaret tried to get there first.

"Don't be silly, Maggie. This may be *your* first baby, but *I* had five kid brothers." He laughed her away, and reached with his other hand for the string that closed one sleeve. He opened the sleeve bow, and groped for an arm.

"The way you wriggle," he addressed his child sternly, as his hand touched a moving knob of flesh at the shoulder, "anyone might think you are a worm, using your tummy to crawl on, instead of your hands and feet."

Margaret stood and watched, smiling. "Wait till you hear her sing, darling—"

His right hand traveled down from the shoulder to where he thought an arm would be, traveled down, and straight down, over firm small muscles that writhed in an attempt to move against the pressure of his hand. He let his fingers drift up again to the shoulder. With infinite care he opened the knot at the bottom of the nightgown. His wife was standing by the bed, saying, "She can do 'Jingle Bells,' and—"

His left hand felt along the soft knitted fabric of the gown, up toward the diaper that folded, flat and smooth, across the bottom end of his child. No wrinkles. No kicking. *No...*

"Maggie." He tried to pull his hands from the neat fold in the diaper, from the wriggling body. "Maggie." His throat was dry; words came hard, low and grating. He spoke very slowly, thinking the sound of each word to make himself say it. His head was spinning, but he had to *know* before he let it go. "Maggie, why...didn't you...tell me?"

"Tell you what, darling?" Margaret's poise was the immemorial patience of woman confronted with man's childish impetuosity. Her sudden laugh sounded fantastically easy and natural in that room; it was all clear to her now. "Is she wet? I didn't know."

She didn't know. His hands, beyond control, ran up and down the soft-skinned baby body, the sinuous, limbless body. *Oh God, dear God*—his head shook and his muscles contracted in a bitter spasm of hysteria. His fingers tightened on his child—*Oh God, she didn't know...*

Sharon Webb is a young writer from Blairsville, Pennsylvania, whose stories of the misadventures of Terra Tarkington, SN (Space Nurse) are a popular feature of Isaac Asimov's Science Fiction Magazine. *This entertaining tale first appeared in the August 1979 issue.*

ITCH ON THE BULL RUN

By Sharon Webb

Satellite Hospital Outpost
Taurus 14, North Horn 978675644
Nath Orbit

Jan. 2

Carmelita O'Hare-Mbotu RN
Teton Medical Center
Jackson Hole Summation City
Wyoming 306548760 United Earth, Sol

Dear Carmie,

This may be the last time you hear from me. I am doomed. Just as beautiful Dr. Brian-Scott and I were beginning an ardent alliance—Armageddon.

Yes, it's true. When I signed up with the Interstellar Nurses' Corps, I signed my life away. I am writing to you from a plague ship. There's been no official word, but where there's steam (to coin a phrase) there's a reactor.

I just got back from a week's pass (Earth time, not Bull

Run time), and found that I had fallen into a nest of pestilence. All of the Aldeberan nurses were hissing about it, but they kept lapsing from Standard into their native tongue so I couldn't get any details. I asked one of the Hyadean orderlies about it, but all he'd do was shake his head and jiggle the crease where his nose ought to be. He wouldn't say a *word*, Carmie; and he's a terrible gossip. When Glockto is at a loss for words, it is *serious*. I did find out that the chief epidemiologist, old Dr. Kelly-Bach, is stricken. Word is that he picked up the plague from an Aurigan patient. Dr. Kelly-Bach's wife, Olga the Grim, is sure to be next. And after Olga? Carmie, I am going to die. And I don't even know what the symptoms are yet.

When you read in the medical journals of the disease that decimated Nath Outpost, think of me, Carmie, and weep.

Yours in dissolution,
Terra

Satellite Hospital Outpost
Taurus 14, North Horn 978675644
Nath Orbit

Jan. 2

Gladiola Tarkington
45 Subsea
Petroleum City
Gulf of Mexico 233433111 United Earth, Sol

Dear Mom,

Everything is fine here, but boring. I just got back from a week's pass. I'm afraid I was terribly extravagant; I spent the week on Hyades IV and bought a Snuggie. I can't wear it on the ship, of course, because Hyadean Snuggies are good for forty degrees below zero, but it will come in handy back on Earth if I ever get there.

Don't worry about the plague.

Love,
Terra

Satellite Hospital Outpost
Taurus 14, North Horn 978675644
Nath Orbit

Jan. 5

Carmelita O'Hare-Mbotu RN
Teton Medical Center
Jackson Hole Summation City
Wyoming 306548760 United Earth, Sol

Dear Carmie,

I told you that I was going to die, but it is much worse than that. *Much worse.* I am to be flayed alive—victim of an insidious and malignant fungus.

We still don't have any official word, but that's because the official word has to come from Dr. Kelly-Bach, and he is in awful shape. Poor Dr. Kelly-Bach is still up and around, ministering to the sick; but his mind wanders, and his heart is not in his work. Carmie, you should see him. He has to wear thick gloves to keep from scratching his hide off. Olga tells me she has to restrain his hands every night, because if she didn't, he would wake up in the morning with most of his epidermis gone. The look in his eye is terrible, Carmie. Sort of maddened. And he moans and sighs a lot.

There is no known cure, Carmie. None. And it is definitely contagious. Only this morning, I found Olga smearing the end of her nose with a local anesthetic, but she said it didn't help much. To make matters worse, Glockto, the orderly, came in about then and begged some for his crease.

Carmie, it is so depressing that I am nearing catatonia. Just when Dr. Brian-Scott and I were developing such a fulfilling relationship, disaster strikes. We will be cut down in our prime.

I know that if he is stricken first, I will stand by him. But what if I'm first? Would he want me if my skin were gone? They say that beauty is only skin deep, but that's a lie, Carmie.

There is only one thing left to do. I've got to figure out a way to get us off this tub.

Machinatingly yours,
Terra

Satellite Hospital Outpost
Taurus 14, North Horn 978675644
Nath Orbit

Jan. 7

Gladiola Tarkington
45 Subsea
Petroleum City
Gulf of Mexico 233433111 United Earth, Sol

Dear Mom,

I'm not sick. I never said I was sick. I don't see why you're worried, because I'm fine.

The Hyadean Snuggie does not carry disease. The only diseases we get around here come from the patients.

I have applied for a transfer, but they said I couldn't have it until Olga Kelly-Bach's skin grows back.

Your loving daughter,
Terra

Satellite Hospital Outpost
Taurus 14, North Horn 978675644
Nath Orbit

Jan. 9

Carmelita O'Hare-Mbotu RN
Teton Medical Center
Jackson Hole Summation City
Wyoming 306548760 United Earth, Sol

Dear Carmie,

Well, they wouldn't let me transfer off this tin coffin, but I've beaten them at their game. I volunteered for special assignment on Pleiades II, and Dr. Brian-Scott is going too. It seems that one of the Pleiades II Mothers is sick. Her egg production slowed down to zero, and we have to find out why. The Pleiades II population is on the decline anyway, and they can't afford to lose a Mother. It sounds like an interesting case, and it sure beats terminal pruritus.

Olga is a *mass* of excoriation, and it is better not to describe the condition of poor Dr. Kelly-Bach. I really fear for his sanity, Carmie. He is so testy, you just can't stand to be around him. (If you wanted to be around him.)

We thought the Aldeberans were immune; but just this morning, one of Dr. Qotermire's scales fell out of his tail during surgery. He seemed awfully distressed about it, and the Aldeberan nurse who was assisting him turned such a pale blue that I thought she would faint. I'm getting off this tub just in time, Carmie. It's one thing to see the disease in humans and Hyadeans, but it's altogether something else to contemplate Dr. Qotemire's defoliation. I don't think I could bear that. It's hard enough to look at Dr. Qotemire when he's in health.

Terra

P.S. How's this for an itinerary? Tomorrow we take the shuttle to Hyades IV and then the express to Pleiades II. Our port-of-entry is Seven Sisters—the only Pleasure Dome in *light-years*! We'll spend the night at the Kubla Khan and then off to see our patient.

Yours in anticipation,
Terra

Satellite Hospital Outpost
Taurus 14, North Horn 978675644
Nath Orbit

Jan. 9

Gladiola Tarkington
45 Subsea
Petroleum City
Gulf of Mexico 233433111 United Earth, Sol

Dear Mom,

My skin is fine. You worry too much. I worry about your worrying about me.

They won't let me come home, Mom. They're sending Dr. Brian-Scott and me to Pleiades II to see a patient there. But don't be concerned. It's probably not true what they say about the Seven Sisters Pleasure Dome.

Much love,
Terra

Pleiades II Express
17th Relay 800880008

Jan. 10

Carmelita O'Hare-Mbotu RN
Teton Medical Center
Jackson Hole Summation City
Wyoming 306548760 United Earth, Sol

Dear Carmie,

Life is bleak. There is no shining dawn for me, Carmie. No rosy edge. Dr. Brian-Scott is stricken with the fungus.

He twitched all the way on the shuttle, and now he's beginning to scratch. Just when our love begins to flower, it is nipped (to coin a phrase) cruelly in the bud. I cannot express to you the way I feel.

Yours in desolation,
Terra

Pleasure Dome
Pleiades II 456765453 Pleiades

Jan. 11

Gladiola Tarkington
45 Subsea
Petroleum City
Gulf of Mexico 233433111 United Earth, Sol

Dear Mom,

You shouldn't get so excited about things, Mom. The Pleasure Dome is really a big nothing. Absolutely tame and harmless.

I'm sure the police will let us go soon.

And don't worry. Even though Dr. Brian-Scott is growing worse by the minute, I am still fine.

Love and kisses,
Terra

Pleasure Dome
Pleiades II 456765453 Pleiades

Jan. 11

Carmelita O'Hare-Mbotu RN
Teton Medical Center
Jackson Hole Summation City
Wyoming 306548760 United Earth, Sol

Dear Carmie,

I am being held prisoner in the Seven Sisters Pleasure Dome. When we arrived last night, Dr. Brian-Scott couldn't stop scratching while we were going through customs and the officials kept giving us funny looks. About the time I thought we were through, these two huge beings came and put us under arrest. (I say "beings" because I don't know *what* they were—they were wearing bulky decontam. suits.)

Well, they marched us off through a sort of tunnel into our cell. It looks like an ordinary Floatel room, but make no mistake, Carmie, it is really a cell. We are locked in. We are being fed and cared for after a fashion, but we've had no physical contact with anybody. A health servo came in and took samples of us though.

In between scratching, Dr. Brian-Scott called the embassy. Everyone was very polite, but adamant. We have to stay here until we get clearance from Pleiades II Health.

So now I am prisoner in a Pest Hole. Who would have thought it would come to this, Carmie? Have you ever been arrested? Have you ever spent the night in a Pleasure Dome cell with a man with the itch? Believe me, it is no fun. No fun at all.

The health servo told us that Aurigan fungus is not touched in any way by any drug known to the civilized galaxy.

What the health servo didn't tell us was that any known pleasurable stimulus makes it worse.

Do you know how helpless it makes you feel to see the man you love writhing on a jelly bed and pleading, "Do something, Terra. *Do something*"?

Well, what could *I* do? He's the doctor.

Grimly yours,
Terra

Pleasure Dome
Pleiades II 456765453 Pleiades

Jan. 12

Carmelita O'Hare-Mbotu RN
Teton Medical Center
Jackson Hole Summation City
Wyoming 306548760 United Earth, Sol

Dear Carmie,
We have been freed. The health servo came in a while ago and told us.

What he said was, "You are free to leave the dome. Do not attempt to return or you will be executed."

Can you imagine, Carmie? Here we are on a mission of mercy and that's the treatment we get. I can't wait to get out of here.

Pleiades II Health said it would be all right to visit our patient outside the dome. It seems that there's a lot of fungus out there anyway, and the natives are immune to most of it, including the Aurigan variety.

If I were not the dedicated professional I am, I wouldn't bother to help the Pleiades Mother. But as you know, Carmie, I am dedicated to the end.

Besides, we don't have anyplace else to go. They won't let us board the express because we're contaminated. We are doomed to wander the hostile surface of Pleiades II—perhaps forever.

> Yours into the wilderness,
> Terra

> Mother's Oviporium
> Vicious Swamp
> Pleiades II 352344480

Jan. 13

Gladiola Tarkington
45 Subsea
Petroleum City
Gulf of Mexico 233433111 United Earth, Sol

Dear Mom,

Well, here we are at the Oviporium. We've seen our patient and Dr. Brian-Scott and I are going to start treatment after lunch, if he is still up and around.

I am fine.

You would be amazed at the sex habits on Pleiades II. Absolutely amazed.

> Yours in wonder,
> Terra

> Mothers' Oviporium
> Vicious Swamp
> Pleiades II 352344480 Pleiades

Jan. 13

Carmelita O'Hare-Mbotu RN
Teton Medical Center
Jackson Hole Summation City
Wyoming 306548760 United Earth, Sol

Dear Carmie,

I found out why they call it a Pleasure Dome. The only pleasure that anyone could conceivably have on this planet is under that dome. Outside, it rains all the time. *All the time*. Everything is musty and mildewy.

The Pleiades II Mother is in bad shape. When we got here, she was curled up in a kind of spastic ball. Since you've led a sheltered life back on Earth, Carmie, you've probably forgotten your Alien Physiology. The Mother is about three meters long and she looks a lot like a millipede. She's stopped laying her eggs and she seems to be in pain. Of course, it's a little hard to be sure, because she's completely blind, deaf, and dumb.

After a while she began to writhe. Her groomers panicked. They stood around whimpering and twiddling their feelers while Dr. Brian-Scott stood around and scratched. Then he did an internal and said, "I think it's (scratch, scratch) a mechanical obstruction (scratch, scratch) of the ovipositor."

I thought that was interesting, and I looked at her tail; but Dr. Brian-Scott said I was looking at the wrong end. The Mother's ovipositor is just under her mouth. (Can you imagine, Carmie?)

Then he said, "We'd better (scratch, scratch) put on protective clothing (scratch, scratch)."

He said that when he finished dilating her ovipositor, the eggs would start rolling out. "As soon as they do, she'll start squirting liters of fluid from the pores in her sides to coat the eggs."

So I have to go put on this plasticine suit to keep the juice off of me. I'll let you know what happens.

Obstetrically yours,
Terra

Mothers' Oviporium
Vicious Swamp
Pleiades II 352344480 Pleiades

Jan. 14
Carmelita O'Hare-Mbotu RN
Teton Medical Center
Jackson Hole Summation City
Wyoming 206548760 United Earth, Sol

Dear Carmie,

I am ecstatic! You'll never guess what happened. When we got suited up, Dr. Brian-Scott dilated the Mother's ovipositor and sure enough, these white eggs started rolling out in a steady stream. She'd catch each one with her anterior legs, and then she'd roll it down her body all the way to her tail. All the while, this brown fluid kept pouring out of openings in the side of her body. By the time the eggs got to her tail they were brown—completely coated with the fluid.

Meanwhile, poor Dr. Brian-Scott was abjectly miserable inside the plasticine suit. It simply *exacerbated* his condition to an unbearable extreme.

While he danced around on one foot and then the other and scratched and scratched with a manic expression on his face, I got to wondering about why the Mother had to squirt all that stuff over the eggs.

He stopped scratching and dancing long enough to say, "It prevents the eggs from rotting. It's so damp here the eggs would be destroyed by fungus in no time."

And that's when I conceived this brilliant idea.

I said, "Well, do you suppose that juice would do any good for the Aurigan fungus?"

The effect on him was amazing. He stood completely still like he had turned to plexiglas or something. Then, after the longest time, he leaped up in the air and began to rip his clothes off.

It was unbelievable. There he was, stripped to his itchy skin in front of everybody. Then he reached out and splashed handfuls of that brown syrupy mess all over himself. As he did it, he made little happy moans and then splashed some more. Carmie, he practically *embraced* the Mother.

I can't tell you how mortified I was. Fortunately, the Mother was blind, deaf, and dumb, or there's no telling what her reaction would have been. I guess the groomers all thought it was part of the treatment.

But it made me mad. He could have killed himself. A more unscientific experiment I have never seen; he could have at least tried a little patch first. Carmie, he's lucky that what was left of his hide didn't come off.

Well, after a while, he was completely brown like the eggs and he had this *beatific* smile on his face.

And when I saw that smile, I stopped being mortified.

Then he said (I remember his every word), "I love you, Terra."

So we're bringing back *containers* of the Mother Juice so we can cure the plague. The Port Authorities say we can board the express if we've both been treated.

I feel like Madame Curie.

Majestically yours,
Terra

Satellite Hospital Outpost
Taurus 14, North Horn 978675644
Nath Orbit

Jan. 16

Gladiola Tarkington
45 Subsea
Petroleum City
Gulf of Mexico 233433111 United Earth, Sol

Dear Mom,

You don't need to come here to see about me. *I'm fine.* I really wish you wouldn't call Dr. Kelly-Bach just now, since he's still weak from the plague.

We all took the cure, and Dr. Brian-Scott says that the brown stains may come off in a few months.

In the meantime, I am going to be a student. In view of my interest in the reproductive habits of the Pleiades II Mothers, Dr. Brian-Scott says he is going to teach me all about the most interesting reproductive habits in the galaxy.

Studiously yours,
Terra

Fredric Brown (1906–72) gave much to science fiction. Among his contributions was an unmatched talent for the short-short story, possibly the most difficult form to do effectively. He also had a wonderful sense of humor, which frequently found its way into his work—What Mad Universe (1949) and Martians, Go Home (1955) being two excellent examples.

"Letter to a Phoenix" (Astounding Science Fiction, August 1949) captures all of the qualities that made him so effective and so popular.

LETTER TO A PHOENIX

By Fredric Brown

There is much to tell you, so much that it is difficult to know where to begin. Fortunately, I have forgotten most of the things that have happened to me. Fortunately, the mind has a limited capacity for remembering. It would be horrible if I remembered the details of a hundred and eighty thousand years—the details of four thousand lifetimes that I have lived since the first great atomic war.

Not that I have forgotten the really great moments. I remember being on the first expedition to land on Mars and the third to land on Venus. I remember—I believe it was in the third great war—the blasting of Skora from the sky by a force that compares to nuclear fission as a nova compares to our slowly dying sun. I was second in command on a Hyper-

78

A Class spacer in the war against the second extragalactic invaders, the ones who established bases on Jupe's moons before we knew they were there and almost drove us out of the Solar System before we found the one weapon they couldn't stand up against. So they fled where we couldn't follow them, then, outside of the Galaxy. When we did follow them, about fifteen thousand years later, they were gone. They were dead three thousand years.

And this is what I want to tell you about—that mighty race and the others—but first, so that you will know how I know what I know, I will tell you about myself.

I am not immortal. There is only one immortal being in the universe; of it, more anon. Compared to it, I am of no importance, but you will not understand or believe what I say to you unless you understand what I am.

There is little in a name, and that is a fortunate thing—for I do not remember mine. That is less strange than you think, for a hundred and eighty thousand years is a long time and for one reason or another I have changed my name a thousand times or more. And what could matter less than the name my parents gave me a hundred and eighty thousand years ago?

I am not a mutant. What happened to me happened when I was twenty-three years old, during the first atomic war. The first war, that is, in which both sides used atomic weapons—puny weapons, of course, compared to subsequent ones. It was less than a score of years after the discovery of the atom bomb. The first bombs were dropped in a minor war while I was still a child. They ended that war quickly, for only one side had them.

The first atomic war wasn't a bad one—the first one never is. I was lucky for, if it had been a bad one—one which ended a civilization—I'd not have survived it despite the biological accident that happened to me. If it had ended a civilization, I wouldn't have been kept alive during the sixteen-year sleep period I went through about thirty years later. But again I get ahead of the story.

I was, I believe, twenty or twenty-one years old when the war started. They didn't take me for the army right away because I was not physically fit. I was suffering from a rather rare disease of the pituitary gland—Somebody's syndrome. I've forgotten the name. It caused obesity, among other things. I was about fifty pounds overweight for my height and had little stamina. I was rejected without a second thought.

About two years later my disease had progressed slightly, but other things had progressed more than slightly. By that time the army was taking anyone; they'd have taken a one-legged one-armed blind man if he was willing to fight. And I was willing to fight. I'd lost my family in a dusting, I hated my job in a war plant, and I had been told by doctors that my disease was incurable and I had only a year or two to live in any case. So I went to what was left of the army, and what was left of the army took me without a second thought and sent me to the nearest front, which was ten miles away. I was in the fighting one day after I joined.

Now I remember enough to know that *I* hadn't anything to do with it, but it happened that the time I joined was the turn of the tide. The other side was out of bombs and dust and getting low on shells and bullets. We were out of bombs and dust, too, but they hadn't knocked out *all* of our production facilities and we'd got just about all of theirs. We still had planes to carry them, too, and we still had the semblance of an organization to send the planes to the right places. Nearly the right places, anyway; sometimes we dropped them too close to our own troops by mistake. It was a week after I'd got into the fighting that I got out of it again—knocked out of it by one of our smaller bombs that had been dropped about a mile away.

I came to, about two weeks later, in a base hospital, pretty badly burned. By that time the war was over, except for the mopping up, and except for restoring order and getting the world started up again. You see, that hadn't been what I call a blow-up war. It killed off—I'm just guessing; I don't remember the fraction—about a fourth or a fifth of the world's population. There was enough productive capacity left, and there were enough people left, to keep on going; there were dark ages for a few centuries, but there was no return to savagery, no starting over again. In such times, people go back to using candles for light and burning wood for fuel, but not because they don't know how to use electricity or mine coal; just because the confusions and revolutions keep them off balance for a while. The knowledge is there, in abeyance until order returns.

It's not like a blow-up war, when nine-tenths or more of the population of Earth—or of Earth and the other planets—

is killed. Then is when the world reverts to utter savagery and the hundredth generation rediscovers metals to tip their spears.

But again I digressed. After I recovered consciousness in the hospital, I was in pain for a long time. There were, by then, no more anesthetics. I had deep radiation burns, from which I suffered almost intolerably for the first few months until, gradually, they healed. I did not sleep—that was the strange thing. And it was a terrifying thing, then, for I did not understand what had happened to me, and the unknown is always terrifying. The doctors paid little heed—for I was one of millions burned or otherwise injured—and I think they did not believe my statements that I had not slept at all. They thought I had slept but little and that I was either exaggerating or making an honest error. But I had *not* slept at all. I did not sleep until long after I left the hospital, cured. Cured, incidentally, of the disease of my pituitary gland, and with my weight back to normal, my health perfect.

I didn't sleep for thirty years. Then *I did sleep,* and I slept for sixteen years. And at the end of that forty-six-year period, I was still, physically, at the apparent age of twenty-three.

Do you begin to see what had happened as I began to see it then? The radiation—or combination of types of radiation— I had gone through, had radically changed the functions of my pituitary. And there were other factors involved. I studied endocrinology once, about a hundred and fifty thousand years ago, and I think I found the pattern. If my calculations were correct, what happened to me was one chance in a great many billions.

The factors of decay and aging were not eliminated, of course, but the rate was reduced by about fifteen thousand times. I age at the rate of one day every forty-five years. So I am not immortal. I have aged eleven years in the past hundred and eighty millennia. My physical age is now thirty-four.

And forty-five years is to me as a day. I do not sleep for about thirty years of it—then I sleep for about fifteen. It is well for me that my first few "days" were not spent in a period of complete social disorganization or savagery, else I would not have survived my first few sleeps. But I did survive them and by that time I had learned a system and could take care of my own survival. Since then, I have slept about four thousand times, and I have survived. Perhaps someday I shall be unlucky. Perhaps someday, despite certain safeguards, someone will discover and break into the cave or vault into which I seal myself, secretly, for a period of sleep. But it is not likely. I have years in which to prepare each of those places and the experience of four thousand sleeps back of me. You could pass such a place a thousand times and never know it was there, nor be able to enter if you suspected.

No, my chances for survival between my periods of waking life are much better than my chances of survival during my conscious, active periods. It is perhaps a miracle that I have survived so many of those, despite the techniques of survival that I have developed.

And those techniques are good. I've lived through seven major atomic—and super-atomic—wars that have reduced the population of Earth to a few savages around a few campfires in a few still habitable areas. And at other times, in other eras, I've been in five galaxies besides our own.

I've had several thousand wives, but always one at a time, for I was born in a monogamous era and the habit has persisted. And I have raised several thousand children. Of course, I have never been able to remain with one wife longer than thirty years before I must disappear, but thirty years is long enough for both of us—especially when she ages at a normal rate and I age imperceptibly. Oh, it leads to problems, of course, but I've been able to handle them. I always marry, when I do marry, a girl as much younger than myself as possible, so the disparity will not become too great. Say I am thirty; I marry a girl of sixteen. Then when it is time that I must leave her, she is forty-six and I am still thirty. And it is best for both of us, for everyone, that when I awaken I do not again go back to that place. If she still lives, she will be past sixty and it would not be well, even for her, to have a husband come back from the dead—still young. And I have left her well provided, a wealthy widow—wealthy in money or in whatever may have constituted wealth in that particular era. Sometimes it has been beads and arrowheads, sometimes wheat in a granary and once—there have been peculiar civilizations—it was fish scales. I never had the slightest difficulty in acquiring my share, or more, of money or its equivalent. A few thousand years' practice and the difficulty becomes the other way—knowing when to stop in order not to become unduly wealthy and so attract attention.

For obvious reasons, I've always managed to do that. For

reasons that you will see, I've never wanted power, nor have I ever—after the first few hundred years—let people suspect that I was different from them. I even spend a few hours each night lying thinking, pretending to sleep.

But none of that is important, any more than I am important. I tell it to you only so you will understand how I *know* the thing that I am about to tell you.

And when I tell you, it is not because I'm trying to sell you anything. It's something you can't change if you want to, and—when you understand it—you won't want to.

I'm not trying to influence you or to lead you. In four thousand lifetimes I've been almost everything—except a leader. I've avoided that. Oh, often enough I have been a god among savages, but that was because I had to be one in order to survive. I used the powers they thought were magic only to keep a degree of order, never to lead them, never to hold them back. If I taught them to use the bow and arrow, it was because game was scarce and we were starving and my survival depended upon theirs. Seeing that the pattern was necessary, I have never disturbed it.

What I tell you now will not disturb the pattern.

It is this: The human race is the only immortal organism in the universe.

There have been other races, and there are other races throughout the universe, but they have died away or they will die. We charted them once, a hundred thousand years ago, with an instrument that detected the presence of thought, the presence of intelligence, however alien and at whatever distance—and gave us a measure of that mind and its qualities. And fifty thousand years later that instrument was rediscovered. There were about as many races as before but only eight of them were ones that had been there fifty thousand years ago and each of those eight was dying, senescent. They had passed the peak of their powers and they were dying.

They had reached the limit of their capabilities—and there is always a limit—and they had no choice but to die. Life is dynamic; it can never be static—at however high or low a level—and survive.

That is what I am trying to tell you, so that you will never again be afraid. Only a race that destroys itself and its progress periodically, that goes back to its beginning, can survive more than, say, sixty thousand years of intelligent life.

In all the universe only the human race has ever reached a high level of intelligence without reaching a high level of sanity. We are unique. We are already at least five times as old as any other race has ever been and it is because we are not sane. And man has, at times, had glimmerings of the fact that insanity is divine. But only at high levels of culture does he realize that he is collectively insane, that fight against it as he will he will always destroy himself—and rise anew out of the ashes.

The phoenix, the bird that periodically immolates itself upon a flaming pyre to rise newborn and live again for another millennium, and again and forever, is only metaphorically a myth. It exists and there is only one of it.

You are the phoenix.

Nothing will ever destroy you, now that—during many high civilizations—your seed has been scattered on the planets of a thousand suns, in a hundred galaxies, there ever to repeat the pattern. The pattern that started a hundred and eighty thousand years ago—I think.

I cannot be sure of that, for I have seen that the twenty to thirty thousand years that elapse between the fall of one civilization and the rise of the next destroy all traces. In twenty to thirty thousand years memories become legends and legends become superstitions and even the superstitions become lost. Metals rust and corrode back into earth while the wind, the rain, and the jungle erode and cover stone. The contours of the very continents change—and glaciers come and go, and a city of twenty thousand years before is under miles of earth or miles of water.

So I cannot be sure. Perhaps the first blow-up that I knew was not the first; civilizations may have risen and fallen before my time. If so, it merely strengthens the case I put before you to say that mankind *may* have survived more than the hundred and eighty thousand years I know of, may have lived through more than the six blow-ups that have happened since what I think to have been the first discovery of the phoenix's pyre.

But—except that we scattered our seed to the stars so well that even the dying of the sun or its becoming a nova would not destroy us—the past does not matter. Lur, Candra, Thragan, Kah, Mu, Atlantis—those are the six I have known, and they are gone as thoroughly as this one will be twenty thousand years or so hence, but the human race, here or in other galaxies, will survive and will live forever.

It will help your peace of mind, here in this year of your current era, to know that—for your minds are disturbed. Perhaps, I do know, it will help your thoughts to know that the coming atomic war, the one that will probably happen in your generation, will not be a blow-up war; it will come too soon for that, before you have developed the really destructive weapons man has had so often before. It will set you back, yes. There will be darkish ages for a century or a few centuries. Then, with the memory of what you will call World War III as a warning, man will think—as he has always thought after a mild atomic war—that he has conquered his own insanity.

For a while—if the pattern holds—he will hold it in check. He will reach the stars again, to find himself already there. Why, you'll be back on Mars within five hundred years, and I'll go there too, to see again the canals I once helped to dig. I've not been there for eighty thousand years and I'd like to see what time has done to it and to those of us who were cut off there the last time mankind lost the space drive. Of course they've followed the pattern too, but the rate is not necessarily constant. We may find them at any stage in the cycle except the top. If they were at the top of the cycle, we wouldn't have to go to them—they'd come to us. Thinking, of course, as they think by now, that they are Martians.

I wonder how high, this time, you will get. Not quite as high, I hope, as Thragan. I hope that never again is rediscovered the weapon Thragan used against her colony on Skora, which was then the fifth planet until the Thragans blew it into asteroids. Of course that weapon would be developed only long after intergalactic travel again becomes commonplace. If I see it coming I'll get out of the Galaxy, but I'd hate to have to do that. I like Earth and I'd like to spend the rest of my mortal lifetime on it if it lasts that long.

Possibly it won't, but the human race will last. Everywhere and forever, for it will never be sane and only insanity is divine. Only the mad destroy themselves and all they have wrought.

And only the phoenix lives forever.

Jack Lewis had about a dozen stories in the science-fiction magazines in the mid-to-late 1950s, most of which were good to excellent. "Who's Cribbing" (Startling Stories, January 1953) is one of the most famous stories of its kind. Samuel Mines was really the editor at Startling when this story was written, and we only trust that the anthology you are now reading has not appeared somewhere else!

WHO'S CRIBBING?

By Jack Lewis

April 2, 1952

Mr. Jack Lewis
90-26 219 St.
Queens Village, N.Y.

Dear Mr. Lewis:

We are returning your manuscript, "The Ninth Dimension." At first glance, I had figured it a story well worthy of publication. Why wouldn't I? So did the editors of *Cosmic Tales* back in 1934 when the story was first published.

As you no doubt know, it was the great Todd Thromberry who wrote the story you tried to pass off on us as an original. Let me give you a word of caution concerning the penalties resulting from plagiarism.

It's not worth it. Believe me.

Sincerely,
Doyle P. Gates
Science Fiction Editor
Deep Space Magazine

April 5, 1952

Mr. Doyle P. Gates, Editor
Deep Space Magazine
New York, N.Y.

Dear Mr. Gates:

I do not know, nor am I aware of the existence of any Todd Thromberry. The story you rejected was submitted in good faith, and I resent the inference that I plagiarized it.

"The Ninth Dimension" was written by me not more than a month ago, and if there is any similarity between it and the story written by this Thromberry person, it is purely coincidental.

However, it has set me thinking. Some time ago, I submitted another story to *Stardust Scientifiction* and received a penciled notation on the rejection slip stating that the story was, "too thromberrish."

Who in the hell is Todd Thromberry? I don't remember reading anything written by him in the ten years I've been interested in science fiction.

Sincerely,
Jack Lewis

April 11, 1952

Mr. Jack Lewis
90-26 219 St.
Queens Village, N.Y.

Dear Mr. Lewis:

Re: Your letter of April 5.

While the editors of this magazine are not in the habit of making open accusations and are well aware of the fact in the writing business there will always be some overlapping of plot ideas, it is very hard for us to believe that you are not familiar with the works of Todd Thromberry.

While Mr. Thromberry is no longer among us, his works, like so many other writers', only became widely recognized after his death in 1941. Perhaps it was his work in the field of electronics that supplied him with the bottomless pit of new ideas so apparent in all his works. Nevertheless, even at this stage of science fiction's development it is apparent that he had a style that many of our so-called contemporary writers might do well to copy. By "copy," I do not mean rewrite word for word one or more of his works, as you have done. For while you state this has been accidental, surely you must realize that the chance of this phenomenon actually happening is about a million times as great as the occurrence of four pat royal flushes on one deal.

Sorry, but we're not that naïve.

Sincerely yours,
Doyle P. Gates
Science Fiction Editor
Deep Space Magazine

April 14, 1952

Mr. Doyle P. Gates, Editor
Deep Space Magazine
New York, N.Y.

Sir:
Your accusations are typical of the rag you publish. Please cancel my subscription immediately.

Sincerely,
Jack Lewis

April 14, 1952

Science Fiction Society
144 Front Street
Chicago, Ill.

Gentlemen:
I am interested in reading some of the works of the late Todd Thromberry.

I would like to get some of the publications that feature his stories.

Respectfully
Jack Lewis

April 22, 1952

Mr. Jack Lewis
90-26 219 St.
Queens Village, N.Y.

Dear Mr. Lewis:
So would we. All I can suggest is that you contact the

publishers if any are still in business, or haunt your second-hand bookstores.

If you succeed in getting any of these magazines, please let us know. We'll pay you a handsome premium on them.

> Yours,
> Ray Albert
> President
> Science Fiction Society

May 11, 1952

Mr. Sampson J. Gross, Editor
Strange Worlds Magazine
St. Louis, Mo.

Dear Mr. Gross:

I am enclosing the manuscript of a story I have just completed. As you see on the title page, I call it "Wreckers of Ten Million Galaxies." Because of the great amount of research that went into it, I must set the minimum price on this one at not less than two cents a word.

Hoping you will see fit to use it for publication in your magazine, I remain,

> Respectfully,
> Jack Lewis

May 19, 1952

Mr. Jack Lewis
90-26 219 St.
Queens Village, N.Y.

Dear Mr. Lewis:

I'm sorry, but at the present time we won't be able to use "Wreckers of Ten Million Galaxies." It's a great yarn though, and if at some future date we decide to use it we will make out the reprint check directly to the estate of Todd Thromberry.

That boy sure could write.

> Cordially,
> Sampson J. Gross
> Editor
> *Strange Worlds Magazine*

May 23, 1952

Mr. Doyle P. Gates, Editor
Deep Space Magazine
New York, N.Y.

Dear Mr. Gates:

While I said I would never have any dealings with you or your magazine again, a situation has arisen which is most puzzling.

It seems all my stories are being returned to me by reason of the fact that except for the byline, they are exact duplicates of the works of this Todd Thromberry person.

In your last letter you aptly described the odds on the accidental occurrence of this phenomenon in the case of one story. What would you consider the approximate odds on no less than half a dozen of my writings?

I agree with you—astronomical!

Yet in the interest of all mankind, how can I get the idea across to you that every word I have submitted was actually written *by me!* I have never copied any material from Todd Thromberry, nor have I ever seen any of his writings. In fact, as I told you in one of my letters, up until a short while ago I was totally unaware of his very existence.

An idea has occurred to me however. It's a truly weird theory, and one that I probably wouldn't even suggest to anyone but a science-fiction editor. But suppose—just suppose—that this Thromberry person, what with his experiments in electronics and everything, had in some way managed to crack through this time-space barrier mentioned so often in your magazine. And suppose—egotistical as it sounds—he had singled out my work as being the type of material he had always wanted to write.

Do you begin to follow me? Or is the idea of a person from a different time cycle looking over my shoulder while I write too fantastic for you to accept?

Please write and tell me what you think of my theory?

Respectfully,
Jack Lewis

May 25, 1952

Mr. Jack Lewis
90-26 219 St.
Queens Village, N.Y.

Dear Mr. Lewis:
    We think you should consult a psychiatrist.

Sincerely,
Doyle P. Gates
Science Fiction Editor
Deep Space Magazine

June 3, 1952

Mr. Sam Mines
Science Fiction Editor
Standard Magazines Inc.
New York 16, N.Y.

Dear Mr. Mines:
    While the enclosed is not really a manuscript at all, I am
submitting this series of letters, carbon copies, and correspondence, in the hope that you might give some credulity
to this seemingly unbelievable happening.
    The enclosed letters are all in proper order and should be
self-explanatory. Perhaps if you publish them, some of your
readers might have some idea how this phenomenon could
be explained.
    I call the entire piece "Who's Cribbing?"

Respectfully,
Jack Lewis

June 10, 1952

Mr. Jack Lewis
90-26 219 St.
Queens Village, N.Y.

Dear Mr. Lewis:
    Your idea of a series of letters to put across a science-
fiction idea is an intriguing one, but I'm afraid it doesn't
quite come off.
    It was in the August 1940 issue of *Macabre Adventures*
that Mr. Thromberry first used this very idea. Ironically
enough, the story title also was "Who's Cribbing?"

Feel free to contact us again when you have something more original.

Yours,
Samuel Mines
Science Fiction Editor
Standard Magazines Inc.

Like A. E. van Vogt, Gordy Dickson (1923–) was born in Canada. His forty or so published sf books include Soldier Ask Not *(1967), part of his "Childe Cycle"; the wonderful* Time Storm *(1977);* The Alien Way *(1965); and* The Dragon and the George *(1976). He won a Hugo Award for "Soldier Ask Not" in 1965 and a Nebula for "Call Him Lord" in 1966.*

This terrifying story (from Analog Science Fiction, *September 1965) is arguably his best, frightening because the bureaucratic foul-ups depicted in it seem so damn plausible.*

COMPUTERS DON'T ARGUE

By Gordon R. Dickson

TREASURE BOOK CLUB
PLEASE DO NOT FOLD,
SPINDLE OR MUTILATE
THIS CARD

Mr: Walter A. Child   Balance: $4.98
Dear Customer: Enclosed is your latest book selection.
"Kidnapped," by Robert Louis Stevenson.

437 Woodlawn Drive
Panduk, Michigan
Nov. 16, 198—

Treasure Book Club
1823 Mandy Street
Chicago, Illinois
Dear Sirs:

I wrote you recently about the computer punch card you sent, billing me for "Kim," by Rudyard Kipling. I did not open the package containing it until I had already mailed you my check for the amount on the card. On opening the package, I found the book missing half its pages. I sent it back to you, requesting either another copy or my money back. Instead, you have sent me a copy of "Kidnapped," by Robert Louis Stevenson. Will you please straighten this out?

I hereby return the copy of "Kidnapped."

Sincerely yours,
Walter A. Child

Treasure Book Club
SECOND NOTICE
PLEASE DO NOT FOLD,
SPINDLE OR MUTILATE
THIS CARD
Mr: Walter A. Child   Balance: $4.98
For "Kidnapped," by Robert Louis Stevenson
(If remittance has been made for the above, please disregard this notice)

437 Woodlawn Drive
Panduk, Michigan
Jan. 21, 198—

Treasure Book Club
1823 Mandy Street
Chicago, Illinois
Dear Sirs:

May I direct your attention to my letter of November 16, 198—? You are still continuing to dun me with computer punch cards for a book I did not order. Whereas, actually, it is your company that owes *me* money.

Sincerely yours,
Walter A. Child

Treasure Book Club
1823 Mandy Street
Chicago, Illinois
Feb. 1, 198–

Mr. Walter A. Child
437 Woodlawn Drive
Panduk, Michigan
Dear Mr. Child:

We have sent you a number of reminders concerning an amount owing to us as a result of book purchases you have made from us. This amount, which is $4.98 is now long overdue.

This situation is disappointing to us, particularly since there was no hesitation on our part in extending you credit at the time original arrangements for these purchases were made by you. If we do not receive payment in full by return mail, we will be forced to turn the matter over to a collection agency.

Very truly yours,
Samuel P. Grimes
Collection Mgr.

437 Woodlawn Drive
Panduk, Michigan
Feb. 5, 198–

Dear Mr. Grimes:

Will you stop sending me punch cards and form letters and make me some kind of a direct answer from a human being? *I* don't owe you money. *You* owe me money. Maybe I should turn your company over to a collection agency.

Walter A. Child

FEDERAL COLLECTION OUTFIT
88 Prince Street
Chicago, Illinois
Feb. 28, 198–

Mr. Walter A. Child
437 Woodlawn Drive
Panduk, Michigan
Dear Mr. Child:

Your account with the Treasure Book Club, of $4.98 plus interest and charges has been turned over to our agency for collection. The amount due is now $6.83. Please send your check for this amount or we shall be forced to take immediate action.

Jacob N. Harshe
Vice President

FEDERAL COLLECTION OUTFIT

88 Prince Street
Chicago, Illinois
April 8, 198—

Mr. Walter A. Child
437 Woodlawn Drive
Panduk, Michigan
Dear Mr. Child:

You have seen fit to ignore our courteous requests to settle your long overdue account with Treasure Book Club, which is now, with accumulated interest and charges, in the amount of $7.51.

If payment in full is not forthcoming by April 11, 198—, we will be forced to turn the matter over to our attorneys for immediate court action.

Ezekiel B. Harshe
President

MALONEY, MAHONEY, MacNAMARA
and PRUITT
Attorneys

89 Prince Street
Chicago, Illinois
April 29, 198—

Mr. Walter A. Child
437 Woodlawn Drive
Panduk, Michigan
Dear Mr. Child:

Your indebtedness to the Treasure Book Club has been referred to us for legal action to collect.

This indebtedness is now in the amount of $10.01. If you will send us this amount so that we may receive it before May 5, 198—, the matter may be satisfied. However, if we do not receive satisfaction in full by that date, we will take steps to collect through the courts.

I am sure you will see the advantage of avoiding a judg-

ment against you, which as a matter of record would do last-
ing harm to your credit rating.

> Very truly yours,
> Hagthorpe M. Pruitt Jr.
> Attorney at law

> 437 Woodlawn Drive
> Panduk, Michigan
> May 4, 198–

Mr. Hagthorpe M. Pruitt, Jr.
Maloney, Mahoney, MacNamara and Pruitt
89 Prince Street
Chicago, Illinois
Dear Mr. Pruitt:

You don't know what a pleasure it is to me in this matter
to get a letter from a live human being to whom I can explain
the situation.

This whole matter is silly. I explained it fully in my letters
to the Treasure Book Company. But I might as well have
been trying to explain to the computer that puts out their
punch cards, for all the good it seemed to do. Briefly, what
happened was I ordered a copy of "Kim," by Rudyard Kipling,
for $4.98. When I opened the package they sent me, I found
the book had only half its pages, but I'd previously mailed
a check to pay them for the book.

I sent the book back to them, asking either for a whole
copy or my money back. Instead, they sent me a copy of
"Kidnapped," by Robert Louis Stevenson—which I had not
ordered; and for which they have been trying to collect from
me.

Meanwhile, I am still waiting for the money back that
they owe me for the copy of "Kim" that I didn't get. That's
the whole story. Maybe you can help me straighten them out.

> Relievedly yours,
> Walter A. Child

P.S.: I also sent them back their copy of "Kidnapped," as
soon as I got it, but it hasn't seemed to help. They have never
even acknowledged getting it back.

MALONEY, MAHONEY, MacNAMARA
and PRUITT
Attorneys

89 Prince Street
Chicago, Illinois
May 9, 198–

Mr. Walter A. Child
437 Woodlawn Drive
Panduk, Michigan
Dear Mr. Child:

I am in possession of no information indicating that any item purchased by you from the Treasure Book Club has been returned.

I would hardly think that, if the case had been as you stated, the Treasure Book Club would have retained us to collect the amount owing from you.

If I do not receive your payment in full within three days, by May 12, 198–, we will be forced to take legal action.

Very truly yours,
Hagthorpe M. Pruitt, Jr.

COURT OF MINOR CLAIMS
Chicago, Illinois

Mr. Walter A. Child
437 Woodlawn Drive,
Panduk, Michigan

Be informed that a judgment was taken and entered against you in this court this day of May 26, 198–, in the amount of $15.66 including court costs.

Payment in satisfaction of this judgment may be made to this court or to the adjudged creditor. In the case of payment being made to the creditor, a release should be obtained from the creditor and filed with this court in order to free you of legal obligation in connection with this judgment. Under the recent Reciprocal Claims Act, if you are a citizen of a different state, a duplicate claim may be automatically entered and judged against you in your own state so that collection may be made there as well as in the State of Illinois.

COURT OF MINOR CLAIMS
Chicago, Illinois
PLEASE DO NOT FOLD,
SPINDLE OR MUTILATE
THIS CARD

Judgment was passed this day of May 27, 198–, under Statute 941

Against: Child, Walter A. of 437 Woodlawn Drive, Panduk, Michigan. Pray to enter a duplicate claim for judgment.

    In: Picayune Court—Panduk, Michigan
    For Amount: $15.66

                    437 Woodlawn Drive
                    Panduk, Michigan
                    May 31, 198–

Samuel P. Grimes
Vice President, Treasure Book Club
1823 Mandy Street
Chicago, Illinois
Grimes:

    This business has gone far enough. I've got to come down to Chicago on business of my own tomorrow. I'll see you then and we'll get this straightened out once and for all, about who owes what to whom, and how much!

                          Yours,
                    Walter A. Child

          From the desk of the Clerk
            Picayune Court

                    June 1, 198–

Harry:

    The attached computer card from Chicago's Minor Claims Court against A. Walter has a 1500-series Statute number on it. That puts it over in Criminal with you, rather than Civil, with me. So I herewith submit it for your computer instead of mine. How's business?

                          Joe

CRIMINAL RECORDS
Panduk, Michigan
PLEASE DO NOT FOLD,
SPINDLE OR MUTILATE
THIS CARD

Convicted: (Child) A. Walter
On: May 26, 198–
Address: 437 Woodlawn Drive, Panduk, Mich.
Statute: 1566 (Corrected) 1567
Crime: Kidnap
Date: Nov. 16, 198–
Notes: At large. To be picked up at once.

POLICE DEPARTMENT, PANDUK, MICHIGAN. TO POLICE DEPARTMENT CHICAGO ILLINOIS. CONVICTED SUBJECT A. (COMPLETE FIRST NAME UNKNOWN) WALTER, SOUGHT HERE IN CONNECTION REF. YOUR NOTIFICATION OF JUDGMENT FOR KIDNAP OF CHILD NAMED ROBERT LOUIS STEVENSON, ON NOV. 16, 198–. INFORMATION HERE INDICATES SUBJECT FLED HIS RESIDENCE, AT 437 WOODLAWN DRIVE, PANDUK, AND MAY BE AGAIN IN YOUR AREA.

POSSIBLE CONTACT IN YOUR AREA: THE TREASURE BOOK CLUB, 1823 MANDY STREET, CHICAGO, ILLINOIS. SUBJECT NOT KNOWN TO BE ARMED, BUT PRESUMED DANGEROUS. PICK UP AND HOLD, ADVISING US OF CAPTURE...

TO POLICE DEPARTMENT, PANDUK, MICHIGAN. REFERENCE YOUR REQUEST TO PICK UP AND HOLD A. (COMPLETE FIRST NAME UNKNOWN) WALTER, WANTED IN PANDUK ON STATUTE 1567, CRIME OF KIDNAPPING.

SUBJECT ARRESTED AT OFFICES OF TREASURE BOOK CLUB, OPERATING THERE UNDER ALIAS WALTER ANTHONY CHILD AND ATTEMPTING TO COLLECT $4.98 FROM ONE SAMUEL P. GRIMES, EMPLOYEE OF THAT COMPANY.

DISPOSAL: HOLDING FOR YOUR ADVICE.

POLICE DEPARTMENT PANDUK, MICHIGAN TO POLICE DEPARTMENT CHICAGO, ILLINOIS.

REF: A. WALTER (ALIAS WALTER ANTHONY CHILD) SUBJECT WANTED FOR CRIME OF KIDNAP, YOUR AREA, REF: YOUR COMPUTER PUNCH CARD NOTIFICATION OF JUDGMENT, DATED MAY 27 198–. COPY OUR CRIMINAL RECORDS PUNCH CARD HEREWITH FORWARDED TO YOUR COMPUTER SECTION.

CRIMINAL RECORDS
Chicago, Illinois
PLEASE DO NOT FOLD,
SPINDLE OR MUTILATE
THIS CARD

SUBJECT (CORRECTION—OMITTED RECORD SUPPLIED)

APPLICABLE STATUTE NO. 1567

JUDGMENT NO. 456789

TRIAL RECORD: APPARENTLY MISFILED AND UNAVAILABLE

DIRECTION: TO APPEAR FOR SENTENCING BEFORE JUDGE JOHN
ALEXANDER MCDIVOT, COURTROOM A, JUNE 9, 198—

From the Desk of
Judge Alexander J. McDivot

June 2, 198—

Dear Tony:

I've got an adjudged criminal coming up before me for
sentencing Thursday morning—but the trial transcript is
apparently misfiled.

I need some kind of information (Ref: A. Walter—Judgment No. 456789, Criminal). For example, what about the
victim of the kidnapping? Was victim harmed?

Jack McDivot

June 3, 198—

Records Search Unit
Re: Ref: Judgment No. 456789—was victim harmed?

Tonio Malagasi
Records Division

June 3, 198—

To: United States Statistics Office
Attn: Information Section
Subject: Robert Louis Stevenson
Query: Information concerning

Records Search Unit
Criminal Records Division
Police Department
Chicago, Ill.

June 5, 198—

To: Records Search Unit
Criminal Records Division

Police Department
Chicago, Illinois
Subject: Your query re Robert Louis Stevenson (File no. 189623)
Action: Subject deceased. Age at death, 44 yrs. Further information requested?

A. K.
Information Section
U. S. Statistics Office

June 6, 198–

To: United States Statistics Office
Attn.: Information Division
Subject: Re: File no. 189623
No further information required.

Thank you.
Records Search Unit
Criminal Records Division
Police Department
Chicago, Illinois

June 7, 198–

To: Tonio Malagasi
Records Division
Re: Ref: judgment No. 456789—victim is dead.

Records Search Unit

June 7, 198–

To: Judge Alexander J. McDivot's Chambers
Dear Jack:
Ref: Judgment No. 456789. The victim in this kidnap case was apparently slain.

From the strange lack of background information on the killer and his victim, as well as the victim's age, this smells to me like a gangland killing. This for your information. Don't quote me. It seems to me, though, that Stevenson—the victim—has a name that rings a faint bell with me. Possibly, one of the East Coast Mob, since the association comes back to me as something about pirates—possibly New York dockage hijackers—and something about buried loot.

As I say, above is only speculation for your private guidance.

Any time I can help...

Best,
Tony Malagasi
Records Division

MICHAEL R. REYNOLDS
Attorney-at-law

49 Water Street
Chicago, Illinois
June 8, 198–

Dear Tim:

Regrets: I can't make the fishing trip. I've been court-appointed here to represent a man about to be sentenced tomorrow on a kidnapping charge.

Ordinarily, I might have tried to beg off, and McDivot, who is doing the sentencing, would probably have turned me loose. But this is the damnedest thing you ever heard of.

The man being sentenced has apparently been not only charged, but adjudged guilty as a result of a comedy of errors too long to go into here. He not only isn't guilty—he's got the best case I ever heard of for damages against one of the larger Book Clubs headquartered here in Chicago. And that's a case I wouldn't mind taking on.

It's inconceivable—but damnably possible, once you stop to think of it in this day and age of machine-made records—that a completely innocent man could be put in this position.

There shouldn't be much to it. I've asked to see McDivot tomorrow before the time of sentencing, and it'll just be a matter of explaining to him. Then I can discuss the damage suit with my freed client at his leisure.

Fishing next weekend?

Yours,
Mike

MICHAEL R. REYNOLDS
Attorney-at-law

49 Water Street
Chicago, Illinois
June 10

Dear Tim:

In haste—
No fishing this coming week either. Sorry.

You won't believe it. My innocent-as-a-lamb-and-I'm-not-kidding client has just been sentenced to death for first-degree murder in connection with the death of his kidnap victim.

Yes, I explained the whole thing to McDivot. And when he explained his situation to me, I nearly fell out of my chair.

It wasn't a matter of my not convincing him. It took less than three minutes to show him that my client should never have been within the walls of the County Jail for a second. But—get this—McDivot couldn't do a thing about it.

The point is, my man had already been judged guilty according to the computerized records. In the absence of a trial record—of course there never was one (but that's something I'm not free to explain to you now)—the judge has to go by what records are available. And in the case of an adjudged prisoner, McDivot's only legal choice was whether to sentence to life imprisonment, or execution.

The death of the kidnap victim, according to the statute, made the death penalty mandatory. Under the new laws governing length of time for appeal, which has been shortened because of the new system of computerizing records, to force an elimination of unfair delay and mental anguish to those condemned, I have five days in which to file an appeal, and ten to have it acted on.

Needless to say, I am not going to monkey with an appeal. I'm going directly to the Governor for a pardon—after which we will get this farce reversed. McDivot has already written the Governor, also, explaining that his sentence was ridiculous, but that he had no choice. Between the two of us, we ought to have a pardon in short order.

Then, I'll make the fur fly ...

And we'll get in some fishing.

Best,
Mike

OFFICE OF THE
GOVERNOR OF ILLINOIS

June 17, 198—

Mr. Michael R. Reynolds
49 Water Street
Chicago, Illinois
Dear Mr. Reynolds:

In reply to your query about the request for pardon for

Walter A. Child (A. Walter), may I inform you that the Governor is still on his trip with the Midwest Governors Committee, examining the Wall in Berlin. He should be back next Friday.

I will bring your request and letters to his attention the minute he returns.

Very truly yours,
Clara B. Jilks
Secretary to the Governor

June 27, 198–

Michael R. Reynolds
49 Water Street
Chicago, Illinois
Dear Mike:

Where is that pardon?
My execution date is only five days from now!

Walt

June 29, 198–

Walter A. Child (A. Walter)
Cell Block E
Illinois State Penitentiary
Joliet, Illinois
Dear Walt:

The Governor returned, but was called away immediately to the White House in Washington to give his views on interstate sewage.

I am camping on his doorstep and will be on him the moment he arrives here.

Meanwhile, I agree with you about the seriousness of the situation. The warden at the prison there, Mr. Allen Magruder, will bring this letter to you and have a private talk with you. I urge you to listen to what he has to say; and I enclose letters from your family also urging you to listen to Warden Magruder.

Yours,
Mike

June 30, 198–

Michael R. Reynolds
49 Water Street
Chicago, Illinois
Dear Mike: (This letter being smuggled out by Warden Magruder)

As I was talking to Warden Magruder in my cell, here, news was brought to him that the Governor has at last returned for a while to Illinois, and will be in his office early tomorrow morning, Friday. So you will have time to get the pardon signed by him and delivered to the prison in time to stop my execution on Saturday.

Accordingly, I have turned down the Warden's kind offer of a chance to escape; since he told me he could by no means guarantee to have all the guards out of my way when I tried it; and there was a chance of my being killed escaping.

But now everything will straighten itself out. Actually, an experience as fantastic as this had to break down sometime under its own weight.

Best,
Walt

FOR THE SOVEREIGN STATE OF ILLINOIS
I, Hubert Daniel Willikens, Governor of the State of Illinois, and invested with the authority and powers appertaining thereto, including the power to pardon those in my judgment wrongfully convicted or otherwise deserving of executive mercy, do this day of July 1, 198– do announce and proclaim that Walter A. Child (A. Walter), now in custody as a consequence of erroneous conviction upon a crime of which he is entirely innocent, is fully and freely pardoned of said crime. And I do direct the necessary authorities having custody of the said Walter A. Child (A. Walter) in whatever place or places he may be held, to immediately free, release, and allow unhindered departure to him...

Interdepartmental Routing Service
PLEASE DO NOT FOLD,
MUTILATE, OR SPINDLE
THIS CARD
Failure to route Document properly.
To: Governor Hubert Daniel Willikens
Re: Pardon issued to Walter A. Child, July 1, 198–

Dear State Employee:

You have failed to attach your Routing Number.

PLEASE: Resubmit document with this card and form 876, explaining your authority for placing a TOP RUSH category on this document. Form 876 must be signed by your Departmental Superior.

RESUBMIT ON: Earliest possible date ROUTING SERVICE office is open. In this case, Tuesday, July 5, 198–.

WARNING: Failure to submit form 876 WITH THE SIGNATURE OF YOUR SUPERIOR may make you liable to prosecution for misusing a Service of the State Government. A warrant may be issued for your arrest.

There are NO exceptions. YOU have been WARNED.

Mildred Clingerman (1918–   ) was a mainstay of The Magazine of Fantasy and Science Fiction *in the 1950s, but stopped appearing in the sf magazines in the early 1960s. Her disappearance was a great loss to the field, because, like R. A. Lafferty, she brought a wonderful and indescribable* strangeness *to her work. Her best stories can be found in* A Cupful of Space *(1961).*

"Letters From Laura" (F & SF, October, 1954) is simply an exchange of letters between a mother and her loving daughter. Well, maybe not so simple.

LETTERS FROM LAURA

By Mildred Clingerman

Monday

Dear Mom:

Stop *worrying*. There isn't a bit of danger. Nobody ever dies or gets hurt or anything like that while time-traveling. The young man at the Agency explained it all to me in detail, but I've forgotten most of it. His eyebrows move in the most fascinating way. So I'm going this weekend. I've already bought my ticket. I haven't the faintest idea where I'm going, but that's part of the fun. Grab Bag Tours, they call them. It costs $60 for one day and night, and the Agency supplies you with food concentrates and water capsules—a whole bag full of stuff they send right along with you. I certainly do *not* want Daddy to go with me. I'll tell him all about it when I get back, and then he can go himself, if he still wants to. The thing Daddy forgets is that all the history he reads is mostly just a pack of lies. Everybody says so nowadays, since time travel. He'd spoil everything arguing with the natives, telling them how they were supposed to act. I have to stop now, because the young man from the Agency is going to take me out to dinner and explain about insurance for the trip.

Love,
Laura

Tuesday

Dear Mom:

I can't *afford* to go first class. The Grab Bag Tours are not the leavings. They're perfectly all right. It's just that you sorta have to rough it. They've been thoroughly explored. I mean somebody has been there at least once before. I never heard of a native attacking a girl traveler. Just because I won't have a guide you start worrying about that. Believe me, some of those guides, from what I hear, wouldn't be very safe, either. Delbert explained it all to me. He's the boy from the Agency. Did you know that insurance is a very interesting subject?

Love,
Laura

Friday

Dear Mom:

Everything is set for tomorrow. I'm so excited. I spent three hours on the couch at the Agency's office—taking the hypno-course, you know, so I'll be able to speak the language. Later Delbert broke a rule and told me my destination, so I rushed over to the public library and read bits here and there. It's ancient Crete! Dad will be so pleased. I'm going to visit the Minotaur in the Labyrinth. Delbert says he is really off the beaten track of the tourists. I like unspoiled things, don't you? The Agency has a regular little room all fixed up right inside the cave, but hidden, so as not to disturb the regular business of the place. The Agency is very particular that way. Time travelers, Delbert says, have to agree to make themselves as inconspicuous as possible. Delbert says that will be very difficult for me to do. Don't you think *subtle* compliments are the nicest? I've made myself a darling costume—I sat up late to finish it. I don't know that it's exactly right, historically, but it doesn't really matter, since I'm not supposed to leave the cave. I have to stay close to my point of arrival, you understand. Delbert says I'm well covered now with insurance, so don't worry. I'll write the minute I get back.

Love,
Laura

Friday

Dear Prue:

Tomorrow I take my first time-travel tour. I wish you could see my costume. Very fetching! It's cut so that my breasts are displayed in the style of ancient Crete. A friend of mine doubts the authenticity of the dress but says the charms it shows off are *really* authentic! Next time I see you I'll lend you the pattern for the dress. But I honestly think, darling, you ought to get one of those Liff-Up operations first. I've been meaning to tell you. Of course, I don't need it myself. I'll tell you all about it (the trip I mean) when I get back.

Love,
Laura

Monday

Dear Prue:

I had the stinkiest time! I'll never know why I let that character at the travel agency talk me into it. The accommodations were lousy. If you want to know what I think, it's all a gyp. These Grab Bag Tours, third-class, are just the *leavings,* that they can't sell any other way. I hate salesmen. Whoever heard of ancient Crete anyway? And the Minotaur. You would certainly expect him to be a red-blooded he-man, wouldn't you? He looked like one. Not cute, you know, but built like a bull, practically. Prue, you just can't *tell* anymore. But I'm getting ahead of myself.

You've heard about that funny dizziness you feel for the first few minutes on arrival? That part is true. Everything is supposed to look black at first, but things kept on looking black even after the dizziness wore off. Then I remembered it was a cave I was in, but I did expect it to be lighted. I was lying on one of those beastly little cots that wiggle everytime

your heart beats, and mine was beating plenty fast. Then I
remembered the bag the Agency packs for you, and I sat up
and felt around till I found it. I got out a perma-light and
attached it to the solid rock wall and looked around. The floor
was just plain old dirty dirt. That Agency had me stuck off
in a little alcove, furnished with that sagging cot and a few
coat hangers. The air in the place was rather stale. Let's be
honest—it smelled. To console myself I expanded my wrist
mirror and put on some more makeup. I was wearing my
costume, but I had forgotten to bring a coat. I was freezing.
I draped the blanket from the cot around me and went exploring. What a place! One huge room just outside my cub-
byhole and corridors taking off in all directions, winding
away into the dark. I had a perma-light with me, and naturally I couldn't get lost with my earrings tuned to point of
arrival, but it was *weird* wandering around all by myself. I
discovered that the corridor I was in curved downward. Later
I found there were dozens of levels in the Labyrinth. Very
confusing.

I was just turning to go back when something reached out
and grabbed for me, from one of those alcoves. I was *thrilled*.
I flicked off the light, dropped my blanket, and ran.

From behind I heard a man's voice. "All right, sis, we'll
play games."

Well, Prue, I hadn't played hide-and-seek in years (except
once or twice at office parties), but I was still pretty good at
it. That part was fun. After a time my eyes adjusted to the
dark so that I could see well enough to keep from banging
into the walls. Sometimes I'd deliberately make a lot of noise
to keep things interesting. But do you know what? That character would blunder right by me, and way down at the end
of the corridor he'd make noises like "Oho" or "Aha." Frankly,
I got discouraged. Finally I heard him grumbling his way
back in my direction. I knew the dope would never catch me,
so I just stepped out in front of him and said "Wellll?" You
know, in that drawly, sarcastic way I have.

He reached out and grabbed me, and then he staggered
back—like you've seen actors do in those old, old movies. He
kept pounding his forehead with his fist, and then he yelled,
"Cheated! Cheated again!" I almost slapped him. Instead I
snapped on my perma-light and let him look me over good.

"Well, Buster," I said very coldly, "what do you mean,
cheated?"

He grinned at me and shaded his eyes from the light. "Darling," he said, "you look luscious, indeed, but what the hell are you doing here?"

"I'm sight-seeing," I said. "Are you one of the sights?"

"Listen, baby, I *am* the sight. Meet the Minotaur." He stuck out this huge paw, and I shook it.

"Who did you think I was?" I asked him.

"No *who,* but *what*," he said. "Baby, you ain't no virgin."

Well, Prue, really. How can you argue a thing like that? He was completely *wrong,* of course, but I simply refused to discuss it.

"I only gobble virgins," he said.

Then he led me down into his rooms, which were really quite comfortable. I couldn't forgive the Agency for that cot, so when I spied his lovely, soft couch draped in pale blue satin, I said, "I'll borrow that if you don't mind."

"It's all yours, kid," the Minotaur said. He meant it, too. You remember how pale blue is one of my best colors? There I was lolling on the couch, looking like the Queen of the Nile, flapping my eyelashes, and what does this churl want to do?

"I'm simply starved for talk," he says. And about what? Prue, when a working girl spends her hard-earned savings on time travel, she has a right to expect something besides *politics.* I've heard there are men, a few shy ones, who will talk very fast to you about science and all that highbrow stuff, hoping maybe you won't notice some of the things they're doing in the *meantime.* But not the Minotaur. Who cares about the government a room's length apart? Lying there, twiddling my fingers and yawning, I tried to remember if Daddy had ever mentioned anything about the Minotaur's being so persnickety. That's the trouble with books. They leave out all the important details.

For instance, did you know that at midnight every night the Minotaur makes a grand tour of the Labyrinth? He wouldn't let me go along. That's another thing. He just says "no" and grins and means it. Now isn't that a typical male trait? I thought so, and when he locked me in his rooms the evening looked like turning into fun. I waited for him to come back with bated breath. But you can't bate your breath forever, and he was gone hours. When he did come back I'd fallen asleep and he woke me up *belching*.

"Please," I said. "Do you have to do that?"

"Sorry, kid," he said. "It's these gaunt old maids. Awful

souring to the stomach." It seems this windy diet was one of
the things wrong with the government. He was very bitter
about it all. Tender virgins, he said, had always been in short
supply and now he was out of favor with the new regime. I
rummaged around in my wrist bag and found an anti-acid
pill. He was delighted. Can you imagine going into a transport over pills?

"Any cute males ever find their way into this place?" I
asked him. I got up and walked around. You can loll on a
couch just so long, you know.

"No boys!" The Minotaur jumped up and shook his fist at
me. I cowered behind some hangings, but I needn't have both-
ered. He didn't even jerk me out from behind them. Instead
he paced up and down and raved about the lies told on him.
He swore he'd never eaten boys—hadn't cared for them at
all. That creep, Theseus, was trying to ruin him politically.
"I've worn myself thin," he yelled, "in all these years of service—" At that point I walked over and poked him in his big,
fat stomach. Then I gathered my things together and walked
out.

He puffed along behind me wanting to know what was the
matter. "Gee, kid," he kept saying, "don't go home mad." I
didn't say goodbye to him at all. A spider fell on him and it
threw him into a hissy. The last I saw of him he was cursing
the government because they hadn't sent him an extermi-
nator.

Well, Prue, so much for the bogey man. Time travel in the
raw!

Love,
Laura

Monday

Dear Mom:
Ancient Crete was nothing but politics, not a bit exciting.
You didn't have a single cause to worry. These people are
just as particular about girls as you are.

Love,
Laura

Tuesday

Dear Mr. Delbert Barnes:
Stop calling me or I will complain to your boss. You cad.
I see it all now. You and your fine talk about how your Agency

"fully protects its clients." That's a very high-sounding name for it. Tell me, how many girls do you talk into going to ancient Crete? And do you provide all of them with the same kind of insurance? Mr. Barnes, I don't want any more insurance from you. But I'm going to send you a client for that trip—the haggiest old maid I know. She has buck teeth and whiskers. Insure *her*.

Laura

P. S. Just in case you're feeling smug about me, put this in your pipe and smoke it. The Minotaur *knew*, I can't imagine how, but *you*, Mr. Barnes, *are no Minotaur*.

A. E. van Vogt (1912–   ), along with Robert Heinlein, Theodore Sturgeon, and one of your editors (can you guess which one?) was one of the great stars of the first "Golden Age" of science fiction (1939–1943). His novels Slan (book form, 1946) and The Weapon Shops of Isher (book form, 1951), and a brace of excellent short stories, established his reputation. Born in Canada, he now lives in Southern California, and is still writing (and publishing).

"Dear Pen Pal" is a delightful story of a planned invasion of Earth. It first appeared in the Winter 1949 issue of the Arkham Sampler, one of the least known (and most beloved among those who knew it) and short-lived sf-and-fantasy magazines.

DEAR PEN PAL

By A. E. van Vogt

Planet Aurigae II

Dear Pen Pal:

When I first received your letter from the interstellar correspondence club, my impulse was to ignore it. The mood of one who has spent the last seventy planetary periods—years, I suppose you would call them—in an Aurigaen prison, does not make for a pleasant exchange of letters. However, life is

115

very boring, and so I finally settled myself to the task of writing you.

Your description of Earth sounds exciting. I would like to live there for a while, and I have a suggestion in this connection, but I won't mention it till I have developed it further.

You will have noticed the material on which this letter is written. It is a highly sensitive metal, very thin, very flexible, and I have enclosed several sheets of it for your use. Tungsten dipped in any strong acid makes an excellent mark on it. It is important to me that you do write on it, as my fingers are too hot—literally—to hold your paper without damaging it.

I'll say no more just now. It is possible you will not care to correspond with a convicted criminal, and therefore I shall leave the next move up to you. Thank you for your letter. Though you did not know its destination, it brought a moment of cheer into my drab life.

Skander

Aurigae II

Dear Pen Pal:

Your prompt reply to my letter made me happy. I am sorry your doctor thought it excited you too much, and sorry, also, if I have described my predicament in such a way as to make you feel badly. I welcome your many questions, and I shall try to answer them all.

You say the international correspondence club has no record of having sent any letters to Aurigae. That, according to them, the temperature on the second planet of the Aurigae sun is more than 500 degrees Fahrenheit. And that life is not known to exist there. Your club is right about the temperature and the letters. We have what your people would call a hot climate, but then we are not a hydrocarbon form of life, and find 500 degrees very pleasant.

I must apologize for deceiving you about the way your first letter was sent to me. I didn't want to frighten you away by telling you too much at once. After all, I could not be expected to know that you would be enthusiastic to hear from me.

The truth is that I am a scientist, and, along with the other members of my race, I have known for some centuries that there were other inhabited systems in the galaxy. Since I am allowed to experiment in my spare hours, I amused myself in attempts at communication. I developed several simple systems for breaking in on galactic communication operations, but it was not until I developed a subspacewave control that I was able to draw your letter (along with several others, which I did not answer) into a cold chamber.

I use the cold chamber as both sending and receiving center, and since you were kind enough to use the material which I sent you, it was easy for me to locate your second letter among the mass of mail that accumulated at the nearest headquarters of the interstellar correspondence club.

How did I learn your language? After all, it is a simple one, particularly the written language seems easy. I had no difficulty with it. If you are still interested in writing me, I shall be happy to continue the correspondence.

Skander

Aurigae II

Dear Pen Pal:

Your enthusiasm is refreshing. You say that I failed to answer your question about how I expected to visit Earth. I confess I deliberately ignored the question, as my experiment had not yet proceeded far enough. I want you to bear with me a short time longer, and then I will be able to give you the details. You are right in saying that it would be difficult for a being who lives at a temperature of 500 degrees Fahrenheit to mingle freely with the people of Earth. This was never my intention, so please relieve your mind. However, let us drop that subject for the time being.

I appreciate the delicate way in which you approach the subject of my imprisonment. But it is quite unnecessary. I performed forbidden experiments upon my body in a way that was deemed to be dangerous to the public welfare. For instance, among other things, I once lowered my surface temperature to 150 degrees Fahrenheit, and so shortened the radioactive cycle-time of my surroundings. This caused an unexpected break in the normal person-to-person energy flow in the city where I lived, and so charges were laid against me. I have thirty more years to serve. It would be pleasant to leave my body behind and tour the universe—but as I said I'll discuss that later.

I wouldn't say that we're a superior race. We have certain qualities which apparently your people do not have. We live longer, not because of any discoveries we've made about ourselves, but because our bodies are built of a more enduring element—I don't know your name for it, but the atomic weight is 52.9#.* Our scientific discoveries are of the kind that would normally be made by a race with our kind of physical structure. The fact that we can work with temperatures of as high as—I don't know just how to put that—has been very helpful in the development of the subspace energies which are extremely hot, and require delicate adjustments. In the later stages these adjustments can be made by machinery, but in the development the work must be done by "hand"—I put that word in quotes, because we have no hands in the same way that you have.

I am enclosing a photographic plate, properly cooled and chemicalized for your climate. I wonder if you would set it up and take a picture of yourself. All you have to do is arrange it properly on the basis of the laws of light—that is, light travels in straight lines, so stand in front of it—and when you are ready *think* "Ready!" The picture will be automatically taken.

Would you do this for me? If you are interested, I will also send you a picture of myself, though I must warn you. My appearance will probably shock you.

Sincerely
Skander

Planet Aurigae II

Dear Pen Pal:

Just a brief note in answer to your question. It is not necessary to put the plate into a camera. You describe this as a dark box. The plate will take the picture when you think, "Ready!" I assure you it will be flooded with light.

Skander

Aurigae II

Dear Pen Pal:

You say that while you were waiting for the answer to my last letter you showed the photographic plate to one of the doctors at the hospital—I cannot picture what you mean by doctor or hospital, but let that pass—and he took the problem up with government authorities. Problem? I don't understand. I thought we were having a pleasant correspondence, private and personal.

*A radioactive isotope of chromium.—Author's Note.

I shall certainly appreciate your sending that picture of yourself.

Skander

Aurigae II

Dear Pen Pal:

I assure you I am not annoyed at your action. It merely puzzled me, and I am sorry the plate has not been returned to you. Knowing what governments are, I can imagine that it will not be returned to you for some time, so I am taking the liberty of enclosing another plate.

I cannot imagine why you should have been warned against continuing this correspondence. What do they expect me to do?—eat you up at long distance? I'm sorry but I don't like hydrogen in my diet.

In any event, I would like your picture as a memento of our friendship, and I will send mine as soon as I have received yours. You may keep it or throw it away, or give it to your governmental authorities—but at least I will have the knowledge that I've given a fair exchange.

With all best wishes
Skander

Aurigae II

Dear Pen Pal:

Your last letter was so slow in coming that I thought you had decided to break off the correspondence. I was sorry to notice that you failed to enclose the photograph, puzzled by your reference to having a relapse, and cheered by your statement that you would send it along as soon as you felt better—whatever that means. However, the important thing is that you did write, and I respect the philosophy of your club which asks its members not to write of pessimistic matters. We all have our own problems which we regard as overshadowing the problems of others. Here I am in prison, doomed to spend the next thirty years tucked away from the main stream of life. Even the thought is hard on my restless spirit, though I know I have a long life ahead of me after my release.

In spite of your friendly letter, I won't feel that you have completely re-established contact with me until you send the photograph.

Yours in expectation
Skander

Aurigae II

Dear Pen Pal:

The photograph arrived. As you suggest, your appearance startled me. From your description I thought I had mentally reconstructed your body. It just goes to show that words cannot really describe an object which has never been seen.

You'll notice that I've enclosed a photograph of myself, as I promised I would. Chunky, metallic looking chap, am I not, very different, I'll wager, than you expected? The various races with whom we have communicated become wary of us when they discover we are highly radioactive, and that literally we are a radioactive form of life, the only such (that we know of) in the universe. It's been very trying to be so isolated and, as you know, I have occasionally mentioned that I had hopes of escaping not only the deadly imprisonment to which I am being subjected but also the body which cannot escape.

Perhaps you'll be interested in hearing how far this idea has developed. The problem involved is one of exchange of personalities with someone else. Actually, it is not really an exchange in the accepted meaning of the word. It is necessary to get an impress of both individuals, of their mind and of their thoughts as well as their bodies. Since this phase is purely mechanical, it is simply a matter of taking complete photographs and of exchanging them. By complete I mean, of course, every vibration must be registered. The next step is to make sure the two photographs are exchanged, that is that each party has somewhere near him a complete photograph of the other. (It is already too late, Pen Pal. I have set in motion the sub-space energy interflow between the two plates, so you might as well read on.) As I have said, it is not exactly an exchange of personalities. The original personality in each individual is suppressed, literally pushed back out of the consciousness, and the image personality from the "photographic" plate replaces it.

You will take with you a complete memory of your life on Earth, and I will take along memory of my life on Aurigae Simultaneously, the memory of the receiving body will be blurrily at our disposal. A part of us will always be pushing up, striving to regain consciousness, but always lacking the strength to succeed.

As soon as I grow tired of Earth, I will exchange bodies in the same way with a member of some other race. Thirty years hence, I will be happy to reclaim my body, and you can then have whatever body I last happened to occupy.

This should be a very happy arrangement for us both. You, with your short life expectancy, will have outlived all your contemporaries and will have had an interesting experience. I admit I expect to have the better of the exchange—but now, enough of explanation. By the time you reach this part of the letter it will be me reading it, not you. But if any part of you is still aware, so long for now, Pen Pal. It's been nice having all those letters from you. I shall write you from time to time to let you know how things are going with my tour.

Skander

Aurigae II

Dear Pen Pal:

Thanks a lot for forcing the issue. For a long time I hesitated about letting you play such a trick on yourself. You see, the government scientists analyzed the nature of that first photographic plate you sent me, and so the final decision was really up to me. I decided that anyone as eager as you were to put one over should be allowed to succeed.

Now I know I didn't have to feel sorry for you. Your plan to conquer Earth wouldn't have gotten anywhere, but the fact that you had the idea ends the need for sympathy.

By this time you will have realized for yourself that a man who has been paralyzed since birth, and is subject to heart attacks, cannot expect a long life span. I am happy to tell you that your once-lonely pen pal is enjoying himself, and I am happy to sign myself with a name to which I expect to become accustomed.

With best wishes
Skander

*A former professor of biological psychology, Dr. Lambe is now
an active member of the writing society. He insists that his
patronym has two syllables—but won't say which two. His
short fiction has appeared in* Omni *and* Analog.

DAMN SHAME

By Dean R. Lambe

Sept. 12, 1985

Albert S. Cranberg, M.D.
P.O. Box 912
Fulton, Wisconsin
Dear "Alice":

Sorry to be so long getting back to you; been busy as a
bitch in heat. Janet swears that if I don't get some time off
soon, she's going to take a vacation without me. The test
series are really beginning to pay off on AC-337, and it's
damn exciting, to say the least! I think I may have mentioned
the *in vitro* results on this stuff the last time I wrote, but of
course, we've seen terrific data with isolated tumor cells before. Now that we've finished the first round of animal trials
and toxicity screens, though, AC-337 is beginning to look
like a winner. Why, in the Bh/286 mice alone (they're the

little buggers with a handy gene for bladder cancer), we've got a 92 percent remission rate, and no gastrointestinal side-effects at all. You'd better believe that I'm anxious to start the dog trials next week.

Well, enough shop talk...oh, mum's the word on AC-337. Not that you would say anything, I'm sure, but Hendricks would have my fair young hide if premature publicity got out on our wonder drug. And you know how the press goes crazy about a "cancer cure."

So anyway, how're you doing out there in the sticks? Never could understand how you and Ruth keep from going crazy, but I guess you're right about small towns being the only sensible place to raise kids these days. Still going the GP route—golf on Wednesdays, poker on Saturday night? Just kidding, I remember how you used to play poker—old stone face, you ain't.

Wish I had more time, but gotta get back to the damn computer. Give my love to Ruth and your crumb crushers. Oh, and when you write, you'd better send it here to the lab...mail at home just seems to get lost in the shuffle.

All the best,
Fred

30 Sept 85

Frederick Jenssen, Ph.D.
Ritter Memorial Institute
3944 Orangegrove Drive
Cloverdale, California
Dear Fred:

Will you for christsakes quit calling me "Alice"?! You'd think that we were still back in the damn frat house. Speaking of which, did you see the class reunion picture in the latest alumni bulletin? Ho boy, George Riviere looks like he'll be completely bald before he's 40, and Ken Shikoku must have gained 20 kilos. I was also surprised to see that Willis Eisner is working on that Amazon Basin project—never figured that screwball for a Corps of Engineers type. Say though, if your California water shortage gets any worse, maybe old Willis can ship you some; he must have plenty to spare these days.

The old alma ma is asking for more contributions again—I imagine you got a letter too. Ruth and I always give all we can; what with so many good private schools folding, I'd like to think that the place will still be there when my kids are ready.

Glad to hear that your work is going well. That AC-337 really sounds promising. I've sure got a lot of patients with the Big C who could use something better than what they're getting now, but I suppose your stuff will come too late for most of them, even if it pans out.

As for what's new at this end; well, not much, as you suspected. Little Ruth broke her arm two weeks ago—greenstick fracture of the radius. She fell off that damn jet skater that she just had to have for her birthday. Kids! When my partner set it, she wouldn't let him put on a mnemoplastic cast. Insisted on the old-fashioned plaster kind. Said her friends couldn't write on a plastic one! Not much else, I guess. Oh, Ruth says to tell Janet that she's welcome to move in with us when she gets tired of your workaholic ways.

Regards,
Al

Nov. 21, 1985

Albert S. Cranberg, M.D.
P.O. Box 912
Fulton, Wisconsin
Dear Al:

The space between our letters gets longer and longer, and that's no way to treat the best man at my wedding (I'll never forgive you for that business with the ring, you bastard). The work keeps going super; AC-337 is starting to look like Nobel Prize material. It's all we can do to keep our mouths shut when we're off-campus, but we've got to play it tight until the FDA prelim for human trials is approved. The three runs in the beagles were *go* all the way; still better than 85 percent remission for both sarcomas and carcinomas of several varieties...damn stuff's almost too good to be true. Keep all your toes crossed for us. We start the primate trials next Tuesday.

Believe it or not, Jack hasn't been a dull boy. Janet and I took a long weekend in Vancouver a couple of weeks ago; much fun and frolic was had by all, and she says that she won't run off with that new stud in her office after all (she's joking...uh, I think).

Hello to Ruth and the kids....

All the best,
Fred

3 Jan 86

Frederick Jenssen, Ph.D.
Ritter Memorial Institute
3944 Orangegrove Drive
Cloverdale, California
Dear Fred:

Happy New Year, you lucky dog. Wish you were here to help me shovel snow! You people must have forgotten what winter's like, but then, I don't envy your drought. At least we can flush our commodes here—if the pipes don't freeze; and we did get to spend the holidays with Ruth's folks in Florida.

Fred, old buddy, I have a rather unusual request...hell, I know I shouldn't even ask, but if your AC-337 is still looking good, could you possibly send me enough for two patients? Yah, I know, the FDA and six other piles of bureaucrats would shit bricks, but these patients have nothing to lose, believe me. One is a 41-year-old schoolteacher, but by no means an old maid. She's been bed-hopping for years, and has never been pregnant—makes a classic case for breast cancer, and she's got it in both barrels, and I'm pretty sure that it's metastasized to her brain. Naturally, she waited too long to come in, and I don't give her more than six months. The other case is a 17-year-old kid who was a star basketball player until a couple of months ago. He's got myeloma in both tibias, and he and his parents wouldn't accept double amputation when taking his legs might have done some good. I'm sure that it'll be into the marrow of femur and pelvis in less than a year.

So what do you say, Fred? I know we'd be shaky legally, but who's to know except a couple of terminal patients. Besides, the Laetrile and marijuana precedents do give us some protection; and you'd gain valuable data probably years

ahead of schedule. Sure, I'll understand if you don't think
you can swing it, but think on it, huh?

Regards,
Al

Jan. 14, 1986

Albert S. Cranberg, M.D.
P.O. Box 912
Fulton, Wisconsin
Dear Al:

Your plea for your two patients really hit me between the
eyes, pal; sometimes day-in, day-out lab work makes a guy
forget what it's all about. A week ago, I'd have had to say no
way, but the FDA prelim just came through, and the third
baboon series came up roses too. Granted, we won't be able
to start human trials until June, but Hendricks has put me
in charge of the whole shooting match (look Ma, a promotion).
So between you, me, and a couple of dying folks, what's a
little AC-337 between friends. I'm sending you a little package, which includes the computer projections on the human
dose-response curve. Naturally, I'll expect you to keep meticulous records. Oh, and you may be interested to know that
our biochem people finally have a handle on how it works.
Seems AC-337 has characteristics of both methotrexate and
urethane, but selectively hits the RNA of tumor cells more
like the former. They're still puzzling over why the protein
synthesis breaks down in so many seemingly different types
of cancer cells, though.

Sure glad I can say yes. And hey, you folks give some real
thought about heading this way for a vacation this summer.

All the best,
Fred

12 April 86

Frederick Jenssen, Ph.D.
Ritter Memorial Institute
3944 Orangegrove Drive
Cloverdale, California
Dear Fred:

Now look who's falling behind in letter-writing. And this
has got to be just a quick note. I've got three runny noses,

a sprained ankle, and two little old ladies who're just lonely, all outside in the waiting room. But I just got the second lab workup on "our" two patients, and want to let you know right away. The first follow-up after I started AC-337 was inconclusive, so I didn't want to send you any false positives. Now... well, I can hardly believe my eyes as I hold these X rays. If what I see continues, that school teacher will be back to the Three Rs this fall, and the kid will be under the hoop with the best of them again. Naturally, my next question is, can you spare any more of the stuff? Could save surgery for a couple other patients. Oh, and how tough is AC-337 to synthesize? Is it going to cost an arm and a leg (no pun intended) when it's finally released?

Regards,
Al

May 2, 1986

Albert S. Cranberg, M.D.
P.O. Box 912
Fulton, Wisconsin
Dear Al:

Damn mail gets slower every month, but boy am I happy you're happy. And you'll be even happier to know that the baboons and chimps have shown no side-effects either; got three female baboons pregnant that had uterine cancer three months ago. How's that for a turn-around! As for synthesis of AC-337, well, the boys and girls in biochem say it'd be a bitch, but no sweat because the source is a botanical—some South American plant of all things (hell, I didn't even know that until a few days ago, and I'm supposed to be in charge). Of course, it's too soon to have done a cost-per-dose projection, and our research costs certainly aren't cheap, but you sawbones shouldn't have to worry about the price.

I really wish I could send you more, but our human trials are about ready to go, and the available supply is all tightly budgeted. As a matter of fact, I have to break this off and get a subtle order out to the supply house for more raw materials (ah, the joys of being project director). Do keep me informed on those patients' progress.

All the best,
Fred

May 2, 1986

Mr. Nathan Anderson
Butler Bio-Medical Supply, Inc.
521 Washburn Avenue
Lawrence, Kansas
Dear Mr. Anderson:

About a year ago, your company supplied us with 60 kilograms of dried specimens of the plant *Pedicularis tefensis*. You may recall that Dr. Carlton's team at the University of Kansas had found some indications of medicinal value in this South American plant. I am pleased to report that our research has confirmed Dr. Carlton's findings.

We are most anxious to continue our investigations with extracts from *Pedicularis tefensis*, and would like to order 400 kilograms for immediate delivery.

Should your company be unable to supply this amount, I would appreciate any information you may have on other suppliers.

Sincerely,
Frederick Jenssen, Ph.D.
Ritter Memorial Institute

May 28, 1986

Dr. Frederick Jenssen
Ritter Memorial Institute
3944 Orangegrove Drive
Cloverdale, California
Dear Dr. Jenssen:

I regret that we no longer have any stock of *Pedicularis tefensis*. As you undoubtedly know, there has been considerable terrorist activity and increased anti-American sentiment in much of South America, and our regular field collectors are simply no longer welcome (or safe) in many areas. My contacts within our industry would indicate that other suppliers would be cut off from their former sources as well.

I am enclosing the name of a Brazilian botanist with whom we have had very good relations in the past, and I hope that he can be of help to you.

Please contact me if you feel that we can be of further service.

> Yours truly,
> Nate Anderson
> Vice Pres., Botanicals
> Butler Bio-Medical Supply, Inc.

29 May 1986

Frederick Jenssen, Ph.D.
Ritter Memorial Institute
3944 Orangegrove Drive
Cloverdale, California
Dear Fred:

Damnit, old buddy, this is literally one hell of a note! Classic "there's good news, and bad news." As for our two patients, well, that's the good news—complete remission. You know we don't like to use the word, but if ever I've seen "cures," then that term applies to our schoolmarm and basketball player. Now for the irony—Ruth's got a lump in her left breast. Got the biopsy results yesterday, and I needn't tell you the verdict.

My ethics are shot to hell over this. I had one dose of AC-337 left, and you know what I did with it. But it won't be enough...please, Fred.

> Please,
> Al

June 12, 1986

Albert S. Cranberg, M.D.
P.O. Box 912
Fulton, Wisconsin
Dear Al:

Ethics be damned, friend! You know I'll find enough somewhere to give Ruth the full series. It's tight, what with all the protocols now on file with the Feds, but I think we're about to have a "computer error" here. I just ran into a little snag on the supply of raw materials, but I'm going directly to the source, so it's nothing for you or Ruth to worry about. We ought to have an ample amount in a couple of months, and I can easily replace what I send you.

Hang in there,
Fred

June 12, 1986

Senhor Dotor João Luís Linhares
Instituto Botânico Ocidental
27 Rua Barbacena
Manaus, Amazonas, Brazil
Dear Dr. Linhares:

Mr. Nathan Anderson of Butler Bio-Medical Supply, Inc. has given me your name as one who might be able to supply extract from the plant *Pedicularis tefensis*. Our research has uncovered useful medicinal properties in this plant, and we are anxious to obtain several hundred kilograms in order to continue our investigations.

I would also appreciate any information that you may have on the possibility of controlled, hothouse cultivation of this species. If possible, I would like to arrange for the immediate shipment of several hundred living plants.

Sincerely,
Frederick Jenssen, Ph.D.
Ritter Memorial Institute

19 July 1986

Dr. Frederick Jenssen
Ritter Memorial Institute
3944 Orangegrove Drive
Cloverdale, California USA
Dear Dr. Jenssen:

I am in receipt of your letter to Dr. João Luís Linhares, and ask that you forgive my poor use of your language. I regret to inform you Dr. Linhares is not among the living, it being particularly saddening that the gentleman died at his own hand. As you may know, Dr. Linhares put in most of his years in the study of the ecology of our tropical rain forest, and it is thought that he could not accept the necessity of flooding for to make our great Amazon Sea. It is unfortunate that this good man lacked the vision of our great Presidente for the progress and good of our peoples.

I also regret that I cannot supply you any *Pedicularis tefensis,* what you would call Tefé Lousewort. I do not know this plant personally, but with consultation of the notes of Dr. Linhares, I find that *Pedicularis tefensis* grows only at a place 50 km. from where the River Tefé flows into the River Amazon. Now, with completion of our great dams, that region is below many meters of water. It is to be assumed that this species is now extinct.

As I am convinced of your interest in our other plants of value medical, I take the liberty of sending you a listing of what is available.

Yours sincerely,
Raimundo P-M. Chavantes, D.Sc.
Instituto Botânico Ocidental

Howard Fast (1914–   ) is one of a relatively small group of authors who have written some excellent science fiction and fantasy in addition to other works for which they are more famous. Others who come to mind are John D. MacDonald, John Jakes, and Michael Shaara. Mr. Fast's literary accomplishments include such famous books as Citizen Tom Paine *(1943),* Spartacus *(1951), and the best-selling* Immigrant series. *Within sf, he has produced a string of notable stories which have been collected as* The Edge of Tomorrow *(1961),* The General Zapped an Angel *(1969), and* A Touch of Infinity *(1973).*

The present selection originally appeared as "The First Men" in the February 1960 issue of The Magazine of Fantasy and Science Fiction.

THE TRAP

By Howard Fast

Bath, England
October 12, 1945

Mrs. Jean Arbalaid
Washington, D.C.

My dear Sister:
I admit to lethargy and perhaps to a degree of indifference—

although it is not indifference in your terms, not in the sense of ceasing to care. I care for you very much and think about you a good deal. After all, we have only each other, and apart from the two of us, our branch of the Feltons has ceased to exist. So, in my failure to reply to three separate letters, there was no more than a sort of inadequacy. I had nothing to say because there was nothing that I wanted to say.

You knew where I was, and I asked Sister Dorcas to write you a postcard or something to the effect that I had mended physically even if my brain was nothing to shout about. I have been rather depressed for the past two months—the doctors here call it melancholia, with their British propensity for Victorian nomenclature—but they tell me that I am now on the mend in that department as well. Apparently, the overt sign of increasing mental health is an interest in things. My writing to you, for example, and also the walks I have taken around the city. Bath is a fascinating town, and I am rather pleased that the rest home they sent me to is located here.

They were terribly short of hospitals with all the bombing and with the casualties sent back here after the Normandy landing, but they have a great talent for making do. Here they took several of the great houses of the Beau Nash period and turned them into rest homes—and managed to make things very comfortable. Ours has a garden, and when a British garden is good, it has no equal anywhere else in the world. In fact, it spurred me to make some rather mawkish advances to Sister Dorcas one sunny day, and she absolutely destroyed my budding sexual desires with her damned understanding and patience. There is nothing as effective in cutting down a clean-cut American lad as a tall, peach-skinned, beautiful and competent British lady who is doubling as a nurse and has a high-bridged nose in the bargain.

I have been ambulant lately, pottering around Bath and poking my nose into each and every corner. The doctor encourages me to walk for the circulation and final healing of my legs, and since Bath is built up and down, I take a good deal of exercise. I go to the old Roman baths frequently, being absolutely fascinated by them and by the whole complex that is built around the Pump Room—where Nash and his pals held forth. So much of Bath is a Georgian city, perhaps more perfect architecturally than any other town in England. But there are also the baths, the old baths of the Middle Ages, and then the Roman baths which date back before that. In fact, the doctors here have insisted that I and other circulatory-problem cases take the baths. I can't see how it differs from an ordinary hot bath, but British physicians still believe in natural healing virtues and so forth.

Why am I a circulatory problem, you are asking yourself; and just what is left of old Harry Felton and what has been shot away and how much of his brain is soggy as a bowl of farina? Yes indeed—I do know you, my sister. May I say immediately that in my meanderings around the town, I am permitted to be alone; so apparently I am not considered to be the type of nut one locks away for the good of each and everyone.

Oh, there are occasions when I will join up with some convalescent British serviceman for an amble, and sometimes I will have a chat with the locals in one of the pubs, and on three or four occasions I have wheeled Sister Dorcas into coming along and letting me hold her hand and make a sort of pass, just so I don't forget how; but by and large, I am alone. You will remember that old Harry was always a sort of loner—so apparently the head is moderately dependable.

It is now the next day, old Jean. October 13. I put the letter away for a day. Anyway, it is becoming a sort of epistle, isn't it? The thing is that I funked it—notice the way I absorb the local slang—when it came down to being descriptive about myself, and I had a talk with Sister Dorcas, and she sent me to the psychiatrist for a listen. He listens and I talk. Then he pontificates.

"Of course," he said to me, after I had talked for a while, "this unwillingness to discuss one's horrors is sometimes worn like a bit of romantic ribbon. You know, old chap—a decoration."

"I find you irritating," I said to him.

"Of course you do. I am trying to irritate you."

"Why?"

"I suppose because you are an American and I have a snobbish dislike for Americans."

"Now you're being tactful."

The psychiatrist laughed appreciatively and congratulated me on a sense of humor. He is a nice fellow, the psychiatrist, about forty, skinny, as so many British professionals are, long head, big nose, very civilized. To me, Jean, that is the very nice thing about the English—the sense of civilization you feel.

"But I don't want you to lose your irritation," he said.

"No danger."

"I mean if we get to liking and enjoying each other, we'll simply cover things up. I want to root up a thing or two. You're well enough to take it—and you're a strong type, Felton. No schizoid tendencies—never did show any. Your state of depression was more of a reaction to your fear that you would never walk again, but you're walking quite well now, aren't you? Yet Sister Dorcas tells me you will not write a word to your family about what happened to you. Why not?"

"My family is my sister. I don't want to worry her, and Sister Dorcas has a big mouth."

"I'll tell her that."

"And I'll kill you."

"And as far as worrying your sister—my dear fellow, we all know who your sister is. She is a great scientist and a woman of courage and character. Nothing you can tell her would worry her, but your silence does."

"She thinks I've lost my marbles?"

"You Americans are delightful when you talk the way you imagine we think you talk. No, she doesn't think you're dotty. Also, I wrote to her a good many months ago, telling her that you had been raked by machine-gun fire across both legs and describing the nature of your injuries."

"Then there it is."

"Of course not. It is very important for you to be able to discuss what happened to you. You suffered trauma and great pain. So did many of us."

"I choose not to talk about it," I said. "Also, you are beginning to bore me."

"Good. Irritation and boredom. What else?"

"You are a goddamn nosey Limey, aren't you?"

"Yes, indeed."

"Never take No for an answer."

"I try not to."

"All right, doc—it is as simple as this. I do not choose to talk about what happened to me because I have come to dislike my race."

"Race? How do you mean, Felton—Americans? White race? or what?"

"The human race," I said to him.

"Oh, really? Why?"

"Because they exist only to kill."

"Come on now—we do take a breather now and then."

"Intervals. The main purpose is killing."

"You know, you are simply feeding me non sequiturs. I ask you why you will not discuss the incident of your being wounded, and you reply that you have come to dislike the human race. Now and then I myself have found the human race a little less than overwhelmingly attractive, but that's surely beside the point."

"Perhaps. Perhaps not."

"Why don't you tell me what happened?"

"Why don't you drop dead?" I asked him.

"Or why don't you and I occupy ourselves with a small pamphlet on Americanisms—if only to enlighten poor devils like myself who have to treat the ill among you who inhabit our rest homes?"

"The trouble is," I said, "that you have become so bloody civilized that you have lost the ability to be properly nasty."

"Oh, come off it, Felton, and stop asking for attention like a seven-year-old. Why don't you just tell me what happened—because you know, it's you who are becoming the bore."

"All right," I agreed. "Good. We're getting to be honest with each other. I will tell you—properly and dramatically—and then will you take your stinking psychiatric ass off my back?"

"If you wish."

"Good. Not that it's any great hotshot story for the books—it simply is what it is to me. I had a good solid infantry company, New York boys mostly; some Jews, some Negroes, five Puerto Ricans, a nice set of Italians and Irish, and the rest white Protestants of English, Scotch, North of Ireland and German descent. I specify, because we were all on the holy mission of killing our fellow man. The boys were well trained and they did their best, and we worked our way into Germany with no more casualties or stupidities than the next company; and then one of those gross and inevitable stupidities occurred. We came under enemy fire and we called our planes for support, and they bombed and strafed the hell out of us."

"Your planes?"

"That's right. It happened a lot more often than anyone gave out, and it was a wonder it didn't happen twice as much. How the hell do you know, when you're way up there and moving at that speed? How do you know which is which, when one and all are trying to cuddle into the ground? So it happened. There was an open farm shed, and one of my riflemen and I dived in there and took cover behind a woodpile. And that was where I found this little German kid, about three years old, frightened, almost catatonic with fear—and just a beautiful kid."

I must have stopped there. He prodded me, and pointed out that the war had drawn small distinction between children and adults, and even less distinction between more beautiful and less beautiful children.

"What did you do?"

"I tried to provide cover for the child," I explained patiently. "I put her in my arms and held my body over her. A bomb hit the shed. I wasn't hurt, but the rifleman there with me—his name was Ruckerman—he was killed. I came out into the open with the kid in my arms, warm and safe. Only the top of her head was gone. A freak hit. I suppose the bomb fragment sheared it clean off, and I stood there with the little girl's brains dripping down on my shoulder. Then I was hit by the German machine-gun burst."

"I see," the psychiatrist said.

"You have imagination, then."

"You tell it well," he said. "Feel any better?"

"No."

"Mind a few more questions, Felton? I am keeping my promise to take my ass off your back, so just say No, if you wish."

"You're very patient with me."

He was. He had put up with my surliness and depression for weeks. Never lost his temper, which was the principal reason why he irritated me so.

"All right. Question away."

"Now that you've told this to me, do you feel any different?"

"No."

"Any better?"

"No."

"That's good."

"Why is it good?" I asked him.

"Well, you see—the incident outraged you, but not in a traumatic sense. Apparently it doesn't hurt or help very much to recall it."

"It's not blocked, if you mean that. I can think about it whenever I wish to. It disgusts me."

"Certainly. As I said, I believe your depression was entirely due to the condition of your legs. When you began to walk, the depression started to lift, and they tell me that in another few weeks your legs will be as good as ever. Well, not for mountain climbing—but short of that, good enough. Tell me, Felton, why were you so insistent upon remaining in England for your convalescence? You pulled a good many strings. You could have been flown home, and the care stateside is better than here. They have all sorts of things and conveniences that we don't have."

"I like England."

"Do you? No girl awaited you here—what do you like about us?"

"There you go with your goddamn, nosy professional touch."

"Yes, of course. But, you see, Captain, you made your indictment universal. Man is a bloody horror. Quite so. Here, too. Isn't he?"

"Oh, do get off my back," I said to him, and that ended the interview; but by putting it down, "he said," "I said," etc., I am able, my dear Jean, to convey the facts to you.

You ask whether I want to come home. The answer is No. Not now, not in the foreseeable future. Perhaps never, but never is a hairy word, and who can tell?

You say that my share of mother's estate brings me over a hundred dollars a week. I have no way to spend any of it, so let the lawyers piddle with it just as they have been doing. I have my own dole, my accumulated pay, and a few hundred dollars I won playing bridge. Ample. As I said, I have nothing to spend it on.

As to what I desire—very little indeed. I have no intentions of resuming the practice of corporate law. The first two years of it bored me, but at least I brought to them a modicum of ambition. Now the ambition is gone, and the only thing that replaces it is distaste. No matter what direction my thinking takes, I always return to the fact that the human race is a rather dreadful thing. That is, my dear, with the exception of yourself and your brilliant husband.

I am better able to write now, so if you write to me and tell me what brilliance and benevolence you and your husband are up to now, I shall certainly answer your letter.

Thank you for bearing with me through my boorish months.

Harry.

2

Washington, D.C.
October 16, 1945

Captain Harry Felton
Bath, England

My dear Harry:

I will not try to tell you how good it was to hear from you. I never was terribly good at putting my feelings down on paper, but believe me I have read and reread your letter, oh, I should say, at least half a dozen times, and I have done little but think of you and what you have been through and your situation at this moment. I am sure you realize, Harry, better than anyone else, that this is not a time for bright words and happy clichés. Nothing I say at this moment is going to make very much difference to you or to your state of mind or, of course, to your state of health. And nothing I offer at this moment in the way of philosophical argument is going to change any of your attitudes. On my part, I am not sure that changing them at this moment is very important. Far more important is Harry Felton, his life and his future.

I have been talking about that to Mark and thinking about it a great deal myself. Harry, we've both of us engaged on a most exciting project which, for the moment, must remain surrounded with all the silly United States Army attitudes of secrecy and classification. Actually, our project is not military and there are no military secrets concerned with it. But at the moment we are operating with Army money and therefore we are surrounded with all sorts of taboos and rules and regulations. Nevertheless, Harry, rest assured that the project is fascinating, important and, quite naturally, difficult.

We need help—I think specifically the kind of help you might provide. And at the same time, I think we can give you what you need most at this moment of your life—a purpose. We cannot give you a profession, and, when you come right down to it, we cannot ask you to be much more than an exalted messenger-boy–reporter. However, the combination of the two will give you a chance to travel, perhaps to see some of the world that you have not yet seen, and, we think, to ask some interesting questions.

Truthfully, our mission requires a very intelligent man. I am not apple-polishing or trying to cheer you with compliments. I am simply stating that we can make you a fairly decent offer that will take your mind off your present situation and at least give you an interest in geography.

At the moment we can pay you only a pittance, but you say in your letter that you are not particularly concerned with money. We will pay all expenses, of course, and you may stay at the best places if you wish.

Just as an indication of the kind of wheels we presently are and the kind of weight we can throw around, Mark has completed your discharge in England; your passport is on its way via diplomatic pouch, and it will be handed to you personally either before this letter arrives or no more than a day later.

The bit in your letter about your legs was reassuring, and I am sure by now you are even further improved. What I would like you to do, at our expense, is to pick up a civilian outfit. If you can buy the clothes you need in Bath, good; if not, you'd better run up to London and buy them there. You will want, for the most part, tropical lightweight stuff since the wind is up for us in the Far East. Though you will travel as a civilian, we are able to offer you a sort of quasi-diplomatic status, and some very good-looking papers and cards that will clear your way whenever there is a difficulty about priorities. I'm afraid that priorities will remain very much in the picture for the next six months or so. We are short of air-travel space as well as a number of other things. But, as I said before, we are very large wheels indeed, and we envisage no trouble in moving you wherever we desire to. That's a dreadful thing to say, isn't it, and it almost places you outside of the picture as a human being with any volition of your own. Believe me, Harry, like your charming British psychiatrist, I am combining irritation with love. No, I know how easy it would be for you to say No, and I also know that a sharp negative will be absolutely your first and instinctive reaction. By now, of course, simply reading my letter, you have said No half a dozen times, and you have also asked yourself just who the devil your sister thinks she is. My dear, dear Harry, she is a person who loves you very much. How easy it would be for me to say to you, "Harry, please come home immediately to the warmth of our hearts and to the welcome of our open arms." All too easy, Harry, and as far as I can tell, thinking the matter through, it would do you absolutely no good. Even if we could persuade you to come back stateside, I am afraid that you would be bored to tears and frustrated beyond belief. I think that I can understand why you do not want to come home, and I think that at this moment in your existence, it is a very proper decision for you to make. That is to say, I agree with you: you should not come home; but, at the same time, you must have something to do. You may feel, Harry, that this messenger-boy business is not the most creative thing in the world, but I think that rather than attempt to explain to you in advance what we are up to and what you will encounter, you should allow yourself to be drawn into it. You need make no absolute commitments. You will see and you will understand more and more, and at any point along the way you are free to quit, to tell us to go to the devil—or to continue. The choice is always yours; you have no obligation and you are not tied down.

On the other hand, this is not to say that we do not very much want you to accept the assignment. I don't have to tell you what Mark's opinion of you is. You will remember—and believe me it has not changed—he shares my love for you, and you command his very great respect along with mine.

Harry, if you are able to accept my offer, cable me immediately. I would like you to be ready to move out in the next day or two after cabling.

Meanwhile, you have all our love and all our best and deepest and most sincere wishes and prayers for a complete recovery. I do love you very much, and I remain,

Your most devoted sister,
Jean.

3

By cable:

MRS. JEAN ARBALAID
WASHINGTON, D.C.
OCTOBER 19, 1945

THAT YOU SHOULD EVEN APOLOGIZE. I ACCEPT YOUR OFFER WITH
UNEQUIVOCAL DELIGHT. ENTIRE OUTFIT AVAILABLE AT BATH
WHERE THE MEN'S HABERDASHERY SHOPS ARE VERY GOOD IN-
DEED. OUTFITTING UP LIKE A VERY PUKKA EAST INDIAN TYPE.
READY TO LEAVE WHENEVER YOUR SPECIFIC INSTRUCTIONS AR-
RIVE. THIS IS THE FIRST TOUCH OF PLEASURE OR EXCITEMENT
THAT I HAVE EXPERIENCED IN A GOOD MANY DREARY MONTHS.
YOU AND MARK DEAR SISTER ADMIRABLE PSYCHOLOGISTS. T1 ANK
YOU BOTH. LOVE AND KISSES. I AWAIT INSTRUCTIONS.

HARRY FELTON

By cable:

HARRY FELTON
BATH, ENGLAND
OCTOBER 21, 1945

THANK YOU HARRY AND OUR BLESSINGS WITH YOU. AIR TRANS-
PORT FROM LONDON AIRPORT ON 23 OCTOBER. SPECIAL PRIORI-
TIES TO CALCUTTA INDIA. AT CALCUTTA PROCEED TO CALCUTTA
UNIVERSITY AND SEE THE INDIAN ANTHROPOLOGIST PROFESSOR
SUMIL GOJEE. QUESTION HIM. GET ALL DETAILS INDIAN CHILD SUP-
POSEDLY STOLEN AND RAISED BY WOLVES VILLAGE OF CHANGA
IN ASSAM. STORY ASSOCIATED PRESS REPORTER OCTOBER 9, 1945.
ASSOCIATED PRESS STORY HAS PROFESSOR GOJEE DEEPLY IN-
VOLVED. PLEASE GET ALL DETAILS AND WRITE FULL REPORT AS
SOON AS POSSIBLE.

JEAN ARBALAID

4

By airmail:

Calcutta, India
November 4, 1945

Mrs. Jean Arbalaid
Washington, D.C.

My dear Sister:

First of all, I want you to know that I have taken your mission very seriously. I have never been contented with errand-boy status, as you will remember if you look back through the years of my life. Therefore, I decided to bring to the problem you set before me an observing eye, a keen ear, an astute mind, and all the skills of a poor lawyer. In any case, the mission has been completed, and I think that to some degree I have fallen in love with India. What a strange and beautiful place it is, especially now in November! I am told that in the summer months it is very different and quite unbearable. But my experience has been of a congenial climate and of a people as hospitable and gentle as I have ever known.

I arrived in Calcutta and saw the Indian anthropologist, Professor Gojee. We had a number of meetings, and I discussed this case with him quite thoroughly. I found him charming, intelligent and very perceptive, and he has been kind enough to have me at his house for dinner on two separate occasions, and to introduce me to his family. Let me tell you, indeed let me assure you, my dear sister, that in Bengal this is no small achievement.

But before I go into my discussions with Professor Gojee and the conclusions we came to, let me give you the general background of the matter.

The original Associated Press story seems to have been quite accurate in all of its details—so far as I can ascertain—and I have done my detective work thoroughly and assiduously. I went personally to the small village of Changa in Assam. It is not an easy place to get to, and requires plane, narrow-gauge train and ox cart. At this time of the year, however, it was a fairly pleasant trip. The village itself is a tiny, rather wretched place, but in Indian terms it is by no means the worst place in the world. It has what very few Indian villages have, especially in this part of Bengal—a tiny schoolhouse. It also has a schoolteacher and a number of people who are literate. This helps a great deal in the process of tracking down any historical data or events connected with the life and history of the village.

The village schoolmaster, whose name is Adap Chaterjee, was very helpful, since his English was excellent and since he knew all the participants in the particular event, and, indeed, was at the village when the child was originally lost. That was twelve years ago.

I am sure, Jean, that you know enough about India to realize that twelve is very much an adult age for a girl in these parts—the majority of them are married by then; and there is no question, none at all, about the age of the child. I spoke to the mother and the father, who originally identified the child by two very distinctive birthmarks. I saw these birthmarks myself in Calcutta, where the child is kept at the university. She has there at the university the best of care, kindness, and all the attention she demands. Of course, at this moment we cannot say how long the university will be able to keep her.

However, everything the mother and father told me about the child in the village of Changa seemed to be entirely compatible with the circumstances. That is, wherever their stories and the statements of other villagers could be checked, this checking proved that they had been telling more or less the truth—considering, of course, that any truth loses some of its vividness over a twelve-year period.

The child was lost as an infant—at eight months—a common story in these parts. The parents were working in the field. The child was set down and then the child was gone. Whether the child crawled at that age or not, I can't say, nor can I find any witness who will provide that particular information. At any rate, all agree that the child was healthy, alert and curious—a fine and normal infant. There is absolutely no disagreement on that point.

Now, I know full well that most European and American scientists regard the whole mythology of a child being raised by wolves or some other animal under jungle conditions as an invention and a fiction. But a great many things that

Western science has regarded as fiction are now proving to be at least the edge of a fact if not the fact itself. Here in India, the child raised in the jungle is regarded as one of the absolutes of existence. There are so many records of it that it seems almost impossible to doubt it. Nor, as you will see, is there any other conceivable explanation for this child.

How the child came to the wolves is something we will never know. Possibly a bitch who had lost her own cubs carried the infant off. That is the most likely story, isn't it? But I do not rule out entirely any act of animosity against the parents by another villager. The child could have been carried off and left deep in the jungle; but, as I said, we will never have the truth on this question.

These wolves here in Assam are not *lupus*, the European variety, but *pallipes*, its local cousin. *Pallipes* is nevertheless a most respectable animal in size and disposition, and not something to stumble over on a dark night. When the child was found, a month ago, the villagers had to kill five wolves to take her, and she herself fought like a devil out of hell. At that point, the child had lived as a wolf for eleven years. This does not mean, however, that *pallipes* is a vicious animal. I recall reading a book not too long ago concerning the Canadian variety of *lupus*, the wolf. The naturalist commented on the fact that *lupus*, raised with a family as a dog might be raised, is, contrary to common legend, even more dependable and gentler than almost any house dog. The same naturalist goes on to say that all of the stories of *lupus* running in packs, viciously tearing down his prey, killing his fellow wolf in wolf-to-wolf fights—that all of this is invention, and not very pleasant invention. This naturalist said that there are absolutely no cases of interpack fighting among wolves, that they do not kill each other, and that they have taught each other and taught their offspring as great a responsibility as can be found in any species.

Personally, I would include man in that statement. My being here on this mission has led me to do a great deal of investigation and reading on wolves, and it all comes down to the fact that at this moment Harry Felton is ready to regard the wolf as an animal quite equal to, if not superior to, man in all moral and ethical behavior—that is, if you are willing to grant ethics to a wolf.

To get back to the problem we have here—namely, the

story of this child's life among the wolves—will the whole story ever emerge? I don't know. To all effects and purposes she is a wolf. She cannot stand upright, the curvature of her spine being beyond correction. She runs on all fours and her knuckles are covered with heavy calluses.

One day at the university, I watched her run. They had put a heavy leather belt around her waist. From it a chain extended to a cable which, in turn, was anchored high up on two opposite walls of a room about twenty feet wide. While I observed her, this time for a period of about fifteen minutes, she ran back and forth the length of the cable, on all fours, using her knuckles as front paws. She ran back and forth in that swaying, horrible, catatonic manner that a caged animal comes to assume.

My first reaction to this was that they were being unduly cruel. Later I learned better. The fact of the matter is that, if anything, they were overly tender, overly gentle and thoughtful with her. It is in the nature of the educated Indian to have enormous reverence for all forms of life. The people at the university combine such reverence with great pity for this child and her fate. If you will remember, my dear Jean, your readings in Buddhism—specifically in the type of Buddhism that is practiced in Bengal—you will recollect that it teaches, among other things, the doctrine of reoccurrence. This means that this poor damned child is caught in an eternal wheel, destined to live this senseless, awful fate of hers over and over for eternity—or at least so they believe. And it evokes their great pity.

They have been trying for days to teach her to use her hands for grasping and holding, but so far unsuccessfully. We are very glib when we talk of what man has done with a thumb in opposition to four fingers; but I assure you that in so far as this wolf-child is concerned, the thumb in opposition to her four fingers is utterly meaningless. She cannot use her thumb in conjunction with her fingers, nor can she properly straighten her fingers or use them in any way for any kind of manipulation—even for the very simple manipulation that her teachers try to lead her into.

Did I mention that she must be naked? She tears off any clothes they dress her in, and there are times when she will attack her leather belt with a kind of senseless ferocity. They attempted to put a cloth sleeping pad in the room, but in this they were unsuccessful, since she promptly tore to pieces each pad they placed there. They were equally unsuccessful in their attempts to teach her to defecate in toilet or chamber pot; in fact, any puppy is more easily housebroken than this child. Eleven years have given her a rigidity of action—or a mechanicality, as the university people here prefer to call it—which appears to preclude any kind of training.

However, the people at the university do not despair, and they hope that in time she will be able to master at least some elements of civilized behavior.

At this point, however, she has not been able to grasp even the meaning of speech, much less make any progress herself in the art of conversation or communication. The problem of communication with this child is absolutely staggering.

The Indian anthropologist, Professor Sumil Gojee (the man you had been in communication with), is very highly regarded both here and in Bombay, where he has been a guest lecturer on one occasion or another. He is a social anthropologist, you know, and he is recognized as a great authority on village life in Bengal. He has been working with the wolf-child for a week now, and during the past four days he has been joined by Professor Armen Ranand from the University of Bombay. Both of them have been very kind to me and have given me unstintingly of their time, which I want you to know is an achievement on my part, since I was unable to explain to them in any coherent fashion just what you are up to and after. That comes back to the fact that I am entirely ignorant of what you are up to and after, and have been able only to guess and to form some rather silly theories of my own which I will not bore you with.

At this point, both men have little hope that any real communication will ever be possible. In our terms and by our measurements, the wolf-child is a total idiot, an infantile imbecile, and it is likely that she will remain so for the rest of her life. This prognosis of mental rigidity puzzled me, and I discussed it at some length with both Professor Gojee and Professor Ranand.

Our first discussion took place while we were observing the child in her room, which has become for the most part her habitat. Do not think that she is held prisoner there in some heartless manner. She is taken for walks, but that is not easy; she is a rather savage little animal, and a great many precautions must be taken every time she is removed from her room. The room is equipped with one of those mirrors that enable you to look into it without being perceived from the inside. The mirror is placed high enough on the wall not to bother the child, and so far as I know she has never become aware of either the mirror or its two-way quality. Watching her on this occasion, Professor Gojee pointed out to me that she was quite different from a wolf.

I said to him, "I would think that being so unhuman she would at least be wolflike in most ways."

"Not at all," Gojee replied. "In the first place, she is twelve years old, which is very old indeed for a wolf. Do you understand? She has spent a lifetime, a wolf lifetime among the wolves, during which her wolf companions have matured and, I imagine, in many cases gone to their deaths. She, however, remained through that period a child. Now you must not believe for a moment that she could have been unaware of her difference from the wolves. She was most aware of the difference, and indeed the wolves were also aware of this difference. The fact that they accepted her, that they fed her, that they took care of her, does not mean that they were foolish enough to mistake her for a wolf. No, indeed! They knew that they were dealing with a very nonwolf type of child; and I am inclined to believe that within the limitations of their mentality the wolves had some hazy notion that this was a human child. This could only have meant that she would be treated differently from the rest of the wolves, and the result of this different treatment would be a series of traumas. In other words, a wolf brought up in a normal wolf environment would, we could expect, be fairly free from neuroses. Now, this is probably a very silly use of terminology. We do not know whether neuroses exist among wolves, and we are not absolutely certain as to the nature of neuroses in the human being. However, we can with some certainty make a case for the neurosis of this child. Whether she is pathological, I am not certain, but certainly her emotional structure has been deformed beyond repair, and her intellectual powers have been stunted beyond belief and deprived of any ability to mature."

"Then what exactly is she?" I asked him.

He turned to Dr. Ranand and, with a rather sad smile, repeated my question. Dr. Ranand, the professor from Bombay, shrugged his shoulders.

"How can I possibly answer that? She is not human; she

is not a wolf. If we were to approach her in terms of her intelligence, then certainly we would say that she is closer to the wolves. But a wolf's intelligence is a completed thing; in other words, a wolf is just as intelligent as a wolf should be. Whether she is as intelligent as a wolf should be, I don't know. Presumably a wolf with her cranial capacity would be capable of a great deal of learning. She, on the other hand, is not capable of the kind of learning we would expect from this theoretical but nonexistent wolf with a super-large cranial capacity. What, then, is the poor child? A human being? No, I don't think she is a human being. A wolf? Quite obviously she is not a wolf." His voice trailed away here. He looked at Professor Gojee helplessly.

"We can conclude this," Professor Gojee said, "she has been denied the opportunity to become a human being."

The next day, a Dr. Chalmers, a British public-health officer, joined us for a period of observation. Like myself, he had been to the village of Changa, investigating her background. He bore out what I had learned there, that there was absolutely no history of imbecilism in her background. Afterwards, he was able to examine the child very carefully. I must say here, Jean, that in order for him to make this examination the child had to be put to sleep. Ether was used, and every care was taken. An anaesthetist from the General Hospital here administered the anaesthesia—under difficult conditions, I will admit. Then the child was unchained and was taken to a medical examination room where Dr. Chalmers conducted his physical examination under the supervision of both Professor Gojee and Professor Ranand. He found absolutely no physical elements to account for the child's mental condition: no malformation of the cranial area and no signs of imbecilism. His findings bore out my own in Changa; that is, the fact that everyone in the village had attested to the normalcy—indeed, alertness and brightness—of the infant. Both Dr. Chalmers and Professor Gojee made a special point of the alertness and adaptability that the infant must have required to enable it to begin its eleven years of survival among the wolves. The child responds excellently to reflex tests, and neurologically, she appears to be sound. She is also strong—beyond the strength of most adults—very wiry, quick in her movements, and possessed of an uncanny sense of smell and hearing.

I watched while the doctor examined the wolf marks upon her—that is, the specific physical idiosyncrasies that were the result of her life among four-legged animals. Her spine was bent in a perpetual curvature that could not be reversed—even with an operation. Her calluses were well developed and most interesting; evidently she ran mostly, if not always, on all fours. Her teeth were strong and there were no signs of decay, although the incidence of tooth decay is rather high in the native village. While Dr. Chalmers is not a psychiatrist, his experience in the Public Health Service has been long and very varied; and, in his opinion, the prognosis for this child is not hopeful. Like Professor Gojee, he does not believe that she will ever progress to a point where she can master even the simplest use of language.

Professor Ranand believes that eventually the child will die. He has examined records of eighteen similar cases. These eighteen cases were selected from several hundred recorded in India during the past century. Of these several hundred recorded cases, a great many could be thrown aside as fiction. These eighteen cases Professor Ranand chose to study carefully were cases which he believed had been documented beyond a possibility of doubt. In every case, he says, the recovered child was an idiot in our terms—or a wolf in objective terms.

"But this child is not a wolf, is she?" I asked him.

"No, certainly not, by no means. The child is a human child."

"An imbecile?" I asked him. "Would you call the child an idiot? Would you call the child a moron? If you did, would you give her any number on the scale of intelligence we use?"

Professor Ranand was upset by this kind of thing and he brushed it aside, and he had some very harsh things to say about our Western methods of measuring intelligence.

"Of course the child is not an idiot," he said; "neither is the child an imbecile. You cannot call the child an imbecile any more than you would call a wolf an idiot or an imbecile because the wolf is not capable of engaging in human actions."

"But the child is not a wolf," I insisted.

"Of course not. We went over that before. The child is not a wolf, not by any means. Then you must ask what the child is and that, too, we have gone over before. It is impossible to state what this child is. This child is something that nature never intended. Now, to you, to you Westerners, this is a clinical point of view, but to us it is something else entirely. You do not recognize any such things as intentions on the part of nature. In so far as your Western science is concerned, nature moves blindly and mechanically with neither purpose nor intent nor direction. I think you have all driven yourselves into blind alleys with your concepts of the origin of the species. I am not arguing with Darwin's theories; I am only saying that your use of Darwin's theories has been as blind as your overall attitude toward the world and the life of the world."

Two days have passed since I wrote that section of my report which you have just read. Yesterday the wolf-child came down with some sort of amoebic dysentery. She seems entirely unable to fight the disease and she is obviously growing weaker. I will send you news as her condition changes.

Meanwhile, I am putting together all of the notes and the verbatim records of conversations that I have taken down concerning the wolf-child. When I have them in some proper and understandable form, I will send them to you. I don't know why this whole experience has depressed me as it has. My spirits were quite high when I arrived in India, and the whole business around this poor child has been, from my own selfish point of view, consistently interesting. At the same time, I made some good friends here, and the people at the university, the native Indian professors as well as the British here, could not have been kinder to me. I have every reason, my dear sister, for saying that I have enjoyed my stay in Bengal—but, at the same time, I feel a terrible sense of tragedy around this child, a sense of tragedy that goes far beyond her own pitiful fate and her own personal tragedy. Perhaps when I work this out in my mind, I will be able to turn it into something constructive.

In any case, be assured that I am your errand boy for as long as you desire. I am intrigued by this matter, and I spend the pre-sleep hour each night guessing what you are up to, what your purpose is, and what you and Mark have in those cunning little scientific minds of yours. I have made some absolutely fascinating guesses, and if you are very nice to me perhaps I will pass them on to you.

Love and kisses,
Harry.

5

By cable:

MRS. JEAN ARBALAID
WASHINGTON, D.C.
NOVEMBER 7, 1945

TODAY AT TWO O'CLOCK OUR TIME HERE THE WOLF-CHILD DIED. THE DIRECT CAUSE OF HER DEATH WAS THE DYSENTERY. THAT IS THERE WAS NO WAY TO STOP THE DEHYDRATION OF THE CHILD WHICH CONTINUED TO A POINT WHERE SHE COULD NO LONGER SUSTAIN HER LIFE. HOWEVER DR. CHALMERS WHO IS BY NO MEANS A MYSTIC BUT A VERY PRACTICAL BRITISH PRACTITIONER FEELS THAT ALMOST ANY INFECTIOUS DISEASE WOULD HAVE LED TO THE SAME RESULT. SHE HAD BEEN DIVESTED OF ANY DESIRE TO LIVE AND IN HER OWN WAY HAD BEEN IN VERY DEEP DEPRESSION SOMETHING I RECOGNIZE AND SYMPATHIZE WITH WHOLLY. I AM SENDING THIS CABLE COLLECT AND AM MAKING NO EFFORT TO ECONOMIZE WITH WORDS. I AM SURE YOU CAN AFFORD IT. WHAT NOW? I AWAIT WORD FROM YOU AT THE HOTEL EMPIRE CALCUTTA.

HARRY FELTON

By cable:

HARRY FELTON
HOTEL EMPIRE
CALCUTTA, INDIA
NOVEMBER 9, 1945

YOU HAVE DONE SUPERBLY HARRY AND WE ARE DEEPLY APPRECIATIVE. HOWEVER, YOUR REPORTS ARE TOO MODEST. WE LOOK UPON YOU AS AN INTELLIGENT AND WELL-INFORMED PERSON AND WE ARE VERY EAGER FOR YOUR OWN REACTION. PLEASE REMAIN IN INDIA AT HOTEL EMPIRE FOR TIME BEING AND WRITE US IMMEDIATELY AIRMAIL YOUR REACTION TO THE CHILD AND YOUR EXPLANATION OF WHAT HAPPENED TO THE CHILD. THIS IS TO BE ABSOLUTELY YOUR OWN EXPLANATION AND IF POSSIBLE NOT TEMPERED OR BIASED IN ANY WAY BY THE SPECIALISTS YOU HAVE DISCUSSED THE CASE WITH.

JEAN ARBALAID

6

By airmail:

Calcutta, India
November 10, 1945

Mrs. Jean Arbalaid
Washington, D.C.

My Dear Jean:

I am flattered by your interest in my opinion. On the other hand, I am not going to negate the value of such an opinion. I think I agree with you that professional people, specialists in one branch or another of the various sciences, tend to have a narrow point of view where they have either a background of experimental evidence or specific existing evidence upon which to base their assertions and conclusions. This is a very admirable and careful method in so far as it goes, but I am afraid it will achieve only what the facts at hand—that is, the provable facts—allow it to achieve.

I can guess that by now you have consulted every available specialist on the question of human children being raised by animals. I am sure you have discussed this thoroughly with the bigwigs at the National Geographic Society and with all the various specialists who know more about animals than the animals know about themselves. Do they all agree that no human child was ever reared by so-called beasts? Do they all agree that the whole thing is a sort of continuing invention, a fiction that each generation perpetuates to confuse itself? If they do, they are in agreement with your Western naturalists here in Calcutta. I have spoken to three of them—two Englishmen and a Frenchman—and they are all absolutely certain of the scientific and historical ground they stand on. The wolf-girl is a fraud; she was not raised by the wolves; she is an idiot child who ran away from the village and spent perhaps weeks, perhaps months, wandering in the forest, deranged and developing calluses where the calluses are. And the odd thing, my dear Jean, is that I cannot prove differently. So much for evidence.

Now, as to my own conclusion which you asked for: I told you in the previous letter that I had been deeply depressed by the incident of this child and by her condition. I have been attempting to understand the origin of this depression in myself and to deal with it—if only to repay an obligation and a promise to a skinny British psychiatrist who pulled me out of the doldrums back in Bath. I think I have found the source of the depression—a sort of understanding of what the girl was afflicted with. I believe she was afflicted simply with the loss of humanity. Now you have every right to say that the loss of humanity is a widespread disease that afflicts most of the human race; and there I cannot argue with you. But regardless of how much or often we turn into killers, mass murderers, sadists, etc., we seem always to preserve some sense of our origin, some link with our beginnings. We are at least recognizable as Homo sapiens. This child, poor thing, cut all her connections. She is no longer recognizable as Homo sapien. Having the form of a human being, she is less than a human being, less indeed than what nature intended her to be.

I am quite impressed by the outlook of Professor Gojee and his associates. I think I must agree with their opinion of Western science. The sad fact is that, while the East is ahead of us in many ways, they have lagged behind in scientific method and discoveries; and therefore, the great intuitive feelings that they have and which they incorporate into some of their religion, concerning the meaning and the destiny of mankind, have remained disassociated from any wide discipline of fact and investigation.

For myself, I tend to agree with them that there must be some purpose to human existence. I am hesitant to ascribe such purpose to the presence of God. I think that their definition and concept is as limited by our intelligence and as constrained by our outlook as most of our other theories. But, speaking only for myself, I have never been truly aware of the essence of humanity until I was present here at a case where humanity was extracted from a human being. We are too pat with our descriptions, designations and accusations of those whom we consider devoid of humanity. I don't really believe that anyone is devoid of humanity in the sense that this poor little wolf-child was. But then that leads me to another question. What is your human being? What is the essence of being human?

I have not been quick to embrace the all-encompassing theories of environment that have come out of the democratic

movement of the nineteenth century. Too often I have felt
that theories of environment have been used to prove political
points and to make for political ammunition. At the same
time, heredity is possibly less important than many people
imagine it to be. I think that to create a human being, you
need the presence, the society and the environment of other
human beings. Directly to answer the question you put to
me—What happened to the child?—I would say that she was
deprived of her humanity. Certainly, she is not a human
being, and neither is she a wolf. A wolf society can produce
wolves; a human society can produce human beings. A human
being trapped in a wolf society is a good deal less than a
human being and perhaps not as much as a wolf. So I would
say that this child occupied a sort of limbo on the scale, or
in the current, of evolution. She is not a part of development;
she is not a thing in herself; she is something that had been
destroyed by a set of circumstances; she is a spoiled mechanism that continued to function in a limited sort of way. Do
you find that a rather dreadful definition—a spoiled mechanism? Perhaps the word "mechanism" is wrong. Would a
spoiled bit of life be better? I don't know, but there are my
opinions for what they are worth.

I have found a charming young lady, Miss Edith Wychkoff
by name, who is the daughter of the colonel of an old Indian
regiment. The whole thing is a cliché except that she is
charming and blue-eyed, and will make the hours here, while
I wait for your reply and for your instructions, much more
endurable.

Please allow me to continue as your free-wheeling, theorizing errand boy. As the above demonstrates, my state of
mind is infinitely better. I send my love to both of you, and
await your reply.

Harry.

7

By cable:

HARRY FELTON
HOTEL EMPIRE
CALCUTTA, INDIA
NOVEMBER 14, 1945

THANK YOU FOR EVERYTHING HARRY. YOU HAVE DONE NOBLY
AND YOUR CONCLUSIONS HAVE BEEN READ AND REREAD AND DIS-
CUSSED SERIOUSLY AND WITH THE GREATEST OF INTEREST. A SIM-
ILAR CASE HAS CROPPED UP IN PRETORIA UNION OF SOUTH AFRICA
AT GENERAL HOSPITAL THERE UNDER DR. FELIX VANOTT. WE HAVE
MADE ALL ARRANGEMENTS WITH AIR TRANSPORT AND YOU WILL
BE WHISKED THERE BEFORE YOU CAN SAY JACK ROBINSON.
DREADFULLY SORRY TO END ROMANCE WITH THE COLONEL'S
DAUGHTER BUT IF YOU ARE VERY SERIOUS ABOUT IT AND DES-
PERATE TO CONTINUE IT WE WILL ARRANGE FOR YOU TO PICK IT
UP LATER. MEANWHILE ON TO PRETORIA.

JEAN ARBALAID

8

By airmail:

Pretoria, Union of South Africa
November 18, 1945

Mrs. Jean Arbalaid
Washington, D.C.

My dear Sister:
You are evidently very big wheels, you and your husband,
and I wish I knew just what your current experiment adds
up to. I suppose that in due time you'll see fit to tell me.
Meanwhile, my speculations continue.

But in any case, your priorities command respect. A full
colonel was bumped, and I was promptly whisked away to
South Africa, a beautiful country of pleasant climate and, I
am sure, great promise.

I saw the child, who is still being kept in the General
Hospital here; and I spent an evening with Dr. Vanott, an
entire day at the hospital, and another evening with a young
and attractive Quaker lady, Miss Gloria Oland, an anthropologist working among the Bantu people for her doctorate.
Her point of origin is Philadelphia and Swarthmore College,
so I was able to play upon all the bonds that unite countrymen
(I will have something to say about that later). But I think
that my acquaintance with Miss Oland has been fruitful,
and, all in all, I will be able to provide you with a certain
amount of background material.

Superficially, this case is remarkably like the incident in Assam. There it was a girl of twelve; here we have a Bantu boy of eleven (an estimate). The girl was reared by a variety of wolf; the boy in this case was reared by baboons—that is, supposing that here, as in India, we can separate fact from fiction, and come to a reasonable assumption that the child actually was stolen and reared by baboons. Let me say at this point that I have done some investigating, and I have been able to add to my notebook over twenty cases of African children stolen by baboons or by some other kind of baboon-like ape and reared by said baboons and apes. Now, these cases are by no means researched; they have not been tracked down; they have not been proven: so along with their interest as background material must go the assumption that most, if not all of them, belong to the mythology. However, if I have been able to turn up this number of cases in so short a time, and by asking as few questions as I did and of as few people, then it seems to me that this kind of thing must be fairly widespread throughout South Africa. Even if the overwhelming majority of stories belong to the mythology, any such mythology must have some basis in fact, however small.

The child was rescued from the baboons by a white hunter, name of Archway—strong, silent type, right out of Hemingway. Unfortunately, unlike most of his fictional counterparts, this Ned Archway is a son of a bitch with a nasty temper and a thoroughgoing dislike for children. So when the boy understandably bit him—for which the boy can only be praised—the white hunter whipped the child to within an inch of his life.

"Tamed him," as Mr. Archway put it to me in one of the local bars over a tall mint julep. Archway is a thoroughgoing gentleman when he is with his betters, and, as much as I dislike that kind of talk, namely, "his betters," it is the only kind that fits. Back home, a sensitive person would catalogue Archway as poor white trash. I think that describes him better than several pages of words.

I asked him for some of the details of the capture and Archway swore me to silence, since evidently his actions were somewhat illegal. He loves to shoot baboons; it proves him "a target master," as he puts it.

"Shot twenty-two of the bloody beasts," he said to me.

"You're a very good shot," I said to him.

"Would have shot the black bastard too," he added. "However, he awakened my curiosity. Nimble little creature. You should have seen him go. You know, I have one of your jeeps—marvelous car, marvelous for the brush country, kind of car that might have been made for this part of Africa. Well, I was in the car and I had with me two of your very rich American women, two of your very rich women—you know the type: brown as smoked goose, long legs drawn hard and thin, and just couldn't wait for the war to be over to get out here on safari. They enjoyed the chase no end. Ran the thing down in the jeep. You know, I don't think I would have ever gotten him if it weren't that the jeep threw a bad scare into him, and he froze. Animals do that, you know."

"He is not an animal," I ventured.

"Oh, of course he is. The Kaffirs are not so different from the baboons anyway, when you come right down to it."

This and a lot more. My conversation with the white hunter was not pleasant, and I don't enjoy repeating it.

May I say that at the hospital here they have a more humane, if not a more egalitarian, point of view. The child is receiving the very best of care and reasonable scientific affection. I asked them at the hospital whether there was any way to trace him back to his point of origin, that is, to his parents or to the village where he originated. They said No, there was no way at all of doing so, not in a thousand years. Evidently these Basutoland baboons are great travelers, and there is no telling where they picked up the child. It might be several hundred or a thousand miles away.

Putting his age at eleven years is a medical guess, but nevertheless reasonable. That he is of Bantu origin there is no doubt; and if I were to put him up as a physical specimen alongside of the white hunter, there is no doubt in my mind who would come out best. The child is very handsome, long-limbed, exceedingly strong, and with no indication of any cranial injury. His head is narrow and long, and his look is intelligent. Like the girl in Assam, he is—in our terms—an idiot and an imbecile, but there is nevertheless a difference. The difference is the difference between the baboon and the wolf. The wolf-child was incapable of any sort of vocalization. Did I mention that at moments of fear she howled? In her howling she was able to give an almost perfect imitation of a wolf's howl—that is, the howl of the local wolf whose habitat is Assam. Aside from this howl, her vocalization was limited to a number of wolf sounds—barks, whines and that sort of thing. Here we have something different indeed.

The vocalization of this eleven-old-old Bantu boy is the vocalization of a baboon. Strangely enough, at least here in Pretoria, there is no indication of any local scientific and serious work being done on the question of baboon vocalization. Again, all we have is a variety of opinion based on mythology. Some of the Kaffirs here will swear that the baboons have a language. Others claim to know a little of the baboon language, and I have had some of the Kaffir hunters make an assortment of sounds for me—after I had paid them well—and proceed to state their own interpretations of what these sounds meant. I think this is less a tribute to the speech abilities of the baboon than to the ingenuity of the local Kaffir when it comes to extracting money from a white man. Miss Oland pooh-poohs any suggestion that the baboons have a language, and I am inclined to go along with her.

There is one reasonably well informed naturalist at the local college with whom I had a short chat over the luncheon table. He, too, derides the notion that there is a language among the baboons. He raises an interesting point, however. He believes that the ability to talk is the motivating factor for man's becoming man, and he also believes that certain frontal sections of the brain are absolutely necessary before a species can engage in conversation. He says that the only species on earth that has any sort of conversational powers whatsoever is man, and he proceeded to break down for me various theories that bees and other insects and some of the great apes can talk to each other. He said that there is a very strong myth in gorilla country that the gorillas are able to talk to each other, but this, too, he rejects unconditionally.

He does admit that there is a series of specific sounds that the gorillas use; but these sounds are explosive grunts used entirely for situations of danger. Each and every one of these sounds relates to some area of fear, and my naturalist cannot include them in what we understand as language. He is willing to admit, however, that the baboons have a series of squeaks and grunts that may communicate, in addition to situations of fear, situations of affection. I am inclined to agree with this, for there seem to be some indications that this Bantu child will in time learn at least some elements of speech.

In that way he differs from the wolf-girl, and he also differs from her in that he is able to use his hands to hold things and to examine things. He also has a more active curiosity, but that, I am assured by the naturalist, is the difference between the wolf and baboon. The baboon is a curious creature, endlessly investigative, and he handles an endless number of objects. So the boy's curiosity and his ability to grasp things with his hands are an indication of his relationship to baboons, I think, more than an indication of his relationship to mankind.

As with the wolf-child, he too has a permanent curvature of the spine. He goes on all fours as the baboons do, and the backs of his fingers, specifically the area of the first knuckle joint, are heavily callused. After tearing off his clothes the first time, he accepted them. This too, is quite different from the case in India, and here again we have a baboon trait. Miss Oland told me of cases where baboons have been trained to wear clothing and to do remarkable tricks. Miss Oland has great hope for the boy's progress in the future, but Dr. Vanott, who has worked with him and tested him in the hospital, doubts that the child will ever talk. How much Dr. Vanott is influenced by local attitudes toward Negroes, I leave for you to decide. Incidentally, in those numerous reports of human children raised by animals, which Professor Ranand of Bombay University professed to believe, there is no case where the child was able subsequently, upon being recovered and brought back into the company of human beings, to learn human speech.

So goes my childhood hero, Tarzan of the Apes, and all the noble beasts along with him. Poor Lord Graystroke. He would have been like this Bantu child—trembling with fear, never released from this fear, cowering into a corner of his cage, staring at his human captors with bewilderment and horror. Has it been said to you that animals do not experience fear in the sense that we human beings do? What nonsense! Fear appears to be woven into the fabric of their lives; and the thing that is most heartbreaking in both of these cases is the constant fear, the fear from which neither child was apparently free, even for a moment.

But the most terrifying thought evoked by this situation is this: What is the substance of man himself, if this can happen to him? The learned folk here have been trying to explain to me that man is a creature of his thought, and that his thought is, to a very large extent, shaped by his environment; and that this thought process—or mentation as they prefer to call it—is based on words. Without words, thought becomes a process of pictures, which is on the animal level and rules out all, even the most primitive, abstract concepts.

In other words, man cannot become man by himself: he is the result of other men and of the totality of human society and experience. I realize that I am putting this forward rather blandly, but it is all new to me; and newcomers tend to simplify and (as you would say, my dear sister) vulgarize a science of which they possess some small knowledge.

Yet my thinking was borne out to some degree during a very pleasant dinner I had with Miss Oland. It was not easy to get her to have dinner with me. You see, I don't think she liked me very much, although I am presuming to say that she likes me a little better now. But in the beginning, her attitude was very much shaped by my objective and somewhat cold investigative attitude toward what had happened to the little boy.

Miss Oland, may I say, is a very intelligent young lady, an attractive young lady, and a very devout Quaker. She takes her religion with great seriousness, and she lives it. It was a nice and perhaps constructive blow to my ego to realize that she looked down upon me with a mixture of dislike and pity. I think, however, that Miss Oland and people like her look down upon most of the human race. I put this surmise of mine to her, and she denied it very hotly. In fact, she was so annoyed by the thought that I wonder whether she will agree to spend another evening with me.

However, there is no doubt in my mind but that people like Miss Oland occupy the role of the outsider. They watch the human race, without actually belonging to it. I have noticed this same attitude in a number of well-educated Jews I have met. But Miss Oland is the first Quaker with whom I ever discussed these things. I would hardly be surprised if her attitude were shared by other Quakers of sensitivity and thoughtfulness.

Miss Oland regards me as a barbarian—less a barbarian, of course, than such an obvious creature as the white hunter Ned Archway. But only by contrast with him do I become admirable, and at that only slightly admirable. As Miss Oland put it to me:

"You profess your superiority to the white hunter, Mr. Felton, and you look down on him as a rather uncivilized sort of man, but for what actually do you condemn him? For shooting the baboons for the fun of it or for beating the child?"

"For both," I replied.

"But he kills only animals, and surely the child will recover from the beating."

"And do you see virtue in killing animals for fun, as you put it?" I asked her.

"No virtue indeed, Mr. Felton, but I see less evil in it than in the slaughter of human beings."

"By that, just what do you mean, Miss Oland?"

"I mean that, like Ned Archway, you have been a hunter. You hunted men."

"What do you mean, I hunted men?"

"You told me you were an infantry captain, didn't you? What other purpose would an infantry captain have but the hunting down and the slaughter of human beings?"

"But that was different."

"How was it different, Mr. Felton?"

"My goodness, I don't have to go into all that, do I? You're not going to trap me with that old, old saw? You lived in the world that Adolf Hitler was remaking. You inhabited the same world that contained the concentration camps, the abattoirs, the gas ovens, the slaughter pits. How can you ask me such an absurd question?"

"Of course the question is absurd," she nodded. "Any question, Mr. Felton, becomes absurd when it is new to you or irritating to you or outside of your particular sphere of mental agreement. My question disturbed you; therefore, it becomes absurd."

"But surely you are not going to defend the Nazis."

"Now that indeed becomes rather absurd, doesn't it, Mr. Felton? You know that I would not defend the Nazis. How could you conceivably think that under any circumstances I would?"

"You're right. I could not conceivably think that. I admit it."

"I am not objecting, Mr. Felton, to your attitude toward the Nazis. I am simply objecting to your attitude toward killing. Obviously, you resent the pointless and witless killing of baboons, but you do not resent the equally pointless and witless slaughter of human beings."

"I like to think, Miss Oland, that I was fighting for the survival of human civilization and human dignity, and that whatever killing I was forced to do was neither thoughtless nor witless."

"Oh come now, Mr. Felton, we are both a little too old for that sort of thing, aren't we? Were you fighting for man's dignity? And by what process did you know that whatever German soldier you happened to kill was not equally aware of what was demanded by man's dignity? Did you know whether he opposed Hitler, if he did not oppose Hitler, how he agreed with Hitler or whether he agreed or disagreed with Hitler? You knew nothing of that; and certainly you knew enough of military structure to know that, like yourself, he had no choice but to face you and fight you."

"He could surrender," I said.

"Could he really, Mr. Felton? Now I am going to ask you a question. Did you shoot first and ask questions afterwards? Or did you ask questions first and shoot afterwards? I have never been on a battlefield, but I have a good imagination, and I have read many stories about what goes on a battlefield. Could he have surrendered, Mr. Felton?"

"No," I admitted, "you're quite right. In most cases he couldn't have surrendered. There were cases where he could and maybe he did, but in most cases he could not have surrendered. Certainly, as an individual, he could not have surrendered. So you are absolutely right there, and I will not argue it. Nevertheless, I also will not relinquish my belief that there was a virtue in our cause in World War II, a virtue in what we fought for and what so many of us died for."

"Then why don't you say that there was virtue in what you killed for, Mr. Felton?"

"I don't like to put it that way because I have never regarded myself as a killer."

"But the plain and naked fact of the matter, Mr. Felton, is that you are a killer. You have killed human beings, haven't you?"

"I have," I admitted weakly.

"I am not trying to pin you down to something nasty, Mr. Felton. I am not trying to derogate you, please believe me. It is only that no man takes any action without some sort of justification. He would go out of his mind if he did, wouldn't he? You ask me to prefer you to Mr. Archway, but I find that very hard to do. Really, I know this hurts you and I know I

am not being polite, but from my point of view you and Archway inhabit the same world."

"And you don't inhabit that world, Miss Oland?" I wanted
to know.

"No, not really. I am a Quaker, Mr. Felton. I think that
my culture, the culture of my family, the culture of my people,
has been different for many generations. We live among you
but not with you. Your world is not our world. It really isn't,
Mr. Felton, and you might do well to think about that. You
seem very seriously interested in what has happened to this
poor child. Maybe thinking about what I have just said would
give you some clue as to what happens when a human child
must live in a baboon's world."

"And at the same time," I said to her, "you have your little
triumph and great, great satisfaction of righteousness."

She did not argue that point. "Yes," she said, "I suppose
I am righteous, Mr. Felton. I wish I knew how to be otherwise,
and perhaps in time I will learn. For the moment I am young
enough to feel righteous and disgusted as well. You have no
idea how frequently I am disgusted, Mr. Felton."

So, you see, I can fail her for politeness and score her very
low as regards hospitality, she having been in Pretoria at
least six months longer than I. At the same time, even though
she is a woman I will not remember fondly, I have to admire
her, and, in the last analysis, I have to admit that she was
speaking the truth.

All of which leads me to ask some very pertinent questions, sister mine. The man raised by the wolf is no longer
a man, and the man raised by the baboons is no longer a
man, and this fate is inevitable, isn't it? No matter what the
man is, you put him with the apes and he becomes an ape
and never very much more than that. My head has been
swimming with all sorts of notions, some of them not at all
pleasant. My dear sister, what the hell are you and your
husband up to? Isn't it time you broke down and told old
Harry, or do you want me to pop off to Tibet and hold converse
with the lamas? I am ready for anything; I will be surprised
by nothing, and I am prepared to go anywhere at all to please
you. But, preferably, hand me something that adds up to a
positive sum and then put a few words of explanation with
it.

Your nasty killer brother,
Harry.

9

By airmail:

Washington, D.C.
November 27, 1945

Mr. Harry Felton
Pretoria, Union of South Africa

Dear Harry:
You are a good and sweet brother, and quite sharp, too. You are also a dear. You are patient and understanding and you have trotted around dutifully in a maze without trying to batter your way out.

Now it comes down to this, Harry: Mark and I want you to do a job for us which will enable you to go here and there across the face of the earth, and be paid for it, too. In order to convince you, and to have your full cooperation and your very considerable creative abilities as well, we must spill out the dark secrets of our work—which we have decided to do, considering that you are an upright and trustworthy character. But the mail, it would seem, is less trustworthy; and since we are working with the Army, which has a constitutional dedication to top-secrecy and similar nonsense, the information goes to you via diplomatic pouch.

As of receiving this, that is, providing that you agree, you may consider yourself employed. Your expenses will be paid—travel, hotel and per diem—within reason, and there will be an additional eight thousand a year, less for work than for indulgence. In fact, as I write it down here, it makes so absolutely intriguing a proposition that I am tempted to throw over my own job and take yours instead.

So please stay put at your hotel in Pretoria until the diplomatic pouch arrives. I promise you that this will be in not more than ten days. They will certainly find you—that is, the diplomatic courier will.

Love, affection and respect,
Jean.

10

By diplomatic pouch:

Washington, D.C.
December 5, 1945

Mr. Harry Felton
Pretoria, Union of South Africa

Dear Harry:

Consider this letter the joint effort of Mark and myself. The thinking is ours and the conclusions are also shared. Also, Harry, consider this to be a very serious document indeed.

You know that for the past twenty years we have both been deeply concerned with child psychology and child development. There is no need to review our careers or our experience in the Public Health Service. Our work during the war, as part of the Child Reclamation Program, led to an interesting theory, which we decided to pursue. We were given leave by the head of the service to make this our own project. The leave is a sort of five-year sabbatical, with the option given to us at the end of five years to extend the leave for five years more, and a third five years then, if necessary. Recently, we were granted a substantial amount of Army funds to work with. In return for this, we have agreed to put our findings at the disposal of the Government.

Now to get down to the theory, which is not entirely untested. As you know, Mark and I have behind us two decades of practical work with children. When I say practical, I cover a good deal of ground. Since we are both physicians, we have worked with children as pediatricians. We have done hospital work with children. We have operated on children as surgeons; and, under certain conditions (as for example, during emergencies in the early years of the war), we have pioneered surgical work with children simply because we were placed in a position which left us no other choice. From this vast experience, we have come to some curious conclusions. I would put it better if I said that we have come to a great many conclusions, but have now focused our interest on one conclusion in particular, namely this: Mark and I have come to believe that within the rank and file of Homo sapiens is the beginning of a new race.

Call this new race "man-plus"—call it what you will. The people who constitute this new race of men are not of recent arrival; they have been cropping up among men—Homo sapiens, that is—for hundreds, perhaps for thousands, of years. But they are trapped in the human environment; they are trapped in the company of man, and they are molded by the company of man and by the human environment as certainly and as implacably as your wolf-girl was trapped among the wolves or your Bantu child among the baboons. So, you see, the process is quite certain.

Everything that you discovered in Assam and in South Africa tended to bear out our own conclusions. Just as the little Assamese girl was divested of her humanity, deprived of her membership in the human race, by being reared among the wolves, so is our theoretical man-plus deprived of his racehood, of his normal plus-humanity, by living among men. Perhaps your Bantu boy would be a closer parallel to what we mean. I will not at this point try to explain more fully. Later on in this letter we will go into other details of our theory; and if you agree to work with us, as your work progresses, so will your understanding of exactly what we are after.

By the way, your two cases of animal child-rearing are not the only attested ones we have. By sworn witness, we have records of seven similar cases: one in Russia, two in Canada, two in South America, one in West Africa and, just to cut us down to size, one in the United States of America. This does not mean that all seven of these cases are wholly authenticated. If we were to turn to each in succession and apply to it the kind of severe interviewing and testing that you have applied to the two cases you investigated, we might find that of the seven cases perhaps all are fictional, perhaps one is based on reality, perhaps all are based on reality. We might come to any one of these conclusions. *A priori*, we are not able to do more than accept the facts and apply to these facts our own judgment.

You may add to this the hearsay and folklore of three hundred and eleven parallel cases which cover a period of fourteen centuries. We have in fifteenth-century Germany, in the folio manuscript of the monk Hubercus, five case histories he claims to have observed personally. In all these cases, in the seven cases witnessed by people alive today, and in all but sixteen of the hearsay cases, the result is more or less precisely what you have seen and described yourself; that is, the child reared by the wolf is divested of humanity.

We have yet been unable to find a case, mythological or otherwise, in which the child reared by the wolf is able subsequently to learn man's speech. Mythology adds up to a little—of course, very little. But speaking in mythological terms, we can find over forty such cases that survived from great antiquity in the mythologies of one nation or another.

But of course, Harry, we are not attempting to prove that animals can rear a human child, or that human children have been so reared, or that any of the facts connected with human children so reared are true. We are merely attempting to use these cases of the rearing of human children by animals as indications of what may face superior-man reared by man. You see, our own work adds up to the parallel conclusions: the child reared by a man is a man. And what is a man? In the broadest historical sense, a man is a creature who builds social organizations, the major purpose of such organizations being man's own destruction. If what I have just written were an ethical or moral judgemnt, it could certainly be challenged and perhaps successfully; however, it is not by any means a judgment; it is simply an historical conclusion. If one examines the history of man with total objectivity, one can only come to the conclusion that man's existence as a social being has been mainly for the purpose of war. All that he has achieved, all that he has built, has been achieved and has been built in the intervals between wars, thereby creating a social organism that can function during a war and in the act of war. This is by no means a judgment, nor is it an historical observation upon man as an individual. Man as an individual would have to be described quite differently. But we must not for one moment forget that we have just come through a holocaust that has consumed fifty million human lives. I refer to World War II, in which we all played our parts. We have now calculated that the toll of human life internationally in World War II was above fifty million men, women and children. This is larger than the entire human population of the earth at the time of the Roman Empire. We are used to large numbers today; it puts a little different light on the figure when we observe to ourselves that we have just succeeded in destroying in a period of less than five years more human beings than existed upon the entire face of the earth two thousand years ago. That is one to think about, isn't it, Harry? But the observation—the historical observation of the role of man—is made here in a purely clinical sense and in terms of man-plus.

You see, if man-plus exists, he is trapped and caged as certainly as any human child reared by animals is caged. In the same way the incipient man-plus is divested of whatever his potential is. The wolf dealing with our little Assamese girl would hardly be able to calculate or even to guess what she might have been in her own civilization. The wolf can only see her as the product of a wolf society. If man-plus exists, we see him and we have always seen him as a product of man's society. Of course, we have no proof that he exists. We have simply created a supposition that he exists, and we have enough evidence at our disposal for us to support this proposition. This of course, is a usual procedure among scientists. Einstein's conception of the shape of the universe and of the curvature of light was hypothetical to begin with; it originated as a creative idea. After he had formulated the hypothesis, he set about proving it in physical terms. And we shall follow a similar method.

Why do we think the super-child exists? Well, there are many reasons, and we have neither the time nor the space here to go into all of them, or into much detail. However, here are two very telling and important reasons:

Firstly we have gathered together the case histories of several hundred men and women who as children had IQ's of 170 or above. Since these men and women are now adults, their testing goes back to the early days of the Binet-Simon method, and it is by no means reliable—that is, if any intelligence testing, any system of IQ, is reliable. We do not operate on the presumption that IQ testing has any objective reliability; we simply use it as a gauge and in lieu of anything better. In spite of the enormous intellectual promise as children of these several hundred men and women, less than ten percent have succeeded in their chosen careers. Considering how small the whole group is, their record of disaster and tragedy deserves attention in itself.

Another ten percent, roughly speaking, have been institutionalized as mental cases beyond recovery—that is, as pathological cases on the path to disintegration. About fourteen percent of the group have had or now require therapy for mental-health problems; in this fourteen percent, roughly half have been in psychoanalysis or are in psychoanalysis or some similar therapy. Nine percent of the group have been suicides. One percent are in prison. Twenty-seven percent have had one or more divorces, nineteen percent are chronic failures at whatever they attempt—and the rest are undistinguished in any important manner. That is to say, they have not achieved even nominal success in the lines of endeavor they finally chose to follow. All of the IQ's have dwindled—and the dwindling of these IQ's, when graphed, bears a relationship to age. About four percent of the group studied have gone under the hundred or normal mark and are now in the condition of social morons.

Since society has never provided the full potential for such a mentality—that is, a mentality such as this group seemed to have had as children—we are uncertain as to what this potential might be. We have no valid, provable reasons to imagine that this group or a similar group would achieve more under other conditions; but against that we have every reason of logic and common sense to suppose. Our guess is that this group has been reduced to a sort of idiocy, an idiocy that puts them on the level with what we call normalcy. But having been put on that level, they could not become men any more than your Assamese child could become a wolf. Unable to live out their lives, unable to become men, they were simply divested of their destiny, biological and otherwise, and in that sense destroyed. So much for the first reason, Harry.

The second reason we put forward is this: We know that man uses only a tiny part of his brain. Extensive testing enables us to put this forward as a provable fact, but we have no idea what blocks the human ego from using the rest of the human brain. We have to ask why nature has given man equipment that he cannot put to use—not atrophied equipment such as the appendix, but equipment that marks or is definitive of the highest life form ever produced by evolution. We must ask why nature has done this. We must also ask whether society, human society, prevents human beings from breaking the barriers that surround their own potential. In other words, have human beings themselves created a cage which prevents them from ever being more than human beings?

There, in brief, are the two reasons I spoke about before. Believe me, Harry, there are many more—enough for us to have convinced some very hard-headed and unimaginative Government people that we deserve a chance to release supermen. Of course, history helps—in its own mean and degraded manner. It would appear that we are beginning another war, this time with Russia; a cold war, as some have already taken to calling it. Among other things, it will be a war of intelligence—a commodity in rather short supply these days, as some of our local mental giants have been frank enough to admit.

Our new breed of computer warriors licked their lips when we sounded them out. They can't wait to have at another blood bath with all their new gimmicks; they have fed their tapes into the machines, and they have come out with new and enticing methods of human destruction. They look upon our man-plus as a secret weapon, little devils who will come up with death rays and super-atom-bombs and all sorts of similar devices when the time is ripe. Well, let them think that way. It is inconceivable to imagine a project like ours, a project so enormous and so expensive, under benign sponsorship. The important thing is that Mark and I have been placed in full charge of the venture—millions of dollars, top priority, the whole works. We are subject to no one; we must report to no one; we have complete independence. We can requisition what we wish within reason, and we have a long period of time—that is, five years with an extension of an additional five years, and the very real possibility of another extension after that.

But nevertheless, Harry, the project is secret. I cannot stress this enough. This secrecy is not simply the childish classification business that the Army goes into; we support them on the question of secrecy. It is as important to us as to the Army, and I simply cannot stress this sufficiently or make it sound more serious than it actually is.

Now, as to your own job—that is, if you want it. And somehow or other, at this point I cannot envision you saying No. The job will develop step by step, and it is up to you to make it. First step: in Berlin, in 1937, there was a Professor Hans Goldbaum. He was half Jewish. He lectured on child psychology at the university, and he was also the head of the Berlin Institute for Child Therapy. He published a small monograph on intelligence testing in children, and he put forward claims—which we are inclined to believe—that he could determine a child's IQ during its first year of life, in its pre-speech period. The use of the term "IQ" is mine, not his. Professor Goldbaum had no use for the intelligence-quotient system that was developed by the Binet-Simon people, and he rejected it entirely. Instead, he devised his own method of intelligence testing, a very interesting method indeed.

He presented some impressive tables of estimations and subsequent checked results; but we do not know enough of his method to practice it ourselves. In other words, we need the professor's help.

In 1937, Professor Goldbaum vanished from Berlin. All of our efforts, combined with the very generous investigatory help of Army Intelligence, have convinced us that he was not murdered by the Nazis but that in some manner he escaped from Berlin. In 1943, a Professor Hans Goldbaum, either the same man in whom we are interested or someone of the same name, was reported to be living in Cape Town. This is the last address we have for him, and I am enclosing the address herewith. Now, as for you, Harry, here goes your job. You should leave for Cape Town immediately. Somehow or other, find the Professor Goldbaum reported to be in Cape Town. Find out whether he is our Professor Goldbaum. If he is not there, but has left, then follow him. Follow him wherever he has gone. Find him. I am not telling you how and, in turn, I do not expect you to ask us how. It is up to you. Find him! Naturally, all expenses will be paid. Of course, he may be dead. If that is the case, inform us immediately.

At this point I am no longer asking whether or not you will take the job. Either you will take it or I cease to be your sister, and I will curse your name and strike it out of all the family journals, etc. We love you and we need your help; in fact, we need it desperately, and at this moment I know of no one else who could substitute for you.

Jean.

11

By airmail:

Cape Town, South Africa
December 20, 1945

Mrs. Jean Arbalaid
Washington, D.C.

My dear Sister:

I could write a book about my week in Cape Town. This is a city I am not in love with, and if I get out of here alive I have no desire to return ever. The days have been very interesting indeed, as you will see, and the nights have been occupied with nightmares about your hare-brained scheme for super-man. Instead of sleeping peacefully, I dream of rows of little devils preparing all sorts of hideous death rays for your Army partners. What are you up to? No, I am not quitting. I am not walking out. A job is a job, and I remain your faithful employee.

Let me tell you something about the professor. Evidently, in one way or another, he was important to the Nazis—that is, important enough for them to desire to eliminate him. There was a very considerable organization of the Nazi bully boys here in Cape Town when the war began, and they had Herr Goldbaum on their list. A few days after he arrived, an attempt was made on his life. He received a superficial bullet wound, but it became infected and he had a rather bad time of it. The Jewish community took care of him and hid him, but then things got a little hot, and they turned him over to some friends they had in the Kaffir compound. I was following the trail, an old and stale trail, but one that became the path of duty and all that. Leave it to your brilliant brother Harry. I did not meet up with any revanchist Nazis who had survived the war and were hiding out for *der Tag,* whenever it might come. No indeed. I simply followed this cold trail into the Kaffir compound, and thereby was picked up by the police and tossed into jail. They had me tagged for a Communist; can you imagine? I thought that just about everything had happened to me, but this was it. It took two days of argument, and the efforts of the American Consul General as well, to prove that I was the very conservative and rather thoughtless brother of one of our most eminent Americans. I am a little tired of the weight your name carries, but thank heavens it carried enough weight to take me out of one of the most uncomfortable jails I have ever occupied or ever read about. It was crawling with bugs—huge, terrifying South African bugs.

After I got out of jail, I did the sensible thing that I should have done in the beginning. I sought an interview with the head of the Jewish community here, a Rabbi Anatole Bibberman. Bibberman, it seems, is an amaetur Assyriologist—and, if I do not make myself entirely plain, Assyriologists are a small group who devote their spare time to the study of ancient Assyria. I imagine a good many of them devote full time to the subject and become pros. Rabbi Bibberman, however, is a spare-time Assyriologist; and it turns out that Professor Goldbaum shared his interest. They spent long hours, I am told, discussing ancient Assyria and Babylon and things of that sort.

The Rabbi told me something that he thought everyone knew—that is, everyone who is interested in Professor Goldbaum. He told me that in 1944 the people in London (and by people I suppose he meant scientists or physicians or something of that sort) discovered that Professor Goldbaum was holed up in Cape Town. They needed him for something or other, and he took off for London. I am leaving for London myself as soon as I finish this letter, and goodbye to Cape Town. As you plan my itinerary for the future, I would appreciate your eliminating Cape Town from the list.

Your ever-loving brother,
Harry.

12

By cable:

MRS. JEAN ARBALAID
WASHINGTON, D.C.
DECEMBER 25, 1945

PERHAPS YOUR TRUST MISPLACED SINCE I TAKE GLEEFUL AND CHILDISH PLEASURE IN SENDING LONG LONG CABLES COLLECT WHICH THE UNITED STATES ARMY PAYS FOR. LIKE ANY OTHER MAN WHO HAS SERVED ANY LENGTH OF TIME IN THIS HIDEOUS WAR WE HAVE JUST FINISHED I SEEM TO HAVE AN UNSHAKABLE

BIAS AGAINST THE UNITED STATES ARMY. BE THAT AS IT MAY I
HAVE FOUND THE PROFESSOR. IT WAS ABSURDLY EASY AND IN A
LETTER TO FOLLOW I WILL GIVE ALL THE DETAILS. HE IS A CHARM-
ING AND DELIGHTFUL LITTLE MAN AND LAST NIGHT I TOOK HIM
FOR A CHRISTMAS EVE DINNER TO SIMPSON'S. IT TURNED OUT THAT
HE IS A VEGETARIAN. CAN YOU IMAGINE A VEGETARIAN AT SIMP-
SON'S ON CHRISTMAS EVE? I SUPPOSE AT THIS POINT I SHOULD PUT
IN A STOP JUST TO INDICATE THAT I AM QUITE AWARE THAT I AM
SENDING YOU A CABLE BUT I HAVE HEARD IT TOLD ON RELIABLE
AUTHORITY THAT THE NEW YORK TIMES REPORTERS CABLE THOSE
ENDLESS STORIES OF THEIRS IN FULL AND NOT IN CABLESE SO I
PRESUME OF THIS TIDBIT. MAY I SAY THAT THE PROFESSOR IS IN-
TRIGUED BY THE LITTLE I HAVE TOLD HIM. I DID NOT KNOW HOW
MUCH TO TELL HIM OR HOW HARD TO PUSH. JUST WHAT DO YOU
WANT ME TO DO WITH HIM? WHAT SHALL I ASK HIM? WHAT SHALL
I TELL HIM? YOU CAN SEE THAT SINCE THIS IS A PUBLIC CABLE I
AM USING GUARDED CIRCUITOUS AND SOMETIMES RATHER SILLY
LANGUAGE. I TRUST YOU UNDERSTAND ME MY DEAR JEAN. WHAT
NOW?

HARRY FELTON.

13

By diplomatic pouch:

Washington, D.C.
December 26, 1945

Mr. Harry Felton
London, England

Dear Harry:

While I am delighted that your spell of depression has
disappeared, you are beginning to worry me just a wee bit
with your silliness. I try to remember whether you were always as light-headed as you now appear to be, and I keep
telling myself and Mark that the war has changed you. In
any case, you are our man on the spot, and we must go along
with you. The truth is, I'm teasing. We do trust you, dear,
but please be more serious. Our project is dead serious. We
believe that despite protestations of your own limitations,
you have enough sense and good instincts to gauge Professor
Goldbaum's method. Talk to him. Unless you believe he is
a complete fraud—and from the little you say, I doubt that—
we want you to sell him on this venture. Sell him! We will

give him whatever he asks—that is, in the way of financial remuneration. A man like Professor Goldbaum, according to all my past experience with such men, should be more or less indifferent to money; but even if he is, Harry, I want you to set his fee and to set it generously. We want to make an arrangement whereby he will continue to work with us for as long as we need him. If it must be less than that, try to specify some contractual terms, at least a year. As far as his future is concerned, I repeat that we are able to take care of his future; we will take care of it financially, and we will take care of it in terms of citizenship. If he desires American citizenship, we can arrange that with no trouble whatsoever. If he wishes to continue as a British national—I presume that is his status now—then we will smooth the way. No difficulty will be encountered.

I am sure that when you discuss the matter with him he will have a number of questions of his own, and he will desire to be enlightened more fully than we have enlightened you. Perhaps we should have briefed you more completely before now; but the truth of the matter is that we had not yet completed our own preparations, nor were we exactly decided on what our procedure would be. At this point we are.

We have been allocated a tract of eight thousand acres in northern California. The eight thousand acres are very attractive. There is a stand of sequoia forest, a lovely lake, and some very beautiful and arable meadowland. There is also a stretch of badland. All in all, it is a variegated and interesting landscape. Here we intend to establish an environment which will be under military guard and under military security. In other words, we propose to make this environment as close to a self-contained world as perhaps ever existed. In the beginning, in the first years of our experiment, the outside world will be entirely excluded. The environment will be exclusive and it will be controlled as absolutely as anything can be controlled within the present world and national situation.

Within this environment, we intend to bring forty children to maturity—to a maturity that will result in man-plus. But please understand, Harry, and convey this to the professor, that when I state something as a positive I am proceeding on a theoretical hypothesis. Man-plus does not exist and may never exist. We are making an experiment based on a presumption. Always come back to that, Harry; never talk as if we were dealing with certainties.

As to the details of the environment—well, most if it will have to wait. I can tell you this: We shall base its functioning on the highest and the gentlest conclusions of man's philosophy through the ages. There is no way to put this into a few sentences. Perhaps I might say that instead of doing unto others as we would have them do unto us, we will attempt to do not unto others as we would not have them do unto us. Of course that says everything and anything, and perhaps nothing as well; but in due time we will tell you the details of the environment as we plan it, and the details of its functioning. The more immediate and important problem is finding the children. We need a certain type of child—that is, a superior child, a very superior child. We would like to have the most extraordinary geniuses in all the world; but, since these children are to be very young, our success in that direction must always be open to question. But we are going to try.

As I said, we intend to raise forty children. Out of these forty children, we hope to find ten in the United States of America; the other thirty will be found by the professor and yourself—outside of the United States.

Half are to be boys. We want an even boy-girl balance, and the reasons for that, I think, are quite obvious. All of the children are to be between the ages of six months and nine months, and all are to show indications of an exceedingly high IQ. As I said before, we would like to have extraordinary geniuses. Now, you may ask me how, how is this location of infant genius going to work? Well, Harry, there's where the professor comes into the picture, as your guide and mentor. How we are going to accomplish the problem at home, we have not fully worked out. But we believe that we have some methods, some hints, some directions that will ultimately lead us to success. In your case, we are depending upon the professor's method—that is, if his method is any good at all. If it is not—well, there are a dozen points where we can fail, aside from his methods.

We want five racial groupings: Caucasian, Indian, Chinese, Malayan and Bantu. Of course, we are sensible to the vagueness of these groupings, and you will have to have some latitude within them. As you know, racial definitions are at worst political and at best extremely imprecise. If you should find, let us say, three or four or five Bantu children who impress you as extraordinary, naturally we want to include them. Again, when we say Bantu we are not being literal. You may find in South Africa a Hottentot child who commands your attention. By all means include the Hottentot child.

The six so-called Caucasian infants are to be found in Europe. We might suggest two Northern types, two Central European types and two Mediterranean types; but this is only a suggestion and by no means a blueprint for you to follow. Let me be more specific: If you should by any chance find seven children in Italy, all of whom are obviously important for our experiment, you must take all seven children, even though only six children are suggested from Europe.

Now the word "take" which I have just used—understand this: no cops and robbers stuff, no OSS tactics, no kidnapping. If you find the most marvelous, the most extraordinary, infant of your entire search, and the parents of that infant will not part with it, that ends the matter right there. This is not simply an ethical point that I am raising, Harry. This is integral to the success of our program, and I think that in time you will understand why.

Now, where will the children come from? We are going to buy children. Let us be brutally frank about it. We are in the market for children. Where will they come from? Unfortunately for mankind but perhaps fortunately for our narrow purpose here, the world abounds with war orphans—and also in parents so poor, so desperate, that they will sell their children if the opportunity arises. When you find a child in such a situation and you want the child and the parents are willing, you are to buy. The price is no object. Of course, I must add here that you should exercise a certain amount of common sense. When I say price is no object, I mean that if you have to pay a hundred thousand or a hundred and fifty thousand dollars for a child, you are to pay the price. If, on the other hand, a price is in the neighborhood of a million dollars, you are to think it over very carefully. This is not to say that we will not pay as high as a million dollars if the necessity arises; but at that price, I want you to be very certain of what you are doing. We have enormous backing and an enormous amount of money to work with; but regardless of how enormous our resources are at this moment, they are going to be spent eventually, and there are limitations. I am afraid that we must work within these limitations.

However, I will have no maudlin sentimentality or scruples about acquiring the children, and I would like you and the professor to share my point of view. We are scientists, and sentimentalism rarely advances science; also, in itself, I find sentimentalism a rather dreadful thing. Let me state emphatically that these children will be loved and cherished as much as it is possible for those who are not blood parents to love and cherish children; and in the case of these children that you acquire by purchase, you will be buying not only a child but, for that child, a life of hope and promise. Indeed, we hope to offer these children the most wonderful life that any child could have.

When you find a child that you want and you are ready to acquire that child, inform us immediately. Air transport will be at your disposal. We are also making all arrangements for wet nurses—that is to say, if you find a nursing infant who should continue to nurse, we will always have wet nurses available. Rest assured that all other details of child care will be anticipated. We will have a staff of excellent pediatricians whom you can call on anywhere on earth. They will fly to where you are.

On the other hand, we do not anticipate a need for physicians. Above all things, we want healthy children, of course within the general conditions of health in any given area. We know that an extraordinary child in certain regions of the earth may well have the most discouraging signs of poor health, undernourishment, etc. But I am sure that you and Professor Goldbaum will be able to measure and assess such cases.

Good luck to you. We are depending on you, and we love you. We do wish that you could have been here with us for Christmas Day; but, in any case, a Merry Christmas to you, and may the future bring peace on earth and good will to all men.

Your loving sister,
Jean.

14

By diplomatic pouch:

Copenhagen, Denmark
February 4, 1946

Mrs. Jean Arbalaid
Washington, D.C.

Dear Jean:

I seem to have caught your top-secret and classified disease, or perhaps I have become convinced that this is a matter wanting some kind of secrecy. That seems hard to believe in such a down-to-earth, practical and lovely place as Copenhagen. We have been here for three days now, and I am absolutely charmed by the city and delighted with the Danes. I set aside today, in any case a good part of today, to sum up my various adventures and to pass on to you whatever conclusions and opinions might be of some profit to you.

From my cables, you will have deduced that the professor and I have been doing a Cook's Tour of the baby market. My dear sister, this kind of shopping spree does not set at all well with me; however, I gave my word, and there you are. I will complete and deliver. I might add that I have also become engrossed with your plans, and I doubt that I would allow myself to be replaced under any circumstances.

By the way, I suppose I continue to send these along to Washington, even though your "environment," as you call it, has been established? I will keep on doing so until otherwise instructed.

As you know, there was no great difficulty in finding the professor. Not only was he in the telephone book, but he is quite famous in London. He has been working for almost a year now with a child-reclamation project, while living among the ruins of the East End, which was pretty badly shattered and is being reclaimed only slowly. He is an astonishing little man, and I have become fond of him. On his part, he is learning to tolerate me.

I think I cabled to you how I took him to dinner at Simpson's only to learn that he was a vegetarian. But did I say that you were the lever that moved him, my dear sister? I had no idea how famous you are in certain circles. Professor

Goldbaum regarded me with awe, simply because you and I share a mother and a father. On the other hand, my respect for unostentatious scientific folk is growing. The second meeting I had with Dr. Goldbaum took place on the terrace of the House of Commons. This little fellow, who would be lost so easily in any crowd, had casually invited three Members of Parliament and one of His Majesty's Ministers to lunch with us. The subject under discussion was children: the future of children, the care of children, the love of children and the importance of children.

Whatever you may say about the government here, its interest in the next generation is honest, moving, and very deep and real. For the first time in British history, the average Englishman is getting a substantial, adequate and balanced diet. They have wonderful plans and great excitement about the future and about children's role in the future. I think it was for this purpose (to hear some of the plans) that Goldbaum invited me to be there. I am not sure that he trusts me—I don't mean this in a personal sense, but rather that I, being simply what I am, and he, being a sensitive man who recognizes what I am—well, why should he trust me? In that sense, he is quite right not to trust me.

At this lunch he drew me into the conversation, explaining to the others that I was deeply interested in children. They raised their eyebrows and inquired politely just where my interest derived from and where it was directed.

Believe me, my only claim to a decent standing in the human race was the fact that I was Mrs. Jean Arbalaid's brother; and when they heard that I was your brother their whole attitude toward me changed. I passed myself off as a sort of amateur child psychologist, working for you and assisting you, which is true in a way, isn't it? They were all very polite to me, and none of them questioned me too closely.

It was a good day, one of those astonishing blue-sky days that are real harbingers of spring, and that come only rarely in London in February. After the luncheon, the professor and I strolled along Bird Cage Walk, and then through Saint James's Park to the Mall. We were both relaxed, and the professor's uncertainty about me was finally beginning to crumble just a little. So I said my piece, all of it, no holds barred. To be truthful, I had expected your reputation to crumble into dust there on the spot, but no such thing. Goldbaum listened with his mouth and his ears and every fiber of his being. The only time he interrupted me was to question me about the Assamese girl and the Bantu boy; and very pointed and meticulous questions they were.

"Did you yourself examine the child?" he asked me.

"Not as a doctor," I replied, "but I did examine her in the sense that one human being can observe another human being. This was not a calm little girl, nor was the Bantu boy a calm little boy; they were both terror-stricken animals."

"Not animals," Goldbaum corrected me.

"No, of course not."

"You see," Goldbaum said, "that point is most important. Animals they could not become; they were prevented, however, from becoming human beings."

There he hit upon the precise point that I had come to and which Professor Gojee had underlined so often. When I had finished with my whole story, and had, so to speak, opened all my cards to Professor Goldbaum's inspection, he simply shook his head—not in disagreement, but with sheer excitement and wordless delight. I then asked him what his reaction to all this was.

"I need time," he said. "This is something to digest. But the concept, Mr. Felton, is wonderful—daring and wonderful. Not that the reasoning behind it is so novel. I have thought of this same thing; so many anthropologists have thought of it. Also, throughout the ages it has been a concept of many philosophies. The Greeks gave their attention to it, and many other ancient peoples speculated upon it. But always as an imaginative concept, as a speculation, as a sort of beautiful daydream. To put it into practice, young man—ah, your sister is a wonderful and a remarkable woman!"

There you are, my sister, I struck while the iron was hot, and told him then and there that you wanted and needed his help, first to find the children and then to work in the environment.

"The environment," he said. "You understand, that is everything, everything. But how can she change the environment? The environment is total, the whole fabric of human society, self-deluded and superstitious and sick and irrational and clinging to the legends and the fantasies and the ghosts. Who can change that?"

I had my answer ready, and I told him that if anyone could, Mrs. Jean Arbalaid could.

"You have a great deal of respect for your sister," he said. "I am told that she is a very gentle woman."

"When she is not crossed," I agreed. "But the point is this, Professor: Will you work with us? That is the question she wants me to put to you?"

"But how can I answer it now? You confront me with perhaps the most exciting, the most earth-shaking notion of all of human history—not as a philosophical notion but as a pragmatic experiment—and then you ask me to say Yes or No. Impossible!"

"All right," I agreed, "I can accept that. How long do you want to think about it?"

"Overnight will be enough," he said. "Now tell me about California. I have never been there. I have read a little about it. Tell me what the state is like and what sort of an environment this would be in a physical sense; I would also like to know something more specific about your sister's relations to what you call 'the Army.' That phrase you use, 'the Army'—it seems quite different from what we understand in European terms or even in British terms."

So it went. My anthropology is passable at best, but I have read all your books. My geography and history are better, and if my answers were weak where your field was concerned, he did manage to draw out of me a more or less complete picture of Mark and yourself, and as much sociological and political information concerning the United States Government, the United States Army, and the relationship of the government and the Army to subprojects, as I could have provided under any circumstances. He has a remarkable gift for extracting information, or, as I am inclined to regard it, of squeezing water from a rock.

When I left him, he said that he would think the whole matter over. We made an appointment for the following day. Then, he said, provided he had agreed to join us, he would begin to instruct me in his method of determining the intelligence of infants.

By the way, just to touch on his methods, he makes a great point of the fact that he does not test but rather determines, leaving himself a wide margin for error. Years before, in prewar Germany, he had worked out a list of about fifty characteristics which he had noted in infants. All of these characteristics had some relationship to factors of intelligence and response. As the infants in whom he had originally noted these characteristics matured, they were tested regularly by standard methods, and the results of these tests were compared with his original observations. Thereby he began to draw certain conclusions, which he tested again and again during the next fifteen years. Out of these conclusions and out of his tests, his checking, his relating testing to observation, he began to put together a list of characteristics that the pre-tested (that is, the new) infant might demonstrate, and he specified how those characteristics could be relied upon to indicate intelligence. Actually, his method is as brilliant as it is simple, and I am enclosing here an unpublished article of his which goes into far greater detail. Suffice it to say he convinced me of the validity of his methods.

I must note that subsequently, watching him examine a hundred and four British infants and watching him come up with our first choice for the group, I began to realize how brilliant this man is. Believe me, Jean, he is a most remarkable and wise man, and anything and everything you may have heard about his talents and knowledge is less than reality.

When I met him the following day, he agreed to join the project. Having come to this conclusion, he had no reservations about it. He seemed to understand the consequences far better than I did, and he told me very gravely just what his joining meant. Afterwards I wrote it down exactly as he said it:

"You must tell your sister that I have not come to this decision lightly. We are tampering with human souls—and perhaps even with human destiny. This experiment may fail, but if it succeeds it can be the most important event of our time—even more important and consequential than this terrible war we have just been through. And you must tell her something else. I once had a wife and three children, and they were put to death because a nation of men had turned into beasts. I personally lived through and observed that transition, that unbelievable and monstrous mass transition of men into beasts—but I could not have lived through it unless I had believed, always, that what can turn into a beast can also turn into a human being. We—and by we I mean the present population of the earth—are neither beast nor man. When I speak the word 'man,' I speak it proudly. It is a goal, not a fact. It is a dream, not a reality. Man does not exist. We are professing to believe that he might exist. But if we go ahead to create man, we must be humble. We are the tool, not the creator, and if we succeed, we ourselves will be far less than the result of our work. You must also tell your sister that when I make this commitment as I do today, it is a commitment without limitation. I am no longer a young man, and if this experiment is to be pursued properly, it must take up most, perhaps the rest, of my life. I do not lightly turn over the rest of my existence to her—and yet I do."

There is your man, Jean, and as I said, very much of a man. The words above are quoted verbatim. He also dwells a great deal on the question of environment, and the wisdom and judgment and love necessary to create this environment. He understands, of course, that in our work—in our attempt to find the children to begin the experiment with—we are relying most heavily upon heredity. He does not negate the factor of heredity by any means, but heredity without the environment, he always underlines, is useless. I think it would be helpful if you could send me a little more information about this environment that you are establishing. Perhaps Professor Goldbaum could make a contribution toward it while it is in the process of being created.

We have now sent you four infants. Tomorrow we leave for Rome, and from Rome for Casablanca. We will be in Rome for at least two weeks and you can write or cable me there. The embassy in Rome will have our whereabouts at any time.

More seriously than ever and not untroubled.

Harry.

15

By diplomatic pouch:

Via Washington, D.C.
February 11, 1946

Mr. Harry Felton
Rome, Italy

Dear Harry:

Just a few facts here—not nearly as many as we would like to give you concerning the environment, but at least enough for Professor Goldbaum to begin to orient himself. We are tremendously impressed by your reactions to Professor Goldbaum, and we look forward eagerly to his completing his work in Europe and joining us as a staff member here in America. By the way, he is the only staff member, as such, that we will have. Later on in this letter, I will make that clear. Meanwhile, Mark and I have been working night and day on the environment. In the most general terms, this is what we hope to accomplish and to have ready for the education of the children:

The entire reservation—all eight thousand acres—will be surrounded by a wire fence, what is commonly known as heavy tennis fencing or playground fencing. The fence will be eleven feet high; it will be topped by a wire carrying live current, and it will be under Army guard twenty-four hours a day. However, the Army guards will be stationed a minimum of three hundred yards from the fence. They will be under orders never, at any time under any circumstances, to approach the main fence nearer than three hundred yards. Outside of this neutral strip of three hundred yards, a second fence will be built—what might be thought of us an ordinary California cow fence. The Army guards will patrol outside of this fence, and only under specific and special circumstances will they have permission to step within it into the neutralized zone. In this way, and through the adroit use of vegetation, we hope that, for the first ten years, at least, people within the reservation will neither see nor have any other indication of the fact that outside of the reservation an armed guard patrols and protects it.

Within the reservation itself we shall establish a home; indeed, the most complete home imaginable. Not only shall we have living quarters, teaching quarters, and the means of any and all entertainment we may require; but we shall also have machine shops, masonry shops, wood-carving shops, mills, all kinds of fabrication devices and plans—in other words, almost everything necessary for absolute independence and self-maintenance. This does not mean that we are going to cut our relationships with the outside. There will certainly be a constant flow of material from the outside into the environment, for we shall require many things that we shall not be able to produce ourselves.

Now for the population of the environment: We expect to enlist between thirty and forty teachers or group parents. We are accepting only young married couples who love children and who will dedicate themselves entirely to this venture.

This in itself has become a monumental task, for enlistment in this project is even more of a commitment than enlistment in the Army was five years ago. We are telling those parents who accept our invitation and who are ready to throw in their lot with the experiment that the minimum time they will be asked to spend with us is fifteen years, and that the maximum time may well be a lifetime. In other words, the people who accept our invitation and come with us to be a part of the environment are, in actuality, leaving the planet Earth. They are leaving their friends and they are leaving their relatives, not for a day, a week, a month, or a year, but in a manner of speaking, forever. It is as if you were to approach twenty married couples and suggest to them that they emigrate from Earth to an uninhabited planet with no possibility of a return.

Can you imagine what this is, Harry? Can you imagine how keenly these people must believe? You might well suppose that nowhere could we find people who would be willing to join us in our venture; but that is far from the case. It is true that we are going all over the world for the parents, just as we are going all over the world for the children. However, we have already enlisted twelve couples, superb people, of several nationalities. We are excited and delighted with every step forward we take. Remember, it is not enough to find couples willing to dedicate themselves to this venture; they must have unique additional qualifications; and the fact that we have found so many with these qualifications is what excites us and gives us faith in the possibility that we will succeed.

Even to begin the experiment, we must dedicate ourselves to the proposition that somewhere in man's so-called civilized development, something went tragically wrong; therefore, we are returning to a number of forms of great antiquity. One of these forms is group marriage. That is not to say that we will cohabit indiscriminately; rather, the children will be given to understand that parentage is a whole, a matter of the group—that we are all their mothers and their fathers, not by blood but by a common love, a common feeling for protection and a common feeling for instruction.

As far as teaching is concerned, we shall teach our children only the truth. Where we do not know the truth, we shall not teach. There will be no myths, no legends, no lies, no superstitions, no false premises and no religions. There will be no gods, no bogeymen, no horrors, no nameless fears. We shall teach love and compassion and cooperation; and with this we shall demonstrate, in our lives and in every action we take, the same love and compassion—hoping, trusting and fighting for all of this to add up to the fullest possible measure of security. We shall also teach them the knowledge of mankind—but not until they are ready for that knowledge, not until they are capable of handling it. Certainly we shall not give them knowledge of the history of mankind or what mankind has become in the course of that history until they have completed the first eight years of their lives. Thus they will grow up knowing nothing of war, knowing nothing of murder, knowing nothing of the thing called patriotism, unaware of the multitude of hatreds, of fears, of hostilities that has become the common heritage of all of mankind.

During the first nine years in the environment, we shall have total control. We have already installed a complete printing press, a photo-offset system; we have all the moving-picture equipment necessary, and we have laboratories to develop the film we take, projection booths and theaters. All the film we need we shall make. We shall write the books; we shall take the film; we shall shape the history as history is taught to them in the beginning—that is, a history of who they are and what they are within the environment. We shall raise them in a sort of Utopia—God willing, without all the tragic mistakes that man has always made in his Utopias. And, finally, when we have produced something strong and healthy and beautiful and sturdy—at that point only will we begin to relate the children to the world as it is. Does it sound too simple or presumptuous? I am almost sorry, Harry, that I cannot make it more complicated, more intriguing, more wonderful, yet Mark and I both agree that the essence of what we are attempting to do is simple beyond belief; it is almost negative. We are attempting to rid ourselves of something that mankind has done to itself; and, if we can rid a group of children of that undefined something, then what will emerge just might be exciting and wonderful and even magnificent beyond belief. That is our hope; but the environment as I describe it above, Harry, is all that we can do—and I think that Professor Goldbaum will understand that full well and will not ask more of us. It is also a great deal more than has ever been done for any children on this earth heretofore.

So good luck to both of you. May you work well and happily and complete your work. The moment it is completed we want Professor Goldbaum to join us in the United States and to become a part of our group and our experiment. I am not asking you to become a part of it, Harry, and I think you can understand why I don't want to put you in a position of having to make the choice. By now I can well understand how deeply you have committed yourself to our experiment. Mark and I both realize that you cannot spell out such a commitment, but, dear Harry, I know you so well and I know what has happened inside of you. If I asked you to join us, you would not allow yourself to say No; but, at the same time, I don't think that your road to happiness consists of taking off for another planet. However you might feel about it, Harry, you are far too attached to the reality of the world as it is. You have not yet found the woman that you must find, but when you do find her, Harry, she and you will have your own way to find.

Your letters, in spite of your attempt to make them highly impersonal, do give us a clue to the change within you. Do you know, Harry, everyone associated with this experiment begins a process of change—and we feel that same curious process of change taking place within us.

When I put down simply and directly on paper what we are doing now and what we intend to do in the future, it seems almost too obvious to be meaningful in any manner. In fact, when you look at it again and again, it seems almost ridiculously simple and pointless and hopeless. What are we doing, Harry? We are simply taking a group of very gifted children and giving them knowledge and love. Is this enough to break through to that part of man which is unused and unknown? We don't know, Harry, but in time we shall see. Bring us the children, Harry, and we shall see.

With love,
Jean.

16

One day in the early spring of 1965, Harry Felton arrived in Washington from London. At the airport he took a cab directly to the White House, where he was expected.

Felton had just turned fifty; he was a tall and pleasant-looking man, rather lean, with graying hair. As president of the board of Shipways, Inc.—one of the country's largest import and export houses, with offices in London and in New York—Felton commanded a certain amount of deference and respect from Eggerton, who was then Secretary of Defense. A cold, withdrawn, and largely unloved man, Eggerton frequently adopted an attitude of immediate superiority, or, if that failed to impress, of judicious and controlled hostility; but he was sufficiently alert and sensitive not to make the mistake of trying to intimidate Felton.

Instead, he greeted him rather pleasantly—that is, pleasantly for Eggerton. The two of them, with no others present, sat down to talk in a small room in the White House. Drinks were served and a tray of sandwiches was brought in case Felton was hungry. Felton was not hungry. He and Eggerton drank each other's good health, and then they began to talk.

Eggerton proposed that Felton might know why he had been asked to Washington.

"I can't say that I do know," Felton replied—a little less than truthfully; but then, Felton did not like Eggerton and did not feel comfortable with him.

"You have a remarkable sister."

"I have been aware of that for a long time."

Felton seemed to take a moment to think about what he had just said, and then he smiled. Whatever made him smile was not revealed to Eggerton who, after a moment, asked him whether he felt that his statement had been humorous.

"No, I didn't feel that," Felton said seriously.

"You are being very careful here, Mr. Felton," the Secretary observed, "but you have trained yourself to be a very close-mouthed person. So far as we are able to ascertain, not even your immediate family has ever heard of man-plus. That's a commendable trait."

"Possibly and possibly not. It's been a long time," Felton said coldly. "Just what do you mean by 'ascertain'? How have you been able to ascertain whether or not I am close-mouthed? That interests me, Mr. Secretary."

"Please don't be naïve, Mr. Felton."

"I have practiced being naïve for a lifetime," Felton said. "It's really not very sensitive on your part to ask me to change in a moment sitting here in front of you. I find that a degree of naïveté fits well with close-mouthedness. What did it come to, Mr. Secretary? Was my mail examined?"

"Now and then," the Secretary admitted.

"My offices bugged?"

"At times."

"And my home?"

"There have been reasons to keep you under observation, Mr. Felton. We do what is necessary. What we do has received large and unnecessary publicity; so I see no point in your claiming ignorance."

"I am sure you do what is necessary."

"We must, and I hope that this will not interfere with our little conversation today."

"It doesn't surprise me. So, in that direction at least, it will not interfere. But just what is this conversation and what are we to talk about?"

"Your sister."

"I see, my sister." Felton nodded. He did not appear surprised.

"Have you heard from your sister lately, Mr. Felton?"

"No, not for almost a year."

"Does it alarm you, Mr. Felton?"

"Does what alarm me?"

"The fact that you have not heard from your sister in so long?"

"Should it alarm me? No, it doesn't alarm me. My sister and I are very close, but this project of hers is not the sort of thing that allows for frequent social relations. Add to that the fact that my residence is in England, and that, while I do make trips to America, most of my time is spent in London and Paris. There have been long periods before when I have not heard from my sister. We are indifferent letter writers."

"I see," Eggerton said.

"Then I am to conclude that my sister is the reason for my visit here?"

"Yes."

"She is well?"

"As far as we know," Eggerton replied quietly.

"Then what can I do for you?"

"Help us if you will," Eggerton said just as quietly. He was visibly controlling himself—as if he had practiced with himself before the meeting and had conditioned himself not to lose his temper under any circumstances, but to remain quietly controlled, aloof and polite. "I am going to tell you what has happened, Mr. Felton, and then perhaps you can help us."

"Perhaps," Felton agreed. "You must understand, Mr. Eggerton, that I don't admire either your methods or your apparent goal. I think you would be wrong to look upon me as an ally. I spent the first twenty-four years of my life in the United States. Since then I have lived abroad with only infrequent visits here. So, you see, I am not even conditioned by what you might think of as a patriotic frame of mind. I am afraid that, if anything, I am a total internationalist."

"That doesn't surprise me, Mr. Felton."

"On second thought, I realize that it wouldn't. I am sure that you have investigated my residences, my frame of mind, my philosophy, and I would also guess that you have enough recordings of my conversations with my most intimate friends to know exactly what my point of view is."

The Secretary of Defense smiled as if to exhibit to Felton the fact that he, the Secretary of Defense, possessed a sense of humor. "No, not quite that much, Mr. Felton, but I must say that I am rather pleased by the respect you have for our methods. It is true that we know a good deal about you and it is also true that we could anticipate your point of view. However, we are not calling upon you in what some might term a patriotic capacity; we are calling upon you because we feel that we can appeal to certain instincts which are very important to you."

"Such as?"

"Human beings, human decency, the protection of mankind, the future of mankind—subjects that cross national boundaries. You would agree that they do, would you not, Mr. Felton?"

"I would agree that they do," Felton said.

"All right then; let us turn to your sister's project, a project which has been under way so many years now. I don't have to be hush-hush about it, because I am sure that you know as much concerning this project as any of us—more perhaps, since you were in at its inception. At that time, you were on the payroll of the project, and for a number of months you assisted your sister in the beginnings of the project. If I am not mistaken, part of your mission was to acquire certain infants which she needed at that stage of her experiment?"

"The way you say 'infants,'" Felton replied, smiling, "raises a suspicion that we wanted them to roast and devour. May I assure you that such was not the case. We were neither kidnappers nor cannibals; our motives were rather pure."

"I am sure."

"You don't say it as if you were sure at all."

"Then perhaps I have some doubts, and perhaps you will share my doubts, Mr. Felton, when you have heard me out. What I intended to say was that surely you, of all people, realize that such a project as your sister undertook must be regarded very seriously indeed or else laughed off entirely. To date it has cost the Government of the United States upwards of one hundred and fourteen million dollars, and that is not something you laugh off, Mr. Felton."

"I had no idea the price was so high," Felton said. "On the other hand, you may have gotten a hundred and fourteen million dollars' worth for your money."

"That remains to be seen. You understand, of course, that the unique part of your sister's project was its exclusiveness. That word is used advisedly and specifically. Your sister made the point again and again and again—and continues to make it, I may say—the point that the success of the project depended entirely upon its exclusiveness, upon the creation of a unique and exclusive environment. We were forced to accept her position and her demands—that is, if we desired the project at all; and it seems that the people who undertook to back the project did desire it. I say we, Mr. Felton, because 'we' is a term we use in government; but you must understand that was a good many years ago, almost twenty years ago, and I myself, Mr. Felton, did not participate in its inception. Now, in terms of the specifications, in terms of the demands that were made and met, we agreed not to send any observers into the reservation for a period of fifteen years. Of course, during those fifteen years there have been many conferences with Mr. and Mrs. Arbalaid and with certain of their associates, including Dr. Goldbaum."

"Then, if there were conferences," Felton said, "it seems to me that you know more about my sister than I do. You must understand that I have not seen my sister almost since the inception of the project."

"We understand that. Nevertheless, the relationship differs. Out of these conferences, Mr. Felton, there was no progress report that dealt with anything more than general progress and that in the most fuzzy and indefinite terms. We were given to understand that the results they had obtained in the reservation were quite rewarding and exciting, but little more, very little more indeed."

"That was to be expected. That's the way my sister works; in fact, it's the way most scientists work. They are engaged in something that is very special to them, very complicated, very difficult to explain. They do not like to give reports of the way stations they may arrive at. They like to complete their work and have results, proven results, before they report."

"We are aware of that, Mr. Felton. We honored our part of the agreement, and at the end of a fifteen-year period we told your sister and her husband that they would have to honor their part of the agreement and that we would have to send in a team of observers. We were as liberal, as flexible, as people in our position could be. We advised them that they would have the right to choose the observers, that they could even limit the path of the observers—limit what the observers would see and the questions the observers could ask—but that we would have to send in such a team."

"And did you?" Felton asked him.

"No, we did not. That's a tribute to the persuasive powers of your sister and her husband. They pleaded for an extension of time, maintaining that it was critical to the success of the entire program, and they pleaded so persuasively that in the end they did win a three-year extension. Some months ago, the three-year period of grace was over. Mrs. Arbalaid came to Washington and begged for a further extension. I was at the meeting where she was heard, and I can tell you, Mr. Felton, that never before in my life had I heard a woman plead for something with the fervor, the insistence, with which Mrs. Arbalaid pleaded for this further extension."

Felton nodded. "Yes, I imagine my sister would plead with some intensity. Did you agree?"

"No. As I said, we refused."

"You mean you turned her down completely—entirely?"

"Not as completely perhaps as we should have. She agreed—when she saw that she could not move us—that our team could come into the reservation in ten days. She begged the ten-day interval to discuss the matter with her husband and to choose the two people who would make up the observation team. The way she put it, we had to agree to it; and then she returned to California."

Eggerton paused and looked at Felton searchingly.

"Well," Felton said, "what happened then? Did my sister select competent observers?"

"You don't know?" Eggerton asked him.

"I know some things. I'm afraid I don't know whatever you're interested in at this moment. I certainly don't know what happened."

"That was three weeks ago, Mr. Felton. Your sister never chose observers; your sister never communicated with us again; in fact, we know nothing about your sister or her reactions or what she said to her husband because we have not heard from her since."

"That's rather curious."

"That is exceedingly curious, Mr. Felton, far more curious than you might imagine."

"Tell me, what did you do when ten days went by and you didn't hear from my sister?"

"We waited a few days more to see whether it was an oversight on her part, and then we tried to communicate with her."

"Well?"

"We couldn't. You know something, Felton? When I think about what I'm going to tell you now I feel like a damn fool. I also feel a little bit afraid. I don't know whether the fear or the fool predominates. Naturally, when we couldn't communicate with your sister, we went there."

"Then you did go there," Felton said.

"Oh, yes, we went there."

"And what did you find?"

"Nothing."

"I don't understand," Felton said.

"Didn't I make myself plain, Mr. Felton? We went there and we found nothing."

"Oh?"

"You don't appear too surprised, Mr. Felton."

"Nothing my sister did ever really surprised me. You mean the reservation was empty—no sign of anything, Mr. Eggerton?"

"No, I don't mean that at all, Mr. Felton. I wish to God I did mean that. I wish it were so pleasantly human and down to earth and reasonable. I wish we thought or had some evidence that your sister and her husband were two clever and unscrupulous swindlers who had taken the government for a hundred and fourteen million dollars. That would have been a joy, Mr. Felton. That would have warmed the cockles of our hearts compared to what we do have and what we did find. You see, we don't know whether the reservation is empty or not, Mr. Felton, because the reservation is not there."

"What?"

"Precisely. Exactly what I said. The reservation is not there."

"Oh, come on now," Felton smiled. "My sister is a remarkable woman, but she doesn't make off with eight thousand acres of land. It isn't like her."

"I don't find your humor entertaining at this moment, Mr. Felton."

"No. No, of course not. I'm sorry. I realize that this is hardly the moment for humor. Only a thing is put to me and the thing makes no sense at all—how could an eight-thousand-acre stretch of land not be where it was? Doesn't that leave a damn big hole?"

"It's still a joke, isn't it, Mr. Felton?"

"Well, how do you expect me to react?" Felton asked.

"Oh, you're quite justified, Mr. Felton. If the newspapers got hold of it, they could do even better."

"Supposing you explain it to me," Felton said. "We're both guessing, aren't we? Maybe we're both putting each other on, maybe we're not. Let's be sensible about it and talk in terms that we both understand."

"All right," the Secretary said, "suppose you let me try, not to explain—that's beyond me—but to describe. The stretch of land where the reservation is located is in the Fulton National Forest: rolling country, some hills, a good stand of sequoia—a kidney-shaped area all in all, and very exclusive in terms of the natural formation. It's a sort of valley, a natural valley, that contains within itself areas of high land, areas of low land, and flat areas as well. Water, too. It was wire-fenced. Around it was a three-hundred-yard wide neutral zone, and Army guards were stationed at every possible approach. I went out there last week with our inspection team: General Meyers; two Army physicians; Gorman, the psychiatrist; Senator Totenwell of the Armed Services Committee; and Lydia Gentry, the educator who is our present Secretary of Education. You will admit that we had a comprehensive and intelligent team that represented a fine cross-section of American society. At least, Mr. Felton, that is my opinion. I still have some veneration for the American society."

"I share your admiration, Mr. Secretary, if not your veneration. I don't think that this should be a contest between you and me, *re* our attitudes toward the United States of America."

"No such contest intended, Mr. Felton. Let me continue. We crossed the country by plane and then we drove the final sixty miles to the reservation. We drove this distance in two Government cars. A dirt road leads into the reservation. The main guard, of course, is on that dirt road, and that road is the only road into the reservation, the only road that a vehicle could possibly take to go into the reservation. The armed guard on this road halted us, of course. They were merely doing their duty. The reservation was directly before us. The sergeant in charge of the guard approached the first car according to orders; and, as he walked toward our car, the reservation disappeared."

"Come on now," Felton said.

"I am trying to be reasonable and polite, Mr. Felton. I think the very least you could do is attempt to adopt the same attitude toward me. I said, 'The reservation disappeared'."

"Just like that?" Felton whispered. "No noise—no explosion—no earthquake?"

"No noise, no explosion, no earthquake, Mr. Felton. One moment a forest of sequoia in front of us—then a gray area of nothing."

"Nothing. Nothing is not a fact, Mr. Secretary. Nothing is not even a description; it's simply a word and a highly abstract word."

"We have no other word for this situation."

"Well, you say 'nothing.' What do you mean? Did you try to go in? If there was nothing in front of you did you try to go through this nothing?"

"Yes, we tried. You can be very certain that we tried, Mr. Felton, and since then the best scientists in America have tried. I do not like to speak about myself as a brave man, but certainly I am not a coward. Yet believe me, it took a while for me to get up enough courage to walk up to that gray edge of nothing and touch it."

"Then you touched it?"

"I touched it."

"If it was nothing, it seems to me you could hardly touch it. If you could touch it, it was something, certainly not nothing."

"If you wish, it was something. It blistered these three fingers."

He held out his hand for Felton to see. The first three fingers of his right hand were badly blistered.

"That looks like a burn," Felton said.

"It is a burn. No heat and no cold, nevertheless it burned my hand. That kind of thing sets you back, Felton."

"I can appreciate that," Felton said.

"I became afraid then, Mr. Felton, I think we all became afraid. We continue to be afraid. Do you understand, Mr. Felton? The world today represents a most delicate and terrible balance of power. When news comes to us that the Chinese have developed an atomic weapon, we become afraid. Out of necessity, our diplomatic attitude must reflect such fear and our attitude toward the Chinese must change. When the French began their atomic stockpile, our attitude toward the French changed. We are a pragmatic and a realistic administration, Mr. Felton, and we do not lie about fear or abjure power; we recognize fear and power, and we are very much afraid of that damn thing out there in California."

"I need not ask you if you tried this or that."

"We tried everything, Mr. Felton. You know, I'm a little ashamed to say this, and it is certainly damned well not for publication—I trust you will honor my request in that direction, Mr. Felton—?"

"I am not here as a reporter for the press," Felton said.

"Of course, yet this is very delicate, very delicate indeed. You asked whether we tried this or that. We tried things. We even tried a very small atomic bomb. Yes, Mr. Felton, we tried the sensible things and we tried the foolish things. We went into panic and we went out of panic and we tried everything we have and it all failed."

"And yet you have kept it a secret?"

"So far, Mr. Felton, we have kept it a secret," the Secretary agreed. "You cannot imagine what wire-pulling that took. We threw our weight here and there, and we threw our weight heavily, and we kept the secret—so far, Mr. Felton."

"Well, what about airplanes? You couldn't bar access to it from the air, could you? You couldn't cut off so wide a lane of air visibility that it would not be seen?"

"No, we immediately observed it from the air; you can be sure we thought of that quickly enough. But when you fly above it you see nothing. As I said, the reservation is in a valley, and all you can see is what appears to be mist lying in the valley. Perhaps it is mist—"

Felton leaned back and thought about it.

"Take your time," the Secretary said to him. "We are not rushing you, Mr. Felton, and believe me we are not pressuring you. We want your cooperation and, if you know what this is, we want you to tell us what it is."

Finally Felton asked him, "What do your people think it is?"

Eggerton smiled coldly and shook his head. "They don't know. There you are. At first, some of them thought it was some kind of force field. I have since learned that *force field* is a generic term for any area of positive action not understood too well. But when they tried to work it out mathematically, the mathematics wouldn't work. When they put it on the computers, the mathematics still refused to work. I don't know the math, Mr. Felton. I'm not a physicist and I'm not a mathematician, so I'm merely reporting what I have been told. And, of course, it's cold, and they're very upset about the fact that it's cold. It seems to confuse them no end. Terribly cold. Don't think only I am mumbling, Mr. Felton. As I said, I am neither a scientist nor a mathematician, but I can assure you that the scientists and the mathematicians also mumble. As for me, Mr. Felton, I am sick to death of the mumbling. I am sick to death of the doubletalk and the excuses. And that's why we decided that you should come to Washington and talk with us. We thought that you might know about this thing that bars us from the reservation, and you might be able to tell us what it is or tell us how to get rid of it."

"I haven't the vaguest idea what it is," Felton said, "but even if I had, what on earth makes you think that I would tell you how to get rid of it?"

"Surely you don't think it's a good thing."

"How can I say whether it's a good thing or a bad thing?" Felton asked him. "I haven't the faintest notion of what it is, and I'm not sure that I know, in today's scheme of things, what is good or what is bad."

"Then you can't help us at all?"

"I didn't say that either. I just might be able to help you." For the first time, Eggerton emerged from his lethargy, his depression. Suddenly he was excited and patient and overly cordial. He tried to force another drink on Felton. When Felton refused, he suggested that champagne be brought. Felton smiled at him, and the Secretary admitted that he was being childish.

"But you don't know how you have relieved me, Mr. Felton."

"I don't see why the little I said should relieve you. I certainly didn't intend to relieve you, and I don't know whether I can help you or not. I said I might help you."

Felton took a letter out of his pocket.

"This came from my sister," he said.

"You told me you had no letter from her in almost a year," the Secretary replied suspiciously.

"Exactly. And I have had this letter for almost a year." There was a note of sadness in Felton's voice. "I haven't opened it, Mr. Secretary, because when she sent it to me she enclosed it in a sealed envelope with a short letter. The letter said that she was well and quite happy, and that I was not to open or read the enclosed letter until it was absolutely necessary to do so. My sister is like that. We think the same way. I think that it's necessary now, don't you?"

The Secretary nodded slowly but said nothing. His eyes were fixed on Felton. Felton scanned the letter, turned it over, and then reached toward the Secretary's desk where there was a letter opener. The Secretary made no move to help him. Felton took the opener, slit the letter, and took out a sheaf of onionskin paper. He opened this sheaf of paper and he began to read aloud.

17

June 12, 1964

My dear Harry:

As I write this, it is twenty-two years since I have seen you or spoken to you. How very long for two people who have such love and regard for each other as we do! And now that you have found it necessary to open this letter and read it, we must face the fact that in all probability we will never see each other again unless we are most fortunate. And Harry, I have watched so many miracles occur that I hesitate to dream of another. I know from your letters that you have a wife and three children, and I have seen their photographs. So far as I can tell, they are wonderful people. I think the hardest thing is to know that I will not see them or come to know them and watch them grow, and at least be some sort of sister to your wife.

Only this thought saddens me. Otherwise, Mark and I are very happy—perhaps as happy as two human beings have any right to be. As you read this letter I think you will come to understand why.

Now, about the barrier—which must exist or you would not have opened the letter—tell them that there is no harm to it and that no hurt will be caused by it. The very worst that can happen is that if one leans against it too long, one's skin may be badly blistered. But the barrier cannot be broken into because it is a negative power rather than a positive one, an absence instead of a presence. I will have more to say about it later, but I don't think I will be able to explain it better. My physics is limited, and these are things for which we, as human beings, have no real concepts. To put it into visual terms or understandable terms for a layman is almost impossible—at least for me. I imagine that some of the children could put it into intelligible words. But I want this to be my report, not theirs.

Strange that I still call them children and think of them as children—when in fact we are the children and they are the adults. But they still have the quality of children that we know best: the innocence and purity that vanishes so quickly with the coming of puberty in the outside world.

Now, dear Harry, I must tell you what came of our experiment—or some of it. Some of it, for how could I ever put down the story of the strangest two decades that man ever lived through? It is all incredible and, at the same time, it is all commonplace. We took a group of wonderful children and we gave them an abundance of love, security and truth—but I think it was the factor of love that mattered most, and because we were able to give them these three very obvious things—love, security and truth—we were able to return them to their heritage, and what a heritage it is, Harry!

During the first year we weeded out those couples who showed less than a total desire to love the children. I mention this because you must not think that any stage of this was easy or that any part of it ran smoothly. We went into the reservation with twenty-three couples; six of them—that is, twelve people—failed to meet our test, and they had to go but they were still good people and they abided by the necessity for silence and security.

But our children are easy to love, and they were easy to love from the very beginning. You see, I call them our children, Harry, because as the years passed they became our children—in every way. The children who were born to the couples in residence here simply joined the group. No one had a father or a mother; we were a living, functioning group in which all the men were the fathers of all the children and all the women were the mothers of all the children.

Now this is very easy to state as a fact, Harry; it is easy to project as a concept; but its achievement was far from easy. Its achievement was something that tore us to pieces. We had to turn ourselves inside out, totally reexamine ourselves to achieve this. This among ourselves, Harry, among the adults who had to fight and work and examine each other inside and outside again and again and again—and tear out our guts and tear our hearts out—so that we could present ourselves to the children as something in the way of human beings. I mean a quality of sanity and truth and security embodied in a group of adult men and women. Far more spectacular achievements than this were accomplished, Harry—but perhaps nothing more wonderful than the fact that we, the adults, could remake ourselves. In doing so, we gave the children their chance.

And what did the chance amount to? How shall I tell you of an American Indian boy, five years old, composing a splendid symphony? Or of the two children, one Bantu, one Italian, one a boy, one a girl, who at the age of six built a machine to measure the speed of light? Will you believe that we, the adults, sat quietly and respectfully and listened to these six-year-olds explain to us a new theory of light? We listened and perhaps some of us understood, but most of us did not. I certainly did not. I might translate it and repeat it in these terms—that since the speed of light is a constant anywhere regardless of the motion of material bodies, the distance between the stars cannot be mentioned or determined in terms of the speed of light, since distance so arrived at is not, and has no equivalence to, distance on our plane of being. Does what I have said make any sense to you? It makes just a little to me. If I put it poorly, awkwardly, blame my own ignorance.

I mention just this one small thing. In a hundred—no, in a thousand—of these matters, I have had the sensations of an uneducated immigrant whose beloved child is exposed to all the wonders of school and knowledge. Like this immigrant, I understand a little of what the children achieve, but very little indeed. If I were to repeat instance after instance, wonder after wonder—at the ages of six and seven and eight and nine—would you think of the poor tortured nervous creatures whose parents boast that they have an IQ of 160 or 170 and, in the same breath, bemoan the fate that did not give them normal children? Do you understand me, Harry? These children of ours, in your world, would have been condemned to disaster—not to simple disaster but to the specific, terrible disaster that befalls the super-knowing, the super-sensitive, the super-intelligent who are ground down, degraded and destroyed just as that Assamese child raised by the wolves was destroyed. Well, our children were and are normal children. Perhaps they are the first truly normal children that this world has seen in a long time—in many thousands of years. If just once you could hear them laugh or sing, you would know how absolutely true my statement is. If only you could see how tall and strong they are, how fine of body and movement. They have a quality that I have never seen in children before.

I suppose, dear Harry, that much about them would shock you just as it would shock most of the population of the outside world. Most of the time, they wear no clothes. Sex has always been a joy and a good thing to them, and they face it and enjoy it as naturally as we eat and drink—more naturally, for we have no gluttons in sex or food, no ulcers of the belly or the soul.

Our children kiss and caress each other and do many things that the world has specified as shocking, nasty, forbidden, dirty, obscene. But whatever they do, they do it with grace and they do it with joy, and they have no guilt nor any knowledge whatsoever of guilt. *Guilt* as a word or fact is meaningless to them.

Is all this possible? Or is it a dream and an illusion? I tell you that it has been my life for almost twenty years now. I live with these children, with boys and girls who are without evil or sickness, who are like pagans or gods, however you would look at it.

But the story of the children and of their day-to-day life

is one that will some day be told properly in its own time and place. Certainly I have neither the time nor the ability to tell it here, Harry. You will have to content yourself with the bits and snatches that I can put down in this letter to you. All the indications that I have put down here add up only to great gifts and great abilities. But, after all, this was inherent in the children we selected. Mark and I never had any doubt about such results; we knew that if we created a controlled environment that was predicated on our hypothesis, the children would learn more than children do on the outside.

Naturally, this part of it came about. How could it have been otherwise—unless, of course, Mark and I had flubbed the whole thing and acted like fools and sentimentalists. But I don't think that there was much danger of that. Without being egotistical I can say that we, and of course Professor Goldbaum (who was with us through all the most difficult years), and our associates—we knew what we were doing. We knew precisely what we were doing and we knew pretty well how to do it.

In the seventh year of their lives, the children were dealing easily and naturally with scientific problems normally taught on the college level or on the postgraduate level in the outside world. But, as I said, this was to be expected, this was normal and we would have been very disappointed indeed if this development had not taken place. It was the unexpected that we hoped for, prayed for, dreamed of and watched for. A flowering, a development of the mind of man that was unpredictable and unknowable, which we could comprehend only negatively by theorizing that a block to such development is locked in every single human being on the outside.

And it came. Originally, it began with a Chinese child in the fifth year of our work. The second incident occurred in an American child, and the third in a Burmese child. Most strangely, it was not thought of as anything very unusual by the children themselves. We did not realize what was happening until the seventh year, that is, two years after the process had begun; and by that time it had happened already in five of the children. The very fact that it took place so gently, so naturally, so obviously, was a healthy symptom.

Let me tell you how we discovered what was happening. Mark and I were taking a walk that day—I remember it so well, a lovely, cool and clear northern California day—when we came upon a group of children in a meadow. There were about a dozen children gathered together in the meadow. Five of the children sat in a little circle, with a sixth child in the center of their circle. The six heads were almost touching. They were full of little giggles, ripples of mirth and satisfaction. The rest of the children sat in a group about ten feet away—watching intently, seriously, respectfully.

As we came closer the children were neither alarmed nor disturbed. The children in the second group put their fingers to their lips, indicating that we should be quiet. So we came rather close, and then we stood and watched without speaking.

After we were there about ten minutes, the little girl in the center of the circle of five children leaped to her feet, crying out ecstatically:

"I heard you! I heard you! I heard you!"

There was a kind of achievement and delight reflected in the sound of her voice that we had not experienced before, not even from our children. Then all of the children there rushed together to kiss and embrace the girl who had been in the middle of the group of five. They did a sort of dance of play and delight around her. All this we watched with no indication of surprise or even very great curiosity on our part. For even though this was the first time anything like this— anything beyond our expectation or comprehension—had ever happened, we had worked out what our own reaction should be to such discoveries and achievements on the part of the children. We had made up our minds that whatever they accomplished, our position would be that it was perfectly natural and completely expected.

When the children rushed to us for our congratulations, we nodded and smiled and agreed that it was all indeed very wonderful.

"Whose turn is it now?" Mark asked.

They called all the men "Father," the women "Mother." A Senegalese boy turned to me and said excitedly, "Now, it's my turn, Mother. I can do—well, I can almost do it already. Now there are six to help me, and it will be much easier."

"Aren't you proud of us?" another child cried.

"So proud," I said. "We couldn't be more proud."

"Are you going to do it now?" Mark asked him.

"Not now, we're tired now. You know, when you go at i'
with a new one, it's terribly tiring. After that, it's not tiring
But the first time it is."

"Then when will you do it?" I asked.

"Maybe tomorrow."

"Can we be here? I mean would you want us here wher
you do it or does it make it harder?"

"No harder," one of them said.

"Of course you can be here," another answered. "We woul‹
like you to be here."

"Both of us?" Mark asked.

"Of course, both of you and any other mother or fathe
who wants to come."

We pressed it no further, but that evening at our regula
staff meeting, Mark described what had happened and re
peated the conversation.

"I noticed the same thing a few weeks ago," Mary Henge
our semantics teacher, said. "I watched them, but either the
didn't see me or they didn't mind my watching them."

"Did you go up close to them?" I asked her.

"No, I was a little uncertain about that. I must have staye‹
about forty or fifty yards away."

"How many were there then?" Professor Goldbaum aske‹
Mary Hengel. He was very intent on his question, smilin
slightly.

"Three. No there was a fourth child in the center—th
three had their heads together. I simply thought it was on
of their games—they have so many—and I walked away afte
a little while."

"They make no secret about it," someone else observed.

"Yes," I said, "we had the same feeling. They just took i
for granted that we knew what they were doing, and the
were quite proud of what they were doing."

"The interesting thing is," Mark said, "that while the
were doing it, no one spoke. I can vouch for that."

"Yet they were listening," I put in. "There is no questio
about that; they were listening and they were listening fo
something, and finally, I imagine, they heard what they wer
listening for. They giggled and they laughed as if some grea
joke were taking place—you know the way children laug
about a game that delights them."

"Of course," said Abel Simms, who was in charge of ou
construction program, "of course they have no knowledge ‹

right and wrong in our terms, and nothing they do ever seems wrong to them, just as nothing they do ever seems right to them; so there is no way to gauge their attitude in that sense toward whatever they were doing."

We discussed it a bit further, and it was Dr. Goldbaum who finally put his finger on it. He said, very gravely:

"Do you know, Jean—you always thought and hoped and dreamed too that we might open that great area of the human mind that is closed and blocked in all human beings. I think they found out how to open it. I think they are teaching each other and learning from each other what is to them a very simple and obvious thing—how to listen to thoughts."

There was a rather long silence after that, and then Atwater, one of our psychologists, said uneasily, "I am not sure I believe it. You know, I have investigated every test and every report on telepathy ever published in this country, and as much as I could gather and translate of what was published in other parts of the world—the Duke experiments and all the rest of it. None of it, absolutely none of it, was dependable, and absolutely none of it gave any provable or reliable or even believable evidence or indication that such a thing as mental telepathy exists. You know, we have measured brain waves. We know how tiny and feeble they are—it just seems to me utterly fantastic that brain waves can be a means of communication."

"Hold on there," said Tupper, an experimental physicist. "The seemingly obvious linkage of brain waves with telepathy is rather meaningless, you know. If telepathy exists, it is not a result of what we call brain waves of the tiny electric pattern that we are able to measure. It's quite a different type of action, in a different manner on a wholly different level of physical reality. Just what that level is, I have no idea. But one of the things we are learning more and more certainly in physics is that there are different levels of reality, different levels of action and interaction of force and counterforce, so we cannot dispose of telepathy by citing brain waves."

"But how about the statistical factor?" Rhoda Lannon, a mathematician, argued. "If this faculty existed, even as a potential in mankind, is it conceivable that there would be no recorded instance of it? Statistically it must have emerged not once but literally thousands of times."

"Maybe it has been recorded," said Fleming, one of our

historians. "Can you take all the whippings and burnings and hangings of history, all the witches, the demigods, the magicians, the alchemists, and determine which of these were telepaths and which were not? Also, there is another way of looking at it. Suppose one telepath alone is totally impotent. Suppose we need two telepaths to make it work and suppose there is a limited distance over which two telepaths can operate. Then the statistical factor becomes meaningless and the accident becomes virtually impossible."

"I think that all in all I agree at least to some extent with Dr. Goldbaum," Mark said. "The children are becoming telepaths. It seems to me there is no question about that; it is the only sensible explanation for what Jean and I witnessed. If you argue, and with reason, that our children do not react to right and wrong and have no real understanding of right and wrong, then we must also add that they are equally incapable of lying. They have no understanding of the lie, or the meaning of the lie or of the necessity of the lie. So, if they told me that they heard what is not spoken, I have to believe them. I am not moved by an historical argument or by a statistical argument, because our concentration here is the environment and the absolute singularity of our environment. I speak of an historical singularity. There is no record in all of human history of a similar group of unusual children being raised in such an environment. Also, this may be—and probably is—a faculty of man which must be released in childhood, or remain permanently blocked. I believe Dr. Haenigson here will bear me out when I say that mental blocks imposed during childhood are not uncommon."

"More than that," Dr. Haenigson, our chief psychiatrist, stated. "No child in our history escapes the need to erect mental blocks in his mind. Without the ability to erect such blocks, it is safe to say that very few children in our society would survive. Indeed, we must accept the fact—and this is not theoretical or hypothetical, this is a fact, a provable fact which we have learned as psychiatrists—that whole areas of the mind of every human being are blocked in early childhood. This is one of the tragic absolutes of human society and the removal—not the total removal, for that is impossible, but the partial removal—of such blocks becomes the largest part of the work of practicing psychiatrists."

Dr. Goldbaum was watching me strangely. I was about to

say something, but I stopped and I waited, and finally Dr. Goldbaum said:

"I wonder whether we have begun to realize what we may have done without even knowing what we were doing. That is the wonderful, the almost unbearable implication of what may have happened here. What is a human being? He is the sum of his memories and his experience—these are locked in his brain, and every moment of experience simply builds up the structure of these memories. We do not know as yet what is the extent or power of the gift these children of ours appear to be developing, but suppose they reach a point where they can easily and naturally share the totality of memory? It is not simply that among themselves there can be no lies, no deceit, no rationalization, no secrets, no guilts—it is far more than that."

Then he looked from face to face, around the whole circle of our staff. At that point we were beginning to understand him and comprehend the condition he was posing. I remember my own reactions at that moment: a sense of wonder and discovery and joy, and heartbreak too, a feeling so poignant that it brought tears to my eyes. But above and beyond all that, I felt a sense of excitement, of enormous and exhilarating excitement.

"You know, I see," Dr. Goldbaum said. "I think that all of you know to one degree or another. Perhaps it would be best for me to speak about it, to put it into words, and to open it up to our thinking. I am much older than any of you—and I have been through and lived through the worst years of horror and bestiality that mankind ever knew. When I saw what I saw, when I witnessed the rise of Hitlerism, the concentration camps, the abattoirs, the ovens, the senseless, meaningless madness that culminated in the use of human skin to make lampshades, of human flesh and fat to make soap, when I saw and watched all this, I asked myself a thousand times: What is the meaning of mankind? Or has it any meaning at all? Is man not, perhaps, simply a haphazard accident, an unusual complexity of molecular structure, a complexity without meaning, without purpose and without hope? I know that you all have asked yourselves the same thing perhaps a hundred, a thousand times. What sensitive or thoughtful human being does not ask this question of himself? Who are we? What are we? What is our destiny?

What is our purpose? Where is sanity or reason in these bits of struggling, clawing, sick, murderous flesh? We kill, we torture, we hurt, we destroy as no other species does. We ennoble murder and falsehood and hypocrisy and superstition. We destroy our own bodies with drugs and poisonous food. We deceive ourselves as well as others. And we hate and hate and hate until every action we take is a result of our hatred.

"Now something has happened. Something new, something different, something very wonderful. If these children can go into each other's minds completely, then they will have a single memory, which is the memory of all of them. All their experience will be common to all of them, all their knowledge will be common to all of them, all the dreams they dream will be common to all of them—and do you know what that means? It means that they will be immortal. For as one of them dies, another child is linked to the whole, and another, and another. For them there will be no death. Death will lose all of its meaning, all of its dark horror. Mankind will begin, here in this place, in this strange little experiment of ours, to fulfill at least one part of its intended destiny—to become a single, wonderful thing, a whole—almost in the old words of your poet, John Donne, who sensed what each of us has sensed at one time or another: that no man is an island unto himself. Our tragedy has been that we are singular. We never lived, we were always fragmented bits of flesh at the edge of reality, at the edge of life. Tell me, has any thoughtful man or woman ever lived life without having a sense of that singleness of mankind and longing for it and dreaming of it? I don't think so. I think we have all had it, and therefore we have, all of us, been living in darkness, in the night, each of us struggling with his own poor little brain and then dying, perishing, with all the memories and the work of a lifetime destroyed forever. It is no wonder that we achieve so little. The wonder is that we have achieved so much. Yet all that we know, all that we have done, will be nothing, primitive, idiotic, nothing compared to what these children will know and do and create. It just staggers my imagination."

So the old man spelled it out, Harry. I can't put it all down here, but do you know, he saw it—at that moment, which was almost the beginning of it, he saw it in all of its far-flung implications. I suppose that was his reward, that he was able to fling his imagination forward into the future, the vast

unrealized future, and see the blinding, incredible promise
that it holds for us.

Well, that was the beginning, Harry; within the next
twelve months, each one of our children was linked to all the
others telepathically. And in the years that followed, every
child born in our reservation was shown the way into that
linkage by the children. Only we, the adults, were forever
barred from joining it. We were of the old and they were of
the new. Their way was closed to us forever—although they
could go into our minds, and did when they had to. But never
could we feel them there or see them there or go into their
minds or communicate with them as they did with each other.

I don't know how to tell you of the years that followed,
Harry. In our little guarded reservation, man became what
he was always destined to be, but I can explain it only im-
perfectly. I can hardly comprehend, much less explain, what
it means to inhabit forty bodies simultaneously, or what it
means to each of the children to have the other personalities
within him or her, a part of each of them. Can I even speculate
on what it means to live as man and woman, always together,
not only in the flesh, but man and woman within the same
mind?

Could the children explain it to us? Did they explain it to
us? Hardly. For this is a transformation that must take place,
from all we can learn, before puberty; and as it happens, the
children accept it as normal and natural—indeed as the most
natural thing in the world. We were the unnatural ones—
and the one thing they never truly comprehended is how we
could bear to live in our aloneness, how we could bear to live
on the edge of death and extinction and with the knowledge
of death and extinction always pressing against us. Again,
could we explain to a man born blind what color is, gradations
of color, form, light, or the meaning of light and form combined? Hardly, any more than they are able to explain their
togetherness to us who live so singularly and so alone.

As for the children's knowledge of us, we are very happy,
indeed grateful, that it did not come at once. In the beginning,
the children could merge their thoughts only when their
heads were almost touching. This is what saved them from
us, because if, in the very beginning, they had been able to
touch our thoughts, they might not have been able to defend
themselves. Bit by bit, their command of distance grew, but
very slowly; and not until our fifteenth year in the reser-

vation did the children begin to develop the power to reach out and probe with their thoughts anywhere on earth. We thank God for this. By then the children were ready for what they found. Earlier, it might have destroyed them.

I might mention here that the children explained to us in due time that their telepathic powers had nothing to do with brain waves. Telepathy, according to the children, is a function of time, but exactly what that means, I don't know, Harry, and therefore I cannot explain it to you.

I must mention that two of our children met accidental death—one in the ninth year and the second in the eleventh year. But the effect of these two deaths upon the other children cannot be compared to the effects of death in our world. There was a little regret, but no grief, no sense of great loss, no tears or weeping. Death is totally different among them than among us; among them, a loss of flesh and only flesh; the personality itself is immortal and lives consciously in the others.

When we spoke to them about a marked grave, or a tombstone, or some other mark that would enable us to keep alive the memory of the two dead children, they smiled sympathetically and said that we could make such a tomb or tombstone if it would give us any comfort. Their concern was only for us, not in any way for the two bodies that were gone.

Yet later, when Dr. Goldbaum died, their grief was deep and terrible, something so deep, so heartbreaking, that it touched us more than anything in our whole experience here—and this, of course, was because Dr. Goldbaum's death was the old kind of death.

The strangest thing, Harry, is that in spite of all these indications and means of togetherness that I have been telling you about, outwardly our children remain individuals. Each of the children retains his or her own characteristics, mannerisms and personality. The boys and girls make love in a normal, heterosexual manner—though all of them share the experience. Can you comprehend that? I cannot; but then neither can I comprehend any other area of their emotional experience except to realize that for them everything is different. Only the unspoiled devotion of mother for helpless child can approximate the love that binds them together. Yet here, too, in their love everything is different, deeper than anything that we can relate to our own experience. Before their transformation into telepaths took place, the children displayed enough petulance and anger and annoyance; but after it took place, we never again heard a voice raised in anger or annoyance. As they themselves put it, when there was trouble among them, they washed it out. When there was sickness among them, they healed it.

After the ninth year, there was no more sickness. By then they had learned to control their bodies. If sickness approached their bodies—and by that I mean infection, germs, virus, whatsoever you might call it—they could control and concentrate the reaction of their bodies to the infection; and with such conscious control and such conscious ability to change the chemical balance of their bodies, to change their heartbeat if necessary, to influence their blood flow, to increase the circulation in one part of the body, to decrease it in another, to increase or decrease the functioning of various organs in the body—with that kind of control, they were absolutely immune to sickness. However they could go further than that. While they could give us no part of the wholeness which they enjoyed as a normal thing of their lives, they could cure our illnesses. Three or four of them would merge their minds and go into our bodies and cure our bodies. They would go into our minds; they would control the organs of our bodies and the balance of our bodies and cure them; and yet we, the recipients of this cure, were never aware of their presence.

In trying to describe all of this to you, Harry, to make it real and to make incidents come alive, I use certain words and phrases only because I have no other words and phrases, I have no language that fits the life of these children. I use the words I know, but at the same time I realize, and you must realize, that my words do not describe adequately—they do not serve the use I am trying to put them to. Even after all these years of living intimately with the children, day and night, I can comprehend only vaguely the manner of their existence. I know what they are outwardly because I see it, I watch it. They are free and healthy and happy as no men and women ever were before. But what their inner life is remains a closed thing to me.

Again and again we discussed this with various members of our group, that is, among ourselves and also among the children. The children had no reticence about it; they were willing, eager, delighted to discuss it with us, but the discussions were hardly ever fruitful. For example, take the conversation I had with one of the children, whose name is Arlene. She is a tall, lovely child whom we found in an orphanage in Idaho. She came to us as the other children did, in infancy. At the time of our conversation, Arlene was fourteen. So much, you see, had happened in the reservation during the intervening years. We were discussing personality, and I told Arlene that I could not understand how she could live and work as an individual when she was also a part of so many others, and these so many others were a part of her.

She, however, could not see that and she rejected the whole concept.

"But how can you be yourself?" I pressed her.

"I remain myself," she answered simply. "I could not stop being myself."

"But aren't the others also yourself?"

"Yes, of course, what else could they be? And I am also them."

This was put to me as something self-evident. You see, it is no easier for them to understand our concepts than it is for us to understand their concepts. I said to her then:

"But who controls your body?"

"I do, of course."

"But just for the sake of a hypothetical situation, Arlene, suppose we take this possibility—that some of the other children should want to control your body instead of leaving the control to you."

"Why?" she asked me.

"If you did something they didn't approve of," I said lamely, digging the hole I had gotten into still deeper.

"Something they disapproved of?" she asked. "Well, how could I? Can you do something that you yourself disapprove of?"

"I am afraid I can, Arlene, and I do."

"Now that I don't understand at all, Jean. Why do you do it?"

"Well, don't you see, I can't always control what I do."

This was a new notion to her. Even able to read our minds, this was a new notion to her.

"You can't control what you do?" she asked.

"Not always."

"Poor *Jean*," she said, "oh, poor *Jean*. How terrible. What an awful way to have to live."

"But it's not so terrible, Arlene," I argued, "not at all. For us it's perfectly normal."

"But how? How could such things be normal?"

So these discussions always seemed to develop and so they always ended. The communication between us, with all the love that the children had for us and all the love that we had for the children, was so limited. We, the adults, had only words for communication; and words are very limited. But by their tenth year, the children had developed methods of communication as far beyond words as words are beyond the dumb motions of animals. If one of them watched something, there was no necessity to describe what he or she watched to the others. The others could see it through the eyes of the child who was watching. This went on not only in waking but in sleeping as well. They actually dreamed together, participated in the same dreams.

Has it ever occurred to you, Harry, that when something hurts you, you don't have to engage in conversation with yourself to tell yourself that it hurts you? When you have a certain feeling, you don't have to explain the feeling to yourself; you have the feeling. And this was the process of communication that was perfectly natural to the children. They felt as a unit, as a body, and yet they remained individuals.

I could go on for hours attempting to describe something utterly beyond my understanding, but that would not help, would it, Harry? You will have your own problems, and I must try to make you understand what happened, what had to happen, and now what must happen in the future.

You see, Harry, by the tenth year, the children had learned all we knew, all we had among us as material for teaching; our entire pooled experience was now used up. In effect, we were teaching a single mind, a mind composed of the unblocked, unfettered talent and brains of forty superb children. Consider that. A mind forty times as large, as agile, as comprehensive as any mind that man had ever known before—a mind so rational, so pure, that to this mind we could only be objects of loving pity. We have among us, as a pair of group parents, Alex Cromwell and his wife. You will recognize Alex Cromwell's name; he is one of our greatest physicists, and it was he who was largely responsible for the first atom bomb. After that, he came to us as one would go to a monastery. He performed an act of personal expiation in the only manner which could give him any hope, any satisfaction, any surcease from the enormous and terrible guilt that he bore. He and his wife taught our children physics, but by the eighth year, mind you, by the eighth year of their lives, the children were teaching Cromwell. A year later, Cromwell could no longer be taught. He was now incapable of following either their mathematics or their reasoning, and their symbolism, of course, was totally outside of the structure of Cromwell's thoughts. Imagine a mind like Cromwell's, led with concern, with tenderness, with gentleness, with the greatest love and consideration that the children could give him—for he is a charming and lovable person—imagine that such a mind could not advance within the area of knowledge that these nine-year-old children possessed.

It is rather terrifying, isn't it? And when you will show this letter (and of course we want you to show this letter) to the people who command the destiny of the United States, this thing I have just written will also be terrifying to them. I think that one of the saddest aspects of our society is the fear of the child that it engenders in the adult. That is a continuing fact of our society. Each generation, as it matures, fears the coming generation, looks at the coming generation as being conscienceless and depraved. No skill of adults, no talent of adults will engender as much fear as this skill, this talent, this brilliance of our children. Remember that, Harry, and expect it.

Let me give you an example of some of the capabilities, some of the powers our children have developed. In the far outfield of our baseball diamond, there was a boulder of perhaps ten tons. Incidentally, I must remark that our children's athletic skill, their physical prowess, is in its own way almost as extraordinary as their mental powers. They have broken every track and field record, often cutting world records by one third and even by one half. I have watched them effortlessly run down our horses. Their movements and their reactions are so quick as to make us appear sluggards by comparison. If they so desire, they can move their arms and legs faster than our eyes can follow; and, of course, one of the games they love is baseball, and they play in a manner you have never seen on the outside. Now to go back to this situation of the boulder: For some years, we, the adults, had spoken of either blasting the boulder apart or of rolling it out of the way with one of our very heavy bulldozers, but it was something we had simply never gotten to. Then, one day, we discovered that the boulder was gone, and in its place was a pile of thick red dust—a pile that the wind was fast leveling.

We brooded over the matter ourselves for a while, made our usual attempt at interpretation, made our guesses, and at last, frustrated, went to the children and asked them what had happened. They told us that they had reduced the boulder to dust—as if it were no more than kicking a small stone out of one's path and just as if everyone could at will reduce a gigantic boulder to dust. Why not?

Cromwell cornered them on this one and he asked one of the children, Billy:

"But how? After all, Billy, you say you reduced the boulder to dust, but how? That's the point. How?"

"Well, the ordinary way," Billy said.

"You mean there's an ordinary way to reduce a boulder to dust?"

"Well, isn't there?" another child asked.

Billy was more patient. He sensed our difficulty and asked gently whether perhaps Cromwell did not know the ordinary way, but had to do it in some more complex way.

"I suppose I could reduce the boulder to dust," Cromwell said. "I would have to use a great deal of heavy explosive. It would take some time; it would make a lot of noise, and it would be rather expensive."

"But the end would be the same, wouldn't it?" Billy asked.

"I suppose so," Cromwell said, "if you mean dust."

"No, I mean the manner," Billy said, "the technique."

"What technique?" Cromwell asked desperately.

"Well, our technique. I mean to make anything dust you have to unbond it. We do it by loosening the molecular structure—not very quickly, you know, it could be dangerous if you did it too quickly—but we just loosen it slowly, steadily, and we let the thing kick itself to pieces, so to speak. That doesn't mean that it actually kicks itself to pieces. It doesn't explode or anything of that sort; it just powders away. You know, it holds its shape for a while, and then you touch it and it becomes powder—it collapses."

"But how do you do that?" Cromwell insisted.

"Well, the best way of course—directly. I mean with your mind. You understand it, and then you reject it as an understood phenomenon and you let it shake itself loose."

But the more he spoke, the further Billy traveled from

Cromwell's area of comprehension; the more he used words, the less the words were able to convey, and finally, with patient and sympathetic smiles, the children dismissed the whole thing and their attempt to enlighten us as well. This was what usually happened, and this was the manner in which it usually happened.

Of course it was not always that way. They used the tools of our civilization, not because they admired these tools or because they needed mechanical things, but simply because they felt that our anxieties were eased by a certain amount of old-fashioned procedure. In other words, they wanted to preserve some of our world for our own sentimental needs. For example, they built an atomic-fusion power plant, out of which we derived and continued to derive our power. Then they built what they called free-fields into all our trucks and cars so that the trucks and cars could rise and travel through the air with the same facility as on the ground. The children could have built sensible, meaningful platforms that would have done the same thing and would have done it in a functional manner. The cars were much less functional; automobiles and trucks are not built to travel through the air. But the children had the kind of concern for the outer aspect of our world that led them to refrain from disarranging it too much.

At this point the use of thought, the degree to which they are able to use their own thoughts to influence atomic structure, is the most remarkable gift that they have beyond the power of telepathy itself. With the power of their thoughts they can go into atoms, they can control atoms, they can rearrange electrons; they can go into the enormous, almost infinite random patterns of electrons and atoms, and move things so that the random becomes directed and changes take place. In this way they are able to build one element out of another, and the curious thing of it is that all this is so elementary to them that they will do it at times as if they were doing tricks to amuse and amaze us, to save us from boredom, as an adult might do tricks for a child and so entertain the child.

So, dear Harry, I have been able to tell you something of what went on here over the years, a little bit of what the children are, a little bit about what they can do—not as much perhaps, as I would want to tell you. I think I would like to create an hour-by-hour diary for you so that there might be a record on your side of what every day, every week of the last nineteen years has held; for, believe me, every day in the week of almost twenty years was exciting and rewarding.

Now I must tell you what you must know; and you shall tell these things to whoever you wish to tell them to. Use only your own judgment. Nothing in this document, Harry, is a secret. Nothing is for your ears alone. Nothing is to be held back. All of it can be given to the world. As for how much of it should be given to all the world, that must be a decision of the people who control the means of information. But let the decision be theirs, Harry. Do not interfere with it. Do not try to influence it; and above all, do not suppress anything that I am writing here.

In the fifteenth year of the experiment, our entire staff met with the children on a very important occasion. There were fifty-two children then, for all of the children born to us were taken into their body of singleness and flourished in their company. I must add that this was possible despite the initially lower IQ's of most of the children born to our mothers and fathers. Once the group has formed itself telepathically and has merged its powers, there is no necessity for high IQ's among the children who are brought into it. In fact, we are speculating on whether the experiment might not have proceeded almost the same way if we had chosen our first forty children at random. This we will never know.

Now, as to this meeting: It was a very formal and a very serious meeting, perhaps the most serious meeting of our experiment. Thirty days were left before the team of observers was scheduled to enter the reservation, according to the terms of our initial agreement with the Army. We had discussed that situation at great length among ourselves, the adults, and with the children, and of course it had been discussed among the children without us. But now it was discussed formally.

The children had chosen Michael to speak for them, but of course they were all speaking. Michael was simply the voice necessary to communicate with us. Michael, I might say, was born in Italy, a tall, delicate, lovely young man, and a most talented artist. Again I might mention that talent, specific talent, remained the property, the gift of the individual. This could not be communicated through the group to another child. Knowledge, yes, but a creative talent remained entirely the gift of the child who had it originally.

Michael took the floor and began by telling us how much the children loved and cherished us, the adults who were once their teachers.

I interrupted him to say that it was hardly necessary for the children ever to spell that out. We might not be able to communicate telepathically but never once was there anything in their actions to make us doubt their love for us.

"Of course," Michael said, "we understand that; yet, at the same time, certain things must be said. They must be said in your language, and unless they are said they do not really exist as they must exist in relation to you. Believe us, we comprehend fully that all that we have, all that we are, you have given us. You are our fathers and mothers and teachers—and we love you beyond our power to say. We know that you consider us something superior to yourselves, something more than yourselves and beyond yourselves. This may be true, but it is also a fact of life that in each step forward, along with what is gained, something else is lost. There is a taking and a giving, a taking on and a putting aside. For years now, we have wondered and marveled at your patience and self-giving, for we have gone into your minds and we have known what pain and doubt and fear and confusion all of you live with. But there is something else that until now you have not known."

He paused and looked at each of us in turn. Then he looked at me searchingly, wonderingly, and I nodded as if to tell him to go ahead and tell us everything and hold nothing back.

"This then," Michael said. "We have also gone into the minds of the soldiers who guard the reservation. More and more, our power to probe grew and extended itself so that now, in this fifteenth year, there is no mind anywhere on earth we cannot seek out and read. I need not tell you how many thousands of minds we have already sought out and read."

He paused, and I looked at Dr. Goldbaum, who shook his head. Tears rolled down his cheeks and he whispered, "Oh my God, my God, what you must have seen. How could you do it and how could you bear it?"

"You never really knew how much we can bear," Michael

said. "Always we had a child-parent relationship. It was a good relationship. Always you sought to protect us, to interpose your body, your presence, between ourselves and the world. But you didn't have to. It hurts me to say it, but you must know that long, long ago you became the children and we became the parents."

"We know it," I said. "Whether or not we spoke about it in so many words, we know it. We have known it for a long time."

"From our seventh year," Michael continued, "we knew all the details of this experiment. We knew why we were here and we knew what you were attempting—and from then until now, we have pondered over what our future must be. We have also tried to help you, whom we love so much, and perhaps we have been of some help in easing your discontents, in keeping you as physically healthy as possible, in helping you through your troubled, terrible nights and that maze of fear and nightmare and horror that you and all other human beings call sleep. We did what we could, but all our efforts to join you with us, to open your minds to each other and our minds to you, all these efforts have failed. Finally we learned that unless the necessary area of the mind is opened before puberty, the brain tissues change, the brain cells lose the potential of development and the mind is closed forever. Of all the things we face, this saddens us most—for you have given us the most precious heritage of mankind and, in return, we are able to give you nothing."

"That isn't so," I said. "You have given us more than we gave you, so much more."

"Perhaps," Michael nodded. "Or perhaps it helps for you to think that and to say that. You are very good and kind people. You have a kind of tenderness, a kind of gentle love that we can never have, for it grows out of your fear, your guilt, and the horror you live with. We have never been able, nor did we want, to know such fear, such guilt and such horror. It is foreign to us. So while we save ourselves the knowledge of these things, we are also deprived of the kind of love, the kind of self-sacrifice that is almost a matter-of-fact part of your nature. That we must say. But now, our fathers and our mothers, now the fifteen years are over; now this team of observers will be here in thirty days."

I shook my head and said quietly but firmly. "No. They

must be stopped. They must not come here; they cannot come here."

"And all of you?" Michael asked, looking from one to another of us. "Do you all feel the same way? Do you all know what will come after that? Can you imagine what will come after that? Do you know what will happen in Washington? This is what you must think about now."

Some of us were choked with emotion. Cromwell, the physicist, said:

"We are your teachers and your fathers and your mothers, but we can't make this decision. You must tell us what to do. You know what to do. You know that, and you know that you must tell us."

Michael nodded, and then he told us what the children had decided. They had decided that the reservation must be maintained. They needed five more years. They decided that I was to go to Washington with Mark and with Dr. Goldbaum—and somehow we were to get an extension of time. They felt that such an extension would not be too difficult to get at this point. Once we got the extension of time, they would be able to act.

"What kind of action?" Dr. Goldbaum asked them.

"There are too few of us," Michael said. "We need more. We must find new children, new infants, and we must bring them into the reservation. In other words, we must leave the reservation, some of us, and we must bring children here and we must educate the children here."

"But why must they be brought here?" Mark asked. "You can reach them wherever they are. You can go into their minds, you can make them a part of you. The children of the whole world are open to us. Why must you bring them here?"

"That may be true," Michael said, "but the crux of the matter is that the children can't reach us. Not for a long, long time. The children would be alone—and their minds would be shattered if we went into their minds. Tell us, what would the people of your world outside do to such children? What happened to people in the past who were possessed of devils, who heard voices, who heard the sound of angels? Some became saints, but many more were burned at the stake, destroyed, beaten to death, impaled, the victims of every horror that man could devise and inflict upon children."

"Can't you protect the children?" someone asked.

"Someday, yes. Now, no. There are simply not enough of us. First, we must help children to move here, hundreds and hundreds of children. Then we must create other reservations, other places like this one. It cannot be done quickly. It will take a long time. For a child, even our kind of child, to grow into an effective mover, it takes at least fifteen years. It is true that when we are eight, nine, ten years old, we know a great deal, we are able to do a great deal; but we are still children. That has not changed. So you see it will take a long, long time. The world is a very large place and there are a great many children. With all this, we must work carefully, very carefully. You see, people are afraid. Your lives, the lives of mankind, are ruled by fear. This will be the worst fear of all. They will go mad with fear, and all they will be able to think about is how to kill us. That will be their whole intention: to kill us, to destroy us."

"And our children could not fight back," Dr. Goldbaum said quietly. "That is something to remember, to think about; that is very important. You see, fighting, killing, hostility—this is the method of mankind. It has been the method of mankind for so long that we have never questioned it. Can a human being kill? Can a human being fight? We simply take it for granted that this is a human attribute. Take the case, for example, of the Israelis. For two thousand years the Jews had not, as a people, engaged in any kind of war, and it was said that they had lost the will to fight to kill; but you see that with the creation of Israel this will returned. So we say that there is no place on earth where man cannot learn very quickly to become a killer. When the people of India, who were such a people of peace, obtained their freedom from England, they turned upon each other in a fratricide unbelievable, unthinkable, monstrous. But our children are different. Our children cannot kill. This we must understand. No matter what danger faced them, no matter what fate they confronted, they could not kill. They cannot hurt a human being, much less kill one. The very act of hurt is impossible. Cattle, our old dogs and cats, they are one thing—but not people, not people."

(Here Dr. Goldbaum referred to the fact that we no longer slaughtered our cattle in the old way. We had pet dogs and cats, and when they became very old and sick, the children caused them peacefully to go to sleep—a sleep from which they never awakened. Then the children asked us if they might do the same with the cattle we butchered for food. But I must make one point specific, Harry, so that you will understand the children a little better: We butchered the cattle because some of us still required meat, but the children ate no meat. They ate eggs and vegetables, the fruit of the ground, but never meat. This eating of meat, the slaughtering of living things for eating, was a thing they tolerated in us with sadness. Discipline, you know, is also not a part of their being—that is, discipline in the sense that we understand it. They do not ask us not to do things. They will ask us positively to do something; but, on the other hand, if we do what to them is repulsive, no matter how obnoxious it may be to them, they will not ask us to stop doing it.)

"But not people," Dr. Goldbaum went on. "God help us, our children cannot hurt people. We are able to do things that we know are wrong. That remains one power we possess which the children lack. They cannot kill and they cannot hurt. Am I right, Michael, or is this only a presumption on my part?"

"Yes, you are right," Michael said. "We must do our work slowly and patiently, and the world must not know what we are doing until we have taken certain measures. We think we need three years more. We would like to have five years more. But, Jean, if you can get us three years, we will bear with that and somehow manage to do what we must do within that period. Now, will you go with Mark and with Dr. Goldbaum, and will you get us these three years, Jean?"

"Yes, I will get the three years," I said. "Somehow I will do what you need."

"And the rest of you," Michael said, "the rest of you are needed too. We need all of you to help us. Of course we will not keep any of you here if you wish to go. But, oh, we need you so desperately—as we have always needed you—and we love you and we cherish you, and we beg you to remain with us."

Do you wonder that we all remained, Harry, that no one of us could leave our children or will ever leave them now except when death takes us away? You see, Harry, they needed the time and they got the time, and that is why I can write this and that is why I can tell you so forthrightly what happened.

Mark and I and Dr. Goldbaum pleaded our case and we

pleaded it well. We were given the years we needed, the additional years; and as for this gray barrier that surrounds us and the reservation, the children tell me that it is a simple device indeed. Of course that doesn't mean a great deal. They have a whole succession of devices that they call simple which are totally beyond the comprehension of any ordinary human being. But to come back to this barrier; as nearly as I can understand, they have altered the time sequence of the entire reservation; not by much—by less than one ten-thousandth of a second. But the result is that your world outside exists this tiny fraction of a second in the future. The same sun shines on us, the same winds blow, and from inside the barrier, we see your world unaltered. But you cannot see us. When you look at us, the present of our existence, the moment of time which we are conscious of at that moment of being in the universe, that moment has not yet come into existence; and instead of that, instead of reality, there is nothing: no space, no heat, no light, only the impenetrable wall of non-existence. Of course you will read this, Harry, and you will say it makes absolutely no sense whatever, and I cannot pretend that I am able to make any sense out of it. I asked the children how to describe it. They told me as best they could, considering that they had to use the same words I use. They ask me to think of an existing area of time, of us traveling along this existing area with a point of consciousness to mark our progress. They have altered this point. And that means absolutely nothing to someone like myself.

I can only add this—from inside the reservation we are able to go outside, to go from the past into the future. After all, the crossover is only one ten-thousandth of a second. I myself have done this during the moments when we were experimenting with the barrier. I felt a shudder, a moment of intense nausea, but no more than that. There is also a way in which we return, but, understandably, I cannot spell that out.

So there is the situation, Harry. We will never see each other again, but I assure you that Mark and I are happier than we have ever been. Man will change; nothing in the world can halt the change. It has already begun. And in that change, man will become what he was intended to be, and he will reach out with love and knowledge and tenderness to all the universes of the firmament. I have written that down, Harry, and as I look upon it I find it the most thrilling idea I have ever encountered. My skin prickles at the mere thought. Harry, isn't this what man has always dreamed of? No war, no hatred, no hunger or sickness or death? How fortunate we are to be alive while this is happening! I think that we should ask no more.

So now I say goodbye to you, my dear brother, and I finish this letter.

With all my love,
Your sister,
Jean Arbalaid.

Felton finished reading, and then there was a long, long silence while the two men looked at each other. Finally the Secretary of Defense spoke, saying:

"You know, Felton, that we shall have to keep knocking at that barrier. We can't stop. We have to keep on trying to find the way to break through."

"I know."

"It will be easier, now that your sister has explained it."

"I don't think it will be easier," Felton said tiredly. "I don't think that she has explained it."

"Not to you and me, perhaps. But we'll put the eggheads to work on it. They'll figure it out. They always do, you know."

"Perhaps not this time."

"Oh, yes," the Secretary of Defense nodded. "After all, Felton, we've got to stop it. We've had threats before, but not this kind of thing. I'm not going to dwell on the fact of this immorality, this godlessness, this nakedness, this depraved kind of sexual togetherness, this interloping into minds, this violation of every human privacy and every human decency. I don't have to dwell on that. You realize as well as I do, Felton, that this is a threat to every human being on the face of the earth. The kids were right. Oh, they understood this well enough, you know. This isn't a national threat; this isn't like Communism; this isn't simply a threat to the sovereignty, to the freedom of the United States, to the American way of life; this isn't just a threat to democracy; this is a threat to God Himself. This is a threat to mankind. This is a threat to everything decent, everything sacred, everything we believe in, everything we cherish. It's a disease, Felton. You know that, don't you? You recognize that—a disease."

"You really feel that, don't you?" Felton said. "You really believe what you are telling me."

"Believe it? Who can disbelieve it, Felton? It's a disease, and the only way to stop a disease is to kill the bugs that cause it. You know how you stop this disease? I'm going to say it and a lot more are going to say it, Felton: You kill the kids. It's the only way. I wish there were another way, but there isn't."

DIARIES

Daniel Keyes (1927–) is one of those authors who will always be remembered for one story, for "Flowers for Algernon" is one of the most famous works in the history of science fiction. Immediately recognized as a classic when it appeared in the April 1959 issue of The Magazine of Fantasy and Science Fiction, *it was expanded into a novel in 1966 and filmed as* Charly *in 1968. It also won the Hugo Award for short fiction in 1960.*

For the record, we would also like to bring your attention to two other fine stories by Daniel Keyes, "Crazy Maro" and "The Quality of Mercy" (both 1960).

FLOWERS FOR ALGERNON

By Daniel Keyes

progris riport 1—martch 5 1965

Dr. Strauss says I shud rite down what I think and evrey thing that happins to me from now on. I dont know why but he says its importint so they will see if they will use me. I hope they use me. Miss Kinnian says maybe they can make me smart. I want to be smart. My name is Charlie Gordon. I am 37 years old and 2 weeks ago was my brithday. I have nuthing more to rite now so I will close for today.

progris riport 2—martch 6

I had a test today. I think I faled it. and I think that maybe now they wont use me. What happind is a nice young man was in the room and he had some white cards with ink spillled all over them. He sed Charlie what do you see on this card.

I was very skared even tho I had my rabits foot in my pockit because when I was a kid I always faled tests in school and I spillled ink to.

I told him I saw a inkblot. He said yes and it made me feel good. I thot that was all but when I got up to go he stopped me. He said now sit down Charlie we are not thru yet. Then I dont remember so good but he wantid me to say what was in the ink. I dint see nuthing in the ink but he said there was picturs there other pepul saw some picturs. I coudnt see any picturs. I reely tryed to see. I held the card close up and then far away. Then I said if I had my glases I coud see better I usally only ware my glases in the movies or TV but I said they are in the closit in the hall. I got them. Then I said let me see that card agen I bet Ill find it now.

I tryed hard but I still coudnt find the picturs I only saw the ink. I told him maybe I need new glases. He rote somthing down on a paper and I got skared of faling the test. I told him it was a very nice inkblot with littel points all around the eges. He looked very sad so that wasnt it. I said please let me try agen. Ill get it in a few minits becaus Im not so fast somtimes. Im a slow reeder too in Miss Kinnians class for slow adults but I'm trying very hard.

He gave me a chance with another card that had 2 kinds of ink spillled on it red and blue.

He was very nice and talked slow like Miss Kinnian does and he explained it to me that it was a *raw shok*. He said pepul see things in the ink. I said show me where. He said think. I told him I think a inkblot but that wasnt rite eather. He said what does it remind you—pretend something. I closd my eyes for a long time to pretend. I told him I pretned a fowntan pen with ink leeking all over a table cloth. Then he got up and went out.

I dont think I passd the *raw shok* test.

                    progris report 3—martch 7

Dr Strauss and Dr Nemur say it dont matter about the inkblots. I told them I dint spill the ink on the cards and I couldn't see anything in the ink. They said that maybe they will still use me. I said Miss Kinnian never gave me tests like that one only spellin and reading. They said Miss Kinnian told that I was her bestist pupil in the adult nite scool becaus I tryed the hardist and I reely wantid to lern. They said how come you went to the adult nite scool all by yourself Charlie. How did you find it. I said I askd pepul and sumbody told me where I shud go to lern to read and spell good. They said why did you want to. I told them becaus all my life I wantid to be smart and not dumb. But its very hard to be smart. They said you know it will probly be tempirery. I said yes. Miss Kinnian told me. I dont care if it herts.

Later I had more crazy tests today. The nice lady who gave it me told me the name and I asked her how do you spellit so I can rite it in my progris riport. THEMATIC APPERCEPTION TEST. I dont know the frist 2 words but I know what *test* means. You got to pass it or you get bad marks. This test lookd easy becaus I coud see the picturs. Only this time she dint want me to tell her the picturs. That mixd me up. I said the man yesterday said I shoud tell him what I saw in the ink she said that dont make no difrence. She said make up storys about the pepul in the picturs.

I told her how can you tell storys about pepul you never met. I said why shud I make up lies. I never tell lies any more becaus I always get caut.

She told me this test and the other one the raw-shok was for getting personalty. I laffed so hard. I said how can you get that thing from inkblots and fotos. She got sore and put her picturs away. I dont care. It was sily. I gess I faled that test too.

Later some men in white coats took me to a difernt part of the hospitil and gave me a game to play. It was like a race with a white mouse. They called the mouse Algernon. Algernon was in a box with a lot of twists and turns like all kinds of walls and they gave me a pencil and a paper with lines and lots of boxes. On one side it said START and on the other end it said FINISH. They said it was *amazed* and that Algernon and me had the same *amazed* to do. I dint see how we could have the same *amazed* if Algernon had a box and I had a paper but I dint say nothing. Anyway there wasnt time because the race started.

One of the men had a watch he was trying to hide so I wouldnt see it so I tryed not to look and that made me nervus.

Anyway that test made me feel worser than all the others because they did it over 10 times with difernt *amazeds* and Algernon won every time. I dint know that mice were so

smart. Maybe thats because Algernon is a white mouse.
Maybe white mice are smarter then other mice.

progris riport 4—Mar 8

Their going to use me! Im so exited I can hardly write.
Dr Nemur and Dr Strauss had a argament about it first. Dr
Nemur was in the office when Dr Strauss brot me in. Dr
Nemur was worryed about using me but Dr Strauss told him
Miss Kinnian rekemmended me the best from all the people
who she was teaching. I like Miss Kinnian becaus shes a very
smart teacher. And she said Charlie your going to have a
second chance. If you volenteer for this experament you mite
get smart. They dont know if it will be perminint but theirs
a chance. Thats why I said ok even when I was scared because
she said it was an operashun. She said dont be scared Charlie
you done so much with so little I think you deserv it most of
all.

So I got scaird when Dr Nemur and Dr Strauss argud
about it. Dr Strauss said I had something that was very good.
He said I had a good *motor-vation*. I never even knew I had
that. I felt proud when he said that not every body with an
eye-q of 68 had that thing. I dont know what it is or where
I got it but he said Algernon had it too. Algernons *motor-
vation* is the cheese they put in his box. But it cant be that
because I didnt eat any cheese this week.

Then he told Dr Nemur something I dint understand so
while they were talking I wrote down some of the words.

He said Dr Nemur I know Charlie is not what you had in
mind as the first of your new brede of intelek** (coudnt get
the word) superman. But most people of his low ment** are
host** and uncoop** they are usualy dull apath** and hard
to reach. He has a good natcher hes intristed and eager to
please.

Dr Nemur said remember he will be the first human beeng
ever to have his intelijence trippled by surgicle meens.

Dr. Strauss said exakly. Look at how well hes lerned to
read and write for his low mentel age its as grate an acheve**
as you and I lerning einstines therey of **vity without help.
That shows the intenss motor-vation. Its comparat** a tre-
men** achev** I say we use Charlie.

I dint get all the words and they were talking to fast but

it sounded like Dr Strauss was on my side and like the other one wasnt.

Then Dr Nemur nodded he said all right maybe your right. We will use Charlie. When he said that I got so exited I jumped up and shook his hand for being so good to me. I told him thank you doc you wont be sorry for giving me a second chance. And I mean it like I told him. After the operashun Im gonna try to be smart. Im gonna try awful hard.

progris ript 5—Mar 10

Im skared. Lots of people who work here and the nurses and the people who gave me the tests came to bring me candy and wish me luck. I hope I have luck. I got my rabits foot and my lucky penny and my horse shoe. Only a black cat crossed me when I was comming to the hospitil. Dr Strauss says dont be supersitis Charlie this is sience. Anyway Im keeping my rabits foot with me.

I asked Dr Strauss if Ill beat Algernon in the race after the operashun and he said maybe. If the operashun works Ill show that mouse I can be as smart as he is. Maybe smarter. Then Ill be abel to read better and spell the words good and know lots of things and be like other people. I want to be smart like other people. If it works perminint they will make everybody smart all over the wurld.

They dint give me anything to eat this morning. I dont know what that eating has to do with getting smart. Im very hungry and Dr Nemur took away my box of candy. That Dr Nemur is a grouch. Dr Strauss says I can have it back after the operashun. You cant eat befor a operashun...

Progress Report 6—Mar 15

The operashun dint hurt. He did it while I was sleeping. They took off the bandijis from my eyes and my head today so I can make a PROGRESS REPORT. Dr. Nemur who looked at some of my other ones says I spell PROGRESS wrong and he told me how to spell it and REPORT too. I got to try and remember that.

I have a very bad memory for spelling. Dr Strauss says its ok to tell about all the things that happin to me but he says I shoud tell more about what I feel and what I think.

When I told him I dont know how to think he said try. All
the time when the bandijis were on my eyes I tryed to think.
Nothing happened. I dont know what to think about. Maybe
if I ask him he will tell me how I can think now that Im
suppose to get smart. What do smart people think about.
Fancy things I suppose. I wish I knew some fancy things
alredy.

Progress Report 7—Mar 19

Nothing is happening. I had lots of tests and different
kinds of races with Algernon. I hate that mouse. He always
beats me. Dr Strauss said I got to play those games. And he
said some time I got to take those tests over again. Thse
inkblots are stupid. And those pictures are stupid too. I like
to draw a picture of a man and a woman but I wont make
up lies about people.

I got a headache from trying to think so much. I thot Dr
Strauss was my frend but he dont help me. He dont tell me
what to think or when Ill get smart. Miss Kinnian dint come
to see me. I think writing these progress reports are stupid
too.

Progress Report 8—Mar 23

Im going back to work at the factery. They said it was
better I shud go back to work but I cant tell anyone what the
operashun was for and I have to come to the hospitil for an
hour evry night after work. They are gonna pay me mony
every month for lerning to be smart.

Im glad Im going back to work because I miss my job and
all my frends and all the fun we have there.

Dr Strauss says I shud keep writing things down but I
dont have to do it every day just when I think of something
or something speshul happins. He says dont get discoridged
because it takes time and it happins slow. He says it took a
long time with Algernon before he got 3 times smarter then
he was before. Thats why Algernon beats me all the time
because he had that operashun too. That makes me feel better. I coud probly do that *amazed* faster than a reglar mouse.
Maybe some day Ill beat Algernon. Boy that would be something. So far Algernon looks like he mite be smart perminent.

Mar 25 (I dont have to write PROGRESS REPORT on top any more just when I hand it in once a week for Dr Nemur to read. I just have to put the date on. That saves time)

We had a lot of fun at the factery today. Joe Carp said hey look where Charlie had his operashun what did they do Charlie put some brains in. I was going to tell him but I remembered Dr Strauss said no. Then Frank Reilly said what did you do Charlie forget your key and open your door the hard way. That made me laff. Their really my friends and they like me.

Sometimes somebody will say hey look at Joe or Frank or George he really pulled a Charlie Gordon. I don't know why they say that but they always laff. This morning Amos Borg who is the 4 man at Donnegans used my name when he shouted at Ernie the office boy. Ernie lost a packige. He said Ernie for godsake what are you trying to be a Charlie Gordon. I dont understand why he said that. I never lost any packiges.

Mar 28 Dr Strauss came to my room tonight to see why I dint come in like I was suppose to. I told him I dont like to race with Algernon any more. He said I dont have to for a while but I shud come in. He had a present for me only it wasnt a present but just for lend. I thot it was a little television but it wasnt. He said I got to turn it on when I go to sleep. I said your kidding why shud I turn it on when Im going to sleep. Who ever herd of a thing like that. But he said if I want to get smart I got to do what he says. I told him I dint think I was going to get smart and he put his hand on my sholder and said Charlie you dont know it yet but your getting smarter all the time. You wont notice for a while. I think he was just being nice to make me feel good because I dont look any smarter.

Oh yes I almost forgot. I asked him when I can go back to the class at Miss Kinnians school. He said I wont go their. He said that soon Miss Kinnian will come to the hospitil to start and teach me speshul. I was mad at her for not comming to see me when I got the operashun but I like her so maybe we will be frends again.

Mar 29 That crazy TV kept me up all night. How can I sleep with something yelling crazy things all night in my ears.

And the nutty pictures. Wow. I dont know what it says when Im up so how am I going to know when Im sleeping.

Dr Strauss says its ok. He says my brains are lerning when I sleep and that will help me when Miss Kinnian starts my lessons in the hospitil (only I found out it isnt a hospitil its a labatory). I think its all crazy. If you can get smart when your sleeping why do people go to school. That thing I dont think will work. I use to watch the late show and the late late show on TV all the time and it never made me smart. Maybe you have to sleep while you watch it.

PROGRESS REPORT 9—April 3

Dr Strauss showed me how to keep the TV turned low so now I can sleep. I dont hear a thing. And I still dont understand what it says. A few times I play it over in the morning to find out what I lerned when I was sleeping and I dont think so. Miss Kinnian says Maybe its another langwidge or something. But most times it sounds american. It talks so fast faster than even Miss Gold who was my teacher in 6 grade and I remember she talked so fast I coudnt understand her.

I told Dr Strauss what good is it to get smart in my sleep. I want to be smart when Im awake. He says its the same thing and I have two minds. Theres the *subconscious* and the *conscious* (thats how you spell it). And one dont tell the other one what its doing. They don't even talk to each other. Thats why I dream. And boy have I been having crazy dreams. Wow. Ever since that night TV. The late late late late late show.

I forgot to ask him if it was only me or if everybody had those two minds.

(I just looked up the word in the dictionary Dr Strauss gave me. The word is *subconscious. adj. Of the nature of mental operations yet not present in consciousness; as, subconscious conflict of desires.*) Theres more but I still dont know what it means. This isnt a very good dictionary for dumb people like me.

Anyway the headache is from the party. My frends from the factery Joe Carp and Frank Reilly invited me to go with them to Muggsys Saloon for some drinks. I dont like to drink but they said we will have lots of fun. I had a good time.

Joe Carp said I shoud show the girls how I mop out the toilet in the factory and he got me a mop. I showed them and everyone laffed when I told that Mr Donnegan said I was the best janiter he ever had because I like my job and do it good and never come late or miss a day except for my operashun.

I said Miss Kinnian always said Charlie be proud of your job because you do it good.

Everybody laffed and we had a good time and they gave me lots of drinks and Joe said Charlie is a card when hes potted. I dont know what that means but everybody likes me and we have fun. I cant wait to be smart like my best frends Joe Carp and Frank Reilly.

I dont remember how the party was over but I think I went out to buy a newspaper and coffe for Joe and Frank and when I came back there was no one their. I looked for them all over till late. Then I dont remember so good but I think I got sleepy or sick. A nice cop brot me back home. Thats what my landlady Mrs Flynn says.

But I got a headache and a big lump on my head and black and blue all over. I think maybe I fell but Joe Carp says it was the cop they beat up drunks some times. I don't think so. Miss Kinnian says cops are to help people. Anyway I got a bad headache and Im sick and hurt all over. I dont think Ill drink anymore.

April 6 I beat Algernon! I dint even know I beat him until Burt the tester told me. Then the second time I lost because I got so exited I fell off the chair before I finished. But after that I beat him 8 more times. I must be getting smart to beat a smart mouse like Algernon. But I dont *feel* smarter.

I wanted to race Algernon some more but Burt said thats enough for one day. They let me hold him for a minit. Hes not so bad. Hes soft like a ball of cotton. He blinks and when he opens his eyes their black and pink on the eges.

I said can I feed him because I felt bad to beat him and I wanted to be nice and make frends. Burt said no Algernon is a very specshul mouse with an operashun like mine, and he was the first of all the animals to stay smart so long. He told me Algernon is so smart that every day he has to solve a test to get his food. Its a thing like a lock on a door that changes every time Algernon goes in to eat so he has to lern

something new to get his food. That made me sad because
if he couldnt lern he would be hungry.

I dont think its right to make you pass a test to eat. How
would Dr Nemur like it to have to pass a test every time he
wants to eat. I think Ill be frends with Algernon.

April 9 Tonight after work Miss Kinnian was at the laboratory. She looked like she was glad to see me but scared. I
told her dont worry Miss Kinnian Im not smart yet and she
laffed. She said I have confidence in you Charlie the way you
struggled so hard to read and right better than all the others.
At werst you will have it for a littel wile and your doing
somthing for sience.

We are reading a very hard book. I never read such a hard
book before. Its called *Robinson Crusoe* about a man who
gets merooned on a dessert Iland. Hes smart and figers out
all kinds of things so he can have a house and food and hes
a good swimmer. Only I feel sorry because hes all alone and
has no frends. But I think their must be somebody else on
the iland because theres a picture with his funny umbrella
looking at footprints. I hope he gets a frend and not be lonely.

April 10 Miss Kinnian teaches me to spell better. She says
look at a word and close your eyes and say it over and over
until you remember. I have lots of truble with *through* that
you say *threw* and *enough* and *tough* that you dont say *enew*
and *tew*. You got to say *enuff* and *tuff*. Thats how I use to
write it before I started to get smart. Im confused but Miss
Kinnian says theres no reason in spelling.

Apr 14 Finished *Robinson Crusoe*. I want to find out more
about what happens to him but Miss Kinnian says thats all
there is. *Why*

Apr 15 Miss Kinnian says Im lerning fast. She read some of
the Progress Reports and she looked at me kind of funny.
She says Im a fine person and Ill show them all. I asked her
why. She said never mind but I shoudnt feel bad if I find out
that everybody isnt nice like I think. She said for a person
who god gave so little to you done more then a lot of people
with brains they never even used. I said all my frends are
smart people but there good. They like me and they never

did anything that wasnt nice. Then she got something in her eye and she had to run out to the ladys room.

Apr. 16 Today, I lerned, the *comma*, this is a comma (,) a period, with a tail, Miss Kinnian, says its importent, because, it makes writing better, she said, sombeody, coud lose, a lot of money, if a comma, isnt, in the, right place, I dont have, any money, and I dont see, how a comma, keeps you from losing it.

But she says, everybody, uses commas, so Ill use, them too,

Apr 17 I used the comma wrong. Its punctuation. Miss Kinnian told me to look up long words in the dictionary to lern to spell them. I said whats the difference if you can read it anyway. She said its part of your education so now on I'll look up all the words Im not sure how to spell. It takes a long time to write that way but I think Im remembering. I only have to look up once and after that I get it right. Anyway thats how come I got the word *punctuation* right. (Its that way in the dictionary). Miss Kinnian says a period is punctuation too, and there are lots of other marks to lern. I told her I thot all the periods had to have tails but she said no.

You got to mix them up, she showed? me" how. to mix! them(up,. and now; I can! mix up all kinds" of punctuation, in! my writing? There, are lots! of rules? to lern; but I'm gettin'g them in my head.

One thing I? like about, Dear Miss Kinnian: (thats the way it goes in a business letter if I ever go into business) is she, always gives me' a reason" when—I ask. She's a gen'ius! I wish! I cou'd be smart' like, her;

(Punctuation, is; fun!)

Apr 18 What a dope I am! I didn't even understand what she was talking about. I read the grammar book last night and it explanes the whole thing. Then I saw it was the same way as Miss Kinnian was trying to tell me, but I didn't get it. I got up in the middle of the night, and the whole thing straightened out in my mind.

Miss Kinnian said that the TV working in my sleep helped out. She said I reached a plateau. Thats like the flat top of a hill.

After I figgered out how punctuation worked, I read over all my old Progress Reports from the beginning. Boy, did I have crazy spelling and punctuation! I told Miss Kinnian I ought to go over the pages and fix all the mistakes but she said, "No, Charlie, Dr. Nemur wants them just as they are. That's why he let you keep them after they were photostated, to see your own progress. You're coming along fast, Charlie."

That made me feel good. After the lesson I went down and played with Algernon. We don't race any more.

April 20 I feel sick inside. Not sick like for a doctor, but inside my chest it feels empty like getting punched and a heartburn at the same time.

I wasn't going to write about it, but I guess I got to, because it's important. Today was the first time I ever stayed home from work.

Last night Joe Carp and Frank Reilly invited me to a party. There were lots of girls and some men from the factory. I remembered how sick I got last time I drank too much, so I told Joe I didn't want anything to drink. He gave me a plain Coke instead. It tasted funny, but I thought it was just a bad taste in my mouth.

We had a lot of fun for a while. Joe said I should dance with Ellen and she would teach me the steps. I fell a few times and I couldn't understand why because no one else was dancing besides Ellen and me. And all the time I was tripping because somebody's foot was always sticking out.

Then when I got up I saw the look on Joe's face and it gave me a funny feeling in my stomack. "He's a scream," one of the girls said. Everybody was laughing.

Frank said, "I ain't laughed so much since we sent him off for the newspaper that night at Muggsy's and ditched him."

"Look at him. His face is red."

"He's blushing. Charlie is blushing."

"Hey, Ellen, what'd you do to Charlie? I never saw him act like that before."

I didn't know what to do or where to turn. Everyone was looking at me and laughing and I felt naked. I wanted to hide myself. I ran out into the street and I threw up. Then I walked home. It's a funny thing I never knew that Joe and Frank and the others liked to have me around all the time to make fun of me.

Now I know what it means when they say "to pull a Charlie Gordon."

I'm ashamed.

PROGRESS REPORT 11

April 21 Still didn't go into the factory. I told Mrs. Flynn my landlady to call and tell Mr. Donnegan I was sick. Mrs. Flynn looks at me very funny lately like she's scared of me.

I think it's a good thing about finding out how everybody laughs at me. I thought about it a lot. It's because I'm so dumb and I don't even know when I'm doing something dumb. People think it's funny when a dumb person can't do things the same way they can.

Anyway, now I know I'm getting smarter every day. I know punctuation and I can spell good. I like to look up all the hard words in the dictionary and I remember them. I'm reading a lot now, and Miss Kinnian says I read very fast. Sometimes I even understand what I'm reading about, and it stays in my mind. There are times when I can close my eyes and think of a page and it all comes back like a picture.

Besides history, geography, and arithmetic, Miss Kinnian said I should start to learn a few foreign languages. Dr. Strauss gave me some more tapes to play while I sleep. I still don't understand how that conscious and unconscious mind works, but Dr. Strauss says not to worry yet. He asked me to promise that when I start learning college subjects next week I wouldn't read any books on psychology—that is, until he gives me permission.

I feel a lot better today, but I guess I'm still a little angry that all the time people were laughing and making fun of me because I wasn't so smart. When I become intelligent like Dr. Strauss says, with three times my I.Q. of 68, then maybe I'll be like everyone else and people will like me and be friendly.

I'm not sure what an I.Q. is. Dr. Nemur said it was something that measured how intelligent you were—like a scale in the drug-store weighs pounds. But Dr. Strauss had a big argument with him and said an I.Q. didn't weigh intelligence at all. He said an I.Q. showed how much intelligence you could get, like the numbers on the outside of a measuring cup. You still had to fill the cup up with stuff.

Then when I asked Burt, who gives me my intelligence

tests and works with Algernon, he said that both of them were wrong (only I had to promise not to tell them he said so).

Burt says that the I.Q. measures a lot of different things including some of the things you learned already, and it really isn't any good at all.

So I still don't know what I.Q. is except that mine is going to be over 200 soon. I didn't want to say anything, but I don't see how if they don't know *what* it is, or *where* it is—I don't see how they know *how much* of it you've got.

Dr. Nemur says I have to take a *Rorshach Test* tomorrow. I wonder what *that* is.

April 22 I found out what a *Rorshach* is. It's the test I took before the operation—the one with the inkblots on the pieces of cardboard. The man who gave me the test was the same one.

I was scared to death of those inkblots. I knew he was going to ask me to find the pictures and I knew I wouldn't be able to. I was thinking to myself, if only there was some way of knowing what kind of pictures were hidden there. Maybe there weren't any pictures at all. Maybe it was just a trick to see if I was dumb enough to look for something that wasn't there. Just thinking about that made me sore at him.

"All right, Charlie," he said, "you've seen these cards before, remember?"

"Of course I remember."

The way I said it, he knew I was angry, and he looked surprised. "Yes, of course. Now I want you to look at this one. What might this be? What do you see on this card? People see all sorts of things in these inkblots. Tell me what it might be for you—what it makes you think of."

I was shocked. That wasn't what I had expected him to say at all. "You mean there are no pictures hidden in those inkblots?"

He frowned and took off his glasses. "What?"

"Pictures. Hidden in the inkblots. Last time you told me that everyone could see them and you wanted me to find them too."

He explained to me that the last time he had used almost the exact words he was using now. I didn't believe it, and I still have the suspicion that he misled me at the time just for the fun of it. Unless—I don't know any more—could I have been *that* feebleminded?

We went through the cards slowly. One of them looked like a pair of bats tugging at something. Another one looked like two men fencing with swords. I imagined all sorts of things. I guess I got carried away. But I didn't trust him any more, and I kept turning them around and even looking on the back to see if there was anything there I was supposed to catch. While he was making his notes, I peeked out of the corner of my eye to read it. But it was all in code that looked like this:

$$WF + A \ DdF\text{-}Ad \ orig. \ WF\text{-}A \ SF + obj$$

The test still doesn't make sense to me. It seems to me that anyone could make up lies about things that they didn't really see. How could he know I wasn't making a fool of him by mentioning things that I didn't really imagine? Maybe I'll understand it when Dr. Strauss lets me read up on psychology.

April 25 I figured out a new way to line up the machines in the factory, and Mr. Donnegan says it will save him ten thousand dollars a year in labor and increased production. He gave me a twenty-five-dollar bonus.

I wanted to take Joe Carp and Frank Reilly out to lunch to celebrate, but Joe said he had to buy some things for his wife, and Frank said he was meeting his cousin for lunch. I guess it'll take a little time for them to get used to the changes in me. Everybody seems to be frightened of me. When I went over to Amos Borg and tapped him on the shoulder, he jumped up in the air.

People don't talk to me much any more or kid around the way they used to. It makes the job kind of lonely.

April 27 I got up the nerve today to ask Miss Kinnian to have dinner with me tomorrow night to celebrate my bonus.

At first she wasn't sure it was right, but I asked Dr. Strauss and he said it was okay. Dr. Strauss and Dr. Nemur don't seem to be getting along so well. They're arguing all the time. This evening when I came in to ask Dr. Strauss about having dinner with Miss Kinnian, I heard them shouting. Dr. Nemur was saying that it was *his* experiment and *his* research, and Dr. Strauss was shouting back that he contributed just as much, because he found me through Miss Kinnian and he performed the operation. Dr. Strauss said that someday thousands of neurosurgeons might be using his technique all over the world.

Dr. Nemur wanted to publish the results of the experiment at the end of this month. Dr. Strauss wanted to wait a while longer to be sure. Dr. Strauss said that Dr. Nemur was more interested in the Chair of Psychology at Princeton than he was in the experiment. Dr. Nemur said that Dr. Strauss was nothing but an opportunist who was trying to ride to glory on *his* coattails.

When I left afterwards, I found myself trembling. I don't know why for sure, but it was as if I'd seen both men clearly for the first time. I remember hearing Burt say that Dr. Nemur had a shrew of a wife who was pushing him all the time to get things published so that he could become famous. Burt said that the dream of her life was to have a big-shot husband.

Was Dr. Strauss really trying to ride on his coattails?

April 28 I don't understand why I never noticed how beautiful Miss Kinnian really is. She has brown eyes and feathery brown hair that comes to the top of her neck. She's only thirty-four! I think from the beginning I had the feeling that she was an unreachable genius—and very, very old. Now, every time I see her she grows younger and more lovely.

We had dinner and a long talk. When she said that I was coming along so fast that soon I'd be leaving her behind, I laughed.

"It's true, Charlie. You're already a better reader than I am. You can read a whole page at a glance while I can take in only a few lines at a time. And you remember every single thing you read. I'm lucky if I can recall the main thoughts and the general meaning."

"I don't feel intelligent. There are so many things I don't understand."

She took out a cigarette and I lit it for her. "You've got to be a *little* patient. You're accomplishing in days and weeks what it takes normal people to do in half a lifetime. That's what makes it so amazing. You're like a giant sponge now, soaking things in. Facts, figures, general knowledge. And soon you'll begin to connect them, too. You'll see how the different branches of learning are related. There are many levels, Charlie, like steps on a giant ladder that take you up higher and higher to see more and more of the world around you.

"I can see only a little bit of that, Charlie, and I won't go much higher than I am now, but you'll keep climbing up and up, and see more and more, and each step will open new worlds that you never even knew existed." She frowned. "I hope...I just hope to God—"

"What?"

"Never mind, Charles. I just hope I wasn't wrong to advise you to go into this thing in the first place."

I laughed. "How could that be? It worked, didn't it? Even Algernon is still smart."

We sat there silently for a while and I knew what she was thinking about as she watched me toying with the chain of my rabbit's foot and my keys. I didn't want to think of that possibility any more than elderly people want to think of death. I *knew* that this was only the beginning. I knew what she meant about levels because I'd seen some of them already. The thought of leaving her behind made me sad.

I'm in love with Miss Kinnian.

PROGRESS REPORT 12

April 30 I've quit my job with Donnegan's Plastic Box Company. Mr. Donnegan insisted that it would be better for all concerned if I left. What did I do to make them hate me so?

The first I knew of it was when Mr. Donnegan showed me the petition. Eight hundred and forty names, everyone connected with the factory, except Fanny Girden. Scanning the list quickly, I saw at once that hers was the only missing name. All the rest demanded that I be fired.

Joe Carp and Frank Reilly wouldn't talk to me about it. No one else would either, except Fanny. She was one of the few people I'd known who set her mind to something and believed it no matter what the rest of the world proved, said, or did—and Fanny did not believe that I should have been fired. She had been against the petition on principle and despite the pressure and threats she'd held out.

"Which don't mean to say," she remarked, "that I don't think there's something mighty strange about you, Charlie.

Them changes. I don't know. You used to be a good, dependable, ordinary man—not too bright maybe, but honest. Who knows what you done to yourself to get so smart all of a sudden. Like everybody around here's been saying, Charlie, it's not right."

"But how can you say that, Fanny? What's wrong with a man becoming intelligent and wanting to acquire knowledge and understanding of the world around him?"

She stared down at her work and I turned to leave. Without looking at me, she said: "It was evil when Eve listened to the snake and ate from the tree of knowledge. It was evil when she saw that she was naked. If not for that none of us would ever have to grow old and sick, and die."

Once again now I have the feeling of shame burning inside me. This intelligence has driven a wedge between me and all the people I once knew and loved. Before, they laughed at me and despised me for my ignorance and dullness; now, they hate me for my knowledge and understanding. What in God's name do they want of me?

They've driven me out of the factory. Now I'm more alone than ever before...

May 15 Dr. Strauss is very angry at me for not having written any progress reports in two weeks. He's justified because the lab is now paying me a regular salary. I told him I was too busy thinking and reading. When I pointed out that writing was such a slow process that it made me impatient with my poor handwriting, he suggested that I learn to type. It's much easier to write now because I can type nearly seventy-five words a minute. Dr. Strauss continually reminds me of the need to speak and write simply so that people will be able to understand me.

I'll try to review all the things that happened to me during the last two weeks. Algernon and I were presented to the American Psychological Association sitting in convention with the World Psychological Association last Tuesday. We created quite a sensation. Dr. Nemur and Dr. Strauss were proud of us.

I suspect that Dr. Nemur, who is sixty—ten years older than Dr. Strauss—finds it necessary to see tangible results of his work. Undoubtedly the result of pressure by Mrs. Nemur.

Contrary to my earlier impressions of him, I realize that Dr. Nemur is not at all a genius. He has a very good mind, but it struggles under the specter of self-doubt. He wants people to take him for a genius. Therefore, it is important for him to feel that his work is accepted by the world. I believe that Dr. Nemur was afraid of further delay because he worried that someone else might make a discovery along these lines and take the credit from him.

Dr. Strauss on the other hand might be called a genius, although I feel that his areas of knowledge are too limited. He was educated in the tradition of narrow specialization; the broader aspects of background were neglected far more than necessary—even for a neurosurgeon.

I was shocked to learn that the only ancient languages he could read were Latin, Greek, and Hebrew, and that he knows almost nothing of mathematics beyond the elementary levels of the calculus of variations. When he admitted this to me, I found myself almost annoyed. It was as if he'd hidden this part of himself in order to deceive me, pretending—as do many people I've discovered—to be what he is not. No one I've ever known is what he appears to be on the surface.

Dr. Nemur appears to be uncomfortable around me. Sometimes when I try to talk to him, he just looks at me strangely and turns away. I was angry at first when Dr. Strauss told me I was giving Dr. Nemur an inferiority complex. I thought he was mocking me and I'm oversensitive at being made fun of.

How was I to know that a highly respected psychoexperimentalist like Nemur was unacquainted with Hindustani and Chinese? It's absurd when you consider the work that is being done in India and China today in the very field of his study.

I asked Dr. Strauss how Nemur could refute Rahajamati's attack on his method and results if Nemur couldn't even read them in the first place. That strange look on Dr. Strauss' face can mean only one of two things. Either he doesn't want to tell Nemur what they're saying in India, or else—and this worries me—Dr. Strauss doesn't know either. I must be careful to speak and write clearly and simply so that people won't laugh.

May 18 I am very disturbed. I saw Miss Kinnian last night for the first time in over a week. I tried to avoid all discussions of intellectual concepts and to keep the conversation on a simple, everyday level, but she just stared at me blankly and asked me what I meant about the mathematical variance equivalent in Dorbermann's *Fifth Concerto.*

When I tried to explain she stopped me and laughed. I guess I got angry, but I suspect I'm approaching her on the wrong level. No matter what I try to discuss with her, I am unable to communicate. I must review Vrostadt's equations on *Levels of Semantic Progression.* I find that I don't communicate with people much any more. Thank God for books and music and things I can think about. I am alone in my apartment at Mrs. Flynn's boardinghouse most of the time and seldom speak to anyone.

May 20 I would not have noticed the new dishwasher, a boy of about sixteen, at the corner diner where I take my evening meals if not for the incident of the broken dishes.

They crashed to the floor, shattering and sending bits of white china under the tables. The boy stood there, dazed and frightened, holding the empty tray in his hand. The whistles and catcalls from the customers (the cries of "hey, there go the profits!"..."*Mazeltov!*"...and "well, *he* didn't work here very long..." which invariably seems to follow the breaking of glass or dishware in a public restaurant) all seemed to confuse him.

When the owner came to see what the excitement was about, the boy cowered as if he expected to be struck and threw up his arms as if to ward off the blow.

"All right! All right, you dope," shouted the owner, "don't just stand there! Get the broom and sweep that mess up. A broom...a broom, you idiot! It's in the kitchen. Sweep up all the pieces."

The boy saw that he was not going to be punished. His frightened expression disappeared and he smiled and hummed as he came back with the broom to sweep the floor. A few of the rowdier customers kept up the remarks, amusing themselves at his expense.

"Here, sonny, over here there's a nice piece behind you..."

"C'mon, do it again..."

"He's not so dumb. It's easier to break 'em than to wash 'em..."

As his vacant eyes moved across the crowd of amused onlookers, he slowly mirrored their smiles and finally broke into an uncertain grin at the joke which he obviously did not understand.

I felt sick inside as I looked at his dull, vacuous smile, the wide, bright eyes of a child, uncertain but eager to please. They were laughing at him because he was mentally retarded.

And I had been laughing at him too.

Suddenly, I was furious at myself and all those who were smirking at him. I jumped up and shouted, "Shut up! Leave him alone! It's not his fault he can't understand! He can't help what he is! But for God's sake...he's still a human being!"

The room grew silent. I cursed myself for losing control and creating a scene. I tried not to look at the boy as I paid my check and walked out without touching my food. I felt ashamed for both of us.

How strange it is that people of honest feelings and sensibility, who would not take advantage of a man born without arms or legs or eyes—how such people think nothing of abusing a man born with low intelligence. It infuriated me to think that not too long ago I, like this boy, had foolishly played the clown.

And I had almost forgotten.

I'd hidden the picture of the old Charlie Gordon from myself because now that I was intelligent it was something that had to be pushed out of my mind. But today in looking at the boy, for the first time I saw what I had been. *I was just like him!*

Only a short time ago, I learned that people laughed at me. Now I can see that unknowingly I joined with them in laughing at myself. That hurts most of all.

I have often reread my progress reports and seen the illiteracy, the childish naïveté, the mind of low intelligence peering from a dark room, through the keyhole, at the dazzling light outside. I see that even in my dullness I knew that I was inferior, and that other people had something I lacked—something denied me. In my mental blindness, I thought that it was somehow connected with the ability to read and write, and I was sure that if I could get those skills I would automatically have intelligence too.

Even a feeble-minded man wants to be like other men.

A child may not know how to feed itself, or what to eat, yet it knows of hunger.

This then is what I was like, I never knew. Even with my gift of intellectual awareness, I never really knew.

This day was good for me. Seeing the past more clearly, I have decided to use my knowledge and skills to work in the field of increasing human intelligence levels. Who is better equipped for this work? Who else has lived in both worlds? These are my people. Let me use my gift to do something for them.

Tomorrow, I will discuss with Dr. Strauss the manner in which I can work in this area. I may be able to help him work out the problems of widespread use of the technique which was used on me. I have several good ideas of my own.

There is so much that might be done with this technique. If I could be made into a genius, what about thousands of others like myself? What fantastic levels might be achieved by using this technique on normal people? On *geniuses?*

There are so many doors to open. I am impatient to begin.

PROGRESS REPORT 13

May 23 It happened today. Algernon bit me. I visited the lab to see him as I do occasionally, and when I took him out of his cage, he snapped at my hand. I put him back and watched him for a while. He was unusually disturbed and vicious.

May 24 Burt, who is in charge of the experimental animals, tells me that Algernon is changing. He is less cooperative, he refuses to run the maze any more; general motivation has decreased. And he hasn't been eating. Everyone is upset about what this may mean.

May 25 They've been feeding Algernon, who now refuses to work the shifting-lock problem. Everyone identifies me with Algernon. In a way we're both the first of our kind. They're all pretending that Algernon's behavior is not necessarily significant for me. But it's hard to hide the fact that some of the other animals who were used in this experiment are showing strange behavior.

Dr. Strauss and Dr. Nemur have asked me not to come to the lab any more. I know what they're thinking but I can't accept it. I am going ahead with my plans to carry their research forward. With all due respect to both of these fine scientists. I am well aware of their limitations. If there is an answer, I'll have to find it out for myself. Suddenly, time has become very important to me.

May 29 I have been given a lab of my own and permission to go ahead with the research. I'm onto something. Working day and night. I've had a cot moved into the lab. Most of my writing time is spent on the notes which I keep in a separate folder, but from time to time I feel it necessary to put down my moods and my thoughts out of sheer habit.

I find the *calculus of intelligence* to be a fascinating study. Here is the place for the application of all the knowledge I have acquired. In a sense it's the problem I've been concerned with all my life.

May 31 Dr. Strauss thinks I'm working too hard. Dr. Nemur says I'm trying to cram a lifetime of research and thought into a few weeks. I know I should rest, but I'm driven on by something inside that won't let me stop. I've got to find the reason for the sharp regression in Algernon. I've got to know *if* and *when* it will happen to me.

June 4

LETTER TO DR. STRAUSS *(copy)*
Dear Dr. Strauss:
     Under separate cover I am sending you a copy of my report entitled, "The Algernon-Gordon Effect: A Study of Structure and Function of Increased Intelligence," which I would like to have you read and have published.
     As you see, my experiments are completed. I have included in my report all of my formulae, as well as mathematical analysis in the appendix. Of course, these should be verified.
     Because of its importance to both you and Dr. Nemur (and need I say to myself, too?) I have checked and rechecked my results a dozen times in the hope of finding an error. I am sorry to say the results must stand. Yet for the sake of science, I am grateful for the little bit that I here add to the knowledge of the function of the human mind and of the laws governing the artificial increase of human intelligence.
     I recall your once saying to me that an experimental *failure* or the *disproving* of a theory was as important

to the advancement of learning as a success would be.
I know now that this is true. I am sorry, however, that
my own contribution to the field must rest upon the
ashes of the work of two men I regard so highly.

Yours truly,
Charles Gordon

encl.: rept.

June 5 I must not become emotional. The facts and the results
of my experiments are clear, and the more sensational aspects
of my own rapid climb cannot obscure the fact that the tri-
pling of intelligence by the surgical technique developed by
Drs. Strauss and Nemur must be viewed as having little or
no practical applicability (at the present time) to the increase
of human intelligence.

As I review the records and data on Algernon, I see that
although he is still in his physical infancy, he has regressed
mentally. Motor activity is impaired; there is a general re-
duction of glandular activity; there is an accelerated loss of
coordination.

There are also strong indications of progressive amnesia.

As will be seen by my report, these and other physical and
mental deterioration syndromes can be predicted with statistically significant results by the application of my formula.

The surgical stimulus to which we were both subjected
has resulted in an intensification and acceleration of all mental processes. The unforeseen development, which I have
taken the liberty of calling the *Algernon-Gordon Effect,* is
the logical extension of the entire intelligence speed-up. The
hypothesis here proven may be described simply in the following terms: Artificially increased intelligence deteriorates
at a rate of time directly proportional to the quantity of the
increase.

I feel that this, in itself, is an important discovery.

As long as I am able to write, I will continue to record my
thoughts in these progress reports. It is one of my few pleas-
ures. However, by all indications, my own mental deterioration will be very rapid.

I have already begun to notice signs of emotional insta-
bility and forgetfulness, the first symptoms of the burnout.

June 10 Deterioration progressing. I have become absent-
minded. Algernon died two days ago. Dissection shows my

predictions were right. His brain had decreased in weight and there was a general smoothing out of cerebral convolutions as well as a deepening and broadening of brain fissures.

I guess the same thing is or will soon be happening to me. Now that it's definite, I don't want it to happen.

I put Algernon's body in a cheese box and buried him in the back yard. I cried.

June 15 Dr. Strauss came to see me again. I wouldn't open the door and I told him to go away. I want to be left to myself. I have become touchy and irritable. I feel the darkness closing in. It's hard to throw off thoughts of suicide. I keep telling myself how important this introspective journal will be.

It's a strange sensation to pick up a book that you've read and enjoyed just a few months ago and discover that you don't remember it. I remembered how great I thought John Milton was, but when I picked up *Paradise Lost* I couldn't understand it at all. I got so angry I threw the book across the room.

I've got to hold onto some of it. Some of the things I've learned. Oh, God, please don't take it all away.

June 19 Sometimes, at night, I go for a walk. Last night I couldn't remember where I lived. A policeman took me home. I have the strange feeling that this has all happened to me before—a long time ago. I keep telling myself I'm the only person in the world who can describe what's happening to me.

June 21 Why can't I remember? I've got to fight. I lie in bed for days and I don't know who or where I am. Then it all comes back to me in a flash. Fugues of amnesia. Symptoms of senility—second childhood. I can watch them coming on. It's so cruelly logical. I learned so much and so fast. Now my mind is deteriorating rapidly. I won't let it happen. I'll fight it. I can't help thinking of the boy in the restaurant, the blank expression, the silly smile, the people laughing at him. No—please—not that again...

June 22 I'm forgetting things that I learned recently. It seems to be following the classic pattern—the last things learned are the first things forgotten. Or is that the pattern? I'd better look it up again....

I reread my paper on the *Algernon-Gordon Effect* and I get the strange feeling that it was written by someone else. There are parts I don't even understand.

Motor activity impaired. I keep tripping over things, and it becomes increasingly difficult to type.

June 23 I've given up using the typewriter completely. My coordination is bad. I feel that I'm moving slower and slower. Had a terrible shock today. I picked up a copy of an article I used in my research, Krueger's *Uber psychische Ganzheit,* to see if it would help me understand what I had done. First I thought there was something wrong with my eyes. Then I realized I could no longer read German. I tested myself in other languages. All gone.

June 30 A week since I dare to write again. It's slipping away like sand through my fingers. Most of the books I have are too hard for me now. I get angry with them because I know that I read and understood them just a few weeks ago.

I keep telling myself I must keep writing these reports so that somebody will know what is happening to me. But it gets harder to form the words and remember spellings. I have to look up even simple words in the dictionary now and it makes me impatient with myself.

Dr. Strauss comes around almost every day, but I told him I wouldn't see or speak to anybody. He feels guilty. They all do. But I don't blame anyone. I knew what might happen. But how it hurts.

July 7 I don't know where the week went. Todays Sunday I know becuase I can see through my window people going to church. I think I stayed in bed all week but I remember Mrs. Flynn bringing food to be a few times. I keep saying over and over Ive got to do something but then I forget or maybe its just easier not to do what I say Im going to do.

I think of my mother and father a lot these days. I found a picture of them with me taken at a beach. My father has a big ball under his arm and my mother is holding me by the hand. I dont remember them the way they are in the picture. All I remember is my father drunk most of the time and arguing with mom about money.

He never shaved much and he used to scratch my face when he hugged me. My mother said he died but Cousin

Miltie said he heard his mom and dad say that my father ran away with another woman. When I asked my mother she slapped my face and said my father was dead. I dont think I ever found out which was true but I don't care much. (He said he was going to take me to see cows on a farm once but he never did. He never kept his promises...)

July 10 My landlady Mrs Flynn is very worried about me. She says the way I lay around all day and dont do anything I remind her of her son before she threw him out of the house. She said she doesn't like loafers. If Im sick its one thing, but if Im a loafer thats another thing and she wont have it. I told her I think Im sick.

I try to read a little bit every day, mostly stories, but sometimes I have to read the same thing over and over again because I dont know what it means. And its hard to write. I know I should look up all the words in the dictionary but its so hard and Im so tired all the time.

Then I got the idea that I would only use the easy words instead of the long hard ones. That saves time. I put flowers on Algernons grave about once a week. Mrs Flynn thinks Im crazy to put flowers on a mouses grave but I told her that Algernon was special.

July 14 Its sunday again. I dont have anything to do to keep me busy now because my television set is broke and I dont have any money to get it fixed. (I think I lost this months check from the lab. I dont remember)

I get awful headaches and asperin doesnt help me much. Mrs Flynn knows Im really sick and she feels very sorry for me. Shes a wonderful woman whenever someone is sick.

July 22 Mrs Flynn called a strange doctor to see me. She was afraid I was going to die. I told the doctor I wasnt too sick and that I only forget sometimes. He asked me did I have any friends or relatives and I said no I dont have any. I told him I had a friend called Algernon once but he was a mouse and we used to run races together. He looked at me kind of funny like he thought I was crazy.

He smiled when I told him I used to be a genius. He talked to me like I was a baby and he winked at Mrs. Flynn. I got mad and chased him out because he was making fun of me the way they all used to.

July 24 I have no more money and Mrs. Flynn says I got to go to work somewhere and pay the rent because I havent paid for over two months. I dont know any work but the job I used to have at Donnegans Plastic Box Company. I dont want to go back there because they all knew me when I was smart and maybe theyll laugh at me. But I don't know what else to do to get money.

July 25 I was looking at some of my old progress reports and its very funny but I cant read what I wrote. I can make out some of the words but they dont make sense.

Miss Kinnian came to the door but I said go away I dont want to see you. She cried and I cried too but I wouldnt let her in because I didn't want her to laugh at me. I told her I didn't like her any more. I told her I didnt want to be smart any more. Thats not true. I still love her and I still want to be smart but I had to say that so shed go away. She gave Mrs Flynn money to pay the rent. I dont want that. I got to get a job.

Please... please let me not forget how to read and write...

July 27 Mr Donnegan was very nice when I came back and asked him for my old job of janitor. First he was very suspicious but I told him what happened to me then he looked very sad and put his hand on my shoulder and said Charlie Gordon you got guts.

Everybody looked at me when I came downstairs and started working in the toilet sweeping it out like I used to. I told myself Charlie if they make fun of you dont get sore because you remember their not so smart as you once thot they were. And besides they were once your friends and if they laughed at you that doesnt mean anything because they liked you too.

One of the new men who came to work there after I went away made a nasty crack he said hey Charlie I hear your a very smart fella a real quiz kid. Say something intelligent. I felt bad but Joe Carp came over and grabbed him by the shirt and said leave him alone you lousy cracker or Ill break your neck. I didn't expect Joe to take my part so I guess hes really my friend.

Later Frank Reilly came over and said Charlie if anybody bothers you or trys to take advantage you call me or Joe and we will set em straight. I said thanks Frank and I got choked up so I had to turn around and go into the supply room so he wouldn't see me cry. Its good to have friends.

July 28 I did a dumb thing today I forgot I wasnt in Miss Kinnians class at the adult center any more like I use to be. I went in and sat down in my old seat in the back of the room and she looked at me funny and she said Charles. I dint remember she ever called me that before only Charlie so I said hello Miss Kinnian Im redy for my lesin today only I lost my reader that we was using. She started to cry and run out of the room and everybody looked at me and I saw they wasnt the same pepul who used to be in my class.

Then all of a sudden I remembered some things about the operashun and me getting smart and I said holy smoke I reely pulled a Charlie Gordon that time. I went away before she come back to the room.

Thats why Im going away from New York for good. I dont want to do nothing like that agen. I dont want Miss Kinnian to feel sorry for me. Evry body feels sorry at the factery and I dont want that eather so Im going someplace where nobody knows that Charlie Gordon was once a genus and how he cant even reed a book or rite good.

Im taking a cuple of books along and even if I cant reed them Ill practise hard and maybe I wont forget every thing I lerned. If I try reel hard maybe Ill be a littel bit smarter than I was before the operashun. I got my rabits foot and my luky penny and maybe they will help me.

If you ever reed this Miss Kinnian dont be sorry for me Im glad I got a second chanse to be smart becaus I lerned a lot of things that I never even new were in this world and Im grateful that I saw it all for a littel bit. I dont know why Im dumb agen or what I did wrong maybe its becaus I dint try hard enuff. But if I try and practis very hard maybe Ill get a littl smarter and know what all the words are. I remember a littel bit how nice I had a feeling with the blue book that has the torn cover when I red it. Thats why Im gonna keep trying to get smart so I can have that feeling agen. Its a good feeling to know things and be smart. I wish I had it rite now if I did I would sit down and reed all the time. Anyway I bet Im the first dumb person in the world who ever found out somthing importent for sience. I remember I did somthing but I dont remember what. So I gess its like I did it for all the dumb pepul like me.

Good-by Miss Kinnian and Dr Strauss and evreybody. And P.S. please tell Dr Nemur not to be such a grouch when pepul laff at him and he would have more frends. Its easy to make frends if you let pepul laff at you. Im going to have lots of frends where I go.

P.P.S. Please if you get a chanse put some flowrs on Algernon's grave in the bak yard ...

A rising star in the science-fiction galaxy, George R. R. (his friends call him "Railroad") Martin has published a novel (Dying of the Light, 1977) and two excellent collections (A Song for Lya and Other Stories, 1976, and Songs of Stars and Shadows, 1977) in his relatively brief career as a professional writer. "A Song for Lya" won the Hugo Award in the novelette category in 1975.

"The Second Kind of Loneliness" (Analog, December 1972) is a lovely, sad, yet inspirational story of the problems of one man.

THE SECOND KIND OF LONELINESS

By George R. R. Martin

June 18

My relief left Earth today.

It will be at least three months before he gets here, of course. But he's on his way.

Today he lifted off from the Cape, just as I did, four long years ago. Out at Komarov Station he'll switch to a moon boat, then switch again in orbit around Luna, at Deepspace Station. There his voyage will really begin. Up to then he's still been in his own backyard.

Not until the *Charon* casts loose from Deepspace Station and sets out into the night will he feel it, *really* feel it, as I felt it four years ago. Not until Earth and Luna vanish behind him will it hit. He's known from the first that there's no turning back, of course. But there's a difference between knowing it and feeling it. Now he'll feel it.

There will be an orbital stopover around Mars, to send supplies down to Burroughs City. And more stops in the belt.

But then the *Charon* will begin to gather speed. It will be going very fast when it reaches Jupiter. And much faster after it whips by, using the gravity of the giant planet like a slingshot to boost its acceleration.

After that there are no stops for the *Charon*. No stops at all until it reaches me, out here at the Cerberus Star Ring, six million miles beyond Pluto.

My relief will have a long time to brood. As I did.

I'm still brooding now, today, four years later. But then, there's not much else to do out here. Ringships are infrequent, and you get pretty weary of films and tapes and books after a time. So you brood. You think about your past and dream about your future. And you try to keep the loneliness and the boredom from driving you out of your skull.

It's been a long four years. But it's almost over now. And it will be nice to get back. I want to walk on grass again, and see clouds, and eat an ice cream sundae.

Still, for all that, I don't regret coming. These four years alone in the darkness have done me good, I think. It's not as if I had left much. My days on Earth seem remote to me now, but I can still remember them if I try. The memories aren't all that pleasant. I was pretty screwed up back then.

I needed time to think, and that's one thing you get out here. The man who goes back on the *Charon* won't be the same one who came out here four years ago. I'll build a whole new life back on Earth. I know I will.

June 20

Ship today.

I didn't know it was coming, of course. I never do. The ringships are irregular, and the kind of energies I'm playing with out here turn radio signals into crackling chaos. By the time the ship finally punched through the static, the station's scanners had already picked it up and notified me.

It was clearly a ringship. Much bigger than the old system rust-buckets like the *Charon*, and heavily armored to withstand the stresses of the nullspace vortex. It came straight on, with no attempt to decelerate.

While I was heading down to the control room to strap in, a thought hit me. This might be the last. Probably not, of course. There's still three months to go, and that's time enough for a dozen ships. But you can never tell. The ringships are irregular, like I said.

Somehow the thought disturbed me. The ships have been part of my life for four years now. An important part. And the one today might have been the last. If so, I want it all down here. I want to remember it. With good reason, I think. When the ships come, that makes everything else worthwhile.

The control room is in the heart of my quarters. It's the center of everything, where the nerves and the tendons and the muscles of the station are gathered. But it's not very impressive. The room is very small, and once the door slides shut the walls and floor and ceiling are all a featureless white.

There's only one thing in the room: a horseshoe-shaped console that surrounds a single padded chair.

I sat down in that chair today for what might be the last time. I strapped myself in, and put on the earphones, and lowered the helmet. I reached for the controls, and touched them, and turned them on.

And the control room vanished.

It's all done with holographs, of course. I *know* that. But that doesn't make a bit of difference when I'm sitting in that chair. Then, as far as I'm concerned, I'm not inside anymore. I'm out *there*, in the void. The control console is still there, and the chair. But the rest has gone. Instead, the aching darkness is everywhere, above me, below me, all around me. The distant sun is only one star among many, and all the stars are terribly far away.

That's the way it always is. That's the way it was today. When I threw that switch I was alone in the universe with the cold stars and the ring. The Cerberus Star Ring.

I saw the ring as if from outside, looking down on it. It's a vast structure, really. But from out here, it's nothing. It's swallowed by the immensity of it all, a slim silver thread lost in the blackness.

But I know better. The ring is huge. My living quarters take up but a single degree in the circle it forms, a circle whose diameter is more than a hundred miles. The rest is circuitry and scanners and power banks. And the engines, the waiting nullspace engines.

The ring turned silent beneath me, its far side stretching away into nothingness. I touched a switch on my console. Below me, the nullspace engines woke.

In the center of the ring, a new star was born.

It was a tiny dot amid the dark at first. Green today, bright green. But not always, and not for long. Nullspace has many colors.

I could see the far side of the ring then, if I'd wanted to. It was glowing with a light of its own. Alive and awake, the nullspace engines were pouring unimaginable amounts of energy inward, to rip wide a hole in space itself.

The hole had been there long before Cerberus, long before man. Men found it, quite by accident, when they reached Pluto. They built the ring around it. Later they found two other holes, and built other star rings.

The holes were small, too small. But they could be enlarged. Temporarily, at the expense of vast amounts of power, they could be ripped open. Raw energy could be pumped through that tiny, unseen hole in the universe until the placid surface of nullspace roiled and lashed back, and the nullspace vortex formed.

And now it happened.

The star in the center of the ring grew and flattened. It was a pulsing disc, not a globe. But it was still the brightest thing in the heavens. And it swelled visibly. From the spinning green disc, flame-like orange spears lanced out, and fell back, and smoky bluish tendrils uncoiled. Specks of red danced and flashed among the green, grew and blended. The colors all began to run together.

The flat, spinning, multicolored star doubled in size, doubled again, again. A few minutes before it had not been. Now it filled the ring, lapped against the silver walls, seared them with its awful energy. It began to spin faster and faster, a whirlpool in space, a maelstrom of flame and light.

The vortex. The nullspace vortex. The howling storm that is not a storm and does not howl, for there is no sound in space.

To it came the ringship. A moving star at first, it took on visible form and shape almost faster than my human eyes could follow. It became a dark silver bullet in the blackness, a bullet fired at the vortex.

The aim was good. The ship hit very close to the center of the ring. The swirling colors closed over it.

I hit my controls. Even more suddenly than it had come, the vortex was gone. The ship was gone too, of course. Once more there was only me, and the ring, and the stars.

Then I touched another switch, and I was back in the

blank white control room, unstrapping. Unstrapping for what might be the last time, ever.

Somehow I hope not. I never thought I'd miss anything about this place. But I will. I'll miss the ringships. I'll miss moments like the ones today.

I hope I get a few more chances at it before I give it up forever. I want to feel the nullspace engines wake again under my hands and watch the vortex boil and churn while I float alone between the stars. Once more, at least. Before I go.

June 23

That ringship has set me to thinking. Even more than usual.

It's funny that with all the ships I've seen pass through the vortex, I've never even given a thought to riding one. There's a whole new world on the other side of nullspace; Second Chance, a rich green planet of a star so far away that astronomers are still unsure whether it shares the same galaxy with us. That's the funny thing about the holes—you can't be sure where they lead until you go through.

When I was a kid, I read a lot about star travel. Most people didn't think it was possible. But those who did always mentioned Alpha Centauri as the first system we'd explore and colonize. Closest, and all that. Funny how wrong they were. Instead, our colonies orbit suns we can't even see. And I don't think we'll *ever* get to Alpha Centauri.

Somehow I never thought of the colonies in personal terms. Still can't. Earth is where I failed before. That's got to be where I succeed now. The colonies would be just another escape.

Like Cerberus?

June 26

Ship today. So the other wasn't the last, after all. But what about this one?

June 29

Why does a man volunteer for a job like this? Why does a man run to a silver ring six million miles beyond Pluto, to guard a hole in space? Why throw away four years of life alone in the darkness?

Why?

I used to ask myself that, in the early days. I couldn't
answer it then. Now I think I can. I bitterly regretted the
impulse that drove me out here, then. Now I think I understand it.

And it wasn't really an impulse. I ran to Cerberus. Ran
Ran to escape from loneliness.

That doesn't make sense?

Yes it does. I know about loneliness. It's been the theme
of my life. I've been alone for as long as I can remember.

But there are two kinds of loneliness.

Most people don't realize the difference. I do. I've sampled
both kinds.

They talk and write about the loneliness of the men who
man the star rings. The lighthouses of space, and all that
And they're right.

There are times, out here at Cerberus, when I think I'm
the only man in the universe. Earth was just a fever dream
The people I remember were just creations of my own mind

There are times, out here, when I want someone to talk
to so badly that I scream, and start pounding on the walls
There are times when the boredom crawls under my skin and
all but drives me mad.

But there are *other* times, too. When the ringships come
When I go outside to make repairs. Or when I just sit in the
control chair, imaging myself out into the darkness to watch
the stars.

Lonely? Yes. But a solemn, brooding, tragic loneliness. A
loneliness tinged with grandeur, somehow. A loneliness that
a man hates with a passion—and yet loves so much he crave
for more.

And then there is the second kind of loneliness.

You don't need the Cerberus Star Ring for that kind. You
can find it anywhere on Earth. I know. I did. I found it every
where I went, in everything I did.

It's the loneliness of people trapped within themselves
The loneliness of people who have said the wrong thing so
often that they don't have the courage to say anything any
more. The loneliness, not of distance, but of fear.

The loneliness of people who sit alone in furnished room
in crowded cities, because they've got nowhere to go and no
one to talk to. The loneliness of guys who go to bars to meet
someone, only to discover they don't know how to strike up

a conversation, and wouldn't have the courage to do so if they did.

There's no grandeur to that kind of loneliness. No purpose and no poetry. It's loneliness without meaning. It's sad and squalid and pathetic, and it stinks of self-pity.

Oh yes, it hurts at times to be alone among the stars.

But it hurts a lot more to be alone at a party. A lot more.

June 30
Reading yesterday's entry. Talk about self-pity...

July 1
Reading *yesterday's* entry. My flippant mask. After four years, I still fight back whenever I try to be honest with myself. That's not good. If things are going to be any different this time, I have to understand myself.

So why do I have to ridicule myself when I admit that I'm lonely and vulnerable? Why do I have to struggle to admit that I was scared of life? No one's ever going to read this thing. I'm talking to myself, about myself.

So why are there some things I still can't bring myself to say?

July 4
No ringship today. Too bad. Earth ain't never *had* no fireworks that could match the nullspace vortex, and I felt like celebrating.

But why do I keep Earth calendar out here, where the years are centuries and the seasons a dim memory? July is just like December. So what's the use?

July 10
I dreamed of Karen last night. And now I can't get her out of my skull.

I thought I buried her long ago. It was all a fantasy anyway. Oh, she liked me well enough. Loved me, maybe. But no more than a half-dozen other guys. I wasn't really *special* to her, and she never realized just how special she was to me.

Nor how much I wanted to be special to her—how much I needed to be special to someone, somewhere.

So I elected her. But it was all a fantasy. And I knew it

was, in my more rational moments. I had no right to be so hurt. I had no special claim on her.

But I thought I did, in my daydreams. And I *was* hurt. It was my fault, though, not hers. Karen would never hurt anyone willingly. She just never realized how fragile I was.

Even out here, in the early years, I kept dreaming. I dreamed of how she'd change her mind. How she'd be waiting for me. Et cetera.

But that was more wish-fulfillment. It was before I came to terms with myself out here. I know now that she won't be waiting. She doesn't need me, and never did. I was just a friend.

So I don't much like dreaming about her. That's bad. Whatever I do, I must *not* look up Karen when I get back. I have to start all over again. I have to find someone who *does* need me. And I won't find her if I try to slip back into my old life.

July 18

A month since my relief left Earth. The *Charon* should be in the belt by now. Two months to go.

July 23

Nightmares now. God help me.

I'm dreaming of Earth again. And Karen. I can't stop. Every night it's the same.

It's funny, calling Karen a nightmare. Up to now she's always been a dream. A beautiful dream, with her long, soft hair, and her laugh, and that funny way she had of grinning. But those dreams were always wish fulfillments. In the dreams Karen needed me and wanted me and loved me.

The nightmares have the bite of truth to them. They're all the same. It's always a replay of me and Karen, together on that last night.

It was a good night, as nights went for me. We ate at one of my favorite restaurants, and went to a show. We talked together easily, about many things. We laughed together too.

Only later, back at her place, I reverted to form. When I tried to tell her how much she meant to me. I remember how awkward and stupid I felt, how I struggled to get things out, how I stumbled over my own words. So much came out wrong.

I remember how she looked at me then. Strangely. How she tried to disillusion me. Gently. She was always gentle. And I looked into her eyes and listened to her voice. But I didn't find love, or need. Just—just pity, I guess.

Pity for an inarticulate jerk who'd been letting life pass him by without touching it. Not because he didn't want to. But because he was afraid to, and didn't know how. She'd found that jerk, and loved him, in her way—she loved everybody. She'd tried to help, to give him some of her self-confidence, some of the courage and bounce that she faced life with. And, to an extent, she had.

Not enough, though. The jerk liked to make fantasies about the day he wouldn't be lonely anymore. And when Karen tried to help him, he thought she was his fantasy come to life. Or deluded himself into thinking that. The jerk suspected the truth all along, of course, but he lied to himself about it.

And when the day came that he couldn't lie any longer, he was still vulnerable enough to be hurt. He wasn't the type to grow scar tissue easily. He didn't have the courage to try again with someone else. So he ran.

I hope the nightmares stop. I can't take them, night after night. I can't take reliving that hour in Karen's apartment.

I've had four years out here. I've looked at myself hard. I've changed what I didn't like, or tried to. I've tried to cultivate that scar tissue, to gather the confidence I need to face the new rejections I'm going to meet before I find acceptance. But I know myself damn well now, and I know it's only been a partial success. There will always be things that will hurt, things that I'll never be able to face the way I'd like to.

Memories of that last hour with Karen are among those things. *God,* I hope the nightmares end.

July 26

More nightmares. Please Karen. I loved you. Leave me alone. Please.

July 29

There was a ringship yesterday, thank God. I needed one. It helped take my mind off Earth, off Karen. And there was no nightmare last night, for the first time in a week. Instead I dreamed of the nullspace vortex. The raging silent storm.

August 1

The nightmares have returned. Not always Karen, now. Older memories too. Infinitely less meaningful, but still painful. All the stupid things I've said, all the girls I never met, all the things I have never done.

Bad. Bad. I have to keep reminding myself. I'm not like that anymore. There's a new me, a me I built out here, six million miles beyond Pluto. Made of steel and stars and null-space, hard and confident and self-assured. And not afraid of life.

The past is behind me. But it still hurts.

August 2

Ship today. The nightmares continue. Damn.

August 3

No nightmare last night. Second time for that, and I've rested easy after opening the hole for a ringship during the day. (Day? Night? Nonsense out here—but I still write as if they had some meaning. Four years haven't even touched the Earth in me.) Maybe the vortex is scaring Karen away. But I never wanted to scare Karen away before. Besides, I shouldn't need crutches.

August 13

Another ship came through a few nights ago. No dream afterwards. A pattern!

I'm fighting the memories. I'm thinking of other things about Earth. The good times. There were a lot of them, really, and there will be lots more when I get back. I'm going to make sure of that.

These nightmares are stupid. I won't permit them to continue. There was so much else I shared with Karen, so much I'd like to recall. Why can't I?

August 18

The *Charon* is about a month away. I wonder who my relief is. I wonder what drove *him* out here?

Earth dreams continue. No. Call them Karen dreams. Am I even afraid to write her name now?

August 20

Ship today. After it was through I stayed out and looked at stars. For several hours, it seems. Didn't seem as long at the time.

It's beautiful out here. Lonely, yes. But such a loneliness! You're alone with the universe, the stars spread out at your feet and scattered around your head.

Each one is a sun. Yet they still look cold to me. I find myself shivering, lost in the vastness of it all, wondering how it got there and what it means.

My relief, whoever it is, I hope he can appreciate this, as it should be appreciated. There are so many who can't, or won't. Men who walk at night, and never look up at the sky. I hope my relief isn't a man like that.

August 24

When I get back to Earth, I *will* look up Karen. I must. How can I pretend that things are going to be different this time if I can't even work up the courage to do that? And they *are* going to be different. So I *must* face Karen, and prove that I've changed. Really changed.

August 25

The nonsense of yesterday. How could I face Karen? What would I *say* to her? I'd only start deluding myself again, and wind up getting burned all over again. No. I must *not* see Karen. Hell, I can even take the dreams.

August 30

I've been going down to the control room and flipping myself out regularly of late. No ringships. But I find that going outside makes the memories of Earth dim.

More and more I know I'll miss Cerberus. A year from now, I'll be back on Earth, looking up at the night sky, and remembering how the ring shone silver in the starlight. I know I will.

And the vortex. I'll remember the vortex, and the ways the colors swirled and mixed. Different every time.

Too bad I was never a holo buff. You could make a fortune back on Earth with a tape of the way the vortex looks when it spins. The ballet of the void. I'm surprised no one's ever thought of it.

Maybe I'll suggest it to my relief. Something to do to fill the hours, if he's interested. I hope he is. Earth would be richer if someone brought back a record.

I'd do it myself, but the equipment isn't right, and I don't have the time to modify it.

September 4

I've gone outside every day for the last week, I find. No nightmares. Just dreams of the darkness, laced with the colors of nullspace.

September 9

Continue to go outside, and drink it all in. Soon, soon now, all this will be lost to me. Forever. I feel as though I must take advantage of every second. I must memorize the way things are out here at Cerberus, so I can keep the awe and the wonder and the beauty fresh inside me when I return to Earth.

September 10

There hasn't been a ship in a long time. Is it over, then? Have I seen my last?

September 12

No ship today. But I went outside and woke the engines and let the vortex roar.

Why do I always write about the vortex roaring and howling? There is no sound in space. I hear nothing. But I watch it. And it does roar. It does.

The sounds of silence. But not the way the poets meant.

September 13

I watched the vortex again today, though there was no ship.

I've never done that before. Now I've done it twice. It's forbidden. The costs in terms of power are enormous, and Cerberus lives on power. So why?

It's almost as though I don't want to give up the vortex. But I have to. Soon.

September 14

Idiot, idiot, idiot. What have I been doing? The *Charon* is less than a week away, and I've been gawking at the stars as if I'd never seen them before. I haven't even started to pack, and I've got to clean up my records for my relief, and get the station in order.

Idiot! Why am I wasting time writing in this damn *book!*

September 15

Packing almost done. I've uncovered some weird things, too. Things I tried to hide in the early years. Like my novel. I wrote it in the first six months, and thought it was great. I could hardly wait to get back to Earth, and sell it, and become an Author. Ah, yes. Read it over a year later. It stinks.

Also found a picture of Karen.

September 16

Today I took a bottle of Scotch and a glass down to the control room, set them down on the console, and strapped myself in. Drank a toast to the blackness and the stars and the vortex. I'll miss them.

September 17

A day, by my calculations. A day. Then I'm on my way home, to a fresh start and a new life. If I have the courage to live it.

September 18

Nearly midnight. No sign of the *Charon.* What's wrong?

Nothing, probably. These schedules are never precise. Sometimes as much as a week off. So why do I worry? Hell, I was late getting here myself. I wonder what the poor guy I replaced was thinking then?

September 20

The *Charon* didn't come yesterday, either. After I got tired of waiting, I took the bottle of Scotch and went back to the control room. And out. To drink another toast to the stars. And the vortex. I woke the vortex and let it flame, and toasted it.

A lot of toasts. I finished the bottle. And today I've got such a hangover I think I'll never make it back to Earth.

It was a stupid thing to do. The crew of the *Charon* might have seen the vortex colors. If they report me, I'll get docked a small fortune from the pile of money that's waiting back on Earth.

September 21

Where is the *Charon?* Did something happen to it? Is it coming?

September 22

I went outside again.

God, so beautiful, so lonely, so vast. Haunting, that's the word I want. The beauty out there is haunting. Sometimes I think I'm a fool to go back. I'm giving up all of eternity for a pizza and a lay and a kind word.

NO! What the hell am I writing! No. I'm going back, of course I am. I need Earth, I miss Earth, I want Earth. This time it *will* be different.

I'll find another Karen, and this time I won't blow it.

September 23

I'm sick. God, but I'm sick. The things I've been thinking. I thought I had changed, but now I don't know. I find myself actually thinking about staying, about signing on for another term. I don't want to. No. But I think I'm still afraid of life, of Earth, of everything.

Hurry, *Charon.* Hurry, before I change my mind.

September 24

Karen or the vortex? Earth or eternity?

Dammit, how can I *think* that! Karen! Earth! I have to have courage, I have to risk pain, I have to taste life.

I am *not* a rock. Or an island. Or a star.

September 25

No sign of the *Charon.* A full week late. That happens sometimes. But not very often. It will arrive soon. I know it.

September 30

Nothing. Each day I watch, and wait. I listen to my scanners, and go outside to look, and pace back and forth through the ring. But nothing. It's never been this late. What's wrong?

October 3

Ship today. Not the *Charon.* I thought it was at first, when the scanners picked it up. I yelled loud enough to wake the vortex. But then I looked, and my heart sank. It was too big, and it was coming straight on without decelerating.

I went outside and let it through. And stayed out for a long time afterward.

October 4

I want to go home. Where are they? I don't understand. I don't understand.

They can't just leave me here. They can't. They won't.

October 5

Ship today. Ringship again. I used to look forward to them. Now I hate them, because they're not the *Charon*. But I let it through.

October 7

I unpacked. It's silly for me to live out of suitcases when I don't know if the *Charon* is coming, or when.

I still look for it, though. I wait. It's coming, I know. Just delayed somewhere. An emergency in the belt maybe.

There are lots of explanations.

Meanwhile, I'm doing odd jobs around the ring. I never did get it in proper shape for my relief. Too busy star watching at the time, to do what I should have been doing.

January 8 (or thereabouts)

Darkness and despair.

I know why the *Charon* hasn't arrived. It isn't due. The calendar was all screwed up. It's January, not October. And I've been living on the wrong time for months. Even celebrated the Fourth of July on the wrong day.

I discovered it yesterday when I was doing those chores around the ring. I wanted to make sure everything was running right. For my relief.

Only there won't be any relief.

The *Charon* arrived three months ago. I—I destroyed it.

Sick. It was sick. I was sick, mad. As soon as it was done, it hit me. What I'd done. Oh, God. I screamed for hours.

And then I set back the wall calendar. And forgot. Maybe deliberately. Maybe I couldn't bear to remember. I don't know. All I know is that I forgot.

But now I remember. Now I remember it all.

The scanners had warned me of the *Charon's* approach. I was outside, waiting. Watching. Trying to get enough of the stars and the darkness to last me forever.

Through that darkness, *Charon* came. It seemed so slow compared to the ringships. And so small. It was my salvation, my relief, but it looked fragile, and silly, and somehow ugly. Squalid. It reminded me of Earth.

It moved toward docking, dropping into the ring from above, groping toward the locks in the habitable section of Cerberus. So very slow. I watched it come. Suddenly I wondered what I'd say to the crewmen, and my relief. I wondered what they'd think of me. Somewhere in my gut, a fist clenched.

And suddenly I couldn't stand it. Suddenly I was afraid of it. Suddenly I hated it.

So I woke the vortex.

A red flare, branching into yellow tongues, growing quickly, shooting off bluegreen bolts. One passed near the *Charon*. And the ship shuddered.

I tell myself, now, that I didn't realize what I was doing. Yet I knew the *Charon* was unarmored. I knew it couldn't take vortex energies. I knew.

The *Charon* was so slow, the vortex so fast. In two heartbeats the maelstrom was brushing against the ship. In three it had swallowed it.

It was gone so fast. I don't know if the ship melted, or burst asunder, or crumpled. But I know it couldn't have survived. There's no blood on my star ring, though. The debris is somewhere on the other side of nullspace. If there is any debris.

The ring and the darkness looked the same as ever.

That made it so easy to forget. And I must have wanted to forget very much.

And now? What do I do *now*? Will Earth find out? Will there ever be relief? I want to go home.

Karen, I—

June 18

My relief left Earth today.

At least I think he did. Somehow the wall calendar was broken, so I'm not precisely sure of the date. But I've got it back into working order.

Anyway; it can't have been off for more than a few hours, or I would have noticed. So my relief *is* on the way. It will take him three months to get here, of course.

But at least he's coming.

MEMOS

Ms. Merril's second contribution is a beautiful (not an easy quality to obtain in this form of the short story) and powerful story that first appeared in the late and lamented Worlds of Tomorrow *(October 1963).*

THE LONELY

By Judith Merril

TO: The Hon. Natarajan Roi Hennessy, Chairman, Committee on Intercultural Relations. Solar Council, Eros.
FROM: Dr. Shlomo Mouna, Sr. Anthropologist, Project Ozma XII, Pluto Station.
DATE: 10/9/92, TC.
TRANSMISSION: VIA: Tight beam, scrambled. SENT: 1306 hrs, TST. RCDV: 1947 hrs, TST.

Dear Nat:

Herewith, a much condensed, heavily annotated, and top-secret coded transcript of a program we just picked up. The official title is GU #79, and the content pretty well confirms some of our earlier assumptions about the whole series, as this one concerns us directly, and we have enough background information, including specific dates, to get a much more complete and stylistic translation than before.

I'd say the hypotheses that these messages represent a "Galactic University" lecture series broadcast from somewhere near Galactic Center, through some medium a damn sight faster than light, now seems very reasonable.

This one seemed to come from Altair, which would date transmission from there only a few years after some incidents described in script. Some of the material also indicates probable nature of original format, and I find it uncomfortable.

Also reraises question of whether Altair, Arcturus, Castor, etc., relay stations are aimed at us? Although the content makes that doubtful.

Full transcript, film, etc., will go out through channels, as soon as you let me know which channels. This time I am not pleading for declassification. I think of some Spaserve reactions and—frankly I wonder if it shouldn't be limited to SC Intercult Chairmen and Ozma Sr. Anthropoids—and sometimes I wonder about thee.

Cheery reading.
Shlomo

TRANSCRIPT, GU #79, Condensed Version, edited by SM, 10/9/92, TC. (NRH: All material in parens is in my words— summarizing, commenting, and/or describing visual material where indicated. Straight text is verbatim, though cut as indicated. Times, measurements, etc., have been translated from Standard Galactic or Aldebaran local to Terran Standard; and bear in mind that words like "perceive" are often very rough translations for SG concepts more inclusive than our language provided for.—SM)

(Open with distance shot of Spaserve crew visiting Woman of Earth statue on Aldebaran VI. Closeup of reverent faces. Shots of old L-1, still in orbit, and jump-ship trailing it. Repeat first shot, then to Lecturer. You may have seen this one before. Sort of electric-eel type. Actually makes sparks when he's being funny.)

The image you have just perceived is symbolic, in several senses. First, the statue was created by the Arlemites, the native race of Aldebaran VI (!! Yes, Virginia, there *are* aborigines!!) in an effort to use emotional symbols to bridge the gap in communications between two highly dissimilar species. Second: due to the farcical failure of this original intent, the structure has now become a vitally significant symbol— you perceived the impact—to the other species involved, the Terrans, a newly emerged race from Sol III. (Note that "you perceived." We must accept the implication that the original broadcasting format provides means of projecting emotional content.) Finally, this twofold symbol relates in one sense (Shooting sparks like mad here. Professional humor pretty much the same all over, hey?) to the phenomenon of the paradox of absolute universality and infinite variety inherent in the symbolism.

(Next section is a sort of refresher-review of earlier lectures. Subject of the whole course appears to be, roughly, "Problems of disparate symbolism in interspecies communications." This lecture—don't laugh—is "Symbols of Sexuality." Excerpts from review:—)

The phenomenon of symbolism is an integral part of the development of communicating intelligence. Distinctions of biological construction, ecological situation, atmospheric and other geophysical conditions, do of course profoundly influence the radically infantile phases of intellectual-emotional-social development in all cultures...(but)...from approximately that point in the linear development of a civilization at which it is likely to make contact with other cultures—that is, from the commencement of cultural maturity, following the typically adolescent outburst of energy in which first contact is generally accomplished...(He describes this level at some length in terms of a complex of: 1, astrophysical knowledge; 2, control of basic matter-energy conversions, "mechanical or psial"; 3, self-awareness of whole culture and of individuals in it; and 4, some sociological phenomena for which I have no referents.)...all cultures appear to progress through a known sequence of i-e-s patterns...(and)...despite differences in the *rate* of development, the composite i-e-s curve for mature cultural development of all known species is familiar enough to permit reliable predictions for any civilization, once located on the curve.

(Then progresses to symbolism. Specific symbols, he says, vary even more, between cultures, than language or other means of conscious communication, as to wit—)

It is self-evident that the specific symbols utilized by, for instance, a septasexual, mechanophilic, auriphased species of freely locomotive discrete individuals, will vary greatly from those of, let us say, a mitotic, unicellular, intensely psioid, communal culture. (Which makes it all the more striking, that) it is specifically in the *use of symbols,* the general consciousness of their significance, the degree of sophistication of the popularly recognized symbols, and the uses to which they are put by the society as a whole, that we have found our most useful constant, so far, for purposes of locating a given culture on the curve.

(Much more here about other aspects of cultural development, some of which are cyclical, some linear—all fascinating but not essential to understanding of what follows.)

Sexuality has until recently been such a rare phenomenon among civilized species that we had casually assumed it to be something of a drawback to the development of intelligence. Such sexual races as we did know seemed to have developed in spite of their biological peculiarity, but usually not until after the mechanical flair that often seemed to accompany the phenomenon had enabled them to escape their planet of origin for a more favorable environment.

I say more favorable because sexuality does seem to develop as an evolutionary compensation where (some terms untranslatable, some very broad, but generally describing circumstances, like extra-dense atmosphere, in which the normal rate of cosmic radiation was reduced to a degree that inhibited mutation and thus, evolution)...

As I said, this seemed almost a freak occurrence, and so it was, and is, here in the heart of the Galaxy. But in the more thinly populated spiral arms, the normal rate of radiation is considerably lower. It is only in the last centuries that we have begun to make contact with any considerable numbers of species from these sectors—and the incidence of sexuality among these peoples is markedly higher than before.

Recently, then, there has been fresh cause to investigate the causes and effects of sexuality; and there has been a comparative wealth of new material to work with.

(Here he goes into a review of the variety of sexual modes, ranging from two to seventeen sexes within a species, and more exotica-erotica of means, manners, and mores than a mere two-sexed biped can readily imagine. Restrain yourself. It's all in the full transcript.)

But let me for the moment confine myself to the simplest and most common situation, involving only two sexes. Recent investigations indicate that there is an apparently inevitable psychological effect of combining two essentially distinct subspecies in one genetic unit. (Sparks like mad.) I perceive that many of you have just experienced the same delight-dismay the first researchers felt at recognizing this so-obvious and so-overlooked parallel with the familiar cases of symbiosis.

The Terrans, mentioned earlier, are in many ways prototypical of sexuality in an intelligent species, and the unusual and rather dramatic events on Aldebaran VI have added greatly to our insights into the psychology of sexuality in general.

In this culture, dualism is very deep-rooted, affecting

every aspect of the i-e-s complex: not just philosophy and engineering, but mathematics, for instance, and mystique.

This cultural attitude starts with a duality, or two-sided symmetry, of body-structure. (Throughout this discussion he uses visual material—photos, diagrams, etc., of human bodies, anatomy, physiology, habitat, eating and mating habits, etc. Also goes off into some intriguing speculation of the chicken-or-egg type: is physical structure influenced by mental attitudes, or is it some inherent tendency of a chromosome pattern with *pairs* of genes from *pairs* of parents?)

In this respect, the Terrans are almost perfect prototypes, with two pairs of limbs, for locomotion and manipulation, extending from a central—single—abdominal cavity, which, although containing some single organs as well as some in pairs, is so symmetrically proportioned that the first assumption from an exterior view would be that everything inside was equally mirror-imaged. Actually, the main breathing apparatus is paired; the digestive system is single—although food intake is through an orifice with paired lips and two rows of teeth. In both "male" and "female" types, the organ of sexual contact is single, whereas the gamete-producers are pairs. There is a single, roundish head set on top of the abdomen, containing the primary sensory organs, all of which occur in pairs. Even the brain is paired!

I mentioned earlier that it is typical of the sexual races that the flair for physical engineering is rather stronger than the instinct for communication. This was an observed but little-understood fact for many centuries; it was not till this phenomenon of dualism (and triadism for the three-sexed, etc.) was studied that the earlier observation was clarified. If you will consider briefly the various sources of power and transport, you will realize that—outside of the psi-based techniques—most of these are involved with principles of symmetry and/or equivalence; these concepts are obvious to the two-sexed. On the other hand, the principle of unity, underlying all successful communication—physical, verbal, psial, or other—and which is also the basis for the application of psi to engineering problems—is for these species, in early stages, an almost mystical quality.

As with most life-forms, the reproductive act is, among sexual beings, both physically pleasurable and biologically compulsive, so that it is early equated with religio-mystic sensations. Among sexual species, these attitudes are intensified by the communicative aspects of the act. (Cartoon-type diagrams here which frankly gave me to think a bit!) We have much to learn yet about the psychology of this phenomenon, but enough has been established to make clear that the concept of unity for these races is initially almost entirely related to the use of their sexuality, and is later extended to other areas—religion and the arts of communication at first—with a mystical—indeed often reverent attitude!

I hardly need to remind you that the tendencies I have been discussing are the primitive and underlying ones. Obviously, at the point of contact, any species must have acquired at least enough sophistication in the field of physics—quanta, unified field theory, and atomic transmutation for a start—to have begun to look away from the essentially blind alley of dualistic thinking. But the extent to which these Terrans were still limited by their early developmental pattern is indicated by the almost unbelievable fact that they developed ultra-dimensional transport *before* discovering any more effective channels of communication than the electromagnetic!

Thus their first contacts with older civilizations were physical; and, limited as they still are almost entirely to aural and visual communication, they were actually unable to perceive their very first contact on Aldebaran VI.

(Shot of Prof. Eel in absolute sparkling convulsions goes to distance shots of planet and antiquated Earth spaceship in orbit: L-1 again. Then suborb launch drops, spirals to surface. Twenty bulky spacesuited figures emerge—not the same as in opening shots. This looks like actual photographic record of landing, which seems unlikely. Beautiful damn reconstruction, if so. Narration commences with Aldebaran date. I substitute Terran Calendar date we know for same, and accept gift of one more Rosetta Stone.)

The time is the year 2053. For more than six decades, this primitive giant of space has ployed its way through the restrictive medium of slow space. Twice before in its travels, the great ship has paused.

First at Procyon, where they found the system both uninhabited and uninviting; and at the time they did not yet know what urgent cause they had to make a landing. (Our date for Procyon exploration, from L-1 log, is 2016, which fits.)

Then at Saiph, two decades later, where they hoped for

ust a bare mimimum of hospitality—no more than safe footing for their launches, in which they could live while they tried to ensure their future survival. But this system's planets offered little hope. One Earth-size enveloped in horror-film type gases and nasty moistures. (One more with dense atmosphere of high acid content: probe from ship corroded in minutes.)

They limped on. A half-decade later they came to a time of decision, and determined not to try for the next nearest star system, but for the closest one from which their radio had received signs of intelligent life: Aldebaran.

What they had learned between Procyon and Saiph was that those of their crew who were born in space were not viable. The ship had been planned to continue, if necessary, long beyond the lifespan of its first crew. The Terran planners had ingeniously bypassed their most acute psychosocial problem, and staffed the ship with a starting crew of just one sex. Forty females started the journey, with a supply of sperm from one hundred genetically selected males carefully preserved on board.

Sex determination in this species is in the male chromosome, and most of the supply had been selected for production of females. The plan was to maintain the ship in transit with single-sexed population and restore the normal balance only at the end of the journey.

The Terrans have apparently reached a level of self-awareness that enables them to avoid the worst dangers of their own divisive quality, while utilizing the advantages of this special (pun intended—Prof. Eel was sparking again) ambivalence. Their biological peculiarities have, among other things, developed a far greater tolerance in the females for the type of physical constraints and social pressures that were to accompany the long, slow voyage. Males, on the other hand, being more aggressive, and more responsive to hostile challenges, would be needed for colonizing a strange planet. Dissertation on mammals here which says nothing new, but restates from an outsider's—rather admiring—viewpoint with some distinction. Should be a textbook classic—if we can ever release this thing.)

That was the plan. But when the first females born on the trip came to maturity, and could not conceive, the plan was changed. Three male infants were born to females of the original complement—less than half of whom, even then, were still alive and of child-bearing age.

(Well, he tells it effectively, but adds nothing to what w
know from the log. Conflicts among the women led to deat
of one boy, eventual suicide of another at adolescence. Re
maining mature male fails to impregnate known fertil
women. Hope of landing while enough fertiles remained t
start again pretty well frustrated at Saiph. Decision to tr
for nearest system eight light years off—with Aldebaran sti
farther. Faint fantastic hope still at landing, with just on
child-bearer left—the Matriarch, if you recall?)

Remembering the reasons for their choice of Aldebarar
you can imagine the reaction when that landing party, firs
lost all radio signals as they descended; then, could find n
trace whatsoever—to their senses—of habitation. The othe
planets were scouted, to no avail. The signals on the Mothe
Ship's more powerful radio continued to come from VI. On
wild hypothesis was followed up by a thorough and fruitles
search of the upper atmosphere. The atmosphere was barel
adequate to sustain life at the surface. Beam tracing re
peatedly located the signal beacon in a mountain of VI, whic
showed—to the Terrans—no other sign of intelligent life.

The only logical conclusion was that they had followed
"lighthouse beacon" to an empty world. The actual expla
nation, of course, was in the nature of the Arlemites, th
natives of Aldebaran VI.

Originating as a social-colonizing lichen, on a heav
planet, with—even at its prime—a barely adequate atm
sphere, the Arlemites combined smallness of individual si
with limited locomotive powers and superior air and wate
retentive ability. They developed, inevitably, as a highl
psioid culture—as far to one end of the psichophysical as th
Terrans are to the other. (My spelling up there. I think
represents true meaning better than "psycho.") The co
stantly thinning choice was between physical relocation an
a conscious evolutionary measure which this mature psioi
race was far better equipped to undertake: the Arlemites no
exist as a planet-wide diffusion of single-celled entities, con
prising just one individual, and a whole species.

(Visual stuff here helps establish concept—as if you or
just extended the space between cells.)

It seems especially ironic that the Arlemites were not onl
one of the oldest and most psioid of peoples—so that they ha
virtually all the accumulated knowledge of the Galaxy a

their disposal—but were also symbiote products. This background might have enabled them to comprehend the Terran mind and the problems confronting the visitors—except for the accidental combination of almost total psi-blindness in the Terrans, and the single-sexed complement of the ship.

The visitors could not perceive their hosts. The hosts could find no way to communicate with the visitors. The full complement of the ship, eventually, came down in launches, and lived in them, hopelessly, while they learned that their viability had indeed been completely lost in space. There was no real effort to return to the ship and continue the voyage. The ranks thinned, discipline was lost, deaths proliferated. Finally, it was only a child's last act of rebelliousness that mitigated the futility of the tragedy.

The last child saw the last adult die, and saw this immobility as an opportunity to break the most inviolable of rules. She went out of the launch—into near-airlessness that killed her within minutes.

But minutes were more than enough, with the much longer time afterwards for examination of the dead brain. It was through the mind of this one child, young enough to be still partially free of the rigid mental framework that made adult Terrans so inaccessible to Arlemites, that the basis was gained for most of the knowledge we now have.

Sorrowingly, the Arlemites generated an organism to decompose the Terrans and their artifacts, removing all traces of tragedy from the planet's surface. Meanwhile, they studied what they had learned, against future needs.

The technological ingenuity of these young sexuals will be apparent when I tell you that only four decades after the departure of that ill-fated ship, they were experimenting with ultra-dimensional travel. Even at the time of the landing at Aldebaran, ultra-di scouts were already exploring the systems closest to Sol. Eventually—within a decade after the child's death—one of these came to Aldebaran, and sighted the still-orbiting Mother Ship.

A second landing was clearly imminent. The Arlemites had still devised no way to aid this species to live in safety on their planet, nor did they have any means to communicate adequately with psi-negatives whose primary perceptions were aural and visual. But they did have, from the child's mind, a working knowledge of the strongest emotional symbols the culture knew, and they had long since devised a warning sign they could erect for visual perception. The statue of the Woman of Earth was constructed in an incredibly brief time through the combined efforts of the whole Arlemite consciousness.

They had no way to know that the new ship, designed for exploration, not colonizing, and equipped with ultra-di drive, which obviated the long slow traveling, was crewed entirely by males. Even had they known, they did not yet comprehend the extreme duality of the two-sexed double-culture. So they built their warning to the shape of the strongest fear-and-hate symbols of—a female.

(Shot of statue, held for some time, angle moving slowly. No narration. Assuming that emotional-projection notion—and I think we must—the timing here is such that I believe they first project what they seem to think a human female would feel, looking at it. I tried women on staff here. They focused more on phallic than female component, but were just as positive in reactions as males.???? Anyhow, like I said, no narration. What follows, though out of parens, is my own reaction.)

It seems more a return than a venture.

The Woman waits, as she has waited...always?...to greet her sons, welcomes us...home?...She sits in beauty, in peacefulness, perfect, complete, clean and fresh-colored...new?...no, *forever*...open, welcoming, yet so impervious...warm and...untouchable?...rather, *untouched*...almost, but never, forgotten Goddess...Allmother, Woman of Earth...enveloped, enveloping, in warmth and peace...

One stands back a bit: this is the peace of loving insight, of unquesting womanhood, of great age and undying youth...the peace of the past, of life that is passed, of that immortality that nothing mortal can ever achieve except through the frozen impression of living consciousness that we call *art*.

The young men are deeply moved and they make jokes. "Allmother," one hears them say, sarcastically, "Old White Goddess, whaddya know?"

Then they look up and are quiet under the smiling stone eyes. Even the ancient obscenely placed spaceship in her lap is not quite absurd, as it will seem in museum models—or tragic, as is the original overhead.

(Prof. Eel goes on to summarize the conclusions that seem obvious to him. Something is awfully wrong; that's obvious to me. How did they manage to build something so powerful out of total miscomprehension? What are we up against, anyhow? And, to get back to the matter of channels, what do you think this little story would do to Spaserve brass egos? Do you want to hold it top secret a while?)

End of Transcript

TO: Dr. Shlomo Mouna, Sr. Anthropologist, Ozma XII, Pluto
FROM: N.R.Hennessy, Solar Council Dome. Eros
DATE: 10/10/92
TRANSMISSION: VIA tight beam, scrambled. SENT: 0312 hrs. RECVD: 1027 hrs.

Dear Shlomo:
     Absolutely, let me see the full package before we release it elsewhere. I've got a few more questions, like: Do they know we're receiving it? How do we straighten them out? Or should we? Instinct says yes. Tactics says it is advantageous to be underestimated. Think best you come with package, and we'll braintrust it. Meantime, in reply to your bafflement—
     "L" class ships, you should have known, are for "Lysistrata." Five of them launched during brief Matriarchy at beginning of World Government on Terra, following Final War. So sort out your symbols *now*.
     And good grief, where did the *other* four land?

                                                            NRH

A.E. van Vogt's second contribution, "Secret Unattainable" (Astounding Science Fiction, *July 1942*) *is a good example of the reaction of science-fiction writers to Nazism and World War II. Never before (to the best of our knowledge) anthologized, it appeared in the author's excellent collection* Away and Beyond *(1952).*

SECRET UNATTAINABLE

By A. E. van Vogt

The file known as Secret Six was smuggled out of Berlin in mid-1945 when Russia was in sole occupation of the city. How it was brought to the United States is one of those dramatic true tales of World War II. The details cannot yet be published since they involve people now in the Russian zone of Germany.

All the extraordinary documents of this file, it should be emphasized, are definitely in the hands of our own authorities; and investigations are proceeding apace. Further revelations of a grand order may be expected as soon as one of the machines is built. All German models were destroyed by the Nazis early in 1945.

The documents date from 1937, and will be given chronologically, without reference to their individual importance.

But first, it is of surpassing interest to draw attention to the following news item, which appeared in the New York *Sun*, March 25, 1941, on page 17. At that time it appeared to have no significance whatever. The item:

GERMAN CREEK BECOMES RIVER

London, March 24 (delayed): A royal Air Force reconnaissance pilot today reported that a creek in northern Prussia, marked on the map as the Gribe Creek, has become a deep, swift river overnight. It is believed that an underground waterway burst its bounds. Several villages in the path of the new river showed under water. No report of the incident has yet been received from Berlin.

There never was any report from Berlin. It should again be pointed out that the foregoing news item was published in 1941; the documents which follow date from 1937, a period of four years. Four years of world-shaking history:

April 10, 1937

From   Secretary, Bureau of Physics
To   Reich and Prussian Minister of Science
Subject   10731–127–S–6

1. Enclosed is the report of the distinguished scientific board of inquiry which sat on the case of Herr Professor Johann Kenrube.

2. As you will see, the majority of the board oppose emphatically the granting of State funds for what they describe as a "fantastic scheme." They deny that a step-up tube would produce the results claimed, and refute utterly the number philosophy involved. Number, they say, is a function, not a reality, or else modern physics has no existence.

3. The minority report of Herr Professor Goureit, while thought-provoking, can readily be dismissed when it is remembered that Goureit, like Kenrube and Kenrube's infamous brother, was once a member of the SPD.

4. The board of inquiry, having in mind Hitler's desire that no field of scientific inquiry should be left unexplored, and as a generous gesture to Goureit, who has a very great reputation and a caustic pen, suggested that, if Kenrube

could obtain private funds for his research, he should be permitted to do so.

    5. Provided Geheime Staats Polizei do not object, I concur.

G.L.

    Author's Note: *The signature G.L. has been difficult to place. There appear to have been several secretaries of the Bureau of Physics Research, following one another in swift order. The best accounts identify him as Gottfried Lesser, an obscure B.Sc. who early joined the Nazi party, and for a period was its one and only science expert. Geheime Staats Polizei is of course Gestapo.*

MEMO   April 17, 1937

From   Chief, Science Branch, Gestapo

    If Kenrube can find the money, let him go ahead. Himmler concurs, provided supervision be strict.

K. Reissel

COPY ONLY   June 2, 1937

From   Co-ordinator Dept., Deutsche Bank

To   Gestapo

    The marginally noted personages have recently transferred sums totaling Reichsmarks four million five hundred thousand to the account of Herr Professor Johann Kenrube. For your information, please.

J. Pleup.

June 11, 1937

From   Gestapo

To   Reich and Prussian Minister of Science

Subject   Your 10731–127–S–6

    Per your request for further details on the private life of J. Kenrube since the death of his brother in June, 1934, in the purge:

    We quote from a witness, Peter Braun: "I was in a position to observe Herr Professor Kenrube very closely when the news was brought to him at Frankfort-on-Main that August, his brother, had been executed in the sacred blood purge.

    "Professor Kenrube is a thin, good-looking man with a very wan face normally. This face turned dark with color, then drained completely of blood. He clenched his hands and said: 'They've murdered him!' Then he rushed off to his room.

"Hours later, I saw him walking, hatless, hair disarrayed, along the bank of the river. People stopped to look at him, but he did not see them. He was very much upset that first day. When I saw him again the next morning, he seemed to have recovered. He said to me: 'Peter, we must all suffer for our past mistakes. The tragic irony of my brother's death is that he told me only a week ago in Berlin that he had been mistaken in opposing the National-sozialistiche Arbeitspartei. He was convinced they were doing great things. I am too much of a scientist ever to have concerned myself with politics.'"

You will note, Excellency, that this is very much the set speech of one who is anxious to cover up the indiscreet, emotional outburst of the previous day. However, the fact that he was able to pull himself together at all seems to indicate that affection of any kind is but shallowly rooted in his character. Professor Kenrube returned to his laboratories in July, 1934, and has apparently been hard at work ever since.

There has been some discussion here concerning Kenrube, by the psychologists attached to this office; and the opinion is expressed, without dissent, that in three years the professor will almost have forgotten that he had a brother.

K. Reissel.

MEMO AT BOTTOM OF LETTER:

I am more convinced than ever that psychologists should be seen and not heard. It is our duty to watch every relative of every person whose life is, for any reason, claimed by the State. If there are scientific developments of worthwhile nature in this Kenrube affair, let me know at once. His attainments are second to none. A master plan of precaution is in order.

Himmler.

October 24, 1937

From   Secretary, Bureau of Physics
To   Reich and Prussian Minister of Science
Subject   Professor Johann Kenrube

The following report has been received from our Special Agent Seventeen:

"Kenrube has hired the old steel and concrete fortress,

Gribe Schloss, overlooking the Gribe Creek, which flows into the Eastern Sea. This ancient fortress was formerly located on a small hill in a valley. The hill has subsided, however, and is now virtually level with the valley floor. We have been busy for more than a month making the old place livable, and installing machinery."

For your information, Agent Seventeen is a graduate in physics of Bonn University. He was for a time professor of physics at Muenchen. In view of the shortage of technicians, Kenrube has appointed Seventeen his chief assistant.

G.L.

May 21, 1938

From   Science Branch, Gestapo
To   Reich and Prussian Minister of Science
Subject   10731–127–S–6

Himmler wants to know the latest developments in the Kenrube affair. Why the long silence? Exactly what is Professor Kenrube trying to do, and what progress has he made? Surely, your secret agent has made reports.

K. Reissel.

June 3, 1938

From   Secretary, Bureau of Physics
To   Chief, Science Branch, Gestapo
Subject   Professor Johann Kenrube

Your letter of the 21st ultimo has been passed on to me. The enclosed précis of the reports of our Agent Seventeen will bring you up to date.

Be assured that we are keeping a careful watch on the developments in this case. So far, nothing meriting special attention has arisen.

G.L.

PRÉCIS OF MONTHLY REPORTS
OF AGENT SEVENTEEN

Our agent reports that Professor Kenrube's first act was to place him, Seventeen, in charge of the construction of the machine, thus insuring that he will have the most intimate knowledge of the actual physical details.

When completed, the machine is expected to occupy the entire room of the old fortress, largely because of the use of step-up vacuum tubes. In this connection, Seventeen describes how four electric dynamos were removed from Kenrube's old laboratories, their entire output channeled through the step-up tubes, with the result that a ninety-four percent improvement in efficiency was noted.

Seventeen goes on to state that orders for parts have been placed with various metal firms but, because of the defense program, deliveries are extremely slow. Professor Kenrube has resigned himself to the possibility that his invention will not be completed until 1944 or '45.

Seventeen, being a scientist in his own right, has become interested in the machine. In view of the fact that, if successful, it will insure measureless supplies of raw materials for our Reich, he urges that some effort be made to obtain priorities.

He adds that he has become quite friendly with Kenrube. He does not think that the Herr Professor suspects how closely he is connected with the Bureau of Science.

June 4, 1938

From   Gestapo
To   Reich and Prussian Minister of Science
Subject   10731–127–S–6

Raw materials! Why was I not informed before that Kenrube was expecting to produce raw materials? Why did you think I was taking an interest in this case, if not because Kenrube is a genius of the first rank; and therefore anything he does must be examined with the most minute care? But—raw materials! Are you all mad over there, or living in a world of pleasant dreams?

You will at once obtain from Herr Professor Kenrube the full plans, the full mathematics of his work, with photographs of the machine as far as it has progressed. Have your scientists prepare a report for me as to the exact nature of the raw materials that Kenrube expects to obtain. Is this some transmutation affair, or what is the method?

Inform Kenrube that he must supply this information or he will obtain no further materials. If he satisfies our requirements, on the other hand, there will be a quickening of supplies. Kenrube is no fool. He will understand the situation.

As for your agent, Seventeen, I am at once sending an agent to act as his bodyguard. Friendly with Kenrube indeed!

Himmler.

June 28, 1938

From   Gestapo
To   Secretary, Bureau of Physics
Subject   Secret Six

Have you received the report from Kenrube? Himmler is most anxious to see this the moment it arrives.

K. Reissel.

July 4, 1938

From   Gestapo
To   Secretary, Bureau of Physics
Subject   Secret Six

What about the Kenrube report? Is it possible that your office does not clearly grasp how important we regard this matter? We have recently discovered that Professor Kenrube's grandfather once visited a very curious and involved revenge on a man whom he hated years after the event that motivated the hatred. Every conceivable precaution must be taken to see to it that the Kenrube machine can be duplicated, and the machine itself protected.

Please send the scientific report the moment it is available.

K. Reissel.

July 4, 1938

From   Secretary, Bureau of Physics
To   Chief, Science Branch, Gestapo
Subject   Professor Johann Kenrube

The report, for which you have been asking, has come to hand, and a complete transcription is being sent to your office under separate cover. As you will see, it is very elaborately prepared; and I have taken the trouble to have a précis made of our scientific board's analysis of the report for your readier comprehension.

G.L.

PRÉCIS OF
SCIENTIFIC ANALYSIS OF KENRUBE'S REPORT
ON HIS INVENTION

General Statement of Kenrube's Theory: That there are two kinds of space in the universe, normal and hyper-space.

Only in normal space is the distance between star systems and galaxies great. It is essential to the nature of things, to the unity of material bodies, that intimate cohesion exist between every particle of matter, between, for instance, the earth and the universe as a whole.

Kenrube maintains that gravity does not explain the perfect and wonderful balance, the singleness of organism that is a galactic system. And that the theory of relativity merely evades the issue in stating that planets go around the sun because it is easier for them to do that than to fly off into space.

Kenrube's thesis, therefore, is that all the matter in the universe conjoins according to a rigid mathematical pattern, and that this conjunction presupposes the existence of hyperspace.

Object of the Invention: To bridge the gap through hyperspace between the Earth and any planet, or any part of any planet. In effect, this means that it would not be necessary to drill for oil in a remote planet. The machine would merely locate the oil stratum, and tap it at any depth; the oil would flow from the orifice of the machine which, in the case of the machine now under construction, is ten feet in diameter.

A ten-foot flow of oil at a pressure of four thousand feet a minute would produce approximately six hundred thousand tons of oil every hour.

Similarly, mining could be carried on simply by locating the ore-bearing veins, and skimming from them the purest ores.

It should be pointed out that, of the distinguished scientists who have examined the report, only Herr Professor Goureit claims to be able to follow the mathematics proving the existence of hyper-space.

COPY ONLY   July 14, 1938
TRANSCRIPTION OF INTERVIEW BY HERR HIMMLER OF PROFESSOR H. KLEINBERG, CHAIRMAN OF THE SCIENTIFIC COMMITTEE OF SCIENCE BRANCH, GESTAPA, INVESTIGATING REPORT OF HERR PROFESSOR JOHANN KENRUBE.

Q. You have studied the drawings and examined the mathematics?

A. Yes.

Q. What is your conclusion?

A. We are unanimously agreed that some fraud is being perpetrated.

Q. Does your verdict relate to the drawings of the invention, or to the mathematics explaining the theory?

A. To both. The drawings are incomplete. A machine made from those blueprints would hum with apparent power and purpose, but it would be a fraudulent uproar; the power simply goes oftener through a vacuumized circuit before returning to its source.

Q. I have sent your report to Kenrube. His comment is that almost the whole of modern electrical physics is founded on some variation of electricity being forced through a vacuum. What about that?

A. It is a half-truth.

Q. What about the mathematics?

A. There is the real evidence. Since Descartes—

Q. Please abstain from using these foreign names.

A. Pardon me. Since Libniz, number has been a function, a variable idea. Kenrube treats of number as an existing *thing*. Mathematics, he says, has living and being. You have to be a scientist to realize how incredible, impossible, ridiculous, such an idea is.

WRITTEN COMMENT ON THE ABOVE

I am not a scientist. I have no set ideas on the subject of mathematics or invention. I am, however, prepared to accept the theory that Kenrube is withholding information, and for this reason order that:

1. All further materials for the main machine be withheld.

2. Unlimited assistance be given Kenrube to build a model of his machine in the great government laboratories at Dresden. When, and not until, this model is in operation, permission will be given for the larger machine to be completed.

3. Meanwhile, Gestapo scientists will examine the machine at Gribe Schloss, and Gestapo construction experts will, if necessary, reinforce the building, which must have been dam-

aged by the settling of the hill on which it stands.

4. Gestapo agents will hereafter guard Gribe Schloss.

Himmler.

From   Secretary, Bureau of Physics
To   Chief, Science Branch, Gestapo
Subject   Herr Professor Kenrube

Enclosed is the quarterly précis of the reports of our Agent Seventeen.

For your information, please.

August Buehnen

Author's Note: *Buehnen, a party man who was educated in one of the Nazi two-year Science Schools, replaced G.L. as secretary of the Bureau of Physics about September, 1938.*

It is not known exactly what became of Lesser, who was a strong party man. There was a Brigadier General G. Lesser, a technical expert attached to the Fuehrer's headquarters at Smolensk. This man, and there is some evidence that he is the same, was killed in the first battle of Moscow.

QUARTERLY PRÉCIS OF REPORTS
OF AGENT SEVENTEEN

1. Herr Professor Kenrube is working hard on the model. He has at no time expressed bitterness over the enforced cessation of work on the main machine, and apparently accepts readily the explanation that the government cannot afford to allot him material until the model proves the value of his work.

2. The model will have an orifice of six inches. This compares with the ten-foot orifice of the main machine. Kenrube's intention is to employ it for the procuration of liquids, and believes that the model will of itself go far to reducing the oil shortage in the Reich.

3. The machine will be in operation sometime in the summer of 1939. We are all eager and excited.

February 7, 1939

From   Secretary, Bureau of Physics
To   Gestapo
Subject   Secret Six

The following precautions have been taken with the full knowledge and consent of Herr Professor Kenrube:

1. A diary in triplicate is kept of each day's progress. Two copies are sent daily to our office here. As you know, the other copy is submitted by us to your office.

2. Photographs are made of each part of the machine before it is installed, and detailed plans of each part are kept, all in triplicate, the copies distributed as described above.

3. From time to time independent scientists are called in. They are invariably impressed by Kenrube's name, and suspicious of his mathematics and drawings.

For your information, please.

August Buehnen.

March 1, 1939

From   Reich and Prussian Minister of Science
To   Herr Heinrich Himmler, Gestapo
Subject   The great genius, Herr Professor Kenrube

It is my privilege to inform Your Excellency that the world-shaking invention of Herr Professor Johann Kenrube went into operation yesterday, and has already shown fantastic results.

The machine is not a pretty one, and some effort must be made to streamline future reproductions of this model, with an aim toward greater mobility. In its present condition, it is strung out over the floor in a most ungainly fashion. Rough metal can be very ugly.

Its most attractive feature is the control board, which consists of a number of knobs and dials, the operator of which, by an arrangement of mirrors, can peer into the orifice, which is located on the right side of the control board, and faces away from it. (I do not like these awkward names, orifice and hyper-space. We must find a great name for this wonderful machine and its vital parts.)

When Buehnen and I arrived, Professor Kenrube was busy opening and shutting little casements in various parts of that sea of dull metal. He took out and examined various items.

At eleven forty-five, Kenrube stationed himself at the control board, and made a brief speech comparing the locator dials of the board to the dial on a radio which tunes in stations. His dials, however, tuned in planets; and, quite simply, that is what he proceeded to do.

It appears that the same planets are always on exactly the same gradation of the main dial; and the principle extends down through the controls which operate to locate sections of planets. Thus it is always possible to return to any point of any planet. You will see how important this is.

The machine had already undergone its first tests, so Kenrube now proceeded to turn to various planets previously selected; and a fascinating show it was.

Gazing through the six-inch orifice is like looking through a glassless window. What a great moment it will be when the main machine is in operation, and we can *go* through the ten-foot orifice.

The first planet was a desolate, frozen affair, dimly lighted by a remote red sun. It must have been airless because there was a whistling sound, as the air rushed out of our room into that frigid space. Some of that deadly cold came trickling through, and we quickly switched below the surface of the planet.

Fantastic planet! It must be an incredibly heavy world, for it is a treasure house of the heavier metals. Everywhere we turned, the soil formation showed a shifting pattern of gold, silver, zinc, iron, tin—thousands of millions of tons.

At Professor Kenrube's suggestion, I put on a pair of heavy gloves, and removed a four-inch rock of almost pure gold. It simply lay there in a gray shale, but it was so cold that the moisture of the room condensed on it, forming a thick hoarfrost. How many ages that planet must have frozen for the cold to penetrate so far below the surface!

The second planet was a vast expanse of steaming swamps and tropical forests, much as Earth must have been forty million years ago. However, we found not a single trace of animal, insect, reptile, or other non-floral life.

The third, fourth, and fifth planets were devoid of any kind of life, either plant or animal. The sixth planet might have been Earth, except that its green forests, its rolling plains showed no sign of animal or intelligent life. But it is on this planet that oil had been located by Kenrube and Seventeen in their private tests. When I left, a pipeline, previously rigged up, had been attached to the orifice, and was vibrating with oil at the colossal flow speed of nearly one thousand miles per hour.

This immense flow has now been continuous for more than twenty-four hours; and I understand it has already been necessary to convert the great water reservoir in the south suburbs to storage space for oil.

It may be *nouveau riche* to be storing oil at great inconvenience, when the source can be tapped at will. But I personally will not be satisfied until we have a number of these machines in action. It is better to be childish and have the oil than logical and have regrets.

I cannot conceive what could go wrong now. Because of our precautions, we have numerous and complete plans of the machines. It is necessary, of course, to insure that our enemies do not learn our secret, and on this point I would certainly appreciate your most earnest attention.

The enormous potentialities of this marvelous instrument expand with every minute spent in thinking about it. I scarcely slept a wink last night.

March 1, 1939

From   Chief, Criminal Investigation Branch, Gestapo
To   Reich and Prussian Minister of Science
Subject   Secret Six

Will you please inform this office without delay of the name of every scientist or other person who has any knowledge, however meager, of the Kenrube machine?

Reinhard Heydrich.

Author's Note: *This is the Heydrich, handsome, ruthless Heydrich, who in 1941 bloodily repressed the incipient Czech revolt, who, after the notorious Himmler became Minister of the Interior, succeeded his former master as head of the Gestapo, and who was subsequently assassinated.*

March 2, 1939

From   Secretary, Bureau of Physics
To   R. Heydrich
Subject   Secret Six

The list of names for which you asked is herewith attached.

August Buehnen.

COMMENT AT BOTTOM OF LETTER

In view of the importance of this matter, some changes should be made in the precautionary plan drawn up a few months ago with respect to these personages. Two, not one, of our agents must be assigned to keep secret watch on each of these individuals. The rest of the plan can be continued as arranged with one other exception: In the event that any of these men suspect that they are being watched, I must be informed at once. I am prepared to explain to such person, within limits, the truth of the matter, so that he may not be personally worried. The important thing is we do not want these people suddenly to make a run for the border.

                                                             Himmler.

SPECIAL DELIVERY
PERSONAL
From   Reich and Prussian Minister of Science
To   Herr Heinrich Himmler
Subject Professor Johann Kenrube
I this morning informed the Fuehrer of the Kenrube machine. He became very excited. The news ended his indecision about the Czechs. The army will move to occupy.

For your advance information, please.

                                             March 13, 1939
From   Gestapo
To   Reich and Prussian Minister of Science
Subject The Dresden Explosion
The incredibly violent explosion of the Kenrube model must be completely explained. A board of discovery should be set up at Dresden with full authority. I must be informed day by day of the findings of this court.

This is a very grim business. Your agent, Seventeen, is among those missing. Kenrube is alive, which is very suspicious. There is no question of arresting him; the only thing that matters is to frustrate future catastrophes of this kind. His machine has proved itself so remarkable that he must be conciliated at all costs until we can be sure that everything is going right.

Let me know *everything*.

                                                             Himmler.

PRELIMINARY REPORT OF AUGUST BUEHNEN

When I arrived at the scene of the explosion, I noticed immediately that a solid circle, a remarkably precise circle, of the wall of the fifth floor of the laboratories—where the Kenrube machine is located—had been sliced out as by some inconceivable force.

Examining the edges of this circle, I verified that it could not have been heat which performed so violent an operation. Neither the brick nor the exposed steel was in any way singed or damaged by fire.

The following facts have been given to me of what transpired:

It had been necessary to cut the flow of oil because of the complete absence of further storage space. Seventeen, who was in charge—Professor Kenrube during this whole time was at Gribe Schloss working on the main machine—was laboriously exploring other planets in search of rare metals.

The following is an extract from my interview with Jacob Schmidt, a trusted laboratory assistant in the government service:

Q. You say, Herr———(Seventeen) took a piece of ore to the window to examine it in the light of the sun?

A. He took it to the window, and stood there looking at it.

Q. This placed him directly in front of the orifice of the machine?

A. Yes.

Q. Who else was in front of the orifice?

A. Dobelmanns, Minster, Freyburg, Tousand-friend.

Q. These were all fellow assistants of yours?

A. Yes.

Q. What happened then?

A. There was a very loud click from the machine, followed by a roaring noise.

Q. Was anyone near the control board?

A. No, sir.

Q. It was an automatic action of the machine?

A. Yes. The moment it happened we all turned to face the machine.

Q. All of you? Herr———(Seventeen), too?

A. Yes, he looked around with a start, just as Minster cried out that a blue light was coming from the orifice.

Q. A blue light. What did this blue light replace?

A. A soil formation of a planet, which we had numbered

447–711–Gradation A–131–8, which is simply its location on the dials. It was from this soil that Herr—— (Seventeen) had taken the ore sample.

Q. And then, just like that, there was the blue light?
A. Yes. And for a few instants that was all there was, the blue light, the strange roaring sound, and us standing there half paralyzed.
Q. Then it flared forth?
A. It was terrible. It was such an intense blue it hurt my eyes, even though I could only see it in the mirror over the orifice. I have not the faintest impression of heat. But the wall was gone, and all the metal around the orifice.
Q. And the men?
A. Yes, and the men, all five of them.

March 18, 1939

From   Secretary, Bureau of Physics
To   Chief, Science Branch, Gestapo
Subject   Dresden Explosion

I am enclosing a précis of the report of the Court of Inquiry, which has just come to hand. The report will be sent to you as soon as a transcription has been typed.

For your information, please.

August Buehnen

PRÉCIS OF REPORT OF COURT OF INQUIRY

1. It has been established:
   (A) That the destruction was preceded by a clicking sound.
   (B) That this click came from the machine.
   (C) That the machine is fitted with automatic finders.
2. The blue flame was the sole final cause of the destruction.
3. No theory exists, or was offered, to explain the blue light. It should be pointed out that Kenrube was not called to testify.
4. The death of Herr——(Seventeen) and of his assistants was entirely due to the momentary impulse that had placed them in the path of the blue fire.
5. The court finds that the machine could have been tampered with, that the click that preceded the explosion could have been the result of some automatic device previously set to tamper with the machine. No other evidence of sabotage exists, and no one in the room at the time was to blame for the accident.

COPY ONLY

FOR MINISTRY OF SCIENCE   March 19, 1939

From   Major H. L. Guberheit
To   Minister for Air
Subject   Destruction of plane, type JU-88

I have been asked to describe the destruction of a plane under unusual circumstances, as witnessed by several hundred officers and men under my command.

The JU-88, piloted by Cadet Pilot Herman Kiesler, was approaching the runway for a landing, and was at the height of about five hundred feet when there was a flash of intense blue—and the plane vanished.

I cannot express too strongly the violence, the intensity, the blue vastness of the explosion. It was titanic. The sky was alive with light reflections. And though a bright sun was shining, the entire landscape grew brilliant with that blue tint.

There was no sound of explosion. No trace of this machine was subsequently found, no wreckage. The time of the accident was approximately ten-thirty A.M., March 13th.

There has been great uneasiness among the students during the past week.

For your information, please.

H. L. Guberheit
Major, C. Air Station 473

COMMENT AT BOTTOM OF LETTER

Excellency—I wish most urgently to point out that the time of this unnatural accident coincides with the explosion of "blue" light from the orifice of the Kenrube machine.

I have verified that the orifice was tilted ever so slightly upward, and that the angle would place the beam at a height of five hundred feet near the airport in question.

The staggering feature is that the airport referred to is *seventy-five miles* from Dresden. The greatest guns ever developed can scarcely fire that distance, and yet the incredible power of the blue energy showed no diminishment. Literally, it disintegrated metal and flesh—everything.

I do not dare to think what would have happened if that devastating flame had been pointed not away from but at the ground.

Let me have your instructions at once, because here is beyond doubt the weapon of the ages.

August Buehnen

March 19, 1939

From   Chief, Science Branch, Gestapo
To   Reich and Prussian Minister of Science
Subject   Secret Six

In perusing the report of the inquiry board, we were amazed to note that Professor Kenrube was not questioned in this matter.

Be assured that there is no intention here of playing up to this man. We absolutely require an explanation from him. Send Herr Buehnen to see Kenrube and instruct him to employ the utmost firmness if necessary.

K. Reissel

March 21, 1939

From   Secretary, Bureau of Physics
To   Chief, Science Branch, Gestapo
Subject   Dresden Explosion

As per your request, I talked with Kenrube at Gribe Schloss.

It was the second time I had seen him, the first time being when I accompanied his Excellency, the Minister of Science, to Dresden to view the model; and I think I should point out here that Herr Professor Kenrube's physical appearance is very different from what I had been led to expect from the description recorded in File Secret Six. I had pictured him a lean, fanatic-eyed type. He *is* tall, but he must have gained weight in recent years, for his body is well filled out, and his face and eyes are serene, with graying hair to crown the effect of a fine, scholarly, middle-aged man.

It is unthinkable to me that this is some madman plotting against the Reich.

The first part of his explanation of the blue light was a most curious reference to the reality of mathematics, and, for a moment, I almost thought he was attempting to credit the accident to this *actuality* of his incomprehensible number system.

Then he went on to the more concrete statement that a great star must have intruded into the plane of the planet under examination. The roaring sound that was heard he attributed to the fact that the component elements of the air in the laboratory were being sucked into the sun, and destroyed.

The sun, of course, would be in a state of balance all its own, and therefore would not come into the room until the balance had been interfered with by the air of the room.

(I must say my own explanation would be the reverse of this; that is, the destruction of the air would possibly create a momentary balance, a barrier, during which time nothing of the sun came into the room except light reflections. However, the foregoing is what Kenrube said, and I presume it is based on his own mathematics. I can only offer it for what it is worth.)

Abruptly, the balance broke down. For a fraction of an instant, then, before the model hyper-space machine was destroyed, the intolerable energies of a blue-white sun poured forth.

It would have made no difference if the airplane that was caught in the beam of blue light had been farther away from Dresden than seventy-five miles—that measureless force would have reached seven thousand five hundred miles just as easily, or seventy-five thousand.

The complete absence of visible heat is no evidence that it was not a sun. At forty million degrees Fahrenheit, heat, as we know it, does not exist.

The great man went on to say that he had previously given some thought to the danger from suns, and that in fact he was in the late mathematical stage of developing an attachment that would automatically reject bodies larger than ten thousand miles in diameter.

In his opinion, efforts to control the titanic energies of suns should be left to a later period, and should be carried out on uninhabited planets by scientists who have gone through the orifice and who have been then cut off from contact with earth.

August Buehnen

COMMENT ATTACHED

Kenrube's explanation sounds logical, and it does seem incredible that he would meddle with such forces, though it is significant that the orifice was tilted "slightly upward." We can dispense with his advice as to when and how we should experiment with sun energies. The extent of the danger seems to be a momentary discharge of inconceivable forces, and then destruction of the machine. If at the moment of discharge the orifice was slightly tilted toward London or New York, and if a sufficient crisis existed, the loss of one more machine would be an infinitesimal cost.

As for Kenrube's fine, scholarly appearance, I think Buehnen has allowed himself to be carried away by the greatness of the invention. The democrats of Germany are not necessarily madmen, but here, as abroad, they are our remorseless enemies.

We must endeavor to soften Kenrube by psychological means.

I cannot forget that *there is not now a working model of the Kenrube machine in existence.* Until there is, all the fine, scholarly-looking men in the world will not convince me that what happened was entirely an accident.

The deadly thing about all this is that we have taken an irrevocable step with respect to the Czechs; and war in the west is now inevitable.

                                                    Himmler

                                                    May 1, 1939
From   Chief, Science Branch, Gestapo.
To   Reich and Prussian Minister of Science
Subject   Secret Six
    The Fuehrer has agreed to exonerate completely August Kenrube, the brother of Herr Professor Kenrube. As you will recall, August Kenrube was killed in the sacred purge of June, 1934. It will now be made clear that his death was an untimely accident, and that he was a true German patriot.

    This is in line with our psychological attack on Professor Kenrube's suspected anti-Nazism.

                                                    K. Reissel.

                                                    June 17, 1939
From   Secretary, Bureau of Physics
To   Chief, Science Branch, Gestapo
Subject   Professor Johann Kenrube
    In line with our policy to make Kenrube realize his oneness with the community of German peoples, I had him address the convention of mathematicians. The speech, of which I enclose a copy, was a model one; three thousand words of

glowing generalities, giving not a hint as to his true opinions on anything. However, he received the ovation of his life; and I think he was pleased in spite of himself.

Afterward, I saw to it—without, of course, appearing directly—that he was introduced to Fräulein Ilse Weber.

As you know, the Fräulein is university-educated, a mature, modern young woman; and I am sure that she is merely taking on one of the many facets of her character in posing to Kenrube as a young woman who has decided quite calmly to have a child, and desires the father to be biologically of the highest type.

I cannot see how any human male, normal or abnormal, could resist the appeal of Fräulein Weber.

August Buehnen.

July 11, 1939

From   Chief, Science Branch, Gestapo
To   Secretary, Bureau of Physics
Subject   Secret Six

Can you give me some idea when the Kenrube machine will be ready to operate? What about the duplicate machines which we agreed verbally would be built without Kenrube's knowledge? Great decisions are being made. Conversations are being conducted that will shock the world, and, in a general way, the leaders are relying on the Kenrube machine.

In this connection please submit as your own some variation of the following memorandum. It is from the Fuehrer himself, and therefore I need not stress its urgency.

K. Reissel.

MEMORANDUM OF ADOLF HITLER

Is it possible to tune the Kenrube machine to our own earth?

July 28, 1939

From   Secretary, Bureau of Physics
To   Chief, Science Branch, Gestapo
Subject   Secret Six

I enclose the following note from Kenrube, which is self-explanatory. We have retained a copy.

August Buehnen

NOTE FROM KENRUBE

Dear Herr Buehnen:

The answer to your memorandum is yes.

In view of the international anxieties of the times, I offer the following suggestions as to weapons that can be devised from the hyper-space machine:

1. Any warship can be rendered noncombatant at critical moments by draining of its oil tanks.

2. Similarly, enemy oil-storage supplies can be drained at vital points. Other supplies can be blown up or, if combustible, set afire.

3. Troops, tanks, trucks, and all movable war materials can be transported to any point on the globe, behind enemy lines, into cities, by the simple act of focusing the orifice at the desired destination—and driving it and them through. I need scarcely point out that my machine renders railway and steamship transport obsolete: The world shall be transformed.

4. It might even be possible to develop a highly malleable, delicately adjusted machine, which can drain the tanks of airplanes in full flight.

5. Other possibilities, too numerous to mention, suggest themselves with the foregoing as a basis.

Kenrube.

COMMENT ATTACHED

This machine is like a dream. With it, the world is ours, for what conceivable combination of enemies could fight an army that appeared from nowhere on their flank, in the centers of their cities, in London, New York, in the Middle-West plains of America, in the Ural Mountains, in the Caucasus? Who can resist us?

K. Reissel.

ADDITIONAL COMMENT

My dear Reissel:

Your enthusiasm overlooks the fact that the machine is still only in the building stage. What worries me is that our hopes are being raised to a feverish height—what greater revenge could there be than to lift us to the ultimate peak of confidence, and then smash it in a single blow?

Every day that passes we are involving ourselves more deeply, decisions are being made from which there is already no turning back. When, oh, when will this machine be finished?

H.

July 29, 1939

From   Secretary, Bureau of Physics
To   Chief, Science Branch, Gestapo
Subject   Secret Six

The hyper-space machine at Gribe Schloss will be completed in February, 1941. No less than five duplicate machines are under construction, unknown to Kenrube. What is done is that, when he orders an installation for the Gribe Schloss machine, the factory turns out five additional units from the same plans.

In addition, a dozen model machines are being secretly constructed from the old plans, but, as they must be built entirely from drawings and photographs, they will take not less, but more, time to build than the larger machines.

August Buehnen

August 2, 1939

From   Secretary, Bureau of Physics
To   Herr Heinrich Himmler
Subject   Professor Johann Kenrube

I have just now received a telegram from Fräulein Ilse Weber that she and the Herr Professor were married this morning, and that Kenrube will be a family man by the middle of next summer.

August Buehnen

COMMENT WRITTEN BELOW

This is great news indeed. One of the most dangerous aspects of the Kenrube affair was that he was a bachelor without ties. Now, we have him. He has committed himself to the future.

Himmler.

FURTHER COMMENT

I have advised the Fuehrer, and our great armies will move into Poland at the end of this month.

H.

August 8, 1939

From   Gestapo
To   Reich and Prussian Minister of Science
Subject   Secret Six

I have had second thought on the matter of Fräulein Ilse Weber, now Frau Kenrube. In view of the fact that a woman, no matter how intelligent or objective, becomes emotionally involved with the man who is the father of her children, I would advise that Frau Kenrube be appointed to some great executive post in a war industry. This will keep her own patriotism at a high level, and thus she will continue to have exemplary influence on her husband. Such influence cannot be overestimated.

Himmler.

January 3, 1940

From   Secretary, Bureau of Physics
To   Chief, Science Branch, Gestapo

In glancing through the correspondence, I notice that I have neglected to inform you that our Agent Twelve has replaced Seventeen as Kenrube's chief assistant.

Twelve is a graduate of Munich, and was for a time attached to the General Staff in Berlin as a technical expert.

In my opinion, he is a better man for our purpose than was Seventeen, in that Seventeen, it seemed to me, had toward the end a tendency to associate himself with Kenrube in what might be called a scientific comradeship, an intellectual fellowship. He was in a mental condition where he quite unconsciously defended Kenrube against our suspicion.

Such a situation will not arise with Twelve. He is a practical man to the marrow. He and Kenrube have nothing in common.

Kenrube accepted Twelve with an attitude of what-does-it-matter-who-they-send. It was so noticeable that it is now clear that he is aware that these men are agents of ours.

Unless Kenrube has some plan of revenge which is beyond

all precautions, the knowledge that he is being watched should exercise a restraint on any impulses to evil that he may have.

                                                    August Buehnen.

Author's Note: *Most of the letters written in the year 1940 were of a routine nature, consisting largely of detailed reports as to the progress of the machine. The following document, however, was an exception:*

                                                    December 17, 1940

From   Reich and Prussian Minister of Science
To   Herr Heinrich Himmler
Subject   Secret Six

The following work has now been completed on the fortress Gribe Schloss, where the Kenrube machine is nearing completion:

1. Steel doors have been fitted throughout.

2. A special, all-steel chamber has been constructed from which, by an arrangement of mirrors, the orifice of the machine can be watched without danger to the watchers.

3. This watching post is only twenty steps from a paved road which runs straight up out of the valley.

4. A concrete pipeline for the transportation of oil is nearing completion.

                                                    August Buehnen.

MEMO AT BOTTOM OF LETTER

To Reinhard Heydrich:

Please make arrangements for me to inspect personally the reconstructed Gribe Schloss. It is Hitler's intention to attend the official opening.

The plan now is to invade England via the Kenrube machine possibly in March, not later than April. In view of the confusion that will follow the appearance of vast armies in every part of the country, this phase of the battle of Europe should be completed by the end of April.

In May, Russia will be invaded. This should not require more than two months. The invasion of the United States is set for July or August.

                                                    Himmler.

January 31, 1941

From   Secretary, Bureau of Physics
To   Chief, Science Branch, Gestapo
Subject   Secret Six

It will be impossible to complete the five extra Kenrube machines at the same time as the machine at Gribe Schloss. Kenrube has changed some of the designs, and our engineers do not know how to fit the sections together until they have studied Kenrube's method of connection.

I have personally asked Kenrube the reason for the changes. His answer was that he was remedying weaknesses that he had noticed in the model. I am afraid that we shall have to be satisfied with this explanation, and complete the duplicate machines after the official opening, which is not now scheduled until March 20th. The delay is due to Kenrube's experimentation with design.

If you have any suggestions, please let me hear them. I frankly do not like this delay, but what to do about it is another matter.

August Buehnen.

February 3, 1941

From   Chief, Science Branch, Gestapo
To   Secretary, Bureau of Physics
Subject   Secret Six

Himmler says to do nothing. He notes that you are still taking the precaution of daily photographs, and that your agent, Twelve, who replaced Seventeen, is keeping a diary in triplicate.

There has been a meeting of leaders, and this whole matter discussed very thoroughly, with special emphasis on critical analysis of the precautions taken, and of the situation that would exist if Kenrube should prove to be planning some queer revenge.

You will be happy to know that not a single additional precaution was thought of, and that our handling of the affair was commended.

K. Reissel.

February 18, 1941

From   Gestapo
To   Reich and Prussian Minister of Science
Subject   Secret Six

In view of our anxieties, the following information, which I have just received, will be welcome:

Frau Kenrube, formerly our Ilse Weber, has reserved a private room in the maternity ward of the Prussian State Hospital for May 7th. This will be her second child, another hostage to fortune by Kenrube.

K. Reissel.

COPY ONLY
MEMO   March 11, 1941

I have today examined Gribe Schloss and environs and found everything according to plan.

Himmler

March 14, 1941

From   Secretary, Bureau of Physics
To   Herr Himmler, Gestapo
Subject   Secret Six

You will be relieved to know the reason for the changes in design made by Kenrube.

The first reason is rather unimportant. Kenrube refers to the mathematical structure involved, and states that, for his own elucidation, he designed a functional instrument whose sole purpose was to defeat the mathematical reality of the machine. This is very obscure, but he had referred to it before, so I call it to your attention.

The second reason is that there are now two orifices, not one. The additional orifice is for focusing. The following illustration will clarify what I mean:

Suppose we have a hundred thousand trucks in Berlin, which we wished to transfer to London. Under the old method, these trucks would have to be driven all the way to the Gribe Schloss before they could be transmitted.

With the new two-orifice machine, one orifice would be focused in Berlin, the other in London. The trucks would drive through from Berlin to London.

Herr Professor Kenrube seems to anticipate our needs before we realize them ourselves.

August Buehnen.

March 16, 1941

From   Gestapo
To   Secretary, Bureau of Physics
Subject   Secret Six

The last sentence of your letter of March 14th to the effect that Kenrube seems to anticipate our needs made me very uncomfortable, because the thought that follows naturally is: Is he also anticipating our plans?

I have accordingly decided at this eleventh hour that we are dealing with a man who may be our intellectual superior in every way. Have your agent advise us the moment the machine has undergone its initial tests. Decisive steps will be taken immediately.

Himmler.

March 19, 1941

DECODED TELEGRAM

KENRUBE MACHINE WAS TESTED TODAY AND WORKED PERFECTLY.

AGENT TWELVE.

COPY ONLY
MEMO   March 19, 1941

To Herr Himmler:

This is to advise that Professor Johann Kenrube was placed under close arrest, and has been removed to Gestapo Headquarters, Berlin.

R. Heydrich.

March 19, 1941

DECODED TELEGRAM

REPLYING TO YOUR TELEPHONE INSTRUCTIONS, WISH TO STATE ALL AUTOMATIC DEVICES HAVE BEEN REMOVED FROM KENRUBE MACHINE. NONE SEEMED TO HAVE BEEN TAMPERED WITH. MADE PERSONAL TEST OF MACHINE. IT WORKED PERFECTLY.

TWELVE

COMMENT WRITTEN BELOW

I shall recommend that Kenrube be retired under guard to his private laboratories, and not allowed near a hyperspace machine until after the conquest of the United States.

And with this, I find myself at a loss for further precautions. In my opinion, all thinkable possibilities have been covered. The only dangerous man has been removed from the zone where he can be actively dangerous; a careful examination has been made to ascertain that he has left no automatic devices that will cause havoc. And, even if he has, five other large machines and a dozen small ones are nearing completion, and it is impossible that he can have tampered with them.

If anything goes wrong now, thoroughness is a meaningless word.

Himmler.

March 21, 1941

From   Gestapo
To   Secretary, Bureau of Physics
Subject   Secret Six

Recriminations are useless. What I would like to know is: What in God's name happened?

Himmler.

March 22, 1941

From   Secretary, Bureau of Physics
To   Herr Heinrich Himmler
Subject   Secret Six

The reply to your question is being prepared. The great trouble is the confusion among the witnesses, but it should not be long before some kind of coherent reply is ready.

Work is being rushed to complete the duplicate machines on the basis of photographs and plans that were made from day to day. I cannot see how anything can be wrong in the long run.

As for Number One, shall we send planes over with bombs?

August Buehnen.

COPY ONLY
MEMO   March 23, 1941
From   Detention Branch, Gestapo

The four agents, Gestner, Luslich, Heinreide, and Muem-

mer, who were guarding Herr Professor Johann Kenrube
report that he was under close arrest at our Berlin headquarters until six P.M., March 21st. At six P.M., he abruptly
vanished.

S. Duerner

COMMENT WRITTEN BELOW

Kenrube was at Gribe Schloss before two P.M., March 21st.
This completely nullifies the six-P.M. story. Place these scoun-
drels under arrest, and bring them before me at eight o'clock
tonight.

Himmler

COPY ONLY

EXAMINATION BY HERR HIMMLER OF F. GESTNER

Q. Your name?
A. Gestner. Fritz Gestner. Long service.
Q. Silence. If we want to know your service, we'll check it
   in the record.
A. Yes, sir.
Q. That's a final warning. You answer my questions, or I'll
   have your tongue.
A. Yes, sir.
Q. You're one of the stupid fools set to guard Kenrube?
A. I was one of the four guards, sir.
Q. Answer yes or no.
A. Yes, sir.
Q. What was your method of guarding Kenrube?
A. By twos. Two of us at a time were in the great white cell
   with him.
Q. Why weren't the four of you there?
A. We thought—
Q. You thought! Four men were ordered to guard Kenrube
   and—By God, there'll be dead men around here before
   this night is over. I want to get this clear: There was
   never a moment when two of you were not in the cell
   with Kenrube?
A. Always two of us.
Q. Which two were with Kenrube at the moment he dis-
   appeared?
A. I was. I and Johann Luslich.
Q. Oh, you know Luslich by his first name. An old friend
   of yours, I suppose?

A. No, sir.

Q. You knew Luslich previously, though?

A. I met him for the first time when we were assigned to guard Herr Kenrube.

Q. Silence! Answer yes or no. I've warned you about that.

A. Yes, sir.

Q. Ah, you admit knowing him?

A. No, sir. I meant—

Q. Look here, Gestner, you're in a very bad spot. Your story is a falsehood on the face of it. Tell me the truth. Who are your accomplices?

A. None, sir.

Q. You mean you were working this alone?

A. No, sir.

Q. You damned liar! Gestner, we'll get the truth out of you if we have to tear you apart.

A. I am telling the truth, Excellency.

Q. Silence, you scum. What time did you say Kenrube disappeared?

A. About six o'clock.

Q. Oh, he did, eh? Well, never mind that. What was Kenrube doing just before he vanished?

A. He was talking to Luslich and me.

Q. What right had you to talk to the prisoner?

A. Sir, he mentioned an accident he expected to happen at some official opening somewhere.

Q. He what?

A. Yes, sir; and I was desperately trying to find out where, so that I could send a warning.

Q. Now, the truth is coming. So you do know about this business, you lying rat! Well, let's have the story you've rigged up.

A. The dictaphone will bear out every word.

Q. Oh, the dictaphone was on.

A. Every word is recorded.

Q. Oh, why wasn't I told about this in the first place?

A. You wouldn't lis—

Q. Silence, you fool! By God, the coöperation I get around this place. Never mind. Just what was Kenrube doing at the moment he disappeared?

A. He was sitting—talking.

Q. Sitting? You'll swear to that?

A. To the Fuehrer himself.

Q. He didn't move from his chair? He didn't walk over to
    an orifice?
A. I don't know what you mean, Excellency.
Q. So you pretend, anyway. But that's all for the time being.
    You will remain under arrest. Don't think we're through
    with you. That goes also for the others.

AUTHOR'S NOTE:
*The baffled fury expressed by the normally calm Himmler in
this interview is one indication of the dazed bewilderment that
raged through high Nazi circles. One can imagine the accu-
sation and counter-accusation and then the slow, deadly realization of the situation.*

                                              March 24, 1941
From   Reich and Prussian Minister of Science
To   Gestapo
Subject   Secret Six
    Enclosed is the transcription of a dictaphone record which
was made by Professor Kenrube. A careful study of these
deliberate words, combined with what he said at Gribe
Schloss, may reveal his true purpose, and may also explain
the incredible thing that happened.
    I am anxiously awaiting your full report.

                                              Himmler.

TRANSCRIPTION OF DICTAPHONE RECORD P–679–423–1;
CONVERSATION OF PROFESSOR JOHANN KENRUBE IN WHITE CELL
26, ON 3/21/41.

    (Note: K. refers to Kenrube, G. to any of the guards.)
K. A glass of water, young man.
G. I believe there is no objection to that. Here.
K. It must be after five.
G. There is no necessity for you to know the time.
K. No, but the fact that it is late is very interesting. You
    see, I have invented a machine. A very queer machine
    it is going to seem when it starts to react according to
    the laws of real as distinct from functional mathematics.
    You have the dictaphone on, I hope?
G. What kind of a smart remark is that?
K. Young man, that dictaphone had better be on. I intend
    talking about my invention, and your masters will skin
    you alive if it's not recorded. Is the dictaphone on?

G. Oh, I suppose so.

K. Good. I may be able to finish what I have to say. I may not.

G. Don't worry. You'll be here to finish it. Take your time.

K. I had the idea before my brother was killed in the purge, but I thought of the problem then as one of education. Afterward, I saw it as revenge. I hated the Nazis and all they stood for.

G. Oh, you did, eh? Go on.

K. My plan after my brother's murder was to build for the Nazis the greatest weapon the world will ever know, and then have them discover that only I, who understood and who accordingly *fitted in* with the immutable laws involved—only I could ever operate the machine. And I would have to be present physically. That way I would prove my indispensability and so transform the entire world to my way of thinking.

G. We've got ways of making indispensables work.

K. Oh, that part is past. I've discovered what is going to happen—to me as well as to my invention.

G. Plenty is going to happen to you. You've already talked yourself into a concentration camp.

K. After I discovered that, my main purpose was simplified. I wanted to do the preliminary work on the machine and, naturally, I had to do that under the prevailing system of government—by cunning and misrepresentation. I had no fear that any of the precautions they were so laboriously taking would give them the use of the machine, not this year, not this generation, not ever. The machine simply cannot be used by people who think as they do. For instance, the model that—

G. Model! What are you talking about?

K. Silence, please. I am anxious to clarify for the dictaphone what will seem obscure enough under any circumstances. The reason the model worked perfectly was because I fitted in mentally and physically. Even after I left, it continued to carry out the task I had set it, but as soon as Herr——(Seventeen) made a change, it began to yield to other pressures. The accident—

G. Accident!

K. Will you shut up? Can't you see that I am trying to give information for the benefit of future generations? I have no desire that my secret be lost. The whole thing is in understanding. The mechanical part is only half the means. The mental approach is indispensable. Even Herr———(Seventeen), who was beginning to be *sympathique,* could not keep the machine sane for more than an hour. His death, of course, was inevitable, whether it looked like an accident or not.

G. Whose death?

K. What it boils down to is this. My invention does not fit into our civilization. It's *the next,* the coming age of man. Just as modern science could not develop in ancient Egypt because the whole mental, emotional, and physical attitude was wrong, so my machine cannot be used until the thought structure of man changes. Your masters will have some further facts soon to bear me out.

G. Look! You said something before about something happening. What?

K. I've just been telling you: I don't know. The law of averages says it won't be another sun, but there are a thousand deadly things that can happen. When Nature's gears snag, no imaginable horror can match the result.

G. But something is going to happen?

K. I really expected it before this. The official opening was set for half-past one. Of course, it doesn't really matter. If it doesn't happen today, it will take place tomorrow.

G. Official opening! You mean an accident is going to happen at some official opening?

K. Yes, and my body will be *attracted.* I—

G. What—Good God! He's gone!
   (Confusion. Voices no longer audible.)

March 25, 1941

From   Reich and Prussian Minister of Science
To   Herr Himmler
Subject   Destruction of Gribe Schloss

The report is still not ready. As you were not present, I have asked the journalist, Polermann, who was with Hitler, to write a description of the scene. His account is enclosed with the first page omitted.

You will note that in a number of paragraphs he reveals incomplete knowledge of the basic situation, but except for this, his story is, I believe, the most accurate we have.

The first page of his article was inadvertently destroyed. It was simply a preliminary.

For your information.

DESCRIPTION OF DESTRUCTION OF GRIBE SCHLOSS, BY HERR PO-LERMANN

—The first planet came in an unexpected fashion. I realized that as I saw Herr———(Twelve) make some hasty adjustments on one of his dials.

Still dissatisfied, he connected a telephone plug into a socket somewhere in his weird-looking asbestos suit, thus establishing telephone communication with the Minister of Science, who was in the steel enclosure with us. I heard His Excellency's reply:

"Night! Well, I suppose it has to be night some time on other planets. You're not sure it's the same planet? I imagine the darkness is confusing."

It was. In the mirror, the night visible through the orifice showed a bleak, gray, luminous landscape, incredibly eerie and remote, an unnatural world of curious shadows, and not a sign of movement anywhere.

And that, after an instant, struck us all with an appalling effect, the dark consciousness of that great planet, swinging somewhere around a distant sun, an uninhabited waste, a lonely reminder that life is rarer than death in the vast universe. Herr———(Twelve) made an adjustment on a dial; and, instantly, the great orifice showed that we were seeing the interior of the planet. A spotlight switched on, and picked out a solid line of red earth that slowly, as the dial turned, became clay; then a rock stratum came into view, and was held in focus.

An asbestos-clothed assistant of Herr———(Twelve) dislodged a piece of rock with a pick. He lifted it, and started to bring it toward the steel enclosure, apparently for the Fuehrer's inspection.

And abruptly vanished.

We blinked our eyes. But he was gone, and the rock with him. Herr———(Twelve) switched on his telephone hurriedly. There was a consultation, in which the Fuehrer participated. The decision finally was that it has been a mistake to examine a doubtful planet, and that the accident had happened because the rock had been removed. Accordingly, no further effort would be made to remove anything.

Regret was expressed by the Fuehrer that the brave assistant should have suffered such a mysterious fate.

We resumed our observant positions, more alert now, conscious of what a monstrous instrument was here before our eyes. A man whisked completely out of our space simply because he had touched a rock from a planet in hyper-space.

The second planet was also dark. At first it, too, looked a barren world, enveloped in night; and then—wonder. Against the dark, towering background of a great hill, a city grew. It spread along the shore of a moonlit sea, ablaze with ten million lights. It clung there for a moment, a crystalline city, alive with brilliant streets. Then it faded. Swiftly it happened. The lights seemed literally to slide off into the luminous sea. For a moment, the black outline of the city remained, then that, too, vanished into the shadows. Astoundingly, the hill that had formed an imposing background for splendor, distorted like a picture out of focus, and was gone with the city.

A flat, night-wrapped beach spread where a moment before there had been a world of lights, a city of another planet, the answer to ten million questions about life on other worlds—gone like a secret wind into the darkness.

It was plain to see that the test, the opening, was not according to schedule. Once more, Herr————(Twelve) spoke through the telephone to His Excellency, the Minister of Science.

His Excellency turned to the Fuehrer, and said, "He states that he appears to have no control over the order of appearance. Not once has he been able to tune in a planet which he had previously selected to show you."

There was another consultation. It was decided that this second planet, though it had reacted in an abnormal manner, had not actually proved dangerous. Therefore, one more attempt would be made. No sooner was this decision arrived at, than there was a very distinctly audible click from the machine. And, though we did not realize it immediately, the catastrophe was upon us.

I cannot describe the queer loudness of that clicking from the machine. It was not a metallic noise. I have since been informed that only an enormous snapping of energy in motion could have made that unusual, unsettling sound.

My own sense of uneasiness was quickened by the sight of Herr————(Twelve) frantically twisting dials. But nothing happened for a few seconds. The planet on which we had seen the city continued to hold steady in the orifice. The darkened beach spread there in the half-light shed by a moon we couldn't see. And then—

A figure appeared in the orifice. I cannot recall all my emotions at the sight of that manlike being. There was a wild thought that here was some supercreature who, dissatisfied with the accidents he had so far caused us, was now come to complete our destruction. That thought ended as the figure came out onto the floor and one of the assistants swung a spotlight on him. The light revealed him as a tall, well-built, handsome man, dressed in ordinary clothes.

Beside me, I heard someone exclaim: "Why, it's Professor Kenrube!"

For most of those present, everything must have, in that instant, been clear. I, however, did not learn until later that Kenrube was one of the scientists assigned to assist Herr————(Twelve) in building the machine, and that he turned out to be a traitor. He was suspected in the destruction of an earlier model, but as there was no evidence and the suspicion not very strong, he was permitted to continue his work.

Suspicion had arisen again a few days previously, and he had been confined to his quarters, from whence, apparently, he had now come forth to make sure that his skillful tampering with the machine had worked out. This, then, was the man who stood before us. My impression was that he should not have been allowed to utter his blasphemies, but I understand the leaders were anxious to learn the extent of his infamy, and thought he might reveal it in his speech. Although I do not profess to understand the gibberish, I have a very clear memory of what was said, and set it down here for what it is worth.

Kenrube began: "I have no idea how much time I have, and as I was unable to explain clearly to the dictaphone all that I had to say, I must try to finish here." He went on, "I am not thinking now in terms of revenge, though God knows my brother was very dear to me. But I want the world to know the way of this invention."

The poor fool seemed to be laboring under the impression that the machine was his. I did not, and do not understand his reference to a dictaphone. Kenrube went on:

"My first inkling came through psychology, the result of meditating on the manner in which the soil of different parts of the earth influences the race that lives there. This race-product was always more than simply the end-shape of a seacoast, or a plains, or a mountain environment. Somehow, beneath adaptations, peculiar and unsuspected relationships existed between the proper ties of matter and the phenomena of life. And so my search was born. The idea of revenge came later.

"I might say that in all history there has never been a revenge as complete as mine. Here is your machine. It is all there; yours to use for any purpose—provided you first change your mode of thinking to conform to the reality of the relationship between matter and life.

"I have no doubt you can build a thousand duplicates, but beware—every machine will be a Frankenstein monster. Some of them will distort time, as seems to have happened in the time of my arrival here. Others will feed you raw material that will vanish even as you reach forth to seize it. Still others will pour obscene things into our green earth; and others will blaze with terrible energies, but you will never know what is coming, you will never satisfy a single desire.

"You may wonder why everything will go wrong. Herr——(Twelve) has, I am sure, been able to make brief, successful tests. That will be the result of my earlier presence, and will not recur now that so many alien presences have affected its—sanity!

"It is not that the machine has will. It reacts to laws, which you must learn, and in the learning it will reshape your minds, your outlook on life. It will change the world. Long before that, of course, the Nazis will be destroyed. They have taken irrevocable steps that will insure their destruction.

"Revenge! Yes, I have it in the only way that a decent human being could desire it. I ask any reasonable being how else these murderers could be wiped from the face of the earth, except by other nations, who would never act until *they* had acted first?

"I have only the vaguest idea what the machine will do with me—it matters not. But I should like to ask you, my great Fuehrer, one question: Where now will you obtain your raw material?"

He must have timed it exactly. For, as he finished, his

figure dimmed. Dimmed! How else describe the blur that his body became? And he was gone, merged with the matter with which, he claimed, his life force was attuned.

The madman had one more devastating surprise for us. The dark planet, from which the city had disappeared, was abruptly gone from the orifice. In its place appeared another dark world. As our vision grew accustomed to this new night, we saw that this was a world of restless water; to the remote, dim horizon was a blue-black, heaving sea. The machine switched below the surface. It must have been at least ten hellish miles below it, judging from the pressure, I have since been informed.

There was a roar that seemed to shake the earth.

Only those who were with the Fuehrer in the steel room succeeded in escaping. Twenty feet away a great army truck stood with engines churning—it was not the first time that I was thankful that some car engines are always left running wherever the Fuehrer is present.

The water swelled and surged around our wheels as we raced up the newly paved road, straight up out of the valley. It was touch-and-go. We looked back in sheer horror. Never in the world has there been such a titanic torrent, such a whirlpool.

The water rose four hundred feet in minutes, threatened to overflow the valley sides, and then struck a balance. The great new river is still there, raging toward the Eastern Sea.

Author's Note: *This is not quite the end of the file. A few more letters exist, but it is unwise to print more, as it might be possible for the GPU to trace the individual who actually removed the file Secret Six from its cabinet.*

It is scarcely necessary to point out that we subsequently saw the answer that Hitler made to Professor Kenrube's question: "Where now will you obtain your raw material?"

On June 22nd, three months almost to the day after the destruction of Gribe Schloss, the Nazis began their desperate invasion of Russia. By the end of 1941, their diplomacy bankrupt, they were at war with the United States.

Born in 1939, Barry Malzberg has published over thirty sf books since he first entered the genre in 1967. Many of these have used the conventions of science fiction to explore the fears and alienation of twentieth-century humans, and some of them have been among the most controversial (and the best) in the history of the field. Particularly outstanding are Guernica Night (1974), Herovits World (1973), the award-winning Beyond Apollo (1972), and The Falling Astronauts (1971).

"After the Great Space War" (from the original anthology Alternities, 1974) captures several of his major themes, and all of the special qualities that make his work unique and important.

AFTER THE GREAT SPACE WAR

By Barry N. Malzberg

Gents:

Well, here I am in the heart of the Rigelian System, a fine, spacious system indeed, composed of binary stars and a veritable forest of planets and a lovely little planet you have picked, most suitable indeed for conquest, with delicately purple-hued natives who talk in musical scat (whop-a-bee-ba; a-whop-a-dee-*doo*) and whisper about the hedges of their world like birds: as you see, there is no xenophobia in my analyses and the warnings and accusations at the time of embarkment (embarkation?) were *totally* unfair. I *love* being an interstellar scout and am much cheered by the Rigelian System, finding these natives endlessly resourceful and amusing even though our contact has thus far been tentative and I have been able to map out only a little of their language with the inductive devices, making communication somewhat hesitant. Evenings I spend in this capsule spreading out against the sky like an operating table; mornings and afternoons I stroll through the forests of this planet, joshing with the natives monosyllabically (a-ba-*boo*-dup) and handing out the very fine supply of interstellar trinkets with which I was so thoughtfully equipped. These simple-minded inhabitants are delighted with them.

Assignment, in short, proceeds with ease and fluency, fluency and ease, and I make it that I should be ready to summon the landing fleet within a shift or three; in the meantime I continue to win their confidence. They seem to think that I am one of their local gods made manifest and although I recall the problems with this reaction against which we have been warned (riot, desolation, flood, reversion to barbarism) am sure that can handle this as have handled everything else. There is something called the Ceremony of Hinges (very approximate translation of their scat but the best I can do at this time) which they would like me to join but if you do not mind, if you do not mind, I think that I will pass this up. For the time being. The last ceremonial, three planets ago as you will recall, gave me an extremely bad cold and moderate feelings of insufficiency which I have yet to entirely overcome.

Wilson

PARTICIPATE IN SO-CALLED CEREMONY OF HINGES. VITAL AT ALL COSTS THAT INTEGRATION WITH THE SUBGROUP PROCEED ON NATURAL LINES. CEREMONY IS PROBABLY PART OF IMPORTANT RITUAL AND INVITATION THEY EXTEND MEANS THEIR CONFIDENCE IS WON. DO NOT HOLD BACK WILSON WE WILL HAVE NO REPETITION OF PAST DIFFICULTIES TO WHICH OF COURSE THERE IS NO NECESSITY TO REFER IN THIS TRANSMISSION.

HEADQUARTERS

Headquarters:

Yes, gents, I do understand and am not making waves. Really I am not (realize the circumstances of the probation on which I have been placed, a matter of which to quote your own approach I see no necessity to refer in this transmission) but it is not, *not* xenophobia which makes me reluctant to participate in the Ceremony of Hinges but merely a certain shy reluctance, a demureness of the spirit if you will. How can I explain this *je ne sais quoi?* How do I know the material of the ceremony? They turn aside my queries. (The translation is indeed rough, certainly the naming gives no clue. Hinges. *Hinges?*) Am willing to move on straightway with honesty and guile alternating in the best tradition of the interstellar scout with steadfastness and dependability predominating but are you really sure that you want me to do this? The sky is a lovely azure (I asure you of this) and pastel blue like the eyes of my many loves during their days and red at night on a sixteen-hour time cycle and the sound of their voices fills the pleasant glade in which I have landed with music at all times. I am happy here, gents, happy and I *love* the natives and accept the circumstances but do you really think that this is worth the risks?

Come now: what does the Ceremony of Hinges have to do with our plans of conquest? I think that the landing fleet should be called in *now*, right now in fact, but await as always your advice even though I feel that our relationship has not quite reached and I am beginning to fear may never quite reach that mutuality of understanding for which *I*, fellows, have striven from the very first. I remind you that the majority of the embarrassing difficulties to which, delicately, neither of us cares to refer have been caused by the sincerity of my attempts to live up to what I take your own wishes to be. I have *tried.* I have tried so hard.

Wilson

YOU POOR FOOL YOU ARE WASTING YOUR TIME AND OURS. WE ARE IN A POSITION OF MAXIMUM OBSERVATION AND IMMINENCE SUSTAINED ONLY AT GREAT EXPENSE. PARTICIPATE IN THE CEREMONY IMMEDIATELY DO YOU GET THAT PARTICIPATE IN THE CEREMONY IMMEDIATELY AT WHICH POINT OUR SOCIOPATHOLOGISTS HAVE CALCULATED YOU WILL HAVE REACHED THE OPTIMUM INTEGRATION AND CAN BE MOST USEFULLY APPLIED WHEN THE LANDING IS ACCOMPLISHED. CUT IT OUT WILSON WE WILL NOT

TOLERATE MUCH MORE OF THIS. ACCOMPLISH A MODAL INFARC-
TION.

HQ

Friends:

Modal infarction?

Well, you see men, I don't *want* to participate in the Ceremony of Hinges. Has not that already become clear? Since
our last talk, furthermore, I have come into new and somewhat ominous indications as the translation machinery
moves on apace that it, the Ceremony that is, may be a birth
ritual of some kind or perhaps a reconstitution of one's history
in which the participant is stuffed with local herbs and additives and passed through living *flame*. I do not know if I
can survive this even though their purposes do appear benign.

Listen, I am not xenophobic. I love *all* aliens and am prepared to love these too, caring ever more deeply about optimum performance of my job which as you know is rapidly
approaching tenure guaranteeing promotion, probation or
not, and want to make as few problems as possible, but are
you sure, I am are you really sure that you want going ahead
with this particular Ceremony?

Listen, I believe that I have *already* won their confidence.
They are now bringing *me* gifts, local plants and animals
somewhat indistinguishable from the natives themselves virtually ring my little capsule and we chatter and reminisce
through the bulkheads nightly. (Wa-ba-ba-beep; la-lo-*ka*.) I
think that it is now time to bring down the landing party.
Modal infarctions, whatever they might be, are fine, I am
willing to dedicate my *life* to the principles of m.i. but is it
really called for at this time? My life, that is to say. Think
about this friends; I certainly have value at the HQ, even
more value than to my humble self considering the training
and warnings that have been invested in me, and I do not
think that the m.i. is suitable at this time.

Perhaps you ought to land before they make the Ceremony
of Hinges a test of my true sincerity and worth to them which
so far they are not. They are not ordering me to participate.
May I repeat this? They are *not* ordering me to participate,
merely wistfully requesting it in the way that I wistfully
requested this one last assignment to prove my good faith
and credentials and then proceeded as you can see to carry.

off said assignment with great success for indeed and you must believe this now, indeed they do love me.

Let me handle this my way. I can explain that our metabolism will not permit us to accommodate the preparatory herbs and additives and while they are bemusedly considering this the landing parties can come in with the incinerative gear and do the job roundly.

As a matter of fact, let's send them in right now. Leave the apologies and explanations to me; I will handle my part of the bargain and you will handle yours. Now strikes me as an excellent time to send them in.

Do not be winsome, gents, or fail me at this hour of great need. I am counting upon you. Send the fleet in.

Wilson

YOU ARE TO PARTICIPATE IN THE CEREMONY OF HINGES AND AT ONCE.

YOU FOOL THIS IS A WORLD AT STAKE WHO DO YOU THINK YOU ARE TO JEOPARDIZE THE CONQUEST OF A WORLD AS VALUABLE AS THIS COULD BE. AS THE REPORTS ALSO INDICATE WE DO NOT TAKE ANY RISKS OR CHANCES. WILSON THE SCOUT IS THE ONE WHO IS EXPENDABLE IN CIRCUMSTANCES LIKE THIS. THE SCOUT IS EXPENDABLE. YOU KNEW THAT AND IT IS THAT CONDITION UNDER WHICH YOU HAVE WORKED AND IT IS TIME FOR YOU TO ACCEPT THE RESPONSIBILITIES OF THE ASSIGNMENT WHICH YOU ARE REMINDED YOU BEGGED AS ONE LAST CHANCE TO PROVE YOUR MERIT. PARTICIPATE IN THE CEREMONY AND THEN SEND US FULL PARTICULARS AND THEN IN DUE COURSE IT WILL BE OUR DECISION AND ONLY OUR DECISION AS TO WHEN AND WHERE TO LAND THE FLEET.

HQ

Gents:

You know not what you ask. It is a far far better thing which I do. I do not think you understand the sacrifice that I am making. Very well. Have it your way. You will feel sorry. Guilt will overwhelm you in due course and you will be sorry that you have made me do this. Nevertheless I am going to go in. Ask not what I can do for you now but what you can do for me. One small step.

Wilson

YOU HAVE MADE THE PROPER DECISION AND WE WISH TO CON-GRATULATE YOU FOR COMING TO TERMS WITH THE SITUATION IN A REALISTIC MANNER AT LAST. WE KNEW THAT IN THE END WE COULD COUNT UPON YOU. AWAIT YOUR FULL REPORT ON THE CER-EMONY OF HINGES WITH GREAT INTEREST.

HEADQUARTERS

HAVE HAD NO REPORT FROM YOU FOR TWO CYCLES. DID YOU PARTICIPATE IN THE CEREMONY OF HINGES, QUESTION MARK. WE WISH AN IMMEDIATE REPORT. EXCUSE YOURSELF FROM FESTIVI-TIES IF STILL CARRYING ON AND CABLE A FULL REPORT. WE AWAIT SAME.

HQ

TWO MORE CYCLES HAVE ELAPSED AND NOW WE ARE MOVING WELL INTO THE THIRD. INTO THE THIRD YOU FOOL. SUPPORT AND MONITORING DEVICES INDICATE THAT YOU ARE VERY MUCH ALIVE. RESPIRATION PULSE HEARTBEAT GROSS FUNCTIONS ALL NORMAL OR WITHIN GROSS NORMAL RANGE. STOP HIDING FROM US WILSON YOU ARE TO REPLY AT ONCE.

HQ!

To: Headquarters Division
Cancel the fleet. The planet is uncongenial to human life.
James O. Wilson

WHAT ARE YOU TALKING ABOUT WILSON THE PARTY IS IN CLOSE ORBIT AND HAS BEEN FOR SOME CONSIDERABLE TIME NOW. MUCH TIME WASTED TOO MUCH SPECIAL OVERTIME INVOLVED. HOW IS PLANET UNCONGENIAL TO HUMAN LIFE, QUESTION MARK. YOU HAVE SURVIVED ON IT.

HQ

FOR YOUR FAILURE TO REPLY YOU HAVE BEEN RELIEVED OF COMMAND EFFECTIVE AT ONCE WHICH IS TO SAY UPON YOUR RE-CEIPT OF THIS TRANSMISSION WHICH IS TO SAY IMMEDIATELY. DE-CISION TO LAND HAS BEEN MADE INDEPENDENTLY AND YOU ARE TO TURN YOURSELF OVER TO FLEET COMMANDER WHO WILL AR-RANGE QUARTERS AND WE WILL TAKE CARE OF YOU OH WILL WE EVER TAKE CARE OF YOU UPON YOUR RETURN TO THE SHIP.

HQ

To: Headquarters Division of the Enemy

My troops and I that is to say we will fight to the last man, no matter the price, no matter the penalty, in order that we may repel the invaders and save for all time the integrity of our world.

James O. Wilson

LAND THE FLEET. LAND THE FLEET AT ONCE. THIS SUPERSEDES ANY AND ALL OTHER ORDERS AND IS NOT TO BE DISREGARDED UNDER ANY CIRCUMSTANCE. LAND THE FLEET AT ONCE AND SECURE EVERYTHING THAT MOVES.

HQ

Headquarters:

Planet landed and secured at 1400 Cycle 23. We are now in control of the populace and surrounding territory all of which is pleasantly amiable and delightful to behold. We report no instances of enemy action nor indeed any signs of an enemy. These people are our friends. All is well. Now we are going at the special invitation of the Conductors to participate in the Ceremony of Leakage. (This is a rough translation; the transmission devices are still not sensitive to gradations of language but you get the idea.) We will report shortly upon our successful participation in this ceremony. Modal infarction is well upon the way. It is not necessary to send in the second division.

Commander

DO NOT REPEAT DO NOT REPEAT DO NOT DO IT. WHERE IS WILSON. DO NOT DO IT DO NOT PARTICIPATE IN ANY CEREMONIES THIS IS AN ABSOLUTE INFLEXIBLE ORDER. WHERE IS WILSON WHY IS PLANET NOT SECURED WHY ARE YOU PARTICIPATING IN CEREMONY EXPRESS ORDERS SAY YOU ARE NOT TO DO NOT DO IT. REPORT AT ONCE SECOND DIVISION IS ON WAY AND WILL LAND WITHIN TWELVE CYCLES TO TAKE INCENDIARY ACTION IF YOU DO NOT ALL OF YOU COOPERATE.

HQ

Friends:

Ceremony of Leakage delightful. All that we could have wished and more besides. We look forward with an anticipation we can barely hide to the promised Pageant of Stains which we have been advised makes the Ceremony of Leakage pale to insignificance just as the C. of L. utterly reduces the Ceremony of Hinges to the tiny taste of grandeur which it is now seen to be.

The planet is secure and while we await the Pageant of Stains we similarly await arrival of the Second Division and behind them the colonists. The colonists are important. Send the colonists. Send all six thousand of the colonists. The planet is entirely secure and we are awaiting them. Send us boatloads of colonists. They may come in from all the systems; send the word that a green and harmless world awaits them. Planet, climate, circumstances extraordinary, natives totally submissive and within our control. Send at least the initial six thousand colonists. They can enjoy with us the Pageant if they arrive soon enough. Hurry.

Commander

SEAL OFF THE PLANET AND PREPARE FOR INCENDIARY ACTION. WE HAVE NO CHOICE REPEAT WE HAVE NO CHOICE. BEGIN CONDITION PINK AT ONCE.

HQ

We await with great anticipation the colonists. Their place in the Pageant has been saved if they hurry. We are waiting for them and we insist that they be sent immediately do you hear me immediately you send those colonists I wopa-ba-bee-do-dee-wham-bam-*boom!*

"Christopher Anvil" (real name Harry Crosby) was one of the most popular and prolific authors in Analog Science Fiction from the mid-1950s to the end of the 1960s. His work featured social satire and extrapolation, frequently brilliant and almost always entertaining. Few writers could equal his skill in showing how slight changes in the structure of society (or various technological breakthroughs) could cause the whole system to undergo profound change.

"The Prisoner" (Astounding, February 1956) was his first published story, a complicated and excellent example of the "memo tale."

THE PRISONER

By Christopher Anvil

ROUTINE 04-12-2308-1623TCT STAFF
COMGEN IV TO OPCHIEF GS CAPITOL
REQUEST PERMISSION ADVANCE DEFENSE LINE TO SYSTEM CODE
R3J RPT R3J

ROUTINE 04-13-2308-0715TCT STAFF
OPCHIEF GS CAPITOL TO COMGEN IV
PERMISSION ADVANCE DEFENSE LINE TO SYSTEM CODE R3J RPT
R3J REFUSED RPT REFUSED

URGENT 04-14-2308-150TCT PERSONAL
COMGEN IV TO OPCHIEF GS CAPITOL
STINKO IT IS VITALLY NECESSARY THAT I TAKE OVER R3J RPT R3J
BEFORE THE OUTS GET HERE STP YOU KNOW THE SIZE OF MY FLEET
STP LOVE TO TANYA AND KIDS MART MARTIN M GLICK COMGEN IV

ROUTINE 04-15-2308-0730TCT PERSONAL
OPCHIEF GS CAPITOL TO COMGEN IV
SORRY MART I CAN'T LET YOU DO IT STP R3J RPT R3J IS TOUGH NUT
TO CRACK AND NOT ENOUGH TIME TO CRACK IT STP ONLY QUAD-
RITE IN SYSTEM IS ON FIFTH PLANET STP TWO PREVIOUS ATTEMPTS
TO TAKE FIFTH PLANET ABORTED STP SYSTEM AS A WHOLE IS NO
GOOD WITHOUT QUADRITE AND WE COULD NOT SUPPLY YOU FROM
HERE YOU KNOW THAT STP CANNOT HAVE YOUR FORCES IN STATE
OF DISORDER WITH MINOR CONFLICT GOING ON WHEN OUTS AR-
RIVE STP I KNOW YOUR POSITION BUT R3J RPT R3J IS NO SOLUTION
STP CAN ONLY HOPE THEY WILL ATTACK ELSEWHERE STP JACKIE
IS FINE STP YOUNG MART HAS GROWN STP GOOD LUCK STP STINKO
J J RYSTENKO OPCHIEF GS

VITAL 04-16-2308-1632TCT STAFF
COMGEN IV TO ALL STATIONS
U EXPLOSION D308L564v013
U EXPLOSION D308L562v013
U EXPLOSION D308L560v013
U EXPLOSION D308L562v015
U EXPLOSION D308L562v011
EXPLOSIONS SIMULTANEOUS TIME OF OBSERVATION 04-16-2308-
1624TCT
VITAL TRANSMIT TRIPLE AT TEN-MINUTE INTERVALS

URGENT 04-162308-1640TCT PERSONAL
COMGEN IV TO OPCHIEF GS CAPITOL
STINKO THEY ARE NOT GOING SOMEWHERE ELSE THEY ARE COM-
ING HERE STP IF THEY GET BY ME THERE IS NOTHING FROM HERE
TO CAP BUT THE GR AND THAT WILL NEVER HOLD THEM STP THEIR
TIMING PERFECT STP MAXIMUM CONFUSION STP IF THEY CAME
ANY SOONER THEY COULD HAVE VOTED IN THE ELECTION STP IN
CIRCUMSTANCES DESPERATELY NECESSARY TO TAKE R3J RPT R3J
STP SEND PERMISSION BEFORE WE WASTE MORE TIME STP MART
MARTIN M GLICK COMGEN IV

(Reply requested today.)
Office of the Secretary for Defense
Dear General Rystenko:

As a member of the new President's cabinet, responsible for the overall direction of the defense effort, I am determined to acquire, as soon as possible, some appreciation of the overall strategic picture.

So long as I do not understand the meaning of certain technical terms, this will be impossible. These terms are regarded as secret, and no civilian has any sure idea of their meaning until he is thrust into an office where his ignorance may be fatal. Looking at the dispatch copies which come to my office, I find the following terms I would like defined: (a) quadrite; (b) GR; (c) CAP; (d) U-explosion; (e) Henkel sphere; (f) SB; (g) abort.

I also want a brief summary, on no more than two sheets of paper, of the overall defense strategy; a similar summary of known enemy capabilities; and a brief point-by-point comparison of our important weapons, considering not only quality but amounts, and present and projected rates of production.

You need not handle this yourself; but if you do not, I want you to check the papers before they come to me. You will be held personally responsible for their accuracy.

Sincerely,
James Cordovan
Secretary for Defense

4-17-2308

Office of The Chief of Operations
Dear Mr. Secretary:

Quadrite is a crystalline substance used as fuel in the nonradioactive, or N-drive. A small safe quantity of radioactive material starts the reaction, which may be stopped by removal of this material. The mass radioactive, or R-drive, is useless against the present enemy because he possesses a means of exploding it before our ships come into ordinary firing range. Thus we use quadrite on warships.

GR means General Reserve. CAP means Capitol. A U-explosion is a large explosion of uranium or other radioactive material by the enemy's device, or, occasionally, by us. Henkel sphere is a large self-contained unit carrying impulse torpedoes and magnetic-inductive direction finders. SB means solar beam; a concentration of the rays of a sun for offensive or defensive purposes. "Abort," as we use it, merely means "fail."

The overall defense strategy is simple. Our forces are located around the surface of a flattened spheroidal defensive border. At the outer edge is a triple layer of warning devices, the U-markers, which explode on approach of the enemy. Next comes several layers of Henkel spheres, stretching from one sun system to the next. Each sun system is equipped with solar beams, so far as possible, so that these sun systems constitute strong points in the defense perimeter, or, if they are cut off, may function for some time as isolated fortresses in the enemy's rear. Behind this outer line of defense lie the fleets, which help service the Henkel spheres, fight to repair small breaches in the defensive perimeter, and, in the event of large breaches, fall back in an orderly manner and assist in forming the next defensive line.

As for the known enemy capabilities, and the comparison of their important weapons with ours, the first item to consider is their manner of attack. They come in in huge masses of ships, moving at a tremendous velocity, and often making two nearly simultaneous attacks at far separated parts of our defense lines. A series of U-explosions signals their penetration through successive lines of our U-markers, and then they hurtle through the lines of Henkel spheres. The spheres automatically discharge their impulse torpedoes on precalculated courses, and at the same time our fleet on the spot sows a series of new layers of spheres along the estimated course of the enemy attack. There is no such thing as a general engagement between the two fleets, because ours is always too weak at the point of attack. It is guarding a vast area which the enemy can, if he chooses, attack at any chosen point with his full force.

Usually, however, just as the situation becomes desperate, and we feel compelled to rush the general reserve to the spot, a second and even stronger attack strikes us at some widely separated point from the first. At this stage, all resemblance to plan and order ceases, and we are forced to resort to expediency. Fleets are rushed from all around the perimeter to the estimated position of the future enemy penetrations. Solar beams are concentrated in a webwork across the line of enemy attack. It is impossible to generalize beyond this point. We do what we can. Usually we are forced to commit the fleet to battle at a heavy loss, which weakens us for the next attack. The enemy cuts a swath through the whole system, burns out a number of vitally important planetary centres en route, and erupts outward through some place which has already been stripped for defense elsewhere. After the enemy has gone, we draw together the bits and pieces, reapportion the weakened forces, and wait for the next blow.

We know very little of enemy weapons, save that they are similar to ours and used in overwhelming concentrations. As for the enemy personnel, only one individual has been captured following a fluke individual dogfight in which Colonel A. C. Nielson was killed and the enemy ship ruined. This enemy individual showed (a) human form, very compact and muscular, with peculiar eyes; (b) fantastic recuperative power, with healing of very severe wounds, such as killed Colonel Nielson, taking place spontaneously and practically visibly; (c) fanatic hostility, shown as soon as the individual recovered consciousness; and which was followed apparently by the use of some poison, as the enemy's body then at once decomposed, too fast to permit further examination on the spot.

As for our present rate of production, it is suitable to replace approximately forty percent of the losses suffered during enemy attack. This refers to warship production. Production of the cheaper Henkel spheres would be quite respectable if it weren't for the fact that it takes ships to put the spheres in position. Projected production of ships was cut further in the last budget.

As for recruitment of personnel, it is barely adequate to man the continually decreasing strength we are able to maintain. Training facilities are inadequate, but the need for men is so drastic we have no time for adequate training. The quality of recruits is poor, since the population does not believe the situation serious, and thus has little respect for the services.

I hope this answers your questions satisfactorily. I shall be glad to help you in any way I can.

Respectfully,
J. J. Rystenko
Chief of Operations

Office of the Secretary for Defense
Bart:

   I am enclosing an answer from General Rystenko, the Chief of Operations, to some questions of mine. I hope you will read it now and let me know what you think. Unless Rystenko is exaggerating for some reason, this is worse than we ever imagined.

Jim Cordovan

4-17-2308

Office of the President
Jim:

   This is horrible. Let me know immediately if you find out anything more about this.

Bart

(Immediate action)

4-17-2308

Office of the President
General Rystenko:

   Report to my office immediately unless you are occupied with matters of vital importance.

Barton Baruch

4-17-2308

Office of the President
Jim:

   Rystenko is all right. But our predecessors have gutted the defense establishment to balance the budget. Cabinet meeting tonight at 8:30.

Bart

URGENT 04-16-2308-2210TCT PERSONAL
COMGEN IV TO OPCHIEF GS CAPITOL
STINKO MY POSITION HOPELESS HERE IN PRESENT CIRCUMSTAN-
CES STP ONLY JUSTIFICATION FOR INACTION WAS TO AVOID IN-
VOLVEMENT IN MINOR WAR AND THUS INABILITY TO REINFORCE
IF ATTACK CAME ELSEWHERE STP ATTACK IS COMING HERE STP IF
I STAY WHERE I AM I AM LIKE A MOUSE IN AN UNBLOCKED HOLE
WITH THE WEASEL COMING ON THE RUN STP I CANT HOLD THEM
HERE STP THIS TIME THEY WILL GO ALL THE WAY TO CAP STP
STINKO I HOPE YOUR PERMISSION IS ON WAY AS I AM GOING TO
TAKE R3J RPT R3J OR DIE TRYING STP LOVE TO TANYA AND THE

KIDS STP GOOD LUCK IF THEY GET THROUGH STINKO STP MART
MARTIN M GLICK COMGEN IV

ROUTINE 04-17-2308-1100TCT STAFF
OPCHIEF GS CAPITOL TO COMGEN IV
IN ABSENCE OF GENERAL RYSTENKO MY DUTY TO INFORM LIEU-
TENANT GENERAL GLICK NO PERMISSION TO ADVANCE TO R3J RPT
R3J WAS SENT OR CONTEMPLATED STP IN EVENT YOU ADVANCE
CONTRARY TO REITERATED COMMANDS TO CONTRARY MY DUTY
TO INFORM YOU YOU ARE HEREBY RELIEVED OF COMMAND AND
HEREBY ORDERED TO TURN OVER COMMAND TO DEPUTY COMGEN
IV AS PRESCRIBED RGC 6-143J SECTION 14 STP Q L GORLEY COLONEL
FOR GENERAL J J RYSTENKO OPCHIEF GS

ROUTINE 04-18-2308-1625TCT STAFF
COMGEN IV TO OPCHIEF GS CAPITOL
ALL RECEIVING APPARATUS OUT OF ORDER STP POSSIBLY BY EN-
EMY ACTION STP ADVANCE ELEMENTS OF FLEET IV APPROACHING
SYSTEM CODE R3J RPT R3J

VITAL 04-18-2308-1640TCT STAFF
COMGEN IV TO ALL STATIONS
U EXPLOSION D288L564v103
U EXPLOSION D288L562v103
U EXPLOSION D288L560v103
U EXPLOSION D288L562v105
U EXPLOSION D288L562v099
EXPLOSIONS SIMULTANEOUS TIME OF OBSERVATION
04-18-2308-1635TCT
VITAL TRANSMIT TRIPLE AT TEN-MINUTE INTERVALS

(Reply requested immediately)

4-18-2308

Office of the Secretary for Defense
General Rystenko:

As you know, OPCHIEF dispatches move through my office as a routine so I will know what your office is doing. Now
I want to know why this General Glick is being kept on a
short leash. I have gone over a set of star charts, and if I can
make anything out of them this System R3J is a vital link
in your defense system. Who is this Q. L. Gorley, colonel,
who sent the order removing General Glick? Why did *he* send
the order? Are you dodging the responsibility for it? Unless

you are occupied in vital matters I want the answers to these questions by tube within fifteen minutes.

J. Cordovan
Secretary for Defense

4-18-2308

Office of the Chief of Operations
Dear Mr. Secretary:

I had no knowledge of Gorley's action till you called it to my attention. I am reinstating Glick immediately.

Rystenko

VITAL 04-18-2308-1125TCT STAFF
OPCHIEF GS CAPITOL TO COMGEN IV
BY ORDER GENERAL J J RYSTENKO OPCHIEF GS EFFECTIVE IMMEDIATELY LIEUTENANT-GENERAL MARTIN M GLICK IS RPT IS IN FULL COMMAND SECTOR IV STP BY ORDER GENERAL J J RYSTENKO OPCHIEF GS FULL DISCRETION RPT FULL DISCRETION GRANTED RPT GRANTED LIEUTENANT-GENERAL MARTIN M GLICK COMGEN IV INCLUDING RPT INCLUDING ANY ACTIONS REGARDING SYSTEM CODE R3J RPT R3J TIME OF ORIGINAL ORDER 02-18-2308-1125TCT VITAL TRANSMIT TRIPLE AT THIRTY-MINUTE INTERVALS

URGENT 02-18-2308-1128TCT PERSONAL
OPCHIEF GS CAPITOL TO COMGEN IV
MY GOD MART I AM SORRY STP YOUR REASONING REGARDING R3J RPT R3J IS PERFECTLY CORRECT STP GORLEY ACTED WITHOUT MY KNOWLEDGE STP WE ARE IN MIDST OF CHANGE OF ADMINISTRATION HERE STP SOME CONFUSION STP YOU HAVE FULL AUTHORITY STP DO WHAT YOU WANT STP BEST OF LUCK AND GOD BE WITH YOU STP STINKO J J RYSTENKO OPCHIEF GS

4-18-2308

Office of the Chief of Operations
Dear Mr. Secretary:

I have sent orders reinstating General Glick and giving him full authority to take System R3J. Two previous attempts to take the only planet in the system that possesses quadrite have failed, with no survivors returning; but it is worth trying.

Rystenko

(Reply requested immediately)

4-18-2308

Office of the Secretary for Defense
General Rystenko:
   That is fine. What about my questions concerning Colonel
Gorley?

J. Cordovan

4-18-2308

Office of the Chief of Operations
Dear Mr. Secretary:
   Colonel Gorley was sent here by the former President. He
acted in an advisory and liaison capacity between this office
and that of the former President. I know his action in this
instance has proved to be unfortunate, but he was entirely
justified by regulations covering the situation. I was with the
President at the moment, and immediate action was necessary to maintain the balance of the situation.

Respectfully,
J. J. Rystenko
Chief of Operations

(Reply requested immediately)

4-18-2308

Office of the Secretary for Defense
General Rystenko:
   Do you mean that Gorley advised the former President on
matters of defense?

J. Cordovan

4-18-2308

Office of the Chief of Operations
Mr. Secretary:
   That is what I mean. Yes.

J. J. Rystenko
Chief of Operations

4-18-2308

Office of the Secretary for Defense
Bart:
   I am enclosing some correspondence between myself and
Rystenko, regarding a Colonel Q. L. Gorley who has just
taken a step I regard as well calculated to throw our defense
arrangements off balance at the decisive moment. I am enclosing the dispatch referred to. You will note that Rystenko

takes a progressively stiffer tone in protecting Gorley. Personally, I think if Gorley was defense adviser to the previous Administration, he must be no good.

Jim

(Reply requested today)

4-18-2308

Office of the Secretary for Defense
Comptroller of the Records:
I would like a digest of all pertinent data in the service record of Colonel Q. L. Gorley, now attached to the office of the Chief of Operations.

James Cordovan
Secretary for Defense

4-18-2308

Office of the President
Jim:
I have been in office three days and it feels like three years, all thanks to the miserable defense picture. If you think Gorley is no good, select some distant and unimportant asteroid and put him in charge of it. Don't bother me with this trivia.

Bart

PS. The time on this dispatch from Gorley to Glick is 1100. Rystenko was not with me then.

4-19-2308

Comptroller of the Records
Dear Mr. Secretary:
I have been able to ascertain that there is a Colonel Q. L. Gorley attached to the Chief of Operations office, but the Master Recorder merely remains blank when I try to obtain his service record. No Colonel Q. L. Gorley is listed in the Officers' Registry. There is a Q. S. Gorley, Captain, now serving with the Tenth Fleet, and a Brigadier General Mason Gorley, Ret'd. Upon code-checking the rolls of the National Space Academy at Bristol Bay, I find no mention of any Q. L. Gorley within the last hundred years.

It is possible to bar access to the service record of any individual if the President or Secretary for Defense approves the action. But this is not the case here. There simply is no record. Do you wish me to cross-check the coded Adminis-

tration records of the past few years to see if any mention is
made of this man in these records?

Respectfully,
Ogden Mannenberg
Comptroller of the Records

(Reply requested today)

4-19-2308

Office of the Secretary for Defense
Comptroller of the Records:
  Yes, by all means cross-check the administrative records
back to the time Gorley was first mentioned.

James Cordovan
Secretary for Defense

(Immediate action)

4-19-2308

Office of the Secretary for Defense
Birdie:
  Get down to the Chief of Operations' office and play the
part of the Undersecretary getting acquainted with the team.
Find out all you can about a Colonel Q. L. Gorley, who is now
attached to the Opchief's office. Gorley appears to have no
service record and I am a little curious about him.

Jim

ROUTINE 04-19-2308-2300TCT STAFF
COMGEN IV TO OPCHIEF GS CAPITOL
FLEET IV NOW BASED ON SECOND RPT SECOND PLANET OF SYSTEM
CODE R3J RPT R3J STP SB BEING PLACED NOW STP ADVANCE HEN-
KEL SPHERE PERIMETER BEING HEAVILY REINFORCED STP BULK
OF FLEET IV NOW MOVING TO OCCUPY FIFTH RPT FIFTH PLANET
OF SYSTEM CODE R3J RPT R3J

ROUTINE 04-19-2308-2314TCT PERSONAL
COMGEN IV TO OPCHIEF GS CAPITOL
STINKO I HAVE OCCUPIED THE SECOND PLANET OF R3J RPT R3J AND
FIND POPULACE AND GOVERNMENT FRIENDLY AND EAGER TO
HELP STP THEY HAD CIVILIZATION BASED ON FISSION FIVE
HUNDRED YEARS AGO BUT THE OUTS WENT THROUGH HERE AND
KNOCKED THEM INTO A QUOTE PILE OF DUNG END QUOTE STP
THEY HAD SPACE TRAVEL BUT KEPT AWAY FROM FIFTH PLANET
AS HAD NO NEED FOR QUADRITE WHICH IS ONLY ATTRACTION STP

ALL THEY CAN TELL ME IS THAT ONE OF THEIR RELIGIOUS LEADERS
PREDICTED MY ARRIVAL AND SAID OF THE FIFTH PLANET QUOTE
HE WHO WILL FEED ON IT SHALL LIVE OF IT STP END QUOTE
SOUNDS GOOD STP AM EN ROUTE NOW STP MART MARTIN M GLICK
COMGEN IV

4-19-2308

Office of the Undersecretary for Defense
Jim:
    I have covered the situation for you down at the Opchief's
office, and I am sure you must be mistaken about Colonel
Gorley. He seems straightforward and solid, and explained
the defense setup to me in such a way that for the first time
it made sense to me. I can think of no one we might pick who
would make a better advisor to the President on military
matters. As for Colonel Gorley having no service record, the
idea is fantastic. Several of the officers present spoke famil-
iarly to Gorley of events which happened while he and they
were at Bristol Bay together in their Academy days. It could
hardly be a case of mistaken identity. Colonel Gorley is a
very striking man, very compact and muscular—a very powerful, magnetic, dynamic type. He has peculiarly keen intelligent eyes, and an incisive, clear, positive manner of
speaking. Personally, I think that instead of investigating
Gorley, we should raise him to high rank and get a little
decision into the war effort.

                                                        Birdie
PS. The only thing resembling criticism I have heard of Gorley was a joking reference that he has a ferocious appetite
and has to diet constantly to keep his weight down. Surely
you won't hold this against him.

ROUTINE 04-20-2308-0756TCT STAFF
COMGEN IV TO OPCHIEF GS CAPITOL
ADVANCE ELEMENTS FLEET IV HAVE LANDED ON PLANET FIVE
RPT FIVE OF SYSTEM CODE R3J RPT R3J STP NO OPPOSITION STP
ONLY INHABITANTS APPEAR TO BE GRAZING ANIMALS OF INTER-
MEDIATE SIZE

4-20-2308

Comptroller of the Records
Dear Mr. Secretary:
    I list below in chronological order the portions of past

Administrative records apparently referring to Colonel Q. L. Gorley:

4-25-2304... Thank you so much for sending me Colonel Gorley. The defense position is more clear to me...

President to Opchief

5-4-2304... I approve the new plan of dynamic containment. I was a bit uncertain as to the effect this would have should the enemy renew offensive action, but Colonel Gorley has assured me it will be possible to concentrate reserves quickly. On this basis I approve the plan. Certainly it seems much less risky...

President to Opchief

2-23-2305... I do not understand your difficulties in repelling the latest enemy attack. What exactly has happened here? Why were you not able to concentrate your reserves quickly enough to prevent the enemy from traversing the whole length and breadth of the system and leaving a trail of ruin behind him such as we have not seen in twenty years of warfare? Who ordered these cuts in production? What do you mean you cannot replace the losses? I have no memory of these Executive Orders you speak of, or of any Colonel Gorley. Send this man to me immediately, or better yet, come yourself...

President to Opchief

2-24-2305... Colonel Gorley has explained the matter to me satisfactorily. Of course it is unfortunate, but these things happen...

President to Opchief

3-1-2305... Colonel Gorley will explain to you the recommended new cuts in the defense budget. The improved foreign situation makes these cuts possible...

Opchief to President

4-2-2306... Rystenko, these losses are horrible. Why has this thing happened twice? The purpose of censorship is not to hold the people in ignorance and hide the festering wounds from view. The point of censorship is to keep information from the enemy and to prevent over-violent public reaction to unimportant temporary reversals. But these disasters are not unimportant! They are terrible defeats! I find your reaction grossly inadequate. Who is this Gorley you are sending to me, as if this would correct the situation?...

President to Opchief

4-4-2306...Colonel Gorley has explained the matter to me satisfactorily. I see now clearly it was bound to happen in this phase of our defensive effort...

President to Opchief

6-2-2306...I approve the new defense budget, as explained to me by Colonel Gorley. I am, of course, pleased though surprised that you can now give us more defensive power at lower cost. Please check this and be sure that the situation has stabilized to this extent...

President to Opchief

6-2-2306...That Colonel Gorley be attached to my office until these complex arrangements are completed...

President to Opchief

6-7-2306...We will miss Gorley, but are sure he will prove as helpful to you as to us...

Opchief to President

9-15-2306...The food must be much better here than in your mess. Poor Gorley has to go on another diet...

President to Opchief

10-23-2306...I am very sorry to have to bother you with these petty trivialities, Mr. President, but they may prove vital. I can't send men to Cryos with such inadequate equipment as this budget allows for. This one trivial substitution of separate interliners and thin semi-detached boots may cost a delay of up to ten minutes when the men go into action. This equipment has already proved itself worthless. I will gladly consider Colonel Gorley's suggestions, but this matter was disposed of years ago. I have also discovered several other aspects of our present arrangements which make me extremely uneasy...

Opchief to President

10-25-2306...I have talked with Colonel Gorley and can see that these plans are perfectly suited to the situation. Perhaps he could remain with our office for some time till these other matters are ironed out...

Opchief to President

4-15-2307...Poor Gorley is on a diet again...

Opchief to President

4-16-2307...Who? Gorley? Am I acquainted with the man?...

President to Opchief

4-29-2307...Terribly shaken by this hideous disaster. Why had this happened to us when our arrangements were supposed to be invulnerable? The enemy has torn your battle line like tissue paper. Why are we so weak everywhere? Your talk of "elastic counter defensive" makes no sense to me whatever. If these fleets were held concentrated at one central point instead of strewn all over the universe, we could return the blow. What do you mean by offering to send "Colonel Gorley" to me? If any personal explaining is to be done, you will come yourself, not send a stooge. Make out immediately a list of all requirements needed to correct this hideous situation.

President to Opchief

4-30-2307...I see now. Gorley has explained it all to me...

President to Opchief

Note: These are all the direct references made to Colonel Q. L. Gorley in the Administration records. Would you like me to cross-check the Departmental records?

Respectfully,
Ogden Mannenberg
Comptroller of the Records

4-20-2308

Office of the Secretary for Defense
Comptroller of the Records:

Thank you. These references are amply sufficient for the present.

James Cordovan
Secretary for Defense

4-20-2308

Office of the President
Jim:

I have now absorbed the substance of the report Rystenko sent you concerning our defenses, and which you forwarded to me. I have slept on it, and thought of it when I was not otherwise occupied. It seems to me: (1) This policy of locating the main bulk of our fleet in a thin shell around the periphery offers us about as much defense as an eggshell does to an egg. (2) Since in the present arrangement the fleet does not engage, it is worth no more than so many civilian ships. (3) Therefore, let us draw all the fleet to the center (with the possible exception of Glick's IVth, which is actively occupied), and replace it around the periphery with civilian ships and crews to service the layers of Henkel spheres. Enough men could be left behind to train these crews, but no more.

My final observation is that everything I have said so far is fairly obvious, therefore why hasn't Rystenko carried it out on his own? He impressed me very favourably in our interview, but further consideration leads me to think he may be one of those men who expend their sense on the package instead of the contents. I am going to talk to him again, and would like your view of the subject.

Bart

4-20-2308

Office of the President
General Rystenko:

I want to see you within the next hour regarding the overall strategy of the war effort, regarding the present re-cruitment and material replacement situation, and regarding the present arrangements for advancement of high officers.

Barton Baruch

4-20-2308

Office of the Chief of Operations
Dear Mr. President:

I shall be at your office at 3:00 P.M. if this is agreeable to you. As it happens, my aide, Colonel Q. L. Gorley, left my office a short while ago to bring you some important data sheets. I am sure you will find him most helpful also on these other matters if you choose to consult him.

Respectfully,
J. J. Rystenko
Chief of Operations

4-20-2308

Office of the President
Jim:

I have just had a very illuminating talk with General

Rystenko's aide, Colonel Gorley, and he has very clearly explained the logic of the present defence set-up to me. I am sending him along to brief you. He is a most capable man, and I am sure you will profit by contact with him.

Bart

VITAL 04-20-2308-1654TCT STAFF
COMGEN IV TO ALL STATIONS
U EXPLOSION D280L564v193
U EXPLOSION D280L562v193
U EXPLOSION D 280L560v193
U EXPLOSION D280L562v195
U EXPLOSION D280L562v191
EXPLOSIONS SIMULTANEOUS
TIME OF OBSERVATION 04-20-2308-1646TCT
VITAL TRANSMIT TRIPLE AT TEN-MINUTE INTERVALS

4-20-2308

Office of the Undersecretary for Defense
Jim:

Colonel Gorley is out here cooling his heels in the anteroom. He is here at the President's personal order, and yet when the receptionist tries to let him in, your door is locked. Have you turned childish?

Birdie

4-29-2308

Office of the Secretary for Defense
Birdie:

Who is Gorley? Is he the one who made the fuss removing a general yesterday or the day before? If he has anything from the President, he can leave it outside. If he wants to see me, he can make an appointment for tomorrow. I am working my way through a pile of business as high as your head, and I do not want to be disturbed till I am finished. Say, while he is out there, pump him discreetly about Rystenko. See if you can find out whether the Opchief used Gorley for a cat's-paw in trying to get rid of that general...what's his name?...Glick.

Jim

4-20-2308

Office of the Secretary for Defense
Chief Dispatcher:
Send the following:
VITAL 04-20-2308-1621TCT PERSONAL
DEFSEC CAPITOL TO COMGEN GR CAPITOL
REPLY IMMEDIATELY YOUR OPINION WILL PRESENT DEFENSES RE-
PEL ENEMY ATTACK OF MAGNITUDE SIMILAR TO THAT EXPERI-
ENCED LAST THREE YEARS STP REPLY IMMEDIATELY CATEGORY
VITAL TO DEFSEC CAPITOL THROUGH CHIEF DISPATCHER STP THIS
INQUIRY AND REPLY CONFIDENTIAL STP JAMES CORDOVAN DEF-
SEC CAPITOL

(Reply requested immediately)

4-20-2308

Office of the Secretary for Defense
Comptroller of the Records:
Find out for me what happened to the body of the enemy
captured after a dogfight in which Colonel A. C. Nielson was
killed.

James Cordovan
Secretary for Defense

VITAL 04-20-2308-1642TCT PERSONAL
COMGEN GR CAP TO DEFSEC CAP THRU CHIEF DISPATCHER
  CONFIDENTIAL
MY OPINION PRESENT DEFENSES WILL COLLAPSE IF ENEMY AT-
TACKS WITH SAME STRENGTH AS FORMERLY STP OR WITH ANY-
THING LIKE SAME STRENGTH AS FORMERLY STP VERNON L HAUSER
COMGEN GR CAPITOL

4-20-2308

Comptroller of the Records
Dear Mr. Secretary:
The body of the captured enemy was brought here under
refrigeration, to be examined by physicians and chemists. It
arrived at night and was placed, still in its box, in a small
room off the autopsy room. The intern on duty ordered the
lid of the box pried up, examined the remains, and noted that
the object within appeared to be in a state of advanced de-
composition, with, however, very little odor. The room was
refrigerated, and next day the surgeons entered to carry out
a preliminary examination, and upon raising the lid found

nothing within but a quantity of water, some of which had seeped out through the sides of the box.

The above summary is condensed from voluminous reports on the occurrence, and equally voluminous reports attempt to explain the matter, but the substance of these latter reports is that the authorities do not know what happened.

Respectfully,
Ogden Mannenberg
Comptroller of the Records

(Reply requested immediately)

4-20-2308

Office of the Secretary for Defense
Comptroller of the Records:

Send me a summary of the physical characteristics of the captured enemy during life.

James Cordovan
Secretary for Defense

4-20-2308

Office of the Undersecretary for Defense
Jim:

Colonel Gorley was ordered by the President to see you now, today. Why try to put him off till tomorrow? You can get back to your work after he has a few minutes to deliver his message.

Birdie

4-20-2308

Office of the Secretary for Defense
Birdie:

I am snowed under. Tomorrow.

Jim

4-20-2308

Comptroller of the Records
Dear Mr. Secretary:

The captured enemy is described as having during life the following physical characteristics: (a) human form; (b) extremely compact and muscular physique; (c) peculiarly keen sharp eyes; (d) very great recuperative power.

Respectfully,
Ogden Mannenberg
Comptroller of the Records

4-20-2308

Office of the Secretary for Defense
Chief Dispatcher:
    Send the following:
VITAL 04-20-2308-1708TCT PERSONAL
DEFSEC CAP TO COMGEN GR CAP CONFIDENTIAL
REPLY IMMEDIATELY THROUGH CHIEF DISPATCHER YOUR OPINION
ON OUTCOME OF COMING ENEMY ATTACK IF ALL OUR FORCES NOW
CONCENTRATED AT CENTRAL POINT LEAVING SMALL TRAINING
CADRES AND CIVILIANS TO MAINTAIN HENKEL SPHERE DEFENSES
STP REPLY CONFIDENTIAL CATEGORY VITAL STP JAMES COR-
DOVAN DEFSEC CAPITOL

VITAL 04-20-2308-1714TCT PERSONAL
COMGEN GR CAP TO DEFSEC CAP THRU CHIEF DISPATCHER
    CONFIDENTIAL
MY OPINION OUR CHANCES GOOD STP THIS IS FIRST SENSIBLE PLAN
TO COME OUT OF CAP IN FOUR YEARS STP BUT YOU WILL NEVER
GET IT BY RYSTENKO OR HIS CREATURE GORLEY SEE GORLEY
DOES NOT GET TO PRESIDENT STP GORLEY IS CLEVER MAN WITH
THE BUTTER KNIFE OR WHATEVER HE USES STP MR SECRETARY
ONLY CHANCE YOUR PLAN GETTING ACROSS IS TO SEE PRESIDENT
REMOVE RYSTENKO APPOINT ANYONE WITH ALL HIS FACULTIES
STP ANY SANE MAN CAN SEE PLAN NOW IN USE IS SUICIDE STP
VERNON L HAUSER COMGEN GR CAP

4-20-2308

Office of the Undersecretary for Defense
Jim:
    Colonel Gorley was *ordered* to see you by the *President*
and he was *ordered* to do it *today.* The colonel is a very
powerful and determined man when his duty is at stake, Jim,
and I think it would be wise not to get in his or the President's
way. I say this as a friend, Jim. Gorley is *going* to *see* you
today.

Birdie

4-20-2308

Office of the Secretary for Defense
Birdie:
    Why didn't you tell me Gorley was here at the direct order
of the President to see me *today*? He can see me when I am
through, probably about an hour-and-a-half from now, or, as

he would put it, about 1854 hours. Birdie, would you repeat what you said about Colonel Gorley's appearance? I think he reminds me of someone I knew as a kid.

Jim

4-20-2308

Office of the Secretary for Defense
Chief Dispatcher:
   Send the following:
VITAL 04-20-2308-1722TCT PERSONAL
DEFSEC CAP TO COMGEN GR CAP CONFIDENTIAL
REPLY IMMEDIATELY THROUGH CHIEF DISPATCHER STP SITUA-
TION HERE HIGHLY PRECARIOUS STP GORLEY HAS ALREADY GOT-
TEN TO PRESIDENT AND USED WHATEVER HE USES STP PRESIDENT
NOW CONVERTED STP GORLEY AWAITING ME IN MY OUTER OFFICE
STP EAGER TO USE WHATEVER HE USES STP MY THOUGHT THAT
ONLY SOLUTION IS THROW AWAY PRESENT SITUATION AND START
ALL OVER STP INCIDENTALLY WHY CAN I NOT PERSONALLY ORDER
REGROUPING OF FORCES STP IS THERE ANOTHER CAPITOL AS I
HAVE HEARD RUMORED ALL SET UP WITH SKELETON CREWS AND
READY TO TAKE OVER IF ANYTHING HAPPENS TO PRESENT ONE
STP WILL YOU CONSENT TO ACT AS OPCHIEF IF SO DIRECTED BY
ME STP I PROPOSE GIVE YOU DIRECT ORDER TO PERFORM VERY
HAZARDOUS THANKLESS MISSION OF VITAL IMPORTANCE STP WILL
YOU OBEY IMMEDIATELY AND WITHOUT QUESTION STP REPLY IM-
MEDIATELY THROUGH CHIEF DISPATCHER STP REPLY CONFIDEN-
TIAL CATEGORY VITAL STP JAMES CORDOVAN DEFSEC CAPITOL

VITAL 04-20-2308-1730TCT PERSONAL
COMGEN GR CAP TO DEFSEC CAP THRU CHIEF DISPATCHER
   CONFIDENTIAL
HOW DOES GORLEY DO IT STP YES YOU CAN ORDER FORCES DIRECT
BUT WHAT GOOD IF PRESIDENT COUNTERMANDS STP YES AUXIL-
IARY CAP EXISTS READY TO TAKE OVER STP BUT IF WE LOSE THE
PRESENT CAP THRU ENEMY ACTION IT WILL BE BECAUSE OF GREAT
WEAKNESS AND THERE WILL BE LITTLE FOR AUX CAP TO DO BUT
SIGN SURRENDER STP YES I WILL BE OPCHIEF IF YOU SO ORDER
STP I WILL FOLLOW ORDERS REGARDLESS HAZARD OR THANK-
LESSNESS STP I WILL ACT IMMEDIATELY WITHOUT QUESTION STP
BUT I CAN FOLLOW YOUR ORDERS ONLY IF NOT COUNTERMANDED
BY HIGHER AUTHORITY THAT IS THE PRESIDENT STP VERNON L
HAUSER COMGEN GR CAP

4-20-2308

Office of the Undersecretary for Defense
Jim:

Come off it, fellow. You can't expect a man like Colonel Gorley to wait around in your outer office when he is on a mission direct from the President. As for Colonel Gorley's appearance, as I said before, the colonel is a splendid figure of a man, very compact and muscular, with peculiarly keen sharp eyes. Eyes indicative, I might add, of great force of character, and you are standing in this man's way and the President's. Colonel Gorley says he thinks it is "unlikely" you knew him as a child. He came from a place where as a child he didn't ever have enough to eat, which explains his periodic little indulgences in food. He is angry with you, Jim, and he is close to the President. I don't think he will wait much longer, Jim, when it is his duty to see you. Wake up, Jim.

Birdie

4-20-2308

Office of the Secretary for Defense
Chief Dispatcher:

Send the following:
VITAL 04-20-2308-1734TCT PERSONAL
DEFSEC CAP TO COMGENS ALL SECTORS
EFFECTIVE IMMEDIATELY GENERAL J J RYSTENKO IS REMOVED RPT REMOVED FROM POST AS OPCHIEF GS STP EFFECTIVE IMMEDIATELY LIEUTENANT-GENERAL VERNON L HAUSER COMGEN GR IS APPOINTED RPT APPOINTED OPCHIEF GS STP I HAVE FULL AND COMPLETE CONFIDENCE IN GENERAL HAUSER STP ANY DELAY IN CARRYING OUT GENERAL HAUSER'S ORDERS IN THE UNUSUAL CIRCUMSTANCES ABOUT TO OCCUR WILL BE A DIRECT THREAT TO THE SECURITY OF THE RACE STP IN THESE TIMES STEADINESS AND INSTANT OBEDIENCE TO ORDERS ARE THE VITAL QUALITIES STP GOD BE WITH YOU AND HOLD YOU STEADY AGAINST THE FOE STP JAMES CORDOVAN DEFSEC CAPITOL

VITAL 04-20-2308-1735TCT STAFF
DEFSEC CAPITOL TO ALL STATIONS
FOR YOUR INFORMATION EXPERIENCE WITH ENEMY CAPTIVE HERE SUGGESTS OUTS POSSESS GREAT HYPNOTIC POWERS AT CLOSE RANGE STP ADVISABLE TAKE NO PRISONERS

VITAL 04-20-2308-1736TCT PERSONAL
DEFSEC CAPITOL TO COMGEN GR CAPITOL
DIRECT ORDER YOU DESTROY RPT DESTROY CAPITOL RPT CAPITOL
AT EARLIEST POSSIBLE MOMENT CONSISTENT WITH SAFETY OF
FORCES UNDER YOUR COMMAND STP THEN CONCENTRATE MAIN
FORCES AS YOU THINK ADVISABLE STP JAMES CORDOVAN DEFSEC
CAP

4-20-2308

Office of the Undersecretary of Defense
Jim:
    You have gone a little too far in defying Colonel Gorley
and the President, and Colonel Gorley has decided to wait
no longer in performing his duty. He is coming in to see you
now, Jim, door or no door.

Birdie

4-20-2308

Office of the Secretary for Defense
Birdie:
    Tell Colonel Gorley I have a service revolver in my hand
and am only too eager to test Gorley's fantastic recuperative
powers against this and one other weapon. Go after him and
tell him this.

Jim

ROUTINE 04-20-2308-1700TCT STAFF
COMGEN IV TO OPCHIEF GS CAPITOL
OCCUPATION OF PLANET FIVE RPT FIVE COMPLETE STP NO RPT NO
OPPOSITION STP NO RPT NO INDICATION OF PREVIOUS ATTEMPTS
TO TAKE PLANET STP HUGE RESERVES OF QUADRITE STP MINING
NOW UNDERWAY

04-20-2308

Office of the Undersecretary for Defense
Jim:
    What do you mean? What is going on here? May I go home,
Jim? I feel strange.

Birdie

4-20-2308

Office of the Secretary for Defense
Birdie:

Thank you for sending Colonel Gorley in to me. He has explained our defense set-up to me most clearly.

Jim

VITAL 04-20-2308-1750TCT STAFF
COMGEN GR CAP TO ALL STATIONS
U EXPLOSION CAPITOL
U EXPLOSION CAPITOL
U EXPLOSION CAPITOL
U EXPLOSION CAPITOL
U EXPLOSION CAPITOL
EXPLOSIONS RAPID SUCCESSIVE NOT BY ENEMY ACTION TIME OF OBSERVATION 04-20-2308-1746TCT
VITAL TRANSMIT TRIPLE AT TEN-MINUTE INTERVALS

Tony Lewis is a good example of the science-fiction fan turned author. He has been active in organized fandom for many years, and now reviews sf for Analog Science Fiction/Science Fact. *We predict that "Request for Proposal"* (Analog, *November 1972) will see more reprintings, for it is a superior example of social-science fiction and of bureaucracy gone mad.*

REQUEST FOR PROPOSAL

By Anthony R. Lewis

DEPARTMENT OF HOUSING AND URBAN
DEVELOPMENT
ROBERT F. KENNEDY RESEARCH CENTER

FROM: Chief, Improvements Branch, Readjustment Division
TO: Branch Members
DATE: 7 March 1984
SUBJECT: COST EFFECTIVE OPTIMIZATION OF IN-
NER-CITY INTERACTION STABILIZATION

1. Reference is made to the President's speech of 1 March dealing with the necessity to solve the problems of inner-city personnel and matériel interactions in a modern cost-effective manner utilizing state-of-the-art technology.

2. Reference is further made to the statement of the Sec-

retary of Housing and Urban Development reaffirming the role of the Department in the solution of the substantive problems of our society and the need for additional funding in this area.

3. Reference is further made to the memo from the Center Director stressing the unique capability of this Center due to its history of university and industrial relations and its in-house facilities and staff.

4. In accordance with paragraphs 1–3, I would like all technical members of the branch to submit to me, by 14 March, their ideas as to how our branch can aid in the implementation of these national goals.

   a. It is not intended that any of these suggestions will be in final form.
   b. Include estimates as to costs and man-hours to be committed.
   c. I would like to see new concepts: remember that the President has requested us to solve the problems—not their symptoms.

Invest in America
Buy United States Savings Bonds

DEPARTMENT OF HOUSING AND URBAN DEVELOPMENT
ROBERT F. KENNEDY RESEARCH CENTER

FROM: Gordon Rogers
TO: Chief, Improvements Branch
DATE: 13 March 1984
SUBJECT: COST EFFECTIVE OPTIMIZATION OF IN-NER-CITY INTERACTION STABILIZATION (Branch Memo of 7 March 1984)

Keeping in mind paragraph 4c of your memo, the problem seems to naturally divide into the areas of matériel and personnel. However, the approach I suggest will be equally effective in both sections of the problem. (This will enable a saving in both procurement and administrative areas.)

The matériel problem is essentially the replacement of obsolescent and obsolete residential (and, to a very small extent, industrial), buildings in a controlled economical method.

Some of the major problems to be expected are: labor-union regulations; local construction ordinances; lack of specialized tools/techniques.

All these essentially add to the time required to perform the task, adding to the cost. The current patchwork method also makes it extremely difficult to perform long-range, large-scale planning for slum clearance and urban renewal.

The personnel problem is closely tied into this with older buildings (which provide too many defense positions) making effective law enforcement difficult. The unplanned city growth (especially in the use of narrow and short streets) hampers effective control of urban disturbances and riots.

The obvious solution to all these problems is the selective use of low-yield tactical nuclear devices as the major components of a modern, effective slum-clearance and riot-control program. It is expected that sufficient devices can be transferred from the Department of Defense, at cost, in the initial stages of the program. Further downstream, alternate sources for the devices can be sought on a competitive bid basis, thereby decreasing costs.

The program could be run by the Department directly or as a contractor to the states.

I estimate the first year's program should run about $4,700,000 and involve forty man-years of technical and support staff.

Invest in America
Buy United States Savings Bonds

DEPARTMENT OF HOUSING AND URBAN
DEVELOPMENT
ROBERT F. KENNEDY RESEARCH CENTER

FROM: Chief, Improvements Branch
TO: Gordon Rogers
DATE: 19 March 1984
SUBJECT: Your Memo of 13 March 1984

Are you serious? You are proposing that we go into these areas and essentially eliminate them and their inhabitants without any warning. What you are proposing is administrative murder—these are living human beings. Perhaps you meant the whole thing as a joke, but, if so, it is in very bad taste. Regardless of how much money could be saved I don't think anyone in this Department (or any other) would justify using the methods you proposed. If you have any sane suggestions in line with my memo of 7 March, I would like to see them.

A copy of this memo is being placed in your permanent personnel file.

Invest in America
Buy United States Savings Bonds

DEPARTMENT OF HOUSING AND URBAN
DEVELOPMENT
ROBERT F. KENNEDY RESEARCH CENTER

FROM: Gordon Rogers
TO: Chief, Improvements Branch
DATE: 21 March 1984
SUBJECT: Your Memo of 19 March

My proposal was made quite seriously and I believe that its scope comes within the charter of this Center. I would like to refer you to the pertinent sections of the President's speech of 1 March (mention of some of these sections was made in the Division Memo of 7 March) calling for solutions to these critical national problems.

It was not my intention to have any solutions performed in secret, as this could lead to the loss of innocent life and a decrease in the high esteem in which the Department and Center are held by the general public. After an area is publicly selected for improvement, Emergency Urban Evacuation Notices can be served on all persons living in the area under the construction title of the Federal Urban Transit Act of 1977. This will give all decent law-abiding citizens in the improvement area no less than forty-eight (48) hours to relocate elsewhere. They would, of course, have first option to rent new housing (if any) in the improved area after improvement operations.

Since all people residing in the country have their addresses listed in the National Data System, Emergency Urban Evacuation Notices can be sent to all the inhabitants. I would also like to point out that since both failure to report changes of address and failure to comply with an Emergency

Evacuation Notice are felonies, we have what is essentially a self-selecting system which will preserve law-abiding citizens and no others.

I hope that with these points made clear you will see fit to approve this suggestion and pass it on to the Division Chief for consideration. In any case I should point out that even if you do not approve this suggestion, since it deals with an issue designated as a "National Priority Issue" it must be forwarded as called for in the Civil Service Regulations (105.8) and the Internal Operation Instructions of the Department of Housing and Urban Development (RA25-3(c)).

Invest in America
Buy United States Savings Bonds

DEPARTMENT OF HOUSING AND URBAN
DEVELOPMENT
ROBERT F. KENNEDY RESEARCH CENTER

FROM: Chief, Improvements Branch
TO: Chief, Readjustment Division
DATE: 28 March 1984
SUBJECT: Proposed Program for COST EFFECTIVE OPTIMIZATION OF INNER-CITY INTERACTION STABILIZATION

This proposal is being forwarded to you as a "National Priority Issue" under section 105.8 of the Civil Service Regulations and Section RA25-3(c) of the Internal Operating Instructions of the Department of Housing and Urban Development.

This proposal has not been approved by the Branch Chief, Improvements Branch.

Although it should be obvious that this proposal is contraindicated on moral and humanitarian grounds alone, I have included a list of technical objections which should be sufficient grounds for rejection of this program.

Enc: technical objections, list

Invest in America
Buy United States Savings Bonds

DEPARTMENT OF HOUSING AND URBAN DEVELOPMENT
ROBERT F. KENNEDY RESEARCH CENTER

FROM: Chief, Readjustment Division
TO: Gordon Rogers
DATE: 2 April 1984
SUBJECT: Proposed Program for COST EFFECTIVE OPTIMIZATION OF INNER-CITY INTERACTION STABILIZATION

The Division has received and reviewed your proposed program and has found the following problems involved. It is our opinion that any one of these would be sufficient to cause rejection of this program.

1. What percentage of the buildings in potential improvement areas are industrial? This is extremely important as it would lead to a lessening of the city's tax base.

2. What provisions will be made for the exacerbation of the housing shortage since the decrease in demand will not be concomitant with the temporary supply decrease? (Assuming proper action with regard to the Emergency Urban Evacuation Notices.)

3. What damages could occur in neighboring nonimprovement areas? How can we predict overlaps and errors? What tolerance in "slop-over" can be allowed in both personnel and matériel?

4. What containment is necessary under the terms of the Nuclear Test Ban Treaty?

5. What would be the added costs if it becomes necessary to prevent the dispersal of fallout? Or, of the reimbursement of affected areas, if this is more economical?

6. What specific problems will there be with labor unions? Will it be better to retrain the people involved or to pension them off?

7. In order to demonstrate cost effectiveness we will have to run a pilot program. Outline briefly, with especial reference to selection of areas and parameters, such a plan for effectiveness-result comparison.

If you cannot satisfy the problems listed above by 9 April 1984, I shall have no choice but to reject your proposed program.

cc: Improvements Branch

Invest in America
Buy United States Savings Bonds

DEPARTMENT OF HOUSING AND URBAN
DEVELOPMENT
ROBERT F. KENNEDY RESEARCH CENTER

FROM: Gordon Rogers
TO: Chief, Readjustment Division
DATE: 9 April 1984
SUBJECT: Your Memo of 2 April 1984

1. Data from the 1980 census indicate that in potential improvement areas less than four percent of the structures (floor area) are classified as industrial. Of these, more than ninety percent are over sixty (60) years old and are considered to be inefficient.

2. The problems of temporary housing may be met as provided for under the Federal Transit Act of 1977. Those people who cannot relocate independently (through family, friends, or private agencies) are to be provided for by the Federal Government either in the Ecology Improvement Relocation Camps or as Urban Inductees (quasi-voluntary) in the Armed Forces or the Peace Corps.

3. With state-of-the-art techniques in nuclear devices, we can, by pattern shaping, reduce the error to less than twenty feet (approximately an average city street width). The greatest error will result from emplacement of the devices. If we can hand emplace, this will be eliminated. The accuracy of emplacement via remote delivery is estimated as twenty feet (ground) or fifty feet (air). (All uncertainties are root-mean-square.) Since the areas immediately adjacent may also be in need of improvements within a short time span—it is not expected that in most cases this will prove a problem.

In a few cases we may have just such a problem and then a choice arises between a decrease in the yields used, necessitating additional manual clearance at the peripheries, or the reimbursement of survivors and/or legatees in the surrounding areas in the case of nonoptimum emplacement. Which will be more economical will, of course, depend upon the details of each specific case. A small contract to a con-

sulting firm to develop a choice algorithm would be in order
here.

4. Semantically, this is not a test. I think we will still be
abiding by the spirit of the treaty, since these events will not
be directed against anyone, but will be of a specific corrective
and .constructive purpose. Recent urban developments in
other countries lead me to believe that our successes in this
program will be quickly imitated elsewhere. Possibly, later
projects could be done on an international basis—with due
regard to security.

5. It is not expected, in the majority of cases, that containment in advance will be practicable due to the possibility
of criminal elements. Present device design indicates that
major fallout components will be neutron-activated environ-
mental artifacts. Calculations indicate that proper emplacement can eliminate up to seventy-six percent of the specific
activity present twenty-four hours after the event. Reim-
bursements to the surrounding areas are covered under Title
7 of the Federal Urban Transit Act of 1977.

6. Studies of documents and speeches indicate that a
lump-sum payment to the union(s) retirement fund plus
assurance of employment on rebuilding projects in the improved areas will be adequate. Possibly a contract with the
national unions involved would be desirable.

7. This will involve a pilot program. In order to gather
necessary background data we should construct (probably at
the Nevada test site) a selection of the different building
styles which would be encountered in major cities in their
potential improvement areas. These would then be staffed
with personnel transferred from the Departments of Defense
and Labor (proper backgrounds, et cetera, to be computer-
selected). Costs for personnel would be on a per capita–per
diem basis and would be extremely low under the Universal
Conscription Act of 1979. If this phase is to be extended as
data from cities are obtained, perhaps some of the personnel
temporarily evacuated (see paragraph 2) would volunteer for
this assignment knowing that it would aid in the improvement of the lives of their socioeconomic class.

These data will enable us to construct algorithms for the
choice of cities as tests for this program and to eliminate
effects due to the differing urban matrices in which the individual improvement areas are embedded.

I trust that this fully answers the questions you raised.

request that this proposed program be forwarded to the Center Director as a "National Priority Issue" under Section 105.8 of the Civil Service Regulations and Section RA25-3(c) of the Internal Operating Instructions of the Department of Housing and Urban Development and in accordance with the expressed desires of the President in his speech of 1 March 1984.

c: Improvements Branch

Invest in America
Buy United States Savings Bonds

DEPARTMENT OF HOUSING AND URBAN
DEVELOPMENT
ROBERT F. KENNEDY RESEARCH CENTER

FROM: Chief, Readjustment Division
TO: Director, Robert F. Kennedy Research Center
DATE: 13 April 1984
SUBJECT: Proposed Program for COST EFFECTIVE OP-
  TIMIZATION OF INNER-CITY INTERACTION STABI-
  LIZATION

1. Herein is forwarded a proposed program in the area of Cost Effective Optimization of Inner-City Interaction Sta-bilization as a "National Priority Issue" under Section 105.8 of the Civil Service Regulations and Section RA25-3(c) of the Internal Operating Instructions of the Department of Hous-ing and Urban Development and Center Directive XLR-2527-03.

2. This proposal is in response to the Center Memo of 7 March 1984.

3. This proposed program has not been approved by Chief, Improvements Branch nor Chief, Readjustment Division.

4. It is felt that this proposal is highly immoral and that it be rejected.

c: Improvements Branch
  Gordon Rogers

Invest in America
Buy United States Savings Bonds

DEPARTMENT OF HOUSING AND URBAN DEVELOPMENT
ROBERT F. KENNEDY RESEARCH CENTER

FROM: Director, Robert F. Kennedy Research Center
TO: Chief, Readjustment Division
DATE: 18 April 1984
SUBJECT: Proposed Program for COST EFFECTIVE OPTIMIZATION OF INNER-CITY INTERACTION STABILIZATION

1. In view of both the public statements of the President and the Secretary of Housing and Urban Development and the fact that this area has been designated a "National Priority Issue" I do not think that we can reject this proposal on any other grounds than deficiencies in the technical aspects

2. The following major questions have not been answered by the proposed program document:

2.1 Control of devices to be used in this program is by AEC and/or Defense. Is it feasible to set up a liaison program to handle transfers of this magnitude?

2.2 How will the actions of the recalcitrant element in the potential improvement areas affect the proper emplacement of devices, bearing in mind that at least forty-eight hours' notification will be given?

2.3 In the construction of any selection algorithm, it is essential to include the factor that any population readjustments due to the program should not decrease the present Administration's representation in the Congress.

3. Please have Mr. Rogers report to me with answers to the problems in paragraph 2 before 25 April 1984.

cc: Improvements Branch

Invest in America
Buy United States Savings Bonds

DEPARTMENT OF HOUSING AND URBAN DEVELOPMENT
ROBERT F. KENNEDY RESEARCH CENTER

19 April 1984

Dr. J. Moriarty (Code 21-5)
Defense Nuclear Agency
Washington, D.C. 20301

Dear Jim:

We've got a possible program going here in line with the President's speech of 1 March setting up the inner-city problems as a National Priority Issue. Before we can go ahead with formal requests for liaison I'd like to talk to you informally about it. Please give me a call on FTS or Autovon soonest.

Gordon Rogers

Invest in America
Buy United States Savings Bonds

DEPARTMENT OF HOUSING AND URBAN DEVELOPMENT
ROBERT F. KENNEDY RESEARCH CENTER

19 April 1984

Col. S. Moran (Code RM-37)
United States Atomic Energy Commission
Washington, D.C., 20545

Dear Sebastian:

In regard to the President's speech of 1 March setting up the inner-city problems as a National Priority Issue, I think we've got a possible program here that would be a natural for cooperation between our two agencies and would be to all our advantages. Give me a call on FTS and we'll talk it over before we do anything formal about it.

Best to you and Irene.

Gordon Rogers

Invest in America
Buy United States Savings Bonds

DEPARTMENT OF HOUSING AND URBAN DEVELOPMENT
ROBERT F. KENNEDY RESEARCH CENTER

FROM: Chief, Readjustment Division
TO: Director, Robert F. Kennedy Research Center
DATE: 25 April 1984
SUBJECT: Proposed Program for COST EFFECTIVE OP-
TIMIZATION OF INNER-CITY INTERACTION STABI-
LIZATION (Your Memo of 18 April 1984)

Mr. Rogers has spoken informally to the appropriate persons in both the Defense Nuclear Agency and the Atomic
Energy Commission and we have been assured of the support
of both agencies in fulfilling the pledges of the President in
his raising of the inner-city problems to a "National Priority
Issue." (See attachment A for confirmatory memos.)

See also attachment B giving details of remote emplacement in the event that access to the potential improvement
area is denied to lawful authorities by recalcitrant elements.

See also attachment C spelling out the constraints to be
placed on the selection algorithms as specified in paragraph
2.3 of your memo of 18 April 1984.

Since I see no possible way to prevent this program from
being actualized in my present position, I wish to tender my
resignation from the Department.

cc: Improvements Branch
     Gordon Rogers
att: A—confirmatory memos from DNA, AEC
      B—legal brief and details of remote emplacement
      C—mathematical constraints on selection algorithm

Invest in America
Buy United States Savings Bonds

DEPARTMENT OF HOUSING AND URBAN
DEVELOPMENT
ROBERT F. KENNEDY RESEARCH CENTER

FROM: Director, Robert F. Kennedy Research Center
TO: Acting Chief, Readjustment Division
DATE: 3 May 1984
SUBJECT: COST EFFECTIVE OPTIMIZATION OF IN-
NER-CITY INTERACTION STABILIZATION

This is to authorize you to proceed immediately with the subject program as defined in our previous communications. Below is a quote from the Secretary of Housing and Urban Development concerning this program:

"This program will be in keeping with the finest traditions of our country and will reflect most favorably upon the Department and upon the Robert F. Kennedy Research Center and upon those individuals directly involved."

cc: Improvements Branch
    Gordon Rogers

Invest in America
Buy United States Savings Bonds

DEPARTMENT OF HOUSING AND URBAN DEVELOPMENT
ROBERT F. KENNEDY RESEARCH CENTER

FROM: Acting Chief, Improvements Branch
TO: Chief, Procurement Branch
DATE: 7 May 1984
SUBJECT: REQUEST FOR PROPOSAL

Procurement Request for Study for the Cost Effective Optimization of Inner-City Interaction Stabilization
1. It is requested that a contract be negotiated with a commercial source to perform the efforts described in the attached work statement and performance schedule, exhibit A.

Invest in America
Buy United States Savings Bonds

DEPARTMENT OF HOUSING AND URBAN DEVELOPMENT
ROBERT F. KENNEDY RESEARCH CENTER

Issue Date: 4 June 1984
Subject: Solicitation No. HUD84-2101R
Title: Cost Effective Optimization of Inner-City Interaction Stabilization

Due Date: 9 July 1984, 1700 (local Washington, D.C. time)
Submit to:
    Negotiated Contracts
    Procurement Branch
    Department of Housing and Urban Development

Gentlemen:

The U.S. Department of Housing and Urban Development, Robert F. Kennedy Research Center, solicits your organization for a proposal for a study aimed at defining the requirements for, and the economics of, the use of low-yield nuclear devices in the optimization of inner-city interaction stabilization.

This solicitation is covered by the following documents...

H. Beam Piper (1903–64) is best remembered as the author of the "Paratime" and "Terran Federation" series which appeared (mostly) in the 1950s. Particularly popular are the novels Little Fuzzy *(1962) and* The Other Human Race *(1964). His finest short fiction was "Omnilingual" (1957), but "He Walked Around the Horses"* (Astounding Science Fiction, April 1948) *is a close second. The story is based on an actual historical mystery, and, for all we know, this is really what happened.*

HE WALKED AROUND THE HORSES

By H. Beam Piper

In November, 1809, an Englishman named Benjamin Bathurst vanished, inexplicably and utterly.

He was en route to Hamburg from Vienna, where he had been serving as his Government's envoy to the court of what Napoleon had left of the Austrian Empire. At an inn in Perleburg, in Prussia, while examining a change of horses for his coach, he casually stepped out of sight of his secretary and his valet. He was not seen to leave the inn-yard. He was not seen again, ever.

At least, not in this continuum...

I

(From Baron Eugen von Krutz, Minister of Police, to His Excellency the Count von Berchtenwald, Chancellor to His Majesty Friedrich Wilhelm III of Prussia.)

25 November, 1809

Your Excellency:

A circumstance has come to the notice of this Ministry, the significance of which I am at a loss to define, but, since it appears to involve matters of state, both here and abroad, I am convinced that it is of sufficient importance to be brought to the personal attention of your Excellency. Frankly, I am unwilling to take any further action in the matter without your Excellency's advice.

Briefly, the situation is this: We are holding, here at the Ministry of Police, a person giving his name as Benjamin Bathurst, who claims to be a British diplomat. This person was taken into custody by the police at Perleburg yesterday, as a result of a disturbance at an inn there; he is being detained on technical charges of causing disorder in a public place, and of being a suspicious person. When arrested, he had in his possession a dispatch-case, containing a number of papers; these are of such an extraordinary nature that the local authorities declined to assume any responsibility beyond having the man sent here to Berlin.

After interviewing this person and examining his papers, I am, I must confess, in much the same position. This is not, I am convinced, any ordinary police matter; there is something very strange and disturbing here. The man's statements, taken alone, are so incredible as to justify the assumption that he is mad. I cannot, however, adopt this theory, in view of his demeanor, which is that of a man of perfect rationality, and because of the existence of these papers. The whole thing is mad; incomprehensible!

The papers in question accompany, along with copies of the various statements taken at Perleburg, and a personal letter to me from my nephew, Lieutenant Rudolf von Tarlburg. This last is deserving of your Excellency's particular attention; Lieutenant von Tarlburg is a very level-headed young officer, not at all inclined to be fanciful or imaginative. It would take a good deal to affect him as he describes.

The man calling himself Benjamin Bathurst is now lodged in an apartment here at the Ministry; he is being treated with every consideration, and, except for freedom of movement, accorded every privilege.

I am, most anxiously awaiting your Excellency's advice, etc., etc.,

Krutz

II

(Report of Traugott Zeller, *Oberwachtmeister, Staatspolizei*, made at Perleburg, 25 November, 1809.)

At about ten minutes past two of the afternoon of Saturday, 25 November, while I was at the police station, there entered a man known to me as Franz Bauer, an inn-servant employed by Christian Hauck, at the sign of the Sword & Scepter, here in Perleburg. This man Franz Bauer made complaint to *Staatspolizeikapitan* Ernst Hartenstein, saying that there was a madman making trouble at the inn where he, Franz Bauer, worked. I was therefore directed, by *Staatspolizeikapitan* Hartenstein to go to the Sword & Scepter Inn, there to act at discretion to maintain the peace.

Arriving at the inn in company with the said Franz Bauer, I found a considerable crowd of people in the common-room, and, in the midst of them, the innkeeper, Christian Hauck, in altercation with a stranger. This stranger was a gentlemanly-appearing person, dressed in traveling clothes, who had under his arm a small leather dispatch-case. As I entered, I could hear him, speaking in German with a strong English accent, abusing the innkeeper, the said Christian Hauck, and accusing him of having drugged his, the stranger's, wine, and of having stolen his, the stranger's, coach-and-four, and of having abducted his, the stranger's, secretary and servants. This the said Christian Hauck was loudly denying, and the other people in the inn were taking the innkeeper's part, and mocking the stranger for a madman.

On entering, I commanded everyone to be silent, in the King's name, and then, as he appeared to be the complaining party of the dispute, I required the foreign gentleman to state to me what was the trouble. He then repeated his accusations against the innkeeper, Hauck, saying that Hauck, or, rather, another man who resembled Hauck and who had claimed to be the innkeeper, had drugged his wine and stolen his coach and made off with his secretary and his servants. At this point, the innkeeper and the bystanders all began shouting denials and contradictions, so that I had to pound on a table with my truncheon to command silence.

I then required the innkeeper, Christian Hauck, to answer the charges which the stranger had made; this he did with a complete denial of all of them, saying that the stranger had had no wine in his inn, and that he had not been inside the inn until a few minutes before, when he had burst in shouting accusations, and that there had been no secretary, and no valet, and no coachman, and no coach-and-four, at the inn, and that the gentleman was raving mad. To all this, he called the people who were in the common-room to witness.

I then required the stranger to account for himself. He said that his name was Benjamin Bathurst, and that he was a British diplomat, returning to England from Vienna. To prove this, he produced from his dispatch-case sundry papers. One of these was a letter of safe-conduct, issued by the Prussian Chancellery, in which he was named and described as Benjamin Bathurst. The other papers were English, all bearing seals, and appearing to be official documents.

Accordingly, I requested him to accompany me to the police station, and also the innkeeper, and three men whom the innkeeper wanted to bring as witnesses.

Traugott Zeller
Oberwachtmeister

Report approved,

Ernst Hartenstein
Staatspolizeikapitan

III

(Statement of the self-so-called Benjamin Bathurst, taken at the police station at Perleburg, 25 November, 1809.)

My name is Benjamin Bathurst, and I am Envoy Extraordinary and Minister Plenipotentiary of the Government of His Britannic Majesty to the court of His Majesty Franz I, Emperor of Austria, or, at least I was until the events following the Austrian surrender made necessary my return to London. I left Vienna on the morning of Monday, the 20th, to go to Hamburg to take ship home; I was traveling in my own coach-and-four, with my secretary, Mr. Bertram Jardine, and my valet, William Small, both British subjects, and a coachman, Joseph Bidek, an Austrian subject, whom I had hired for the trip. Because of the presence of French troops, whom I was anxious to avoid, I was forced to make a detour west as far as Salzburg before turning north toward Magdeburg, where I crossed the Elbe. I was unable to get a change of horses for my coach after leaving Gera, until I reached Perleburg, where I stopped at the Sword & Scepter Inn.

Arriving there, I left my coach in the inn-yard, and I and my secretary, Mr. Jardine, went into the inn. A man, not this fellow here, but another rogue, with more beard and less paunch, but more shabbily dressed, but as like him as though he were his brother, represented himself as the innkeeper, and I dealt with him for a change of horses, and ordered a bottle of wine for myself and my secretary, and also a pot of beer apiece for my valet and the coachman, to be taken outside to them. Then Jardine and I sat down to our wine, at a table in the common-room, until the man who claimed to be the innkeeper came back and told us that the fresh horses were harnessed to the coach and ready to go. Then we went outside again.

I looked at the two horses on the off-side, and then walked around in front of the team to look at the two nigh-side horses, and as I did, I felt giddy, as though I were about to fall, and everything went black before my eyes. I thought I was having a fainting-spell, something I am not at all subject to, and I put out my hand to grasp the hitching-bar, but could not find it. I am sure, now, that I was unconscious for some time, because when my head cleared, the coach and horses were gone, and in their place was a big farm-wagon, jacked up in front, with the right front wheel off, and two peasants were greasing the detached wheel.

I looked at them for a moment, unable to credit my eyes, and then I spoke to them in German, saying, "Where the devil's my coach-and-four?"

They both straightened, startled; the one who was holding the wheel almost dropped it.

"Pardon, Excellency," he said. "There's been no coach-and-four here, all the time we've been here."

"Yes," said his mate, "and we've been here since just after noon."

I did not attempt to argue with them. It occurred to me—and it is still my opinion—that I was the victim of some plot; that my wine had been drugged, that I had been unconscious for some time, during which my coach had been removed and this wagon substituted for it, and that these peasants had been put to work on it and instructed what to say if questioned. If my arrival at the inn had been anticipated, and everything put in readiness, the whole business would not have taken ten minutes.

I therefore entered the inn, determined to have it out with this rascally innkeeper, but when I returned to the commonroom, he was nowhere to be seen, and this other fellow, who has also given his name as Christian Hauck, claimed to be the innkeeper and denied knowledge of any of the things I have just stated. Furthermore, there were four cavalrymen, Uhlans, drinking beer and playing cards at the table where Jardine and I had had our wine, and they claimed to have been there for several hours.

I have no idea why such an elaborate prank, involving the participation of many people, should be played on me, except at the instigation of the French. In that case, I cannot understand why Prussian soldiers should lend themselves to it.

Benjamin Bathurst

IV

(Statement of Christian Hauck, innkeeper, taken at the police station at Perleburg, 25 November, 1809.)

May it please your Honor, my name is Christian Hauck, and I keep an inn at the sign of the Sword & Scepter, and have these past fifteen years, and my father, and his father, before me, for the past fifty years, and never has there been a complaint like this against my inn. Your Honor, it is a hard thing for a man who keeps a decent house, and pays his taxes, and obeys the laws, to be accused of crimes of this sort.

I know nothing of this gentleman, nor of his coach nor his secretary nor his servants; I never set eyes on him before he came bursting into the inn from the yard, shouting and raving like a madman, and crying out, "Where the devil's that rogue of an innkeeper?"

I said to him, "I am the innkeeper; what cause have you to call me a rogue, sir?"

The stranger replied:

"You're not the innkeeper I did business with a few minutes ago, and he's the rascal I have a crow to pick with. I want to know what the devil's been done with my coach, and what's happened to my secretary and my servants."

I tried to tell him that I knew nothing of what he was talking about, but he would not listen, and gave me the lie, saying that he had been drugged and robbed, and his people kidnapped. He even had the impudence to claim that he and his secretary had been sitting at a table in that room, drinking wine, not fifteen minutes before, when there had been four non-commissioned officers of the Third Uhlans at that table since noon. Everybody in the room spoke up for me, but he would not listen, and was shouting that we were all robbers, and kidnappers, and French spies, and I don't know what all, when the police came.

Your Honor, the man is mad. What I have told you about this is the truth, and all that I know about this business, so help me God.

Christian Hauck

V

(Statement of Franz Bauer, inn-servant, taken at the police station at Perleburg, 25 November, 1809.)

May it please your Honor, my name is Franz Bauer, and I am a servant at the Sword & Scepter Inn, kept by Christian Hauck.

This afternoon, when I went into the inn-yard to empty a bucket of slops on the dung-heap by the stables, I heard voices and turned around, to see this gentleman speaking to Wilhelm Beick and Fritz Herzer, who were greasing their wagon in the yard. He had not been in the yard when I had turned around to empty the bucket, and I thought that he must have come in from the street. This gentleman was asking Beick and Herzer where was his coach, and when they told him they didn't know, he turned and ran into the inn.

Of my own knowledge, the man had not been inside the inn before then, nor had there been any coach, or any of the people he spoke of, at the inn, and none of the things he spoke of happened there, for otherwise I would know, since I was at the inn all day.

When I went back inside, I found him in the common-room, shouting at my master, and claiming that he had been drugged and robbed. I saw that he was mad, and was afraid that he would do some mischief, so I went for the police.

Franz Bauer

his (X) mark

VI

(Statements of Wilhelm Beick and Fritz Herzer, peasants, taken at the police station at Perleburg, 25 November, 1809.)

May it please your Honor, my name is Wilhelm Beick, and I am a tenant on the estate of the Baron von Hentig. On this day, I and Fritz Herzer were sent in to Perleburg with a load of potatoes and cabbages which the innkeeper at the Sword & Scepter had bought from the estate-superintendent. After we had unloaded them, we decided to grease our wagon, which was very dry, before going back, so we unhitched and began working on it. We took about two hours, starting just after we had eaten lunch, and in all that time, there was no coach-and-four in the inn-yard. We were just finishing when this gentleman spoke to us, demanding to know where his coach was. We told him that there had been no coach in the yard all the time we had been there, so he turned around and ran into the inn. At the time, I thought that he had come out of the inn before speaking to us, for I know that he could not have come in from the street. Now I do not know where he came from, but I know that I never saw him before that moment.

Wilhelm Beick

his (X) mark

I have heard the above testimony, and it is true to my own knowledge, and I have nothing to add to it.

Fritz Herzer

his (X) mark

VII

(From *Staatspolizeikapitan* Ernst Hartenstein, to His Excellency, the Baron von Krutz, Minister of Police.)

25 November, 1809

Your Excellency:

The accompanying copies of statements taken this day

will explain how the prisoner, the self-so-called Benjamin Bathurst, came into my custody. I have charged him with causing disorder and being a suspicious person, to hold him until more can be learned about him. However, as he represents himself to be a British diplomat, I am unwilling to assume any further responsibility, and am having him sent to your Excellency, in Berlin.

In the first place, your Excellency, I have the strongest doubts of the man's story. The statement which he made before me, and signed, is bad enough, with a coach-and-four turning into a farm-wagon, like Cinderella's coach into a pumpkin, and three people vanishing as though swallowed by the earth. Your Excellency will permit me to doubt that there ever was any such coach, or any such people. But all this is perfectly reasonable and credible, beside the things he said to me, of which no record was made.

Your Excellency will have noticed, in his statement, certain allusions to the Austrian surrender, and to French troops in Austria. After his statement had been taken down, I noticed these allusions, and I inquired, what surrender, and what were French troops doing in Austria. The man looked at me in a pitying manner, and said:

"News seems to travel slowly, hereabouts; peace was concluded at Vienna on the 14th of last month. And as for what French troops are doing in Austria, they're doing the same thing Bonaparte's brigands are doing everywhere in Europe."

"And who is Bonaparte?" I asked.

He stared at me as though I had asked him, "Who is the Lord Jehovah?" Then, after a moment, a look of comprehension came into his face.

"So; you Prussians concede him the title of Emperor, and refer to him as Napoleon," he said. "Well, I can assure you that His Britannic Majesty's Government haven't done so, and never will; not so long as one Englishman has a finger left to pull a trigger. General Bonaparte is a usurper; His Britannic Majesty's Government do not recognize any sovereignty in France except the House of Bourbon." This he said very sternly, as though rebuking me.

It took me a moment or so to digest that, and to appreciate all its implications. Why, this fellow evidently believed, as a matter of fact, that the French Monarchy had been overthrown by some military adventurer named Bonaparte, who was calling himself the Emperor Napoleon, and who had made war on Austria and forced a surrender. I made no attempt to argue with him—one wastes time arguing with madmen—but if this man could believe that, the transformation of a coach-and-four into a cabbage-wagon was a small matter indeed. So, to humor him, I asked him if he thought General Bonaparte's agents were responsible for his trouble at the inn.

"Certainly," he replied. "The chances are they didn't know me to see me, and took Jardine for the Minister, and me for the secretary, so they made off with poor Jardine. I wonder, though, that they left me my dispatch-case. And that reminds me; I'll want that back. Diplomatic papers, you know."

I told him, very seriously, that we would have to check his credentials. I promised him I would make every effort to locate his secretary and his servants and his coach, took a complete description of all of them, and persuaded him to go into an upstairs room, where I kept him under guard. I did start inquiries, calling in all my informers and spies, but, as I expected, I could learn nothing. I could not find anybody, even, who had seen him anywhere in Perleburg before he appeared at the Sword & Scepter, and that rather surprised me, as somebody should have seen him enter the town, or walk along the street.

In this connection, let me remind your Excellency of the discrepancy in the statements of the servant, Franz Bauer, and of the two peasants. The former is certain the man entered the inn-yard from the street; the latter are just as positive that he did not. Your Excellency, I do not like such puzzles, for I am sure that all three were telling the truth to the best of their knowledge. They are ignorant common-folk, I admit, but they should know what they did or did not see.

After I got the prisoner into safe-keeping, I fell to examining his papers, and I can assure your Excellency that they gave me a shock. I had paid little heed to his ravings about the King of France being dethroned, or about this General Bonaparte who called himself the Emperor Napoleon, but I found all these things mentioned in his papers and dispatches, which had every appearance of being official documents. There was repeated mention of the taking, by the French, of Vienna, last May, and of the capitulation of the Austrian Emperor to this General Bonaparte, and of battles being fought all over Europe, and I don't know what other fantastic things. Your Excellency, I have heard of all sorts of madmen—one believing himself to be the Archangel Gabriel, or Mohammed, or a werewolf, and another convinced that his bones are made of glass, or that he is pursued and tormented by devils—but, so help me God, this is the first time I have heard of a madman who had documentary proof for his delusions! Does your Excellency wonder, then, that I want no part of this business?

But the matter of his credentials was even worse. He had papers, sealed with the seal of the British Foreign Office, and to every appearance genuine—but they were signed, as Foreign Minister, by one George Canning, and all the world knows that Lord Castlereagh has been Foreign Minister these last five years. And to cap it all, he had a safe-conduct, sealed with the seal of the Prussian Chancellery—the very seal, for I compared it, under a strong magnifying-glass, with one that I knew to be genuine, and they were identical!—and yet, this letter was signed, as Chancellor, not by Count von Berchtenwald, but by Baron vom und zum Stein, the Minister of Agriculture, and the signature, as far as I could see, appeared to be genuine! This is too much for me, your Excellency; I must ask to be excused from dealing with this matter, before I become as mad as my prisoner!

I made arrangements, accordingly, with Colonel Keitel, of the Third Uhlans, to furnish an officer to escort this man in to Berlin. The coach in which they come belongs to this police station, and the driver is one of my men. He should be furnished expense-money to get back to Perleburg. The guard is a corporal of Uhlans, the orderly of the officer. He will stay with the *Herr Oberleutnant*, and both of them will return here at their own convenience and expense.

I have the honor, your Excellency, to be, etc., etc.

Ernst Hartenstein
Staatspolizeikapitan

VIII

(From *Oberleutnant* Rudolf von Tarlburg, to Baron Eugen von Krutz.)

26 November, 1809

Dear Uncle Eugen:

This is in no sense a formal report; I made that at the Ministry, when I turned the Englishman and his papers over

to one of your officers—a fellow with red hair and a face like
a bulldog. But there are a few things which you should be
told, which wouldn't look well in an official report, to let you
know just what sort of a rare fish has gotten into your net.

I had just come in from drilling my platoon, yesterday,
when Colonel Keitel's orderly told me that the colonel wanted
to see me in his quarters. I found the old fellow in undress
in his sitting-room, smoking his big pipe.

"Come in, Lieutenant; come in and sit down, my boy!" he
greeted me, in that bluff, hearty manner which he always
adopts with his junior officers when he has some particularly
nasty job to be done. "How would you like to take a little trip
in to Berlin? I have an errand, which won't take half an hour,
and you can stay as long as you like, just so you're back by
Thursday, when your turn comes up for road-patrol."

Well, I thought, this is the bait. I waited to see what the
hook would look like, saying that it was entirely agreeable
with me, and asking what his errand was.

"Well, it isn't for myself, Tarlburg," he said. "It's for this
fellow Hartenstein, the *Staatspolizeikapitan* here. He has
something he wants done at the Ministry of Police, and I
thought of you because I've heard you're related to the Baron
von Krutz. You are, aren't you?" he asked, just as though he
didn't know all about who all his officers are related to.

"That's right, Colonel; the Baron is my uncle," I said.
"What does Hartenstein want done?"

"Why, he has a prisoner whom he wants taken to Berlin
and turned over at the Ministry. All you have to do is to take
him in, in a coach, and see he doesn't escape on the way, and
get a receipt for him, and for some papers. This is a very
important prisoner; I don't think Hartenstein has anybody
he can trust to handle him. A state prisoner. He claims to be
some sort of a British diplomat, and for all Hartenstein
knows, maybe he is. Also, he is a madman."

"A madman?" I echoed.

"Yes, just so. At least, that's what Hartenstein told me.
I wanted to know what sort of a madman—there are various
kinds of madmen, all of whom must be handled differently—
but all Hartenstein would tell me was that he had unrealistic
beliefs about the state of affairs in Europe."

"Ha! What diplomat hasn't?" I asked.

Old Keitel gave a laugh, somewhere between the bark of
a dog and the croaking of a raven.

"Yes, naturally! The unrealistic beliefs of diplomats are what soldiers die of," he said. "I said as much to Hartenstein, but he wouldn't tell me anything more. He seemed to regret having said even that much. He looked like a man who's seen a particularly terrifying ghost." The old man puffed hard at his famous pipe for a while, blowing smoke up through his moustache. "Rudi, Hartenstein has pulled a hot potato out of the ashes, this time, and he wants to toss it to your uncle, before he burns his fingers. I think that's one reason why he got me to furnish an escort for his Englishman. Now, look; you must take this unrealistic diplomat, or this undiplomatic madman, or whatever in blazes he is, in to Berlin. And understand this." He pointed his pipe at me as though it were a pistol. "Your orders are to take him there and turn him over at the Ministry of Police. Nothing has been said about whether you turn him over alive, or dead, or half one and half the other. I know nothing about this business, and want to know nothing; if Hartenstein wants us to play gaol-warders for him, then, *bei Gott*, he must be satisfied with our way of doing it!"

Well, to cut short the story, I looked at the coach Hartenstein had placed at my disposal, and I decided to chain the left door shut on the outside, so that it couldn't be opened from within. Then, I would put my prisoner on my left, so that the only way out would be past me. I decided not to carry any weapons which he might be able to snatch from me, so I took off my sabre and locked it in the seat-box, along with the dispatch-case containing the Englishman's papers. It was cold enough to wear a greatcoat in comfort, so I wore mine, and in the right side pocket, where my prisoner couldn't reach, I put a little leaded bludgeon, and also a brace of pocket-pistols. Hartenstein was going to furnish me a guard as well as a driver, but I said that I would take a servant who could act as guard. The servant, of course, was my orderly, old Johann; I gave him my double hunting-gun to carry, with a big charge of boar-shot in one barrel and an ounce ball in the other.

In addition, I armed myself with a big bottle of cognac. I thought that if I could shoot my prisoner often enough with that, he would give me no trouble.

As it happened, he didn't, and none of my precautions—except the cognac—were needed. The man didn't look like a lunatic to me. He was a rather stout gentleman, of past middle age, with a ruddy complexion and an intelligent face. The only unusual thing about him was his hat, which was a peculiar contraption, looking like the pot out of a close-stool. I put him in the carriage, and then offered him a drink out of my bottle, taking one about half as big myself. He smacked his lips over it and said, "Well, that's real brandy; whatever we think of their detestable politics, we can't criticize the French for their liquor." Then, he said, "I'm glad they're sending me in the custody of a military gentleman, instead of a confounded gendarme. Tell me the truth, Lieutenant; am I under arrest for anything?"

"Why," I said, "Captain Hartenstein should have told you about that. All I know is that I have orders to take you to the Ministry of Police, in Berlin, and not to let you escape on the way. These orders I will carry out; I hope you don't hold that against me."

He assured me that he did not, and we had another drink on it—I made sure, again, that he got twice as much as I did—and then the coachman cracked his whip and we were off for Berlin.

Now, I thought, I am going to see just what sort of a madman this is, and why Hartenstein is making a state affair out of a squabble at an inn. So I decided to explore his unrealistic beliefs about the state of affairs in Europe.

After guiding the conversation to where I wanted it, I asked him:

"What, *Herr* Bathurst, in your belief, is the real, underlying cause of the present tragic situation in Europe?"

That, I thought, was safe enough. Name me one year, since the days of Julius Caesar, when the situation in Europe hasn't been tragic! And it worked, to perfection.

"In my belief," says this Englishman, "the whole damnable mess is the result of the victory of the rebellious colonists in North America, and their blasted republic."

Well, you can imagine, that gave me a start. All the world knows that the American Patriots lost their war for independence from England; that their army was shattered, that their leaders were either killed or driven into exile. How many times, when I was a little boy, did I not sit up long past my bedtime, when old Baron von Steuben was a guest at Tarlburg-Schloss, listening open-mouthed and wide-eyed to his stories of that gallant lost struggle! How I used to shiver at his tales of the terrible Winter camp, or thrill at the battles, or weep as he told how he held the dying Washington in his arms, and listened to his noble last words, at the Battle of Doylestown! And here, this man was telling me that the Patriots had really won, and set up the republic for which they had fought! I had been prepared for some of what Hartenstein had called unrealistic beliefs, but nothing as fantastic as this.

"I can cut it even finer than that," Bathurst continued. "It was the defeat of Burgoyne at Saratoga. We made a good bargain when we got Benedict Arnold to turn his coat, but we didn't do it soon enough. If he hadn't been on the field that day, Burgoyne would have gone through Gates' army like a hot knife through butter."

But Arnold hadn't been at Saratoga. I know; I have read much of the American War. Arnold was shot dead on New Year's Day of 1776, during the attempted storming of Quebec. And Burgoyne had done just as Bathurst had said; he had gone through Gates like a knife, and down the Hudson to join Howe.

"But, *Herr* Bathurst," I asked, "how could that affect the situation in Europe? America is thousands of miles away, across the ocean."

"Ideas can cross oceans quicker than armies. When Louis XVI decided to come to the aid of the Americans, he doomed himself and his regime. A successful resistance to royal authority in America was all the French Republicans needed to inspire them. Of course, we have Louis' own weakness to blame, too. If he'd given those rascals a whiff of grapeshot, when the mob tried to storm Versailles in 1790, there'd have been no French Revolution."

But he had. When Louis XVI ordered the howitzers turned on the mob at Versailles, and then sent the dragoons to ride down the survivors, the Republican movement had been broken. That had been when Cardinal Talleyrand, who had then been merely Bishop of Autun, had come to the fore and become the power that he is today in France; the greatest King's Minister since Richelieu.

"And, after that, Louis' death followed as surely as night after day," Bathurst was saying. "And because the French had no experience in self-government, their republic was foredoomed. If Bonaparte hadn't seized power, somebody else would have; when the French murdered their King, they delivered themselves to dictatorship. And a dictator, unsupported by the prestige of royalty, has no choice but to lead his people into foreign war, to keep them from turning upon him."

It was like that all the way to Berlin. All these things seem foolish, by daylight, but as I sat in the darkness of that swaying coach, I was almost convinced of the reality of what he told me. I tell you, Uncle Eugen, it was frightening, as though he were giving me a view of Hell. *Gott im Himmel,* the things that man talked of! Armies swarming over Europe; sack and massacre, and cities burning; blockades, and starvation; kings deposed, and thrones tumbling like tenpins! battles in which the soldiers of every nation fought, and in which tens of thousands were mowed down like ripe grain; and, over all, the Satanic figure of a little man in a gray coat, who dictated peace to the Austrian Emperor in Schoenbrunn, and carried the Pope away a prisoner to Savona.

Madman, eh? Unrealistic beliefs, says Hartenstein? Well, give me madmen who drool spittle, and foam at the mouth, and shriek obscene blasphemies. But not this pleasant-seeming gentleman who sat beside me and talked of horrors in a quiet, cultured voice, while he drank my cognac.

But not all my cognac! If your man at the Ministry—the one with red hair and the bulldog face—tells you that I was drunk when I brought in that Englishman, you had better believe him!

Rudi.

IX

(From Count von Berchtenwald, to the British Minister.)

28 November, 1809

Honored Sir:

The accompanying *dossier* will acquaint you with the problem confronting this Chancellery, without needless repetition on my part. Please to understand that it is not, and never was, any part of the intentions of the Government of His Majesty Friedrich Wilhelm III to offer any injury or indignity to the Government of His Britannic Majesty George III. We would never contemplate holding in arrest the person, or tampering with the papers, of an accredited envoy of your Government. However, we have the gravest doubt, to make a considerable understatement, that this person who calls himself Benjamin Bathurst is any such envoy, and we do not think that it would be any service to the Government of His Britannic Majesty to allow an impostor to travel about Europe in the guise of a British diplomatic representative. We certainly should not thank the Government of His Britannic Majesty for failing to take steps to deal with some person who, in England, might falsely represent himself to be a Prussian diplomat.

This affair touches us almost as closely as it does your own Government; this man had in his possession a letter of safe conduct, which you will find in the accompanying dispatch-case. It is of the regular form, as issued by this Chancellery, and is sealed with the Chancellery seal, or with a very exact counterfeit of it. However, it has been signed, as Chancellor of Prussia, with a signature indistinguishable from that of the Baron vom und zum Stein, who is the present Prussian Minister of Agriculture. Baron Stein was shown the signature, with the rest of the letter covered, and without hesitation acknowledged it for his own writing. However, when the letter was uncovered and shown to him, his surprise and horror were such as would require the pen of a Goethe or a Schiller to describe, and he denied categorically ever having seen the document before.

I have no choice but to believe him. It is impossible to think that a man of Baron Stein's honorable and serious character would be party to the fabrication of a paper of this sort. Even aside from this, I am in the thing as deeply as he; if it is signed with his signature, it is also sealed with my seal, which has not been out of my personal keeping in the ten years that I have been Chancellor here. In fact, the word "impossible" can be used to describe the entire business. It was impossible for the man Benjamin Bathurst to have entered the inn-yard—yet he did. It was impossible that he should carry papers of the sort found in his dispatch-case, or that such papers should exist—yet I am sending them to you with this letter. It is impossible that Baron vom und zum Stein should sign a paper of the sort he did, or that it should be sealed by the Chancellery—yet it bears both Stein's signature and my seal.

You will also find in the dispatch-case other credentials ostensibly originating with the British Foreign Office, of the same character, being signed by persons having no connection with the Foreign Office, or even with the Government but being sealed with apparently authentic seals. If you send these papers to London, I fancy you will find that they will there create the same situation as that caused here by this letter of safe-conduct.

I am also sending you a charcoal sketch of the person who calls himself Benjamin Bathurst. This portrait was taken without its subject's knowledge. Baron von Krutz's nephew Lieutenant von Tarlburg, who is the son of our mutual friend Count von Tarlburg, has a *little friend*, a very clever young lady who is, as you will see, an expert at this sort of work she was introduced into a room at the Ministry of Police and placed behind a screen, where she could sketch our prisoner's face. If you should send this picture to London, I think that there is a good chance that it might be recognized. I can vouch that it is an excellent likeness.

To tell the truth, we are at our wits' end about this affair I can not understand how such excellent imitations of these various seals could be made, and the signature of the Baron vom and zum Stein is the most expert forgery that I have ever seen, in thirty years' experience as a statesman. This would indicate careful and painstaking work on the part of somebody; how, then, do we reconcile this with such clumsy mistakes, recognizable as such by any schoolboy, as signing the name of Baron Stein as Prussian Chancellor, or Mr George Canning, who is a member of the opposition party and not connected with your Government, as British Foreign Secretary?

These are mistakes which only a madman would make There are those who think our prisoner is a madman, because of his apparent delusions about the great conqueror, General Bonaparte, *alias* the Emperor Napoleon. Madmen have been known to fabricate evidence to support their delusions, it is true, but I shudder to think of a madman having at his disposal the resources to manufacture the papers you will find in this dispatch-case. Moreover, some of our foremost medical men, who have specialized in the disorders of the mind, have interviewed this man Bathurst and say that, save for his fixed belief in a non-existent situation, he is perfectly rational.

Personally, I believe that the whole thing is a gigantic hoax, perpetrated for some hidden and sinister purpose, possibly to create confusion, and undermine the confidence ex-

isting between your Government and mine, and to set against
one another various persons connected with both Governments, or else as a mask for some other conspiratorial activity. Without specifying any Sovereigns or Governments who
might wish to do this, I can think of two groups, namely, the
Jesuits, and the outlawed French Republicans, either of
whom might conceive such a situation to be to their advantage. Only a few months ago, you will recall, there was a
Jacobin plot unmasked at Koln.

But, whatever this business may portend, I do not like it.
I want to get to the bottom of it as soon as possible, and I
will thank you, my dear Sir, and your Government, for any
assistance you may find possible.

I have the honor, Sir, to be, etc., etc., etc.,

Berchtenwald

X

FROM BARON VON KRUTZ, TO THE COUNT VON BERCH-
TENWALD. MOST URGENT; MOST IMPORTANT.
TO BE DELIVERED IMMEDIATELY AND IN PERSON, RE-
GARDLESS OF CIRCUMSTANCES.

28 November, 1809

Count von Berchtenwald:

Within the past half-hour, that is, at about eleven o'clock
tonight, the man calling himself Benjamin Bathurst was shot
and killed by a sentry at the Ministry of Police, while attempting to escape from custody.

A sentry on duty in the rear courtyard of the Ministry
observed a man attempting to leave the building in a suspicious and furtive manner. This sentry, who was under the
strictest orders to allow no one to enter or leave without
written authorization, challenged him; when he attempted
to run, the sentry fired his musket at him, bringing him
down. At the shot, the Sergeant of the Guard rushed into the
courtyard with his detail, and the man whom the sentry had
shot was found to be the Englishman, Benjamin Bathurst.
He had been hit in the chest with an ounce ball, and died
before the doctor could arrive, and without recovering consciousness.

An investigation revealed that the prisoner, who was confined on the third floor of the building, had fashioned a rope from his bedding, his bed-cord, and the leather strap of his bell-pull; this rope was only long enough to reach to the window of the office on the second floor, directly below, but he managed to enter this by kicking the glass out of the window. I am trying to find out how he could do this without being heard; I can assure your Excellency that somebody is going to smart for this night's work. As for the sentry, he acted within his orders; I have commended him for doing his duty, and for good shooting, and I assume full responsibility for the death of the prisoner at his hands.

I have no idea why the self-so-called Benjamin Bathurst, who, until now, was well-behaved and seemed to take his confinement philosophically, should suddenly make this rash and fatal attempt, unless it was because of those infernal dunderheads of madhouse-doctors who have been bothering him. Only this afternoon, your Excellency, they deliberately handed him a bundle of newspapers—Prussian, Austrian, French, and English—all dated within the last month. They wanted, they said, to see how he would react. Well, God pardon them, they've found out!

What does your Excellency think should be done about giving the body burial?

Krutz

(From the British Minister to the Count von Berchtenwald.)

December 20th, 1809

Mr. Dear Count von Berchtenwald:

Reply from London to my letter of the 18th *ult.*, which accompanied the dispatch-case and the other papers, has finally come to hand. The papers which you wanted returned— the copies of the statements taken at Perleburg, the letter to the Baron von Krutz from the police captain, Hartenstein, and the personal letter of Krutz's nephew, Lieutenant von Tarlburg, and the letter of safe-conduct found in the dispatch-case—accompany herewith. I don't know what the people at Whitehall did with the other papers; tossed them into the nearest fire, for my guess. Were I in your Excellency's place, that's where the papers I am returning would go.

I have heard nothing, yet, from my dispatch of the 29th *ult.* concerning the death of the man who called himself Benjamin Bathurst, but I doubt very much if any official notice will ever be taken of it. Your Government had a perfect right to detain the fellow, and, that being the case, he attempted to escape at his own risk. After all, sentries are not required to carry loaded muskets in order to discourage them from putting their hands in their pockets.

To hazard a purely unofficial opinion, I should not imagine that London is very much dissatisfied with this *denouement*. His Majesty's Government are a hard-headed and matter-of-fact set of gentry who do not relish mysteries, least of all mysteries whose solution may be more disturbing than the original problem.

This is entirely confidential, your Excellency, but those papers which were in that dispatch-case kicked up the devil's own row in London, with half the Government bigwigs protesting their innocence to high Heaven, and the rest accusing one another of complicity in the hoax. If that was somebody's intention, it was literally a howling success. For a while, it was even feared that there would be Questions in Parliament, but eventually, the whole vexatious business was hushed.

You may tell Count Tarlburg's son that his little friend is a most talented young lady; her sketch was highly commended by no less an authority than Sir Thomas Lawrence, and here, your Excellency, comes the most bedeviling part of a thoroughly bedeviled business. The picture was instantly recognized. It is a very fair likeness of Benjamin Bathurst, or, I should say, Sir Benjamin Bathurst, who is King's Lieutenant-Governor for the Crown Colony of Georgia. As Sir Thomas Lawrence did his portrait a few years back, he is in an excellent position to criticize the work of Lieutenant von Tarlburg's young lady. However, Sir Benjamin Bathurst was known to have been in Savannah, attending to the duties of his office, and in the public eye, all the while that his double was in Prussia. Sir Benjamin does not have a twin brother. It has been suggested that this fellow might be a half-brother, born on the wrong side of the blanket, but, as far as I know, there is no justification for this theory.

The General Bonaparte, *alias* the Emperor Napoleon, who is given so much mention in the dispatches, seems also to have a counterpart in actual life; there is, in the French army, a Colonel of Artillery by that name, a Corsican who Gallicized his original name of Napolione Buonaparte. He is a most brilliant military theoretician; I am sure some of your own officers, like General Scharnhorst, could tell you about him. His loyalty to the French Monarchy has never been questioned.

This same correspondence to fact seems to crop up everywhere in that amazing collection of pseudo-dispatches and pseudo-state-papers. The United States of America, you will recall, was the style by which the rebellious colonies referred to themselves, in the Declaration of Philadelphia. The James Madison who is mentioned as the current President of the United States is now living, in exile, in Switzerland. His alleged predecessor in office, Thomas Jefferson, was the author of the rebel Declaration; after the defeat of the rebels, he escaped to Havana, and died, several years ago, in the Principality of Lichtenstein.

I was quite amused to find our old friend Cardinal Talleyrand—without ecclesiastical title—cast in the role of chief advisor to the usurper, Bonaparte. His Eminence, I have always thought, is the sort of fellow who would land on his feet on top of any heap, and who would as little scruple to be Prime Minister to His Satanic Majesty as to His Most Christian Majesty.

I was baffled, however, by one name, frequently mentioned in those fantastic papers. This was the English General, Wellington. I haven't the least idea who this person might be.

I have the honor, your Excellency, etc., etc., etc.,

Sir Arthur Wellesley

"Murray Leinster" (the late Will F. Jenkins, 1896–1975) had one of the longest and most successful careers in the history of science fiction, beginning in 1919 and continuing until the late 1960s. He also had a distinguished writing career outside of sf. Within the genre he produced more than forty books and well over a hundred stories, including his popular "Med Service" series, and "Exploration Team," which won a 1956 Hugo Award.

"The Power" (Astounding Science Fiction, September 1945) exhibits all the skill and the imaginative strength that Will Jenkins brought to all of his work.

THE POWER

By Murray Leinster

Memorandum from Professor Charles, Latin Department, Haverford University, to Professor McFarland, the same faculty:

Dear Professor McFarland:
In a recent batch of fifteenth-century Latin documents from abroad, we found three which seem to fit together. Our interest is in the Latin of the period, but their contents seem to bear upon your line. I send them to you with a free translation. Would you let me know your reaction?

Charles.

To Johannus Hartmannus, Licentiate in Philosophy,
Living at the house of the goldsmith Grote,
Lane of the Dyed Flee,
Leyden, the Low Countries:

Friend Johannus:
    I write this from the Goth's Head Inn, in Padua, the second

day after Michaelmas, Anno Domini 1482. I write in haste because a worthy Hollander here journeys homeward and has promised to carry mails for me. He is an amiable lout, but ignorant. Do not speak to him of mysteries. He knows nothing. Less than nothing. Thank him, give him to drink, and speak of me as a pious and worthy student. Then forget him.

I leave Padua tomorrow for the realization of all my hopes and yours. This time I am sure. I came here to purchase perfumes and mandragora and the other necessities for an Operation of the utmost imaginable importance, which I will conduct five nights hence upon a certain hilltop near the village of Montevecchio. I have found a Word and a Name of incalculable power, which in the place that I know of must open to me knowledge of all mysteries. When you read this, I shall possess powers at which Hermes Trismegistos only guessed, and which Albertus Magnus could speak of only by hearsay. I have been deceived before, but this time I am sure. I have seen proofs!

I tremble with agitation as I write to you. I will be brief. I came upon these proofs and the Word and the Name in the village of Montevecchio. I rode into the village at nightfall, disconsolate because I had wasted a month searching for a learned man of whom I had heard great things. Then I found him—and he was but a silly antiquary with no knowledge of mysteries! So riding upon my way I came to Montevecchio, and there they told me of a man dying even then because he had worked wonders. He had entered the village on foot only the day before. He was clad in rich garments, yet he spoke like a peasant. At first he was mild and humble, but he paid for food and wine with a gold piece, and villagers fawned upon him and asked for alms. He flung them a handful of gold pieces and when the news spread the whole village went mad with greed. They clustered about him, shrieking pleas, and thronging ever the more urgently as he strove to satisfy them. It is said that he grew frightened and would have fled because of their thrusting against him. But they plucked at his garments, screaming of their poverty, until suddenly his rich clothing vanished in the twinkling of an eye and he was but another ragged peasant like themselves and the purse from which he had scattered gold became a mere coarse bag filled with ashes.

This had happened but the day before my arrival, and the

man was yet alive, though barely so because the villagers had cried witchcraft and beset him with flails and stones and then dragged him to the village priest to be exorcised.

I saw the man and spoke to him, Johannus, by representing myself to the priest as a pious student of the snares Satan has set in the form of witchcraft. He barely breathed, what with broken bones and pitchfork wounds. He was a native of the district, who until now had seemed a simple ordinary soul. To secure my intercession with the priest to shrive him ere he died, the man told me all. And it was much!

Upon this certain hillside where I shall perform the Operation five nights hence, he had dozed at midday. Then a Power appeared to him and offered to instruct him in mysteries. The peasant was stupid. He asked for riches instead. So the Power gave him rich garments and a purse which would never empty so long—said the Power—as it came not near a certain metal which destroys all things of mystery. And the Power warned that this was payment that he might send a learned man to learn what he had offered the peasant, because he saw that peasants had no understanding. Thereupon I told the peasant that I would go and greet this Power and fulfil his desires, and he told me the Name and the Word which would call him, and also the Place, begging me to intercede for him with the priest.

The priest showed me a single gold piece which remained of that which the peasant had distributed. It was of the age of Antonius Pius, yet bright and new as if fresh minted. It had the weight and feel of true gold. But the priest, wryly, laid upon it the crucifix he wears upon a small iron chain about his waist. Instantly it vanished, leaving behind a speck of glowing coal which cooled and was a morsel of ash.

This I saw, Johannus! So I came speedily here to Padua, to purchase perfumes and mandragora and the other necessities for an Operation to pay great honor to this Power whom I shall call up five nights hence. He offered wisdom to the peasant, who desired only gold. But I desire wisdom more than gold, and surely I am learned concerning mysteries and Powers! I do not know any but yourself who surpasses me in true knowledge of secret things. And when you read this, Johannus, I shall surpass even you! But it may be that I will gain knowledge so that I can transport myself by a mystery to your attic, and there inform you myself, in advance of this letter, of the results of this surpassing good fortune which causes me to shake with agitation whenever I think of it.

Your friend Carolus,

at the Goth's Head Inn in Padua.

... fortunate, perhaps, that an opportunity has come to send a second missive to you, through a crippled man-at-arms who has been discharged from a mercenary band and travels homeward to sit in the sun henceforth. I have given him one gold piece and promised that you would give him another on receipt of this message. You will keep that promise or not, as pleases you, but there is at least the value of a gold piece in a bit of parchment with strange symbols upon it which I enclose for you.

Item: I am in daily communication with the Power of which I wrote you, and daily learn great mysteries.

Item: Already I perform marvels such as men have never before accomplished by means of certain sigils or talismans the Power has prepared for me.

Item: Resolutely the Power refuses to yield to me the Names or the incantations by which these things are done so that I can prepare such sigils for myself. Instead, he instructs me in divers subjects which have no bearing on the accomplishment of wonders, to my bitter impatience which I yet dissemble.

Item: Within this packet there is a bit of parchment. Go to a remote place and there tear it and throw it upon the ground. Instantly, all about you, there will appear a fair garden with marvelous fruits, statuary, and pavilion. You may use this garden as you will, save that if any person enter it, or you yourself, carrying a sword or dagger or any object however small made of iron, the said garden will disappear immediately and nevermore return.

This you may verify when you please. For the rest, I am like a prisoner trembling at the very door of Paradise, barred from entering beyond the antechamber by the fact of the Power withholding from me the true essentials of mystery, and granting me only crumbs—which, however, are greater marvels than any known certainly to have been practiced before. For example, the parchment I send you. This art I have proven many times. I have in my scrip many such sigils, made for me by the Power at my entreaty. But when I have secretly taken other parchments and copied upon them the very symbols to the utmost exactitude, they are valueless.

There are words or formulas to be spoken over them or—I think more likely—a greater sigil which gives the parchments their magic property. I begin to make a plan—a very daring plan—to acquire even this sigil.

But you will wish to know of the Operation and its results. I returned to Montevecchio from Padua, reaching it in three days. The peasant who had worked wonders was dead, the villagers having grown more fearful and beat out his brains with hammers. This pleased me, because I had feared he would tell another the Word and Name he had told me. I spoke to the priest and told him that I had been to Padua and secured advice from high dignitaries concerning the wonder-working, and had been sent back with special commands to seek out and exorcise the foul fiend who had taught the peasant such marvels.

The next day—the priest himself aiding me!—I took up to the hilltop the perfumes and wax tapers and other things needed for the Operation. The priest trembled, but he would have remained had I not sent him away. And night fell, and I drew the magic circle and the pentacle, with the Signs in their proper places. And when the new moon rose, I lighted the perfumes and the fine candles and began the Operation. I have had many failures, as you know, but this time I knew confidence and perfect certainty. When it came time to use the Name and the Word I called them both loudly, thrice, and waited.

Upon this hilltop there are many greyish stones. At the third calling of the Name, one of the stones shivered and was not. Then a voice said dryly:

"Ah! So that is the reason for this stinking stuff! My messenger sent you here?"

There was a shadow where the stone had been and I could not see clearly. But I bowed low in that direction:

"Most Potent Power," I said, my voice trembling because the Operation was a success, "a peasant working wonders told me that you desired speech with a learned man. Beside your Potency I am ignorant indeed, but I have given my whole life to the study of mysteries. Therefore I have come to offer worship or such other compact as you may desire in exchange for wisdom."

There was a stirring in the shadow, and the Power came forth. His appearance was that of a creature not more than an ell and a half in height, and his expression in the moonlight was that of sardonic impatience. The fragrant smoke seemed to cling about him, to make a cloudiness close about his form.

"I think" said the dry voice, "that you are as great a fool as the peasant I spoke to. What do you think I am?"

"A Prince of Celestial race, your Potency," I said, my voice shaking.

There was a pause. The Power said as if wearily:

"Men! Fools forever! Oh, man, I am simply the last of a number of my kind who traveled in a fleet from another star. This small planet of yours has a core of the accursed metal, which is fatal to the devices of my race. A few of our ships came too close. Others strove to aid them, and shared their fate. Many, many years since, we descended from the skies and could never rise again. Now I alone am left."

Speaking of the world as a planet was an absurdity, of course. The planets are wanderers among the stars, traveling in their cycles and epicycles as explained by Ptolemy a thousand years since. But I saw at once that he would test me. So I grew bold and said:

"Lord, I am not fearful. It is not needful to cozen me. Do I not know of those who were cast out of Heaven for rebellion? Shall I write the name of your leader?"

He said "Eh?" for all the world like an elderly man. So, smiling, I wrote on the earth the true name of Him whom the vulgar call Lucifer. He regarded the markings on the earth and said:

"Bah! It is meaningless. More of your legendary! Look you, man, soon I shall die. For more years than you are like to believe I have hid from your race and its accursed metal. I have watched men, and despised them. But—I die. And it is not good that knowledge should perish. It is my desire to impart to men the knowledge which else would die with me. It can do no harm to my own kind, and may bring the race of men to some degree of civilization in the course of ages."

I bowed to the earth before him. I was aflame with eagerness.

"Most Potent One," I said joyfully. "I am to be trusted. I will guard your secrets fully. Not one jot nor tittle shall ever be divulged!"

Again his voice was annoyed and dry.

"I desire that this knowledge be spread so that all may learn it. But—" Then he made a sound which I do not understand, save that it seemed to be derisive—"What I have to say may serve, even garbled and twisted. And I do not think you will keep secrets inviolate. Have you pen and parchment?"

"Nay, Lord!"

"You will come again, then, prepared to write what I shall tell you."

But he remained, regarding me. He asked me questions, and I answered eagerly. Presently he spoke in a meditative voice, and I listened eagerly. His speech bore an odd similarity to that of a lonely man who dwelt much on the past, but soon I realized that he spoke in ciphers, in allegory, from which now and again the truth peered out. As one who speaks for the sake of remembering, he spoke of the home of his race upon what he said was a fair planet so far distant that to speak of leagues and even the span of continents would be useless to convey the distance. He told of cities in which his fellows dwelt—here, of course, I understood his meaning perfectly—and told of great fleets of flying things rising from those cities to go to other fair cities, and of music which was in the very air so that any person, anywhere upon the planet, could hear sweet sounds or wise discourse at will. In this matter there was no metaphor, because the perpetual sweet sounds in Heaven are matters of common knowledge. But he added a metaphor immediately after, because he smiled at me and observed that the music was not created by a mystery, but by waves like those of light, only longer. And this was plainly a cipher, because light is an impalpable fluid without length and surely without waves!

Then he spoke of flying through the emptiness of the empyrean, which again is not clear, because all can see that the heavens are fairly crowded with stars, and he spoke of many suns and other worlds, some frozen and some merely barren rock. The obscurity of such things is patent. And he spoke of drawing near to this world which is ours, and of an error made as if it were in mathematics—instead of in rebellion—so that they drew close to Earth as Icarus to the sun. Then again he spoke in metaphors, because he referred to engines, which are things to cast stones against walls, and in a larger sense for grinding corn and pumping water. But he spoke of engines growing hot because of the accursed metal in the core of Earth, and of the inability of his kind to resist Earth's pull—more metaphor—and then he spoke of a screaming descent from the skies. And all of this, plainly, is a metaphorical account of the casting of the Rebels out of Heaven, and an acknowledgment that he is one of the said Rebels.

When he paused, I begged humbly that he would show me a mystery and of his grace give me protection in case my converse with him became known.

"What happened to my messenger?" asked the Power.

I told him, and he listened without stirring. I was careful to tell him exactly, because of course he would know that—as all else—by his powers of mystery, and the question was but another test. Indeed, I felt sure that the messenger and all that taken place had been contrived by him to bring me, a learned student of mysteries, to converse with him in this place.

"Men!" he said bitterly at last. Then he added coldly. "Nay! I can give you no protection. My kind is without protection upon this earth. If you would learn what I can teach you, you must risk the fury of your fellow countrymen."

But then, abruptly, he wrote upon parchment and pressed the parchment to some object at his side. He threw it upon the ground.

"If men beset you," he said scornfully, "tear this parchment and cast it from you. If you have none of the accursed metal about you, it may distract them while you flee. But a dagger will cause it all to come to naught!"

Then he walked away. He vanished. And I stood shivering for a very long time before I remembered me of the formula given by Apollonius of Tyana for the dismissal of evil spirits. I ventured from the magic circle. No evil befell me. I picked up the parchment and examined it in the moonlight. The symbols upon it were meaningless, even to one like myself who has studied all that is known of mysteries. I returned to the village, pondering.

I have told you so much at length, because you will observe that this Power did not speak with the pride or the menace of which most authors on mysteries and Operations speak. It is often said that an adept must conduct himself with great firmness during an Operation, lest the Powers he has called up overawe him. Yet this Power spoke wearily, with irony, like one approaching death. And he had spoken of death, also. Which was of course a test and a deception, because are not the Principalities and Powers of Darkness immortal? He had some design it was not his will that I should know. So I saw that I must walk warily in this priceless opportunity.

In the village I told the priest that I had had encounter with a foul fiend, who begged that I not exorcise him, promising to reveal certain hidden treasures once belonging to the Church, which he could not touch or reveal to evil men because they were holy, but could describe the location of to me. And I procured parchment, and pens, and ink, and the next day I went alone to the hilltop. It was empty, and I made sure I was unwatched and—leaving my dagger behind me— I tore the parchment and flung it to the ground.

As it touched, there appeared such a treasure of gold and jewels as truly would have driven any man mad with greed. There were bags and chests and boxes filled with gold and precious stones, which had burst with the weight and spilled out upon the ground. There were gems glittering in the late sunlight, and rings and necklaces set with brilliants, and such monstrous hoards of golden coins of every antique pattern...

Johannus, even I went almost mad! I leaped forward like one dreaming to plunge my hands into the gold. Slavering, I filled my garments with rubies and ropes of pearls, and stuffed my scrip with gold pieces, laughing crazily to myself. I rolled in the riches. I wallowed in them, flinging the golden coins into the air and letting them fall upon me. I laughed and sang to myself.

Then I heard a sound. On the instant I was filled with terror for the treasure. I leaped to my dagger and snarled, ready to defend my riches to the death.

Then a dry voice said: "Truly you care naught for riches!"

It was savage mockery. The Power stood regarding me. I saw him clearly now, yet not clearly because there was a cloudiness which clung closely to his body. He was, as I said, an ell and a half in height, and from his forehead there protruded knobby feelers which were not horns but had somewhat the look save for bulbs upon their ends. His head was large and—But I will not attempt to describe him, because he could assume any of a thousand forms, no doubt, so what does it matter?

Then I grew terrified because I had no Circle or Pentacle to protect me. But the Power made no menacing move.

"It is real, that riches," he said dryly. "It has color and weight and the feel of substance. But your dagger will destroy it all."

Didyas of Corinth has said that treasure of mystery must be fixed by a special Operation before it becomes permanent and free of the power of Those who brought it. They can transmute it back to leaves or other rubbish, if it be not fixed.

"Touch it with your dagger," said the Power.

I obeyed, sweating in fear. And as the metal iron touched a great piled heap of gold, there was a sudden shifting and then a little flare about me. And the treasure—all, to the veriest crumb of a seed-pearl!—vanished before my eyes. The bit of parchment reappeared, smoking. It turned to ashes. My dagger scorched my fingers. It had grown hot.

"Ah, yes," said the Power, nodding. "The force-field has energy. When the iron absorbs it, there is heat." Then he looked at me in a not unfriendly way. "You have brought pens and parchment," he said, "and at least you did not use the sigil to astonish your fellows. Also you had the good sense to make no more perfumish stinks. It may be that there is a grain of wisdom in you. I will bear with you yet a while. Be seated and take parchment and pen—Stay! Let us be comfortable. Sheathe your dagger, or better, cast it from you."

I put it in my bosom. And it was as if he thought, and touched something at his side, and instantly there was a fair pavilion about us, with soft cushions and a gently playing fountain.

"Sit," said the Power. "I learned that men like such things as this from a man I once befriended. He had been wounded and stripped by robbers, so that he had not so much as a scrap of accursed metal about him, and I could aid him. I learned to speak the language men use nowadays from him. But to the end he believed me an evil spirit and tried valorously to hate me."

My hands shook with my agitation that the treasure had departed from me. Truly it was a treasure of such riches as no King has ever possessed, Johannus! My very soul lusted after that treasure! The golden coins alone would fill your attic solidly, but the floor would break under their weight, and the jewels would fill hogsheads. Ah, Johannus! That treasure!

"What I will have you write," said the Power, "at first will mean little. I shall give facts and theories first, because they are easiest to remember. Then I will give the applications of the theories. Then you men will have the beginning of such civilization as can exist in the neighborhood of the accursed metal."

"Your Potency!" I begged abjectly. "You will give me another sigil of treasure?"

"Write!" he commanded.

I wrote. And, Johannus, I cannot tell you myself what it is that I wrote. He spoke words, and they were in such obscure cipher that they have no meaning as I con them over. Hark you to this, and seek wisdom for the performance of mysteries in it! "The civilization of my race is based upon fields of force which have the property of acting in all essentials as substance. A lodestone is surrounded by a field of force which is invisible and impalpable. But the fields used by my people for dwellings, tools, vehicles, and even machinery are perceptible to the senses and act physically as solids. More, we are able to form these fields in latent fashions; and to fix them to organic objects as permanent fields which require no energy for their maintenance, just as magnetic fields require no energy supply to continue. Our fields, too, may be projected as three-dimensional solids which assume any desired form and have every property of substance except chemical affinity."

Johannus! Is it not unbelievable that words could be put together, dealing with mysteries, which are so devoid of any clue to their true mystic meaning? I write and I write in desperate hope that he will eventually give me the key, but my brain reels at the difficulty of extracting the directions for Operations which such ciphers must conceal! I give you another instance: "When a force-field generator has been built as above, it will be found that the pulsatory fields which are consciousness serve perfectly as controls. One has but to visualize the object desired, turn on the generator's auxiliary control, and the generator will pattern its output upon the pulsatory consciousness-field..."

Upon this first day of writing, the Power spoke for hours, and I wrote until my hand ached. From time to time, resting, I read back to him the words that I had written. He listened, satisfied.

"Lord!" I said shakily. "Mighty Lord! Your Potency! These

mysteries you bid me write—they are beyond comprehension!"

But he said scornfully:

"Write! Some will be clear to someone. And I will explain it little by little until even you can comprehend the beginning." Then he added. "You grow weary. You wish a toy. Well! I will make you a sigil which will make again that treasure you played with. I will add a sigil which will make a boat for you, with en engine drawing power from the sea to carry you wheresoever you wish without need of wind or tide. I will make others so you may create a palace where you will, and fair gardens as you please..."

These things he has done, Johannus. It seems to amuse him to write upon scraps of parchment, and think, and then press them against his side before he lays them upon the ground for me to pick up. He has explained amusedly that the wonder in the sigil is complete, yet latent, and is released by the tearing of the parchment, but absorbed and destroyed by iron. In such fashion he speaks in ciphers, but otherwise sometimes he jests!

It is strange to think of it, that I have come little by little to accept this Power as a person. It is not in accord with the laws of mystery. I feel that he is lonely. He seems to find satisfaction in speech with me. Yet he is a Power, one of the Rebels who was flung to earth from Heaven! He speaks of that only in vague, metaphorical terms, as if he had come from another world like *the* world, save much larger. He refers to himself as a voyager of space, and speaks of his race with affection, and of Heaven—at any rate the city from which he comes, because there must be many great cities there—with a strange and prideful affection. If it were not for his powers, which are of mystery, I would find it possible to believe that he was a lonely member of a strange race, exiled forever in a strange place, and grown friendly with a man because of his loneliness. But how could there be such as he and not a Power? How could there be another world?

This strange converse has now gone on for ten days or more. I have filled sheets upon sheets of parchment with writing. The same metaphors occur again and again. "Forcefields"—a term without literal meaning—occurs often. There are other metaphors such as "coils" and "primary" and "secondary" which are placed in context with mention of wires of copper metal. There are careful descriptions, as if in the plainest of language, of sheets of dissimilar metals which are to be placed in acid, and other descriptions of plates of similar metal which are to be separated by layers of air or wax of certain thicknesses, with the plates of certain areas! And there is an explanation of the means by which he lives. "I, being accustomed to an atmosphere much more dense than that on Earth, am forced to keep about myself a field of force which maintains an air density near that of my home planet for my breathing. This field is transparent, but because it must shift constantly to change and refresh the air I breathe, it causes a certain cloudiness of outline next my body. It is maintained by the generator I wear at my side, which at the same time provides energy for such other force-field artifacts as I may find convenient."—Ah, Johannes! I grow mad with impatience! Did I not anticipate that he would some day give me the key to this metaphorical speech, so that from it may be extracted the Names and the Words which cause his wonders, I would give over in despair.

Yet he has grown genial with me. He has given me such sigils as I have asked him, and I have tried them many times. The sigil which will make you a fair garden is one of many. He says that he desires to give to man the knowledge he possesses, and then bids we write ciphered speech without meaning, such as: "The drive of a ship for flight beyond the speed of light is adapted from the simple drive generator already described simply by altering its constants so that it cannot generate in normal space and must create an abnormal space by tension. The process is—" Or else—I choose at random, Johannus—"The accursed metal, iron, must be eliminated not only from all circuits but from nearness to apparatus using high-frequency oscillations, since it absorbs their energy and prevents the functioning..."

I am like a man trembling upon the threshold of Paradise, yet unable to enter because the key is withheld. "Speed of light!" What could it mean in metaphor? In common parlance, as well speak of the speed of weather or of granite! Daily I beg him for the key to his speech. Yet even now, in the sigils he makes for me, is greater power than any man has ever known before!

But it is not enough. The Power speaks as if he were lonely beyond compare; the last member of a strange race upon earth; as if he took a strange, companion-like pleasure in merely talking to me. When I beg him for a Name or a Word which would give me power beyond such as he doles out in sigils, he is amused and calls me fool, yet kindly. And he speaks more of his metaphorical speech about forces of nature and fields of force—and gives me a sigil which should I use it will create a palace with walls of gold and pillars of emerald! And then he amusedly reminds me that one greedy looter with an axe or hoe of iron would cause it to vanish utterly!

I go almost mad, Johannus! But there is certainly wisdom unutterable to be had from him. Gradually, cautiously, I have come to act as if we were merely friends, of different race and he vastly the wiser, but friends rather than Prince and subject. Yet I remember the warnings of the most authoritative authors that one must be ever on guard against Powers called up in an Operation.

I have a plan. It is dangerous, I well know, but I grow desperate. To stand quivering upon the threshold of such wisdom and power as no man has ever dreamed of before, and then be denied...

The mercenary who will carry this to you, leaves tomorrow. He is a cripple, and may be months upon the way. All will be decided ere you receive this. I know you wish me well.

Was there ever a student of mystery in so saddening a predicament, with all knowledge in his grasp yet not quite his?

Your friend
Carolus.

Written in the very bad inn in Montevecchio.

Johannus! A courier goes to Ghent for My Lord of Brabant and I have opportunity to send you mail. I think I go mad, Johannus! I have power such as no man ever possessed before, and I am fevered with bitterness. Hear me!

For three weeks I did repair daily to the hilltop beyond Montevecchio and take down the ciphered speech of which I wrote you. My scrip was stuffed with sigils, but I had not one word of Power or Name of Authority. The Power grew mocking, yet it seemed sadly mocking. He insisted that his words held no cipher and needed but to be read. Some of them he phrased over and over again until they were but instructions for putting bits of metal together, mechanicwise. Then he made me follow those instructions. But there was no Word, no Name—nothing save bits of metal put together cunningly. And how could inanimate metal, not imbued with power of mystery by Names or Words or incantations, have power to work mystery?

At long last I become convinced that he would never reveal the wisdom he had promised. And I had come to such familiarity with this Power that I could dare to rebel, and even to believe that I had chance of success. There was the cloudiness about his form, which was maintained by a sigil he wore at his side and called a "generator." Were that cloudiness destroyed, he could not live, or so he had told me. It was for that reason that he, in person, dared not touch anything of iron. This was the basis of my plan.

I feigned illness, and said that I would rest at a peasant's thatched hut, no longer inhabited, at the foot of the hill on which the Power lived. There was surely no nail of iron in so crude a dwelling. If he felt for me the affection he protested, he would grant me leave to be absent in my illness. If his affection was great, he might even come and speak to me there. I would be alone in the hope that his friendship might go so far.

Strange words for a man to use to a Power! But I had talked daily with him for three weeks. I lay groaning in the hut, alone. On the second day he came. I affected great rejoicing, and made shift to light a fire from a taper I had kept burning. He thought it a mark of honor, but it was actually a signal. And then, as he talked to me in what he thought my illness, there came a cry from without the hut. It was the village priest, a simple man but very brave in his fashion. On the signal of smoke from the peasant's hut, he had crept near and drawn all about it an iron chain that he had muffled with cloth so that it would make no sound. And now he stood before the hut door with his crucifix upraised, chanting exorcisms. A very brave man, that priest, because I had pictured the Power as a foul fiend indeed.

The Power turned and looked at me, and I held my dagger firmly.

"I hold the accursed metal," I told him fiercely. "There is a ring of it about this house. Tell me now, quickly, the Words and the Names which make the sigils operate! Tell me the secret of the cipher you had me write! Do this and I will slay this priest and draw away the chain and you may go hence unharmed. But be quick, or—"

The Power cast a sigil upon the ground. When the parchment struck earth, there was an instant's cloudiness as if some dread thing had begun to form. But then the parchment smoked and turned to ash. The ring of iron about the hut had destroyed its power when it was used. The Power knew that I spoke truth.

"Ah!" said the Power dryly. "Men! And I thought one was my friend!" He put his hand to his side. "To be sure! I should have known. Iron rings me about. My engine heats..."

He looked at me. I held up the dagger, fiercely unyielding.

"The Names!" I cried. "The Words! Give me power of my own and I will slay the priest!"

"I tried," said the Power quietly, "to give you wisdom. And you will stab me with the accursed metal if I do not tell you things which do not exist. But you need not. I cannot live long in a ring of iron. My engine will burn out; my force-field will fail. I will stifle in the thin air which is dense enough for you. Will not that satisfy you? Must you stab me, also?"

I sprang from my pallet of straw to threaten him more fiercely. It was madness, was it not? But I was mad, Johannus!

"Forbear," said the Power. "I could kill you now, with me! But I thought you my friend. I will go out and see your priest. I would prefer to die at his hand. He is perhaps only a fool."

He walked steadily toward the doorway. As he stepped over the iron chain, I thought I saw a wisp of smoke begin, but he touched the thing at his side. The cloudiness about his person vanished. There was a puffing sound, and his garments jerked as if in a gust of wind. He staggered. But he went on, and touched his side again and the cloudiness returned and he walked more strongly. He did not try to turn aside. He walked directly toward the priest, and even I could see that he walked with a bitter dignity.

And—I saw the priest's eyes grow wide with horror. Because he saw the Power for the first time, and the Power was an ell and a half high, with a large head and knobbed feelers projecting from his forehead, and the priest knew instantly that he was not of any race of men but was a Power and one of those Rebels who were flung out from Heaven.

I heard the Power speak to the priest, with dignity. I did not hear what he said. I raged in my disappointment. But the priest did not waver. As the Power moved toward him, the priest moved toward the Power. His face was filled with horror, but it was resolute. He reached forward with the crucifix he wore always attached to an iron chain about his waist. He thrust it to touch the Power, crying, *"In nomine Patri—"*

Then there was smoke. It came from a spot at the Power's side where was the engine to which he touched the sigils he had made, to imbue them with the power of mystery. And then—

I was blinded. There was a flare of monstrous, bluish light, like a lightning-stroke from Heaven. After, there was a ball of fierce yellow flame which gave off a cloud of black smoke. There was a monstrous, outraged bellow of thunder.

Then there was nothing save the priest standing there, his face ashen, his eyes resolute, his eyebrows singed, chanting psalms in a shaking voice.

I have come to Venice. My scrip is filled with sigils with which I can work wonders. No men can work such wonders as I can. But I use them not. I labor daily, nightly, hourly, minute by minute, trying to find the key to the cipher which will yield the wisdom the Power possessed and desired to give to men. Ah, Johannus! I have those sigils and I can work wonders, but when I have used them they will be gone and I shall be powerless. I had such a chance at wisdom as never man possessed before, and it is gone! Yet I shall spend years— aye!—all the rest of my life, seeking the true meaning of what the Power spoke! I am the only man in all the world who ever spoke daily, for weeks on end, with a Prince of Powers of Darkness, and was accepted by him as a friend to such a degree as to encompass his own destruction. It must be true that I have wisdom written down! But how shall I find instructions for mystery in such metaphors as—to choose a fragment by chance—"plates of two dissimilar metals, immersed in an acid, generate a force for which men have not yet a name, yet which is the basis of true civilization. Such plates..."

I grow mad with disappointment, Johannus! Why did he not speak clearly? Yet I will find out the secret...

Memorandum from Peter McFarland, Physics Department, Haverford University, to Professor Charles, Latin, the same faculty:

Dear Professor Charles:
   My reaction is, Damnation! Where is the rest of this stuff?
                                                    McFarland.